WAVES OF DECEPTION

A Marcus Dresden Thriller

BRIAN GROGAN

Frog Foot Press
United States

Published in the United States by Frog Foot Press, LLC, Frederick Maryland.

You can contact the author at:

bgroganbooks.com

brian@bgroganbooks.com

This is the first book in the breakout *Marcus Dresden* thriller series. I wouldn't want you to miss book two, any deals or promotions and I definitely wouldn't want you to miss out on ***FREE book*** offers. So please sign up for my ***newsletter*** and don't miss a single thrill.

You can sign up here:

bgroganbooks.com

Dedication

To Liam and Desmond
I'll leave you a box of ashes, a wad of ones and this book – don't spend it all in one place.

Also, to
G. Doherty, D. Collins, K. Kimura, M. Mills and M. Murphy
All Men of Valor.

One

Island of Mindanao, Philippines

The four men leaned hard into the steep trail as they marched upward. With each step, dark jungle mud moved up around their sandaled feet like the fluid tentacles of an octopus. They tensed and flexed their lean, muscled backs and shoulders under the weight of the heavy weapons and ammunition slung around their necks. Their dark skin glistened from the heat and humidity, the hard march taking its toll.

Agapito and Uwang at the rear chatted happily in hushed tones. Really just boys, they relished the idea of being out of the training camp, down in the valley behind them. At the top of the ridge was relief from the grind of weapons, explosive, and tactical training—but mostly from the harsh treatment of the instructors. The third man up from the back, Issay, glanced at the two boys and grunted his disapproval. At the front of the small squad, Lolo chewed hard on a mouth full of betel nut. He spat a large glob of the red juice onto the trail, then hushed the two boys at the back. The boys grumbled for a moment, then went quiet, Issay snorting in their direction.

Lolo pushed the men upward, stopping only once to check his cell phone. The men gained elevation, the dense jungle giving way to smaller trees and brush. The thinner foliage would normally let in more light, but night was coming on fast. Every so often, Lolo looked to the ridgeline where their comrades and training partners were. Edgar was there—Lolo's cousin. The man who'd convinced him to join the ASG. The small marching team would relieve Edgar's team of their three-day post.

When Lolo's team came within twenty meters of the ridgeline they stopped and took a knee. The leader yelled out a bona-fide, a code only Edgar would know. There was no reply. He tried again, and then one more time, a little louder.

Suddenly, the sky lit up with a frightening red glow as two ten-thousand-candle-power flares shot into the darkness. Lolo's men drew their weapons up to the ready. Tall, boxy-looking figures appeared at the summit. The men opened fire on the eerie apparitions wobbling toward them, continuing until the flares burned out and they could no longer see the shapes on the ridge.

The jungle went quiet save for a flurry of frantic bird calls, which died away slowly. The men found cover and waited, listening for what seemed like an hour. Nothing. The moon crept up over a distant mountain. Lolo sent a text to his cousin. Still nothing. It took another hour for the moon to rise high enough to provide light to see.

The four-man squad moved in slow, hopeful they had averted another ambush. As they came upon the outpost, the men spotted four cardboard shipping boxes lying on the ground. The rectangular crates were littered with dozens of bullet holes. The men approached cautiously, weapons at the ready. Agapito trained his weapon on the box while Uwang removed the lid.

Looking inside, Agapito and Uwang leaped back at once. Issay fell to the ground and scrambled backwards in the mud. Lolo stood frozen, staring into the box as a lone eye gawked back at him—Edgar's. Lolo's cousin was bound and gagged and missing large chunks of flesh all over his body. Crimson fluid oozed from his wounds like maple syrup from a tree spike. The lining of the box was blood-soaked and splattered with shards of bone, brain, and muscle. The metallic smell of blood and gunpowder wafted upward. Lolo ordered the rest of the boxes opened, and all revealed more of the same. The four men were dead, torn to pieces by Lolo and his crew.

The team searched the area for their comrades' weapons and equipment. Nothing. The site had been sanitized except for a large, plain white envelope affixed to a tree, stabbed through with a broad knife. Lolo yanked the blade out and threw it to the ground, then opened the envelope and read the note aloud:

Salaam alaikum. Go no further, ASG dogs, or suffer the consequences!

Two

Central Coast, California

Marcus Dresden woke to the sound of waves—a thunderous, ever-rolling crash. He sat up, his head swirling. A damp, salty breeze cut through the room from an open window. He sat motionless as another swell crashed. *The waves are real.* Getting out of bed, he stood in front of the open window. Dresden could hear the swells spilling onto the beach, but he couldn't see them. It was still dark out.

"The report was right, AP," Dresden called back into the dark room.

His Great Pyrenes lay sprawled out at the foot of his bed. The dog didn't move, just let out a slow, guttural sigh.

Turning on a dim light in the closet, Dresden slipped his long legs into a pair of surfboard shorts, then moved downstairs. AP raised his cinder-block head and watched the man disappear. The dog let out another grunt, got up, and lumbered down the stairs.

In the kitchen, AP lay back down next to his bowl, a pool of slobber collecting under his jaw.

His eyes drooped. Dresden ran his fingers through AP's fur as he filled the dog's food bowl.

"You wanna come?" Dresden said. He grabbed his phone, earbuds, and headlamp as he walked to the garage door.

The dog rolled onto his side, away from Dresden.

"Your choice, buddy. A trail run and some beach time would do you some good, you ol' loaf." Dresden waited a moment, then shrugged his shoulders as if in some silent agreement.

"Okay, you need some alone time, I get it. Have it your way."

Outside, Dresden turned on his headlamp, swiped at his phone, and selected a playlist. He took off at a warmup pace, his lungs gulping in the cool, wet air. The smell of sunbaked kelp was sour and pungent in his nose. Where the road met the trailhead, a fine mist had begun to settle in. The skin on Dresden's back and shoulders steamed like a sauna stone. He stopped a few yards down the trail, pulled the phone from his pocket, and tapped play. The rhythmic drumbeat of New Order's "Blue Monday" boomed into his earbuds. Dresden started up the trail again at a decidedly quicker pace, leaning forward, arms and legs pumping as he climbed.

The light from Dresden's headlamp created a cocoon of illumination, and the music in his ears deprived his hearing. The two effects produced a surreal, dreamlike state as he ran. He moved down the trail, bobbing and weaving like a prizefighter, concentrating on the details—every rock, every bush. Each curve in the path provided an opportunity for disaster. A twisted ankle. A skinned knee or worse. Dresden reveled in the laser-like focus; it was akin to some kind of tantric meditation. With each step, the blur of a restless night's sleep sloughed its way out of his head.

The dirt track wound up to Horseback Hill Reservoir. Dresden stopped at the top. From there, during the daylight hours, he could survey the spread of Escondite below him. The small town, the bay, the pier, even Morro Rock in the distance to the south. This morning, all he could make out were streetlights twinkling through the mist like stars in a cloudy night's sky.

Dresden made his way back down into town, the descent more treacherous than the ascent. Loose dirt made him lose traction. Rocks and sand filled his shoes. His pace was slower, but still challenging, quads burning through the steeper sections. He hit the hard pack, shook out his shoes, and kept moving. As he ran down the empty streets, he turned off the music. The sound of waves spilling onto the beach filled the sudden absence in his ears as he approached the coast.

At the foot of the Escondite pier, where he squinted to make out the mountains of water rolling in, his phone hummed. He hesitated, not wanting to interrupt his wave study. Finally, he glanced at the screen. *Michael - First Watch, PI.* His broad shoulders drooped. *Damn it, not now!* When he was sure the line would go dead, Dresden tapped his earbud to answer the call.

"Yeah?"

"Marcus? I need you in the PI."

"Bear?"

"Yeah!"

Dresden could hear the distinctive sound of Southeast Asian traffic in the background. The horns, the music, the mufflers. They were all too familiar. He could smell the grilled street meat mixed with diesel exhaust and burning rubber. There was no doubt Bear was in the Philippines.

"PI? When?"

"Tomorrow."

"Can't. Kelli's got her first practice this afternoon. Can't miss it." He cupped his eyes to make out the waves better. They moved through the pier pylons, crashing and sending gales of white water onto the deck.

"Shit! Shit. Come on man, don't make me call HQ. I don't need the heat. It's hot enough down—" A loud motorbike drowned out whatever Bear was going to say. When Dresden could hear him again, he was saying, "Okay, okay, how about the day after next?" He sounded exasperated. Maybe even nervous. His heavy breathing scratched its way through Dresden's earbuds.

The sun had just broken over the palomino-colored hills behind Dresden as he watched large sections of unrideable waves roll toward the beach. On the south side, straight out from Delta Street, a section of the wave held up. It lasted for a short twenty yards, but it was perfect.

"Yo! Dude, you still with me?" Bear barked.

"Yup!"

"So, you good?"

"No," Dresden said. Bear cursed loudly into his ear. "But I'll forward you my itinerary when I get it." He tapped his earbud to hang up.

Dresden hated doing that to Bear, but the call had pretty much soured his mood. He would have to tell Kelli he couldn't spend the weekend. She would say she understood, but Dresden knew better. His daughter's silences were loaded with disappointment.

Back at his house, Dresden surveyed a surfboard rack at the rear of his garage. He chose an eight-foot minigun from the selection of eight boards. The narrow, needle-like shape would be perfect. Pulling the board off the rack, he laid it on the carpet in the center of the garage. Kneeling next to it, he applied a healthy portion of wax to the surface.

Once finished, Dresden slipped the board into the rack attached to his beach cruiser, mounted the bike, then got off again. Opening the door to the house, he whistled for AP, then noticed him lying right where he'd left him.

"Last chance, buddy. You coming?"

The dog spit slobber on the floor but didn't move.

"Seriously man? You got issues." Dresden shook his head and closed the door.

"Hey there, neighbor," Will said as Dresden rolled his bike out of his garage.

"Hey Will. How's it going?" Dresden said, regretting the words as soon as they fell from his mouth.

"Good. Headed up to Cambria today. Going to visit the relatives, you know?"

Will had no relatives in Cambria. No living ones, that is. "Well, lay a flower on Edna's grave for me, would you Will? Thanks."

"You going out? Kind of small for you, isn't it Mark?"

Dresden winced at the name. It was Marcus.

"We take what we can get, Will. I gotta head down to LA later to see Kelli. No time to search the coast."

"Ah, Kelli. What a lovely girl you got there. It's been a long time since she's been here. What yah guys gonna go do?" Will slurred the last two words, then burped.

Dresden smelled the booze now. Will was still drunk, or starting early. "Going to Kelli's first college basketball practice down in Long Beach."

"Oh. You give her a big hug for us, okay? We really miss her," Will said.

Dresden looked at the ground and rubbed the back of his neck. "You got it. Now, I gotta—"

"I tell people about you sometimes. I tell them I live next to this guy who surfs those giant waves. They figure you're part crazy or mostly stupid. Those—those are *their* words of course, not ... not mine, you understand?" Will's eyes darted from Dresden to the ground and back again. "I figure we all got vices, right?"

"Sure do, Will. Alright, well the waves are only going to get smaller, so—"

"Right, well, okay. Oh yeah, and make sure you tell Kelli hello for me," Will repeated, "And make sure you bring her up here soon."

Dresden mounted his bike. "Got it, Will."

He looked back as he rolled away. Will stood alone, blankly staring up at the sky. He looked like a newborn lamb, bleary-eyed and wobbly. *Poor guy doesn't even know how bad he's got it,* Dresden thought.

Three

Central Coast, California

At the pier, tourists and locals alike gathered in small, insular groups along the rail of the boardwalk. Big waves always brought out the looky-loos like a car crash. Three twenty-something surfers were hanging on the railing near Delta Street. Two were tall, like Dresden but lanky. The third was short and stocky. They had two girls with them. Dresden had no doubt they were spinning stories of how they'd conquered waves like these a dozen times before. They ignored Dresden as he headed down to the water's edge.

Out past the breakers, Dresden was alone, the waves sounding off like a symphony. He closed his eyes and listened. A moment later, the first swell of the next set became visible— it was big. He checked his position in the lineup, telling himself over and over to sit tight. The urge to paddle outside never seemed to go away.

The third wave thundered toward him. He studied the mammoth wall of water as it approached, then swung his board around and paddled at a cant to the wave. The water picked him up as he gave two deep digs then popped to his feet. The board seemed to float, his feet hovering above it. A second later the board made contact with the wave, followed by his feet. The sudden jolt of speed jacked him backward. Aiming his surfboard down the face of the wave, he turned hard at the bottom, jetting to the top for another turn. Water sprayed out from beneath his board like a thumb over the nozzle of a hose before he headed to the bottom again. Another turn and he took flight over the lip of the wave. A feeling of exhilaration coursed through his body, and he leaped over the top as it came crashing down.

Back at the lineup, Dresden could see the next set building on the horizon. He glanced at his watch. Just enough time for a couple more. He turned and paddled into the next wave like before.

This time, though, the lip pitched hard and broke before Dresden anticipated. He felt his board come out from under him. He was falling, suffering the trifecta. First, he hit the water hard at an odd angle. Then his board, driven by hundreds of pounds of water, smacked into his shoulder and hip. Lastly, the crushing full force of the wave shoved him deep under the water toward the bottom. Like a massive jackhammer, the wave's power held Dresden under, spinning him end over end. Finally, Dresden pushed off the bottom in search of air.

He broke through the surface and drew a long breath. His board was racing at him, followed by the next wall of water. Diving fast, he swam out to sea. Dresden felt the tumbling lip clip his heels as he penetrated deep into the wave. He dug harder, lungs burning. His vision narrowed. Blackness crept into his periphery like the closing curtains of a movie theater. Dresden angled his body up and cleared the surface, gulping at the air. He collected his board and paddled back out to the lineup.

"Yo, yard sale!"

Dresden turned around to see Lance O'Rourke paddling toward him.

"Who you callin' yard sale? Junkyard!"

"What's up, bro?" Lance offered Dresden a fist.

Dresden bumped it in return. "Nothin' much. I thought you were going to Maverick's this morning?"

"I was, but I got a late start comin' up from San Diego yesterday. Had to stay in Atascadero. Got up this morning and the report said Mav's was flat,"

"Bummer."

"Yeah, well I figured I'd come see you since you were bailin' on me. My part-time big wave surf buddy."

Lance flashed a toothy grin at Dresden, sitting up on his board. He ran his fingers through a mop of auburn hair, flipping it back to get it out of his eyes. Lance looked more like a wrestler than the stereotypical surfer, which made him perfect for the big waves. Lance was born to chase the big Kahuna.

"I never do," Dresden said.

"Sure."

Lance swirled his fingers in the water, a ploy he'd told Dresden was meant to appease the surf gods and increase the height of the waves by 25 percent. Hocus pocus, Dresden called it. Lance was an odd mixture. Not quite hippie, not quite suburban jock, and not all country. But definitely a scramble of it all. At thirty-two, he'd joined the Teams late. Stayed in eight years. An extreme skier and part-time rodeo clown before joining the Navy, he breezed through training and landed in one of Dresden's last platoons.

"Sorry man, I have to head in soon," Dresden said as he eyed another set rolling toward them.

"You know the rule, bro," Lance said, referring to the unspoken pillar of surfing: never get out of the water feeling worse than when you went in.

Dresden lined himself up, paddled, and dropped into the wave, successfully riding it to shore.

Lance caught a half-dozen waves as Dresden sat on the beach watching. He drew circles in the sand, thinking about calling Bear back. Kelli was going to be really disappointed, and then it got worse—Dresden's phone rang. It was Emily, his ex-wife. He let the call go to voicemail and dropped the phone onto his towel. Glancing between the phone and Lance and back again, he finally punched at her name on the screen.

"Hello!" Emily answered.

Dresden's face winced like he'd jumped into a bath full of ice.

"Hi, you called?" he asked, breathing slowly.

"I did," Emily said, her voice softening but saying nothing else.

A crackling sound punctuated the silence.

"So, what's up?" Dresden asked, still managing his breathing.

"Have you left yet?" Emily said, a sliver of accusation slipping through.

"No."

"When were you planning to leave?"

"In about an hour."

"Are you sure you'll make it on time?"

"I imagine so."

"How about you imagine less and actually do it, okay?" Emily said.

Dresden fought the urge to fire back.

"Okay. I'll make it. But I can't stay the weekend—" He braced himself for what would come, then cut her off instead before she could once again tell him what a bad father he was. How he needed to put his kids first and stop making up all manner of reasons to be gone and not spend time with them. And the big one: how he blamed everything on someone or something else.

"Emily it's not my fault. I gotta go out of town for work. I should get going so I can make it on time."

Emily didn't respond right away; a TV or radio played in the background.

"How's Rodney?" Dresden said.

"Good, great as always," Emily said with a long sigh. "Marcus, you're retired. Why are you even working? You of all people. Why don't you do something meaningful with your time? Like get to know your kids."

Why did she have to bring this up every single time?

"Your kids worry about you, especially Casper. You know that, and you choose to ignore it. It must be nice for you, all cozy and warm, tucked away in that beach hideout ..."

"Emily—Emily!" Dresden had been trying to interject, repeating her name throughout the rant, and finally breaking through.

"What!"

"Really, I have to go," Dresden said.

"Okay, bye. Send pics," Emily said before he hung up.

Sighing, he flipped the phone onto his towel.

Lance moved up the beach toward him. "What's up, bro?"

"Emily."

"Oh," Lance said, sitting down in the sand next to him. Lance had tried marriage once. Found out after a couple years he wasn't cut out for it. A ramblin' man by heart, he had even less aptitude for domestic bliss than Dresden. A girlfriend in every port—that was what the instructors at BUD/S used to say. Lance bought it hook, line, and sinker.

"She's good people, just not good for you, my friend," Lance added.

"Maybe so," Dresden said.

"Come up to Santa Cruz with me. Hang out and see if Mav's goes off. If it does, that will give you the proper perspective."

"Can't," Dresden said. "Gotta head to LA to see Kelli. Plus, I don't want to be a third wheel. Get between you and whichever girl you're shacked up with at the moment."

"I got a girl. But she's out east. So, no worries there."

"Oh really, when did this come about?"

"A while ago."

Dresden looked over at Lance. He did look different. His eternal restlessness that seemed to weigh him down was lighter. There was something Dresden couldn't pinpoint, though. A sort of serenity, maybe. Or could it be disquiet? Dresden looked down the beach toward the pier. A couple walking hand in hand moved slowly toward them. He glanced at his watch.

"Dude, shit, I gotta go!" Dresden said. "Kelli will kill me if I'm late."

"Nice one!" Lance yelled after him as he ran up the beach. "Way to leave me hangin' dude. Again!"

Will was nowhere to be seen when Dresden rounded the corner to his house. This time it was Marybeth, the neighbor across the street. Marybeth consistently feigned distain for Dresden. He thought she was probably a lesbian that had just never put it together, and so instead decided to live alone and hate men. But for some reason, they got on just fine. In fact, Dresden preferred her curt, short communications to Will's billowy, semi-drunk attempts at prose. Dresden waved as he approached, but Marybeth didn't return the greeting. Instead she turned away and continued to water her flowers.

"Mary, I'm gonna need a favor. I gotta go out of town for longer than I first thought. Think you can watch AP for a week or so?" Dresden studied her. She had a sturdy frame and barrel-like shoulders that led directly to her head.

"You know that dog knows me better than you given how often you dump him off on me." Marybeth sniffed into the air.

"I don't doubt that. I'll bring him over in a bit with some food—"

"No, no, for god's sake, don't bring any more damn food. I still have three-quarters of a bag left in my garage," Marybeth said, the corner of her embroidered vest flipping up on the breeze.

"Thanks, Mary. I really appreciate it."

"Yeah, yeah. You know you are the world's worst neighbor, right?" she said over her shoulder. Her black hair, streaked with silver, was bound into a ponytail that whipped side to side.

"Sure thing, Mary. I got to hustle."

Dresden put his surf gear up, packed for both LA and the PI, then took a painfully cold shower to wake himself up for the long drive. In the bathroom mirror, he tugged at his wavy, sun-bleached blonde hair, checking his hair line. No receding. Pretty good for forty-four, he mused. Some minor crow's feet, but no waddle. Waddle. What a ridiculous word.

His phone buzzed as he started flossing his teeth—a text from Lance. Dresden grabbed a towel to dry his hair and sat on the bed to read the message.

Their music game was sophomoric at best, a game of one-upmanship. Something to pass the time back when Dresden and Lance were in the Teams, trying to survive the hurry-up-and-wait military life. They'd found they both loved music, the deep tracks. The rare stuff. They dreamed of a return to old-time radio, when DJs knew their music and programming wasn't in the hands of some corporate blowhard. So, they continuously built their communal playlist of sorts, and dreamed of running their own station. The playlist was nearly a decade old.

Lance's text read, *"Act Naturally" by Buck Owens. Come on its Buck Owens, the Bakersfield Beat, need I say more?*

Dresden Googled the song on his phone, then played it. He hummed along as he finished drying his hair.

When the song finished, Dresden picked up his bag and headed downstairs. He called for AP, but there was no response. He waited and wrote Lance back, *The "Contenders" by the Kinks. No reason other than Dave Davies' blistering guitar work.*

He stuck his phone in his backpack and went to find AP. The dog was sunning himself in the den off the garage.

"Let's go there, you old mutt. You're gonna hang out with Auntie Mary for a few days," Dresden said. The dog lifted his head and stared at him.

"Yeah, I said it. *Mary.*"

AP got to all fours and led Dresden straight to the neighbor's house. He walked into Marybeth's backyard without hesitation, not even a glance back.

"See! Told you," Marybeth said. "The dog don't like you. You know why? Cause you are a terrible neighbor, that's why." She slammed the backyard gate on him. Dresden laughed to himself, walking to his Toyota Tundra. At his truck, he stopped and stared at the woman's back gate. What an odd bird, but AP liked her, and that was all that mattered.

Four

Davao City, Island of Mindanao, Philippines

The AC fan in the Toyota Landcruiser whirred loudly. The vents up front were closed tight. Dresden manipulated his single vent in the back seat, trying desperately to cool off. No luck. He moved to open his window but thought better of it. Outside, dust billowed up and over the entire vehicle. Dresden caught glimpses of banana trees, and blue sky interrupted from time to time by a passing cloud, but not much else. He looked out the back window. Despite the limited visibility, the chase vehicle, another black Toyota Landcruiser, was right on their bumper, and their vehicle was on the bumper of the lead. Dresden peered at the speedometer—fifty-eight miles per hour. Fast for the rutted dirt road. It unnerved him; he didn't like being a passenger with "unfamiliars" at the wheel.

"Yo, Marcus, how you doin' back there?" a voice came over the radio.

The man in the front passenger seat turned to hand the radio microphone to Dresden, flashing a toothy grin. His white teeth gleamed in deep contrast to his dark brown face. The man's boney fingers around the handset loosened, offering it to Dresden.

"Hot," Dresden said into the mic.

"Sorry, bro. Better you climatize anyway," Bear said. His voice cut in and out, static filling the spaces between.

"So, you said at the airport ..."

Dresden's phone vibrated in his pocket. He scrambled to get it out. A missed call from Kelli. His phone buzzed again. This time a text message.

Dad, I know you are really busy and probably won't get this for a day or two, but I just wanted you to know you are getting a text from the freshman starting guard for The Dolphins.

Holy crap! She'd made it.

The vehicle hit a hole in the road and jerked forward, hard. His phone fell out of his hand and into his lap, then to the floor. "Damn!" Dresden barked from the back seat. His stomach twisted with a burning feeling. Grabbing the phone off the floor, he stared at it. He'd missed another moment. An important moment, for sure. He should have told Bear no.

The fast-moving caravan climbed deep into the mountains, the ruts and curves getting worse as they rose. The vehicle bounced in every direction and the radio crackled with Tagalog, the native tongue. When the driver took a curve too fast, Dresden slid hard into the door panel, a sharp pain shooting through his hip. The butt stock of an M-4 rifle sheathed in the door panel slammed against him.

The vehicle slowed but traveled on for another ten minutes. When the dust settled, Dresden could see more of the banana groves that surrounded them. The rich green leaves and long batches of fruit hung like bristled carwash brushes. It was bucolic. Dresden knew that underneath the beauty lay a truth many Westerners chose to ignore. Bananas in the Philippines, like sugar cane in Hawaii, were more than just a cash crop. Many of the plantations were owned by international conglomerates. "Owned" was a euphemism, though. Many of the "landowners" were small-time, local businessmen who mortgaged their livelihoods and assets to the large corporations to be able to sell their products for a fair price. Most, if not all of the plantation owners were on a life sentence of debt payments to some corporation. Dresden had seen firsthand what happened when those payments were missed. His stomach burned again. This plantation was different, though—owned outright by one man: Emilio DeSoto.

The convoy came to a stop on a slope. The man in the passenger seat turned and held up his hand, signaling Dresden to stay. Feeling like a pup at a dog park, he sat staring out the window as his pooch pals played without him.

Through a light cloud of dust, he watched as the men conducted a short security survey. They were treating Dresden like the "principal" in a VIP detail, but he was feeling more like a steaming pig at a luau.

Michael "Bear" Berowski walked over to Dresden's side of the truck. Bear's short torso and long legs gave him an odd gait. He loped along like a giraffe. A former Marine-Recon guy for over twenty years, he and Dresden had bumped into each numerous times in Iraq, Afghanistan, and the PI. Bear winked and opened Dresden's door.

"Right this way, sir." He bowed and swept his arm toward the top of the ridgeline.

"Cut the shit, Bear."

Bear laughed. "Roger that. Follow me."

They walked about thirty yards to the edge of the banana grove, which gave way to more indigenous trees and bushes, and a vantage on the valley far below. The other side of the mountain.

"Alright Bear, what the hell am I looking at?" Dresden said.

Bear motioned for the guards to back off and give them room. When they were slow to move, he barked some orders at them, and they retreated to the parked vehicles, casting glares at Bear. He and Dresden watched in silence as the men slung their weapons over their shoulders, squatted or leaned against the trucks, and lit up smokes.

"You see that down there?" Bear moved to a spot on the ridgeline where he could see clearly down into the valley, then handed Dresden a pair of binoculars. Raising the lenses, he scanned the valley for a moment until he noticed the distinct markers of a military or para-military compound—a series of buildings situated around a square patch of dirt, a couple watch towers, and what looked like an obstacle course and some military vehicles.

"Yup."

"Okay, so that's an ASG training camp," Bear said. He took a swig from a water bottle.

Dresden knew the Abu Sayyif Group well, a militant terror organization focused on the liberation of the island of Mindanao as a Muslim state. The ASG, a more fanatical splinter group of the MILF, or Moro Islamic Liberation Front, had torn away from its predecessor on philosophical grounds. The ASG had also courted Osama Bin Laden, and many of its members had fought alongside the Mujahideen in Afghanistan. It was a dangerous group prone to extreme acts of violence. The first beheading of a captive ever recorded on video was done by the ASG, a tactic Middle Eastern terror groups would later adopt.

"Okay, what about it?"

"We are standing at the border line, what they consider their property line with DeSoto."

"Did you ever see that movie, *The Sandlot*?" Dresden said. He lowered the binoculars and looked over at Bear.

Bear was finishing off his water bottle and took a few seconds to respond. "Uh, yeah."

"You're killing me, Smalls. You're killin' me, okay?" Dresden said.

"Okay boss, got it. So, the property actually belongs to some rich guy from some other country, maybe Malaysia. Anyway, in an effort to help the 'cause,' he allows the ASG to use the property. I'm not sure it was all congenial like that, but nevertheless the ASG have been there since I've been workin' DeSoto's security. I knew they were on the other side of the mountain."

Dresden nodded, waiting for the rest of the story.

He watched as Bear kicked at the dirt. Bear had fucked up, and Dresden knew it. He also knew Bear was struggling with how best to limit the damage to himself. A few weeks earlier, the ASG guys had posted a watched right where Dresden was standing. Bear claimed it was to watch over their camp down in the valley. Turned out that wasn't it at all. The ASG were casing DeSoto's property, his plantation. Then about a week ago, eight heavily armed men showed up to harass some of DeSoto's field workers. They beat up the foreman bad and pinned a note to him with safety pins, ramming them right through the man's skin.

Bear handed the note with its bloody corners to Dresden. The message was handwritten in Tagalog on the back side of a takeout menu. Dresden looked at the wrinkled scrawl, then handed it back to Bear without reading it. Bear summarized the note for him. The ASG were reclaiming the land from an ass-kissing capitalist landowner with the intent to return it to the rightful owners—the followers of Islam. Dresden watched Bear fold up the note, then looked out over the lush green hills. He asked Bear where he'd been when the attack happened. After a long moment and Bear kicking at the dirt some more, the man spilled.

"Okay boss, look, I was left out of the loop. A couple of my guys got a heads-up but didn't tell me. Those guys down there are DeSoto's private, private security. They're all, like, thieves and killers and cons. DeSoto has this idea that if you give a guy like that a home, some money, and some respect, they will be loyal as dogs." Bear hung his head and rubbed the back of his neck with a soaked neckerchief.

"He may be right," Dresden said as he lowered the binoculars. "So, what went down here?"

"Well that's the funny part. DeSoto's guys went all native and got in with the watch, saying they'd help them get DeSoto's property. They got them all hopped up on betel nut and booze, then wrapped them up like Christmas geese. My guys set up some pyrotechnics, and when the watch relief came to take over, they got the party started."

"Where are the bodies?" Dresden said.

"In the cooler at DeSoto's house."

Of course DeSoto would have a cooler big enough for four bodies to fit in. Dresden laughed to himself. But more curious was why the ASG guys hadn't taken their dead comrades back down the mountain. And how did DeSoto's men tangle with some ASG guys and come away without even a scratch?

Dresden put this to Bear. With a comic flare, the other man explained that DeSoto's men, the same men now smoking and making nervous small talk, had staged themselves far away from the "ambush" site. When they finally heard the ASG guys freaking out, they started driving up the dirt road blasting "Flight of the Valkyries"—some real *Apocalypse Now* shit, Bear said. The ASG guys freaked out again and ran back down their side of the mountain.

Bear's story sounded plausible. But Dresden hadn't flown all the way to the PI to have Bear flap his gums. The next two hours limped along as he surveyed the scene. Sweat ran down his back like a leaky faucet as he stared out at the banana grove, watching the workers. Fully clothed from head to foot, they chopped massive bunches of bananas and loaded them into crates, moving methodically down long lines of trees and out of sight.

Dresden took photos and jotted down notes in a green wheel book. He scratched at tree bark with a penknife and brushed dirt aside to reveal shell casings. Like a police detective, he collected the evidence in plastic bags. Dresden had once attended a six-hour class on crime scene investigations led by a surly, red-nosed ex-Chicago police officer. The guy had handed out a twelve-point investigation checklist at the end of the class.

Now, Dresden pulled the same document from his cargo pocket and flipped through the tattered pages. He needed evidence, not to build a case but to substantiate a report on the incident—on whether or not First Watch was culpable. His reports had been used to get First Watch out of some hot water in the past.

Standing, he walked down the trail the ASG men had come up several nights before. He wanted their perspective. What had they seen? Something wasn't adding up. There was one common denominator, of course—Emilio DeSoto. But why would the ASG go after DeSoto? The *note*. The message to DeSoto from the ASG. He needed to read it.

Dresden pulled a plot map from his pocket. The property lines weren't distinct, but they were there. If the map was the least bit accurate, DeSoto's property line was farther down the mountain, toward the ASG camp. That meant the ASG guys had really stepped over the line, way before Bear knew about it. A quarter-mile down the trail, Dresden found a small pistol range set into the steep hillside. The structure was well into DeSoto's property.

When he got back to the attack site atop the hill, Bear stood waiting.

"Boss, you about done?"

"Maybe. Where are DeSoto's men?"

"Still down at the vehicles."

"Have them come up here."

"Uh, okay ... what for?"

"Bear, just get them up here."

The man's shoulders slumped. He walked down the hill to the trucks.

A few minutes later, DeSoto's men were congregated in front of Dresden, giving away their unease with furtive glances at him and each other. Dresden studied the map for another moment, then folded it up and put it away in his cargo pocket. He asked Bear for the note, then read it twice through. After putting it in his pocket as well, he patiently attempted eye contact with each of DeSoto's men, and was successful with about half. Finally, in fluent Tagalog, Dresden asked one of the men, Tony, to follow him down the hill, back down the trail toward the ASG camp. The man hesitated, only moving forward a couple steps. He looked back at the other men, then followed Dresden.

They walked down the trail to the pistol range, where they stayed for over forty minutes. Tony stuttered through his answers to some of the questions and plain refused to respond to others.

As the two men returned to the top of the ridge, Dresden spotted Bear pacing in a short, tight line. Puffs of dust rose from the dry, hard dirt. DeSoto's men were still milling about the ambush site. They wore thin masks to shroud their anxiety.

As Dresden marched past Bear, he said, "Let's go. Let's go see DeSoto,"

"What? Marcus, wait! We can't go *see* DeSoto just like that," Bear yelled after him.

Dresden stopped, then turned to look at Bear and the other men. Everyone stopped in their tracks.

"We can, and we will!" Dresden took a step toward them.

"But ... but why? What happened?" Bear said.

Dresden studied DeSoto's men, watching as three of them ground hard on lumps of betel nut stuck in their jaws. Two others took deep drags from their cigarettes. If this little stunt started a war with the ASG, DeSoto would kill them. Bear would get fired for mishandling this; Dresden was certain of that. But DeSoto's men had much more to lose.

"That note you gave me, Bear, does not say what you think it says," Dresden said.

DeSoto's men exchanged looks.

Dresden pulled the note from his pocket and carefully unfolded it. Again, in fluent Tagalog, he read it aloud. DeSoto's men started to whisper. Dresden stopped. They hushed and came to a semblance of attention. Bear shuffled like he needed to pee.

"So—so what does it say?" Bear said.

"You don't speak Tagalog, right? All these months down here, and you don't speak or read even the basics, do you?" Dresden said.

Bear hesitated; his skin flushed further. "No."

"The note says, *essentially* ..." Dresden stopped and looked up at Bear, who looked away. "That DeSoto had agreed, at some point, to help the ASG by providing property for them to live and train on. That he hadn't come through and was now reneging on his promise and was therefore a traitor, Western-ass-kissing capitalist. That now they, the ASG, were going to take *all* his property."

"How did you—" was all Bear could manage.

"How? Let me ask you; have you been out of sight of any of these guys since the incident?" Dresden waved his hand at DeSoto's men. "Have you spoken to your two men? Did you question these fine gentlemen?" He waved his hand again. "Did you know they didn't think the ASG guys would shoot up their own guys, that was an accident? Did you know that DeSoto's property reaches about a mile back down that hill, toward the ASG camp? No, you didn't know any of that, 'cause *they* weren't going to let you. They also knew you didn't know Tagalog. They knew you inherited this post in a hurry after the last site manager became ill and had to leave. They knew you didn't have a good lay of the land. They knew a lot you didn't. But most importantly, what you knew didn't matter. Because DeSoto gave the order, so they followed it, period. If they hadn't, they would've ended up dead like the last First Watch site lead. A stomach virus, wasn't it?"

Bear's face went pale with the implication.

Dresden paused, folding the note back up, then looked at the man. "Consider yourself lucky, Bear. DeSoto must like you. You're still alive."

He turned and walked to the Land Cruisers, barking a word in Tagalog that made DeSoto's men jump and scramble to the trucks. Bear, unable to move of his own accord, was ushered along and loaded in a vehicle.

The ride back to town was that of dead men walking. The radio on the dash remained silent. The men in the front seat opened their vents wide, cooling the cab off to something tolerable. They faced forward, never looking back. Soon the driver slowed his speed. The alpha male had been established. It gave Dresden an opportunity to reflect on what had happened and what he would say to DeSoto.

A phone rang with a pop tune ringtone, and the man in the front passenger seat answered quickly.

"Yes sir," he said, this time in English. The man hung up without another word. He looked at Dresden in the rearview mirror.

"Mr. DeSoto cannot see you today, Mr. Dresden. He sends his most sincere apologies. Most likely tomorrow." The man returned to staring straight ahead.

"Fine. Take me to my hotel."

"Yes sir."

Dresden looked out the window. Now in the lead vehicle, he could see more of the banana fields. The plantation swept across the landscape like an ocean of green leaves fanning in the breeze. Dresden rummaged for his phone. Emily had text him.

You made my baby CRY, you're such an ASSHOLE!

"Shit!" Dresden said.

The man in the passenger seat stiffened and glanced nervously into the rearview mirror. "It's not about you," Dresden reassured him.

Back at the Marco Polo hotel, the vehicle whipped into the semi-circle passenger drop-off. They pulled away at high speed before Dresden could even close the door. The other two vehicles were gone. No doubt DeSoto's men were eager to get back and cover their asses. Bear had made no attempt to contact him, to set up a time to discuss their next move before they met with DeSoto. Not smart.

Dresden liked Davao. More provincial than Manila. It hadn't changed much in the decade since his last "visit." It was still a little too busy and noisy for his taste, but okay for a few days of diversion. On past trips, he'd ferreted out the quieter, off-the-beaten-path places to go within the city. Dresden would have preferred a waterside café but most of the waterfront near the hotel was devoted to various barangay, not leisure. Instead, he found what he wanted in some of the more unusual enclaves within the bustle of the city.

His stomach rumbled and growled, but he couldn't go straight to the café. Dresden wandered the streets, winding and weaving for nearly twice as long as it should have taken. He ducked down alleys and narrow side streets, spotting the black four-door Camry more than once. Dresden lost the car twice, yet it found him again each time. This was by design, of course. There were too many places a car couldn't go. When Dresden slipped down an alley, a man on a motorcycle followed. Someone was watching him. That someone, Dresden assumed, was DeSoto. He would have expected nothing less from the man.

Cold tea with sweet milk and an aromatic lemongrass soup with fish and squid satisfied Dresden's hunger. He sat back in his chair, rubbing his stomach while watching the traffic outside. The cozy place was empty but shared a foyer with a noisy internet café. A bass beat of chill music thumped away, spilling into the restaurant despite all the doors and windows being closed. A small window A/C unit struggled to keep the space cool. Dresden wiped his brow and sipped his tea, eyeing the street again before he pulled out his phone. He put in his earbuds and called Kelli on WhatsApp.

She answered with a big yawn. Her room was dark. It was five in the morning California time, and a day behind.

"Hey Dad," she said with a broad smile.

"Hey there, champ! Sorry, you look like the starting guard of some college out in California. I must have the wrong number," Dresden said, and lifted his finger as if about to hang up.

"Oh, Dad. Really? It's too late—or early for that."

"Okay. I'm really sorry I didn't stay ..."

"Did you get a text from Mom?" Kelli interrupted.

Dresden hesitated. "Yeah," he said.

"Then just drop it. If you'd wanted to stay, you would have. Apologizing because Mom made you is not really what I'm looking for," Kelli said. She sat up in bed. "So, how's the trip so far?"

"Good. I thought it would be the same old thing, but it looks like it might get interesting." He stared at the motorcycle surveillance guy across the street. "Anyway, how does it feel? You know ... knowing you made the team?"

"Weird! Totally weird. I'm, like, walking around and I get this chill and feel all giddy!"

"That's an awesome feeling, isn't it?"

"Yeah, totally!"

The motorcycle guy tinkered with his bike, occasionally looking over at the restaurant. He couldn't see Dresden through the tinted windows. A second man showed up and pretended to help the motorcycle man. *This just stinks of DeSoto,* Dresden thought. *Just keeping an eye on me, I see.*

"Dad, you okay?"

"Huh? Yeah, I should probably go."

"Oh, okay. Well, I should probably get back to sleep. Big day tomorrow. Or, today."

"Me too. Okay, teddy bear, you have a good sleep." Dresden started to hang up.

"Dad, I'm doing good, okay? But, Casper … Casper needs to hear from you. You know? He *needs* it. He's doing some pretty amazing stuff with Osuna. I know he'd love to tell you. Call him. Soon. Okay?"

"Oh, okay. I will. I'll give him a call, soon." The two guys were now in a heated argument. It was getting weird. "Maybe I'll even go see him. But I gotta go. Sleep tight, teddy bear."

Dresden hung up, paid his bill, then slipped over into the darkness of the internet café, unnoticed. Tucked away near the rear, he watched a third man cross the street and enter the restaurant. When he discovered Dresden wasn't there, he barked at the waiter. The waiter threw his arms around and said something Dresden couldn't make out. The man sprinted out of the café, back to the motorcycle. After a bit of gesticulating, the three men split up.

Dresden made his way back to his hotel, following a different route of twists and turns. A block away, he picked out the black Camry parked on Roxas avenue, opposite the hotel entrance. Skirting around it, he sat in the lobby for a while, as much to text Casper as to watch for his new friends. No one showed.

Dresden drifted into a memory of how much Casper loved to "patrol" through the woods.

They would find sticks for guns and then creep hunched over through the trees and brush on a mission to storm an enemy stronghold. "Just like Daddy does," Casper would say. That was before Casper's "condition" manifested itself. Before Casper became afraid. Dresden stared blankly at nothing, then wrote a short text to his son.

How you doing buddy? Let's go on Patrol soon, okay?

Feeling suddenly stupid, he started to erase the text. Casper was a grown man. *Shit. Who cares?* He rewrote the message and hit send before he had a chance to rethink it.

Five

Davao City, Island of Mindanao, Philippines

"Marcus! Good to see you, my old friend," Emilio DeSoto said as he rose from behind his desk. Dresden moved forward, but a man stepped in front and put a hand against his chest. Dresden looked down at the fireplug of a man who looked powerful despite his size—he knew better than to underestimate this man's potential for violence. DeSoto barked, and the man slipped to the side with the grace of a cat. The boss made his way around the palatial desk to greet Dresden.

DeSoto's office was a bountiful contrast of light and dark. The furniture, floors, and walls were all made of a deep, lush teak wood. Large windows and sliding doors led to an ample patio that ushered in the bright PI sunlight. The ceilings were adorned with slow-moving fans that did little more than shift around the humid, acrid air. The central AC vents on the floor were shut, a tactic of DeSoto's to hurry along his meetings with gringos. The office was just one room in a twenty-room house that sat in a secluded compound, ten minutes outside of Davao City central.

Dresden recognized one of the guards—the motorcycle man from the night before. Bear stood off to the side with two of the men from the banana field detail, and four others were posted around the room. None of them familiar.

DeSoto embraced him warmly, and Dresden reciprocated the gesture, catching the befuddled look on Bear's face.

"Marcus, please, please sit down. Drink?" DeSoto asked. His voice was tinged with hints of his Cambridge education. DeSoto had been born into wealth, which was now in the billions. He was an untouchable hanging out in his native country where the rules were loose, his money went farther, and his influence was boundless. Power oozed out of his silk polo like Texas crude from the ground. DeSoto was a handsome, heavy-set man with a military bearing. He could have doubled for PI's favorite son, Manny Pacquiao.

The wealthy man handed Dresden a glass of filtered water, room temperature, with lime and a pinch of sea salt. "Still your favorite?"

Dresden nodded as DeSoto sat down across from him. He leaned back and folded his legs, teetering a tumbler of bourbon on his knee.

"So, it appears as though you discovered our little ruse," DeSoto said.

"I have, Emilio." Dresden took a drink. "This makes providing you with a sufficient security detail a tad bit more difficult."

"Well, I wasn't really trying to hide it. Your man, there," DeSoto said, stabbing a thick thumb in Bear's direction, "was clueless, of course, but when I heard you were coming, I figured it would be fun to see how long it would take you to figure it out."

"Emilio, while I appreciate a good detective story, that's not why I'm here. And the reason I'm here has become more complicated. To find out you're running your own security detail alongside ours and that you may be playing patsy with terrorists makes no sense to me," Dresden said. He leaned back in his chair, cupping his drink with both hands then taking a long drink of the water.

DeSoto was not new to debate, but he *was* known to be quick-tempered. Dresden thought he might be pushing the envelope of their connection, what some might even have called friendship, but at the moment he didn't care.

"Marcus, my apologies. I neglected to ask about your father."

There it is, Emilio. Cut to the family, all gangster style.

"No idea," he said aloud. "We haven't spoken in the last, well hell, I don't know how long it's been. But it's been a while. I imagine you know more than I do."

"That I do, Marcus."

Dresden sighed. "I'm not here to negotiate terms for First Watch, I'm here—"

"I know why you're here. Your man there called you because he doesn't approve of our arrangement and he needed some muscle to push me."

Dresden glanced at Bear, whose eyes were as round as saucers. "But you know, Marcus, I don't like to be pushed," DeSoto continued. He rolled his glass between his palms, small beads of water dropping to the floor.

"That I do. Still, the question I have is why? Why won't you let First Watch do the job you hired them to do? The idea is that you have significant assets outside of yourself to protect. Assets that are integrated and interlinked." Dresden stopped, took a deep breath, then continued, "You know what, I don't know why I'm rehashing what you already know. The program First Watch offers is supposed to be comprehensive. Why won't you let it work? Why are you playing fucking cowboy?" The fireplug man made a move toward Dresden but DeSoto grunted, and he froze.

DeSoto uncrossed his legs and leaned forward. He stared deep into Dresden's eye, started to say something, then stopped. The man looked down at the ground. With a few sharp words, he ushered everyone except Dresden out of the room. As the last man closed the door behind him, DeSoto spoke in a low tone, "Marcus, you of all people should know. You know what it is like to have workers in your house all the time. You know what kind of people they are."

Dresden's skin prickled. What kind of people? *This* was the Emilio he knew. Asshole. A brilliant, commanding asshole, but an A-1 asshole, nonetheless.

"They will steal from you, Marcus," DeSoto went on. "I can't imagine those same people with guns in their hands, having complete access to me and what I have built."

"And yet your closest security guys are all serious criminals. How does that make any sense?"

Dresden watched DeSoto's hands. If he got agitated, he would work the pinky finger on his right hand as if the joint were seizing up. The finger lay lifeless on his knee as DeSoto talked. Dresden half-listened to him explain how it was his business and he had to run it the way he saw fit. That sometimes meant doing things others might think unreasonable or off-color. No matter what way DeSoto spun it, Dresden always figured he was attempting to justify corruption. This is the way you have to do business, he would say. It's not always a straight line, you know. Fucking crocked self-centered bastard. Dresden had little tolerance for explaining away illegal, amoral, or unethical behavior—a byproduct of being the son of man just like DeSoto.

"So, what about this ASG business? Why would you let a bunch of thugs like that run amok on your land?"

"It's not what it seems. I let them build a small range on their side of the mountain. That was my *promise,* as it were. They wanted more. I didn't give it to them. They pushed. I pushed back, four of them are dead, end of story. And you know this is Mindanao, not the mainland. Not the US! Here you have to *deal* with the thugs. The MILF. The JI. The ASG. I give a little, they leave us alone. But if they throw a rock, I throw a boulder, no question. Your guys aren't going to sign off on that kind of business, unless they are mental. I don't want that kind of guy around here, around me. So, I hired First Watch as a force multiplier—remember back when we did that? Down in Sulu. I want those thugs, all those outside of this compound, to know we have the best men, best weapons, best technology ..."

"Even if that means you won't use it properly."

"Even if that means *I* won't use it properly," DeSoto repeated. He grinned as if Dresden had just gotten the point, easing his way back into his chair. The man downed the drink in one gulp, then whistled. The doors opened and his men came back in along with Bear.

Dresden placed his glass just off the coaster on the dark wood table in front of him and stood.

"We will have dinner tonight. I will have a car pick you up around eight," DeSoto said. He stood and reached to shake Dresden's hand.

Dresden released the grip and moved toward the office door, then stopped and turned.

"Just make sure it's not a blacked-out Camry," Dresden said.

DeSoto let out an enormous laugh, and his men dutifully joined in. Dresden walked out as the laughter died.

The people in the airport terminal rushed by, unnoticed by Dresden until the Filipina brushed his leg. It wasn't the contact that made him look up from his book but her smell, her perfume – fresh flowers. The scene in front of Dresden was one of structured chaos, people purposefully moving from point to point, from gate to gate. But Dresden saw fire, not people. A blaze burned into the night, high above the stilt houses and mountains in the background. The woman's smell sent him spiraling back to a time he wished he could all but forget. A time that replayed in his mind, in his sleep, and when he was perfectly awake, like now. The houses burned for what seemed like an eternity. It would be an eternity to Dresden if the vision kept coming. At least this time the screams of the people were soundless. Dresden shook his head and looked down at his book to find he'd torn the spine almost a quarter of the way down. His phone rang. It was Lance. Dresden took a breath, thankful for the distraction, and answered.

"What up big kahuna?"

"Shit, that's what," Lance said.

"Dude. Okay, so spill," Dresden said.

Lance had returned to Oman three days earlier. He was on the tail end of a security assignment with an Omani billionaire, Badar Almasi. Like DeSoto, the man was one of First Watch's big clients. Private sector contracts, that's what they called it. Lapdogs seemed more appropriate, Dresden thought. A bunch of ex-SOF guys for the likes of Almasi to show off to his enemies when he left his compound in Muscat. Lance was the head lapdog.

He told Dresden he'd just had a sit down with Almasi's minder, Jaffer. He'd tried to explain to the man that without getting Almasi's travel schedule out in advance, Lance and his men were simply a reactionary force. They couldn't do any preplanning for the travel. They simply had to react to whatever came up, which was not something Lance wanted to do. He said that Jaffer had the balls to say that Lance didn't need Almasi's itinerary as Almasi already had a team of people making sure he was taken care of when he traveled. An advance team.

"Whore houses and thousand-dollar-a-plate dinners doesn't constitute a fucking advanced security sweep," Lance said.

"What's in the contract? Dresden asked, keeping to the brass tacks.

"What do you mean?"

"You know, what does the contract say you have to do? Is providing an advance travel team spelled out in the contract?"

"Oh that. No, it's not. But fuck that, man. It's the right thing to do,"

That's it, Dresden thought. *That's the real deal.* Doing the right thing was why Lance got out of the Teams. He'd gotten tired real quick of those guys riding desks not letting the pipe hitters do their job. They cherry-picked the good stuff, the ops that would mean they could get a bird or a star. Never mind that SOF guys—hell, all the military, ground pounders, and jet jockeys in general—left to do the right thing would have gotten the job done ten years earlier. Saved thousands of lives and millions, maybe even billions of dollars. That should have been enough to warrant quite a few advancements for the leadership, the cake eaters. It didn't happen, and Lance got out.

"The right thing. You sure you're doing the right thing?"

"Yeah I'm fuckin' sure I'm doing the right thing," Lance said, then was quiet for a moment. "Maybe not. Has First Watch been sending you some weird emails asking for clients' information?"

"Hmm, no, can't say that they have. But then again, I don't deal with the clients like you do. What kind of information are we talking about?"

Emails, Lance explained. Emails with a list of questions to ask the clients. Like a questionnaire or a survey. Simple enough, except he'd noticed some of them seemed odd. Things like how often you access your bank accounts via your personal computer. And do you password protect your computer, and where do you keep your password stored? Standard IT questions, except the more generic questions in the survey would be multiple choice. The questions Lance thought odd required handwritten answers.

"Don't you think that's kind of creepy, Marcus?"

"I guess. So, did you get the questions answered?"

"No—well, yes, like the first three or four times. But now that jackass Jaffer is stalling, and the HQ guys are pissing up a rope about it.

"Three or four? Damn man, how many emails have they sent in all?"

"Thirteen over the last three months."

"Shit!"

Dresden explained he thought it might be part of the company's move toward more private sector contracts, especially the ultra-rich. So maybe they were trying to build a database of information on these types of clients so they could better tailor their product line. It sounded good enough to Dresden. Lance seemed to half buy it, but more importantly it got him off the subject.

"Where are you?" Lance asked.

"Manila. The airport."

"You going down to Bali. Get some surf in?"

"No, heading back. I got about a week, then I have to head to HQ to teach a class."

"Sure. Sounds much more fun than getting totally barreled in Bali. Hey, bro, I got to go. Thanks for listening. I can't fucking wait to get outta this place."

"I hear you man. I'll catch up with you at the *Reunion*."

"Looking forward to it! Out here, bro."

Dresden hung up the phone. The smell of the woman's perfume was gone, replaced with jet fuel and fried food. He inspected the damage he'd done to his book, Michael Chabon's *The Yiddish Policeman's Union*. Torn, but still readable. As Dresden searched for his page, his phone buzzed. Lance had sent him a text. He must not have been *that* busy. Dresden chuckled as he read the message: *"The Simple Song" by Chris Stapleton.* His friend hadn't sent a reason with it.

Dresden fired back. It took a while, but Lance finally wrote back, *My girl loves it*. Dresden watched the crowd in front of him hustle by in a blur. He didn't know what to say. The immediate reaction would be to give Lance shit for bringing one of his flings into their game. But something told Dresden not to. He wrote back an equally short response: *Must be serious*. Dresden waited and watched a Japanese couple do Tia Chi in a small space they'd carved out in the waiting area across the maddening river of people between them. Ten minutes later, Lance responded: *It is!*

Six

Arline, Tennessee

An early-morning downpour forced the AC system at First Watch Headquarters to work overtime. Heavy, musky air filled the classroom. A fine lacquer of dampness covered everything, including the students. At the podium, Dresden flapped his arms a little to air himself out.

The small group of men and women, nineteen in all, ranged in age from mid-twenties to early forties. Everyone had a background—law enforcement, military, intelligence. A serious bunch for sure, and only half-interested in what Dresden was saying.

"We are in a business of shadows and grayness. A business of negative results being the desired outcome. A business the bean counters and data crunchers have tried time and time again to quantify, to label, to nullify through the judicious application of plain logic. The end result? We are right back where we started, in the shadows." Dresden paused, and no one looked up "Sooo ... everyone in this room is pretty much fucked!" he said, and stomped out from behind the podium. The audience jumped and stared at him.

Dresden flung his arms out to the side, wobbling his head. "Listen, get your heads out of your notebooks and off your tablets. You are all passing the class as of today. All you have to do is stay open-minded and participate, actively participate. So, get comfortable. It's going to be a good week. Agreed?" Dresden said.

The students nodded with enthusiasm, like elementary school children finding out they were on a permanent recess. They closed their notebooks and slid down in their seats, getting as comfortable as one could in a stifling thirty-by-thirty box with no windows and fluorescent lighting.

"The name of this class is ..." Dresden picked up the paper in front of him and read, "The Principles of The Infinite Threat Paradigm. Hmm, okay, let's drop the principles part of the class name. The Infinite Threat Paradigm. Infinite. Endless danger. Never-ending attack scenarios. Bad guys constantly trying to fuck you up—all distilled down to the basics.

"So, why come up with a theory or concept about never-ending threat possibilities?" Dresden asked.

"So, we know what we have to defend against," someone called out.

"Okay, that's one possibility. Anyone else?"

"So we can develop a security system that can more effectively address the current threats. Be agile in our approach."

Dresden took a couple more answers, then said, "You're all *wrong*. And you're all *right* at the same time. You are all right if you believe in the standard approach to developing security systems. And you will all be wrong if you continue to follow that line of thinking," Dresden said.

The class was dry at best. But when he started using his surfing and wave analogy, interest was usually piqued, if not for a short time. Dresden proposed to his listeners that when surfing, the surfer has a series of variables to contend with. Some of these variables have some soft to medium control factors—the surfer and his surfboard. The other variables are just that, variables, with few or no control factors. To make matters worse, or better in the case of surfing, there are an infinite number of combinations that can be thrown at the surfer, and all in a matter of seconds. And that's just one wave. The next wave brings with it another set of challenges, often entirely different from the previous one. You could say the wave almost evolves and adapts to challenge the surfer. And in response, the surfer must never let his guard down.

"If you assume the next wave, or in our case the next threat or attack, will be the same as the last, you are likely to find yourself wanting and that *you* perpetuated the deception. It's funny how often *we* allow these threats or waves to deceive us and we fail to meet the challenge." Dresden paused. He watched as a flicker of understanding sparked in the room. Heads nodded and a few of them couldn't resist taking notes.

Jennifer Nolan slid into the rear of the classroom. She motioned for Dresden to take a break. Several of the students turned to see what had drawn his attention.

"I apologize, everyone—I think one of those waves just rolled my way," Dresden said as he walked to the rear of the room.

"Jennifer, it's great to see you, but don't you think this could wait until after my class?" He reached his hand out, and she shook it.

"Roker wants to see you," Jennifer said.

"Now?"

"Yes, right now."

Dresden turned back to his students, who were all trying their best to eavesdrop and not look like it. They were security professionals, after all. "Uh, read ahead, okay? Chapter Two—The Dichotomy of Security."

Dresden and Jennifer stepped into the hallway. The woman walked swiftly, prompting Dresden to jog to catch up. She looked out of place at First Watch. Tall, with chestnut hair bouncing as she strode out. She moved like a panther and was equally as dangerous and mysterious. Roker's voiceless right-hand man—or woman. A cohort better suited to Madison Avenue than the backwoods of Tennessee.

Jennifer looked sidelong at Dresden. "Are you going to ask?" she said.

Dresden cocked his head and smiled, but kept his gaze forward, purposefully avoiding her intense, sky-blue eyes. "No," he said.

"You know you want to know. You want to know why the rush. Why he needs to see you right now."

"Well, no, not really."

"Ugh! Marcus, you are impossible. You're walking into a minefield, and you don't even know it."

"It moves me deeply that you care so much."

"Care? You arrogant ass, I'm trying—" Jennifer stopped.

He paused, noticing a dark look streak across her face.

"Dresden, I'm worried about Roker," Jennifer said.

He looked at her again. More closely this time. He'd rarely seen her fret this way. Her eyes slid down at the edges, giving her a sad sort of look. Her mouth and its tiny wrinkles popped out under her nose. Dresden lost himself in the details for a moment. They had stopped outside Roker's office door.

"Worried?"

"No time, Marcus," Jennifer whispered out of the side of her mouth, not looking at him.

"I want to know how it goes in there, okay?" She put her hand on the door handle to open it.

"Okay, I'll tell you at the pool. At lunch," Dresden said.

Jen's eyes narrowed. "Fine, you better." She opened the door.

Dresden stepped into the dark room; his eyes needed time to adjust. He looked at the floor, where the gleaming hardwood reflected the scene from outside. Bright sun peeked out from behind an errant rain cloud; blue skies, green trees. Moving into the center of the room, walking on clouds, he headed toward Roker's billiard-sized desk.

With five times as much floor space as furniture, Dresden felt he should be playing basketball, not meeting with First Watch's headmaster. Dresden moved to a single uncomfortable-looking sofa sitting on its own like a castaway. No good. He moved to a modern, highbacked chair and leaned across its back, adjusting and readjusting. Then he gave up and sat down. All the while, Tom Roker stood with his back to Dresden, looking out the floor-to-ceiling windows.

Roker had a linebacker's physique. Conditioned muscles bulged like rolling hills from his back, neck, and arms. He wore his black hair short. A shade of gray shone just above his ears. Dresden had a couple inches on the man, but Roker outweighed him by fifteen or twenty pounds. In his expertly tailored suit, Roker cut an imposing figure.

The man had been born to business. Running the world's largest private security company came easily to him. Roker managed it all with the tenacity and relentlessness born of his father and his father's father before him. Any worry Jennifer had was surely a mere road bump, Dresden thought. Roker had held it all together for nearly two decades. He'd weathered internal strife, external pressure, and the outrageous expectations of his clients. First Watch sank nearly 70 percent of its resources into Federal contacts from all the three-lettered agencies, and some of the OGAs, too. DOD most of all—easy pickings, as they had been at war for as long as he'd been in business. The other 30 percent was in the private sector.

Recently, that had begun to shift. Dresden heard a rumor that the Board of Directors was not happy with First Watch's bottom line and wanted Roker to move more aggressively to shift their efforts to the private sector. Of course the Board was worried. Worried that too many eggs came from one basket. Worried that the hen was nearing the end of its laying life.

Roker did not turn to face Dresden as he spoke. "Emilio DeSoto is not just a client of ours; he is a very wealthy and powerful man." Roker's voice was baritone and scratchy. "I wouldn't expect many to understand where he is in the order of things, but of all people, I would expect it from you. I *do* expect it from you. That's why you *were* in the position you were in."

"Tom, is this going to take long? I have a class full of students waiting on me," Dresden said, ignoring the emphasis.

Roker turned from the window and walked around his desk. His gait was jerky, like his upper body was too much for his legs to handle. He sat on the edge of his desk, legs outstretched, hands clasped in his lap. His shoulders, normally pulled back straight, were slumped forward, rolled in. Looking up, he met Dresden's stare. The man did look tired—real tired.

"I sent you an email apology for calling DeSoto a fucking cowboy. What more do you need?" Dresden said.

There was no malice in Roker's eyes. However, they shifted left to right and back again, quickly. Roker went to a rolling cart and poured two glasses of water. As he walked back, his shoes slapped the hardwood, echoing around the room. Dresden took the glass and put it on the floor next to his chair.

"I . . ." Roker started to say, returning to his perch on the desk.

He took a long breath, but not a deep one. Strained, like an asthmatic. "You insulted one of our most loyal clients. Not to mention a close personal friend. A friend, I might remind you, to both you and me."

"Do you really think I insulted him? If the truth is insulting, then I guess I'm going to piss a lot of people off. Come to think of it, I probably have pissed a lot of people off. So, you might as well fire me right now, right here. Oh, wait, you already did, didn't you Tom?" Dresden picked up his glass of water, took a drink, and watched Roker over the brim.

The man got up from the edge of his desk with a pained look, walked to the opposite side, removed his suit coat, and laid it over his chair back. He loosened and removed his tie and laid it over his coat with a mechanical flare. Roker's desk was empty save for two pieces of paper and a handmade plaque. The inscription read:

BUD/S Class Honor Man. In recognition of outstanding, sustained overall performance during 26 weeks of UDT/SEAL training, Thomas Roosevelt Roker is hereby awarded the title of Class Honor Man.

Roker came around and sat in the chair next to Dresden.

"You're smart, Marcus," Roker said. He paused. "Everyone knows that. But you don't have to prove it all the time. And you especially don't have to do it with our big clients. And even more so with Emilio. I know you think he owes you after what happened down in Sulu. But that was a long time ago. So fucking let it go."

"Mmm," Dresden said.

Roker put his glass down on the floor next to his chair. A damp ring settled around the base of the glass. He got up and retrieved two napkins from the cart, handing one to Dresden and placing the other under his own glass.

"It's a little different on this side of the boss's desk, isn't it, Tom?"

Roker looked at Dresden, who thought he saw a smile come over the man's face, but it was gone as soon as it appeared.

"Marcus, the wolves are circling. I need to make a move. A bold move. I have an upstart ops boss, Sean Branch, thinks he can schmooze the Board into following some scheme he's got cooked up. I got folks in congress that keep trying to hang stuff on our guys. I have to make a move to keep them all at the fence line long enough to ..." Roker trailed off and seemed to get lost in his thoughts.

"Firing me seems like a good start?" Dresden said, trying to bring Roker back.

"Enough joking."

"Okay, okay."

Roker got up and moved back to the windows. Dresden saw now what Jennifer was worried about. The oak was cracking at the seams. The man talked to the glass again but explained he had a plan and needed men he could trust to help him. A grand plan, if not a secret one, to save his company. The company *he* built. To keep it under *his* control, out of the hands of the Board and the likes of Branch. He wanted Dresden to get off the bench, as he put it, and come on full time. If Dresden didn't, he was to consider his current class as his last job for First Watch. "Friendship aside, of course. You understand," Roker added.

Dresden wanted to leave. To walk out and slam the door behind him. Instead he got up and walked over to Roker. His boss and former teammate didn't move, just sighed. They stood quietly, looking out over the training facility.

They could spy less than half of the property from this vantage point. An obstacle course serpentined in and out of the woods to the right. Several figures worked their way through ropes, wood poles, barbed wire, and mud pits. In front of them was a large parking lot, and beyond were two motor tracks—one dirt, with all manner of natural barriers and obstacles; the other, an asphalt track with a quagmire of urban diversions and dangers. Two military tactical vehicles moved over a portion of the dirt track strewn with massive boulders that threatened to flip the vehicles on their side. A caravan of SUVs moved through a town setting with concrete barriers, burning tires, and debris to thwart their progress on the second track. To the left was a series of large brick buildings that housed a three-story ballistic kill house, indoor ranges, and a couple large swimming pools, one of which reached a depth of forty-five feet. The facility was a testament to Roker's ingenuity and fortitude.

"This place never ceases to amaze me, Tom."

"Thank you, Marcus," Roker said.

They were silent again.

"Your father would have been proud. He *is* proud. He would have loved this place. He would have called it a soldier's Disneyland."

"I know. You tell me that every time you're here," Roker said. The right side of his mouth turned up.

"Am I still fired?" Dresden said.

"Yes," Roker said.

Dresden gave an unexpected laugh that surprised even him. A flicker of frustration sparked at the same time he spotted Jennifer exiting the front of the building, heading toward the pool. *Fired? Okay. Fired because I don't want to play your stupid little games, Tom.* He stole a glance at Roker. The man was staring out the window still. Let him deal with this shit storm on his own. *But fire me? That makes no fucking sense.* He watched Jennifer and knew he'd better leave or he was going to punch Roker square in the jaw.

"Okay, well then that settles it," he said as he turned and walked to the office door.

"Marcus! What the hell? I really don't think you get it. You are fired, period," Roker said.

Dresden made it to the door, downed the last gulp of water, and looked around for somewhere to put the glass. He set it on the floor.

"Love what yah did with the office, Tom," Dresden said, thick with sarcasm.

Roker didn't reply.

"I get it, Tom. I'm fired. I'll clean out my nonexistent desk and take the sad walk to the parking lot on Friday."

Still, Roker said nothing.

"You'll be able to see me out that window. Don't worry," Dresden said as he slammed the door behind him.

Jennifer came out of the woman's locker room walking with the authority of a drill sergeant, a towel stuck under her arm like a riding crop. Her hair was pulled tight into a braid that draped over her pale, muscular shoulders. Dresden stood at the deep end of the pool and studied some large, heavy stones at his feet. He pretended not to notice Jennifer. Dresden looked up when a towel hit him in the back of his head "Aw, there you are. Took you long enough," he said.

Jennifer stared, expressionless.

"What?" Dresden asked.

"So?"

"So what?"

"Ugh. Come on. How did it go with Roker?" Jennifer said.

"No, no, no. This is workout time, not chit-chat time. Get your head in the game, young lady," Dresden said, throwing the towel back at Jennifer. She caught it and gave him a scowl.

Dresden squatted and picked up one of the stones, moved to the edge of the pool, and with a brief look over his shoulder dropped the stone into the water. Jennifer tossed aside her towel and donned her goggles quickly. Dresden watched as the stone rocketed to the bottom of the fifteen-foot pool. Jennifer jumped in headfirst, following it. He smiled, then took a deep breath and jumped in after her.

At the bottom of the pool, Jennifer scooped up the fifty-pound stone and brought it in to her stomach. She planted her feet, then lunged forward, walking along the bottom. Dresden swam down and grabbed onto her shoulders. She leaned forward, pulling him the length of the pool.

At the end, she dropped the stone, swam to the surface and pulled herself out onto the pool deck. She started a round of burpees as Dresden exited the pool right behind her and joined in. When he was done, he jumped in the pool and went to the bottom, retrieving the stone in the same way Jennifer had. Jennifer dove down and latched onto his shoulders. This went on until each of them had carried the stone three times.

Afterward they sat, legs dangling in the water, panting when Jennifer blurted out, "I'm seeing someone."

Dresden was taken back by her sudden need to share. They were friends and that was it. Dresden wondered if Jennifer thought it best to stave off any ideas he might have. Not that he did. She was a pretty girl and a great workout partner, but not his type—if he had one.

"Okay," Dresden said, moving to the bleachers to get his towel. Jennifer followed.

"Good for you. Serious?"

She toweled herself off, then sat down. "I think so. It's long distance. But that should change soon."

"Good for you—and him."

"So, what do you think about Roker?" Jennifer asked, abruptly changing the subject.

Dresden laughed. "Man, you are on point, aren't you?"

"Yes, yes I am. So?"

"I can't really talk about it."

"Why not!" Jennifer boomed, the sound bouncing of the walls.

Dresden smiled. He liked it when Jennifer got excited. "Well, the main reason is I was fired."

"What!" Again with the boom.

"Roker fired me." He tried his best to hide his frustration.

"I will talk to him," Jennifer said.

"No, no need. I'm not coming on full-time. Especially if he wants me to tag along on some secret agenda he's got kicking around in his brainpan."

Jennifer stopped drying her hair and looked at Dresden.

"Agenda?"

Crap! "Yeah! I figured you knew. Figured since you're like his right rib, you would know it all. Hell, he didn't tell me anything, anyway. I was hoping you could tell me."

Dresden couldn't tell if Jennifer was boring holes in him or she'd gone to another world. Her glare was too much, and he looked away at the pool.

A few seconds later, he stole a look and she came around.

"You wanna get some coffee?" Dresden tried.

"No. I clearly have work to do," Jennifer said, and without a word stormed toward the locker room.

Great.

Seven

Coronado, California

Four heads rose slowly out of the water. A collective murmur gripped the crowd around Dresden. Lance, seated next to him, tossed popcorn into his mouth. A small boy next to Lance craned his neck to see. His ten-year-old fingers clamped, white-knuckled around the bench seat of the bleachers. A man's voice tinged with drama came over a loudspeaker behind them. He told the onlookers the story of the "naked warriors" on the night before D-Day. The four men crept up the beach toward the stands, clad only in tan shorts, with knives on their belts. The warriors carried swim fins and green canvas sacks. They placed the canvas bags on what looked like large concrete blocks with spikes jutting from them. Really, they were plywood. The obstacles were made to resemble those used by the Germans in 1944 to thwart the landing of Allied forces on the beaches of France.

"So, you quit, huh? Lance said, missing his mouth with a handful of popcorn.

"Didn't quit. Roker fired me," Dresden said. He watched as the young boy leaned farther forward while the men tied the sacks onto the blocks.

The announcer continued, "The naked warriors, their job complete, returned to the sea." The men formed a line a hundred yards out past the breakers, their position barely visible until they each raised an arm in the air. A small patrol craft came by and scooped them up one by one. The tension built as the sound of the boat faded.

"No shit? And you let him?" Lance said.

"I'm not going on full-time. Plus, I'm not sure what he's up to. I don't need that kind of headache," Dresden said.

Without warning, the blocks exploded, sending sand and plywood flying a hundred feet into the sky. The crowd cheered and clapped. Children screamed with excitement. Dresden watched the boy next to Lance jump up and down. For a brief second, the boy was Casper. The man over the loudspeaker announced the mission was a success. The beaches were again free of obstacles. The boats could land. The land troops could storm the beach. The great war would be won.

"What do you mean, 'what he's up to'?" Lance said.

"He's got some plan for First Watch. Maybe it has something to do with the emails you got, I don't know," Dresden said. "And there's some guy named Branch—the ops boss, I think. Roker says he's trying to get on the good side of the Board by proposing a plan for the company as well.

"Branch. God, I hate that dude. A real creep, I say. He sent all the site managers a video on the need to 'imbed' ourselves with our clients," Lance said. "Doesn't surprise me something weird is going on. Business. Yuck. I'd never want to be in business."

Dresden watched the crowd empty off the bleachers and move over to the picnic area. Why was Roker doing this? He'd never seen him this worried before. And why the secrecy?

"So, what are you going to do now?" Lance asked, hopping down off the bleachers into the soft sand.

"Don't know. I was pretty pissed off when I left Tennessee," Dresden said, "but after a week and some time at home, the wound has scabbed over. I don't really care much; ah forget it, yeah I'm still pissed," He would need to figure something out. Not for the money but to keep his sanity. Or he'd turn out like Mary or Will—weird or drunk.

"I bet. I guess you can start drinking like every other out-of-work deadbeat," Lance chided.

"I've got my business set up. Maybe I'll just go it alone. You know, do the same thing but with no middleman."

The two of them walked toward the beer truck. Lanced flipped the tap down and filled a plastic cup with beer. He offered it to Dresden, who declined. They found a group of old guys swapping war stories. Dresden lost himself in the tales of bravado and misfortune, of conquest and failure. There was an empty seat next to him. Dresden saw Casper sitting there when he was ten. Big eyes. Mouth agape. Face flushing at the curse words. This was why Casper loved coming to the reunions—the stories, the Team guys. This was why he incessantly asked how old he had to be to join the Teams, even after he knew he had a disease that meant that dream could never come true. And it was why Emily said he couldn't go anymore, even before the divorce.

A hot poker stabbed Dresden in the chest. Maybe he *should* start drinking again.

Lance nudged him, bringing him back to the present. He looked around at the last two guys from the circle, who were walking away.

"It's rock portage at the Center. Danny's burger and a show?" Lance asked.

"Sounds great," Dresden said.

Dresden and Lance watched as the BUD/S students struggled to land their rubber boats on the rock jetty.

The horizon split the sun silhouetting the instructors standing on the pile of jagged boulders out front of the iconic Del Coronado hotel. The instructors yelled through megaphones as they hopped from rock to rock telling the students how much they sucked. Dresden and Lance laughed at their taunts and the students' feeble efforts to succeed where success was not possible.

"What about you, man?" Dresden said through a mouthful of his burger.

"Same old shit for the next month or so," Lance said.

The two men were quiet for a moment. They ate and watched the collection of boats and men battle the waves to nail a perfect landing. The idea of asking Lance to expound on his plans troubled Dresden. For as long as he'd known him, their conversations were light. Surfing, the Teams, sometimes women, movies, and maybe politics from time to time. And of course, music. Lance kept his feelings and deeper thoughts close to his chest. And Dresden preferred not to pry at anyone, especially his closest friends. Of course, Emily said that was what made him such a bad friend. But he sensed something was different with Lance.

Dresden started, then stopped, then said, "That's not what I'm talking about. I mean, what are you—"

"I know what you meant bro," Lance said, cutting Dresden off. Dresden looked over at his friend.

The man's face shifted its expression as quickly as the waning shadows of the day. Lance sighed. "Look, I'm out after this gig in Oman is up." He stopped and let the comment hang there as if weighing it for himself. "I wasn't going to tell anyone, 'cause I know how everyone gets. So, don't try and pull any weird bullshit on me."

"You know me better than that."

"Yeah I do. But still ..."

"What's this about, Lance? You're kind of freakin' me out," Dresden said, honestly worried.

Lance looked over at him. He smiled, then seemed to dive deep into a thought for a moment. When he came back, he said, "That girl I told you about. Well, it's serious. I have the house in Santa Cruz nearly paid off. I have a grip of money saved up from all the First Watch gigs. I'm good. So, I was thinkin', well I thought I might ask her ..." Lance let the words trail off.

"I'm happy for you, man. It's a good thing. Really," Dresden said.

"Really? You think so? Lance said.

"Most definitely, dude."

"Cool. Of course nothing will change, you know. We'll still hang out and charge Mavericks when it goes off," Lance said expectantly. A thin stream of mustard coursed from the corner of his mouth as he smiled wide at Dresden.

A pang of jealousy welled up inside him, a longing to have the chance to start over. To be where Lance was now, at the precipice of a new beginning. Of course everything would change, but it'd be for the better. That was Dresden's hope for Lance. He felt he needed to say something more. Something profound and meaningful, something honest. But nothing came. A song would have to suffice.

"Hey man, I got a song for *you*. You remember 'The White Blank Page' by Mumford and Sons?"

"Hell yeah I do," Lance said. He looked as if he were mulling it over. Maybe playing it in his head. "Perfect, man. Beautiful. Thanks. I think we should add it to the list too."

"Agreed," Dresden said. He reached over and patted his friend on the shoulder. "Agreed."

"Thanks again for being my friend all these years, Marcus. I only give you shit 'cause I love you, bro. You're good people, and there aren't many of those out there. You know that, right?"

"Yeah. Okay. You're welcome, man. And the feeling's mutual. The good people gotta stick together. Look out for each other."

"Agreed."

Eight

Porto Venere, Italy

The morning sun lifted the curtain of darkness on the small point of land in the northwest of Italy. The postcard views turned on like picture windows in a department store. Dresden, conditioned over decades to rise near dawn, made sure he was out on the narrow, winding coastal roads before the cars. Cyclists were gods in this part of the world; runners were mere targets. Dresden made his way back into the sleepy Liguria village, along the waterfront and out to the Chiesa di San Pietro. At the church of Saint Peter, Dresden scuffed along the ancient stone paths. A sense of smallness came over him as he thought of the timelessness of the rocks beneath him. The men or slaves that had laid them were long gone, dust now. The walkway remained.

Dresden leaned over a stone wall, peeking down at the blue-green water, and breathed in the Mediterranean Sea air. He watched tiny boats cross the Bay of Poets, a salty breeze streaming across his face as he stretched his legs and cooled down from his run.

Lungs hydrated and muscles limber, he walked back to his pension on via Capellini, a few blocks from the church.

At breakfast, a small, bent man hovered over the three-table dining room. Dresden was his only customer.

"Where is your wife?" the man said, his voice like gravel, his English broken.

"No wife," Dresden said.

"No wife? Then what are you doing here? No wife. No romance. Porto Venere is romance."

"Work."

"Work! There is no work here. Only the work of romance."

"Then I'll have to work on that," Dresden said. He gave the man a thumbs up.

The man scoffed at him, retreating to the back room. Dresden could hear him telling someone something in Italian. The man scoffed again. Dresden assumed he was gossiping about his uncouth, obliviously American guest.

With his first appointment scheduled for the afternoon, Dresden took his coffee to a table outside. The sun peeked through the latticework of vines and wrought iron covering the small patio, warming Dresden. He read and dozed, then dozed some more, and before he knew it he'd done much more than doze. He jumped up and went to his room to change.

Dresden hurried the few blocks from his hotel along the waterfront to a trattoria. Like so much of Europe, it looked the same. *Fourteen years,* Dresden thought, as the corners of his mouth stretched. As he breathed in the same smells and studied the tablecloth. It hadn't changed either. Nothing had changed. He chose a table with a view of the boats bobbing at their docks and Palmeria Island across the bay. His angle of concern, though, was the single route into and out of the town—a two-lane road that dropped into the village like the end of a roller coaster ride.

Valerio Rosetti showed up twenty minutes after Dresden had seated himself. He'd not been served, but as the door opened and Valerio walked in, a waiter and attendant appeared as if from nowhere. Dresden stood to greet his friend. Watching, the attendant swallowed hard as Valerio slapped away Dresden's hand and mauled him like a bear. He slammed his back several times, then kissed him on both cheeks. The waiter stood by, head hanging.

Dresden noticed faint wrinkles around Valerio's large round nose, and his dark blues eyes glistened under the shadow of a thick brow. The man ran a hand through his tight, curly black hair, then dawned a serious look.

"It has been way too long, my friend!" Valerio said. He held Dresden's shoulders and looked him up and down. "You are fit, you look good."

"You too, Valerio. If not a little bigger …" Dresden said.

"It has been nearly fifteen years. I have lifted a lot of weights in that time," Valerio said. "Sit, sit." He growled something in Italian at the waiter, who scurried off with his attendant and returned with a bountiful meat and cheese plate.

"So, you are going to meet my great uncle. He is anxious to meet you," Valerio said.

"I'm looking forward to it too. I'm happy for the distraction." Dresden eyed the boats again for a second. "I needed this more than you know. So thank you, Val."

"The thanks go to you, my friend. I've been telling my uncle he needs better security. But he does not want to work with something like First Watch. So, when I heard you quit, well, here you are," Valerio said, and waved one hand in the air while he rolled meat and cheese with the other.

"So how is, uh, your wife?"

"Emily. She's not my wife anymore."

"Aw, I am sorry to hear that. It's not good to be alone you know. Girlfriend?"

"That's what I hear, and no, no girlfriend."

"That's not good."

Dresden smiled. Valerio hadn't changed, not one bit. "By the way, I didn't quit. I was *fired.*" The word jabbed him like a bee sting.

They continued to talk as they finished the plate of meat and cheese. Valerio ordered olives. As Dresden stuck the last one in his mouth, the waiter showed up with coffees. Valerio leaned back, crossed his legs, and sipped at his. Dresden noticed, over the other man's shoulder, a black four-door Audio roll to a stop in front of the trattoria. Dresden looked at his watch and then back up, and Valerio followed his gaze.

"Ah, our ride. Let's go," the man said. He downed his drink, stood, and moved to the door.

"The bill?" Dresden said. Valerio kept walking.

"No bill sir," the attendant said, a large and apologetic grin stretched tight across his face.

Without hesitation, Valerio loaded up in the back seat of the Audi, and Dresden followed suit. The driver nodded to both of them but said nothing. They left Porto Venere and headed north, into the mountains behind the port city of La Spezia.

Near the top of the mountain the driver turned onto a private gravel road. A large iron gate opened as the Audi approached. The driver sped through. Dresden turned to watch the gate bounce its way closed, but he lost sight before it did.

The tires crackled beneath the car as they pulled up to the front of the house, a four-story stone and stucco structure that Dresden assumed must have been several hundred years old. It looked unfinished, which Dresden knew was not uncommon—tax breaks, after all. He started to get out as the driver helped him with his door. The man was slightly taller than Dresden, with a thick brow and a rhinoceros neck. One tooth was missing from his smile, as well as most of his left ear. *Driver and bodyguard.*

Valerio put his arm around Dresden's shoulder and walked him into the house. He'd spent nearly two years in Italy over the span of a decade, and in that time, he'd picked up a good bit of the language and many of the customs. Unfortunately, most of it he'd long forgotten.

The two men waited in the magnificent foyer—marble floors, carpets of blood red and royal purple, near-life-size portraits on the walls, framed in burnished gold. A ten-foot chandelier hung overhead. Classic. Beautiful. Amazing.

Loud chatter vaulted from a room off the foyer, down a hall to the side of a wide, sweeping staircase. Italian voices. He heard a woman and then a man. An older man. It sounded like they were arguing, but Dresden knew better. He looked over at Valerio, who grinned and waited, teetering back and forth on his toes.

A slender, elegant man came out of the back room. Dresden made to walk toward him. Valerio stopped him and moved toward the man instead. He shook the man's hand, and Dresden saw Valerio bow slightly as well, or at least he thought he did.

"Marcus, I would like you to meet Mr. Massignani."

Dresden took Massignani's hand. His grip was of a man who'd once possessed real physical power. The man studied Dresden in return, with eyes both sad and bold. His voice was like silk, refined. Dresden held the man's hand a moment too long. He was overwhelmed by it all—the ancient house, Valerio's bow, and now this man in front of him. *Too much.*

"Mr. Dresden, I have heard a great many things about you. I have been looking forward to meeting you for some time. I admit even at my age I'm still a busy man and do not have much time to spend with you. However, I would like to hear your initial thoughts—as you drove in and came into my home, I imagine you were assessing my security. What did you see?"

"I—" Dresden stopped. A woman came out of the room down the hall. She stopped and looked directly at him, raising her chin. A shadow cut across her diagonally, shrouding her, yet still her sapphire blue dress shone like a bright, cloudless sky. She turned and dashed off. He watched the vapor of her image dissipate before wrenching his attention back to Mr. Massignani. The man dipped his head and smiled as if he knew what Dresden was thinking.

"Yes, sir. I was. You are in a fairly remote location, which of course is good and bad. The approach to your home is not inviting, and that is a plus. I didn't see any camera systems or sensors on the driveway—not to say they aren't there," Dresden added, "but most notable were the gate and your driver. The gate is automatic, which is good. However, it is not very sturdy and moves too slow, and your driver did not wait until it was closed before proceeding.

"Good! I like this. Good," the man said. He glanced at Valerio.

"Sir, I have one question though, if I may," Dresden said. Mr. Massignani nodded. "Why do you think you need me to evaluate your security? Is there a particular threat or concern you're attempting to defend against?"

The man studied him, and Dresden worried he may have asked the wrong question.

"Mr. Dresden, I have many friends. But I'm told I have just as many enemies. I have never seen these enemies. My nephew, my overprotective nephew," Mr. Massignani said as he looked over at Valerio, "says that they are out there. He says you are the best at figuring out what I will need."

"Well, sir, I appreciate that," Dresden said.

He lifted himself up on his toes and looked behind the man again.

"With your permission, I will take a look around and get back to you with an initial assessment. How does that sound?"

"Very agreeable." Mr. Massignani winked at Valerio and nodded to Dresden, then floated away.

For an hour, Dresden wandered around the house and grounds. There was actually very little security to speak of. Dresden could see why Valerio was concerned for his great uncle. If the man had any enemies at all, they could get to him unrestricted. If he had anything of value, there would be little to stop anyone from taking it.

Dresden sat on a wall writing notes, the city of La Spezia and the bay spread out below him. The sun dipped behind him, casting long shadows on the city. A cool, salty breeze with the faintest hint of burning trash blew up the mountainside.

"So, what do you think?"

Dresden jumped and turned to find the woman in the blue dress standing before him. Without thinking, he took her in from her bare feet to her emerald green eyes. He caught her brow pop up, blushed, and found his voice again.

"It's fine."

"Fine?" Her dress billowed, and she pressed it down with long fingers and slender arms.

"Yes. No. Have you been following me? Hi, my name's Marcus," Dresden stammered.

"Maria." She giggled, putting her fist to her mouth.

"Good to meet you, Maria."

"So, do you have a more definitive assessment than *fine*?" Maria said.

"Oh, sure, but I don't want to bore you with … boring security stuff," Dresden said. *Ugh, what is this, high school? Shit, man, get it together.*

"You won't bore me at all. I deal a little in security as well," Maria said. She moved to the wall and sat next to him. "I'm helping my grandfather set up better security for his online businesses and personal electronic accounts. You know, info-sec," Maria said.

Dresden nodded. "So, let me get this straight. Mr. Massignani is your grandfather, and Valerio's uncle."

"Yes, and *great* uncle to Val."

"And you're helping set up your grandfather's electronic security. What are you actually working on?" Dresden said. He scratched at the stubble on his chin.

"Firewalls. Access authorization. Domain admins, things like that."

"Ah. Firewalls and … and. I don't do cyber. Or info-sec, or you know—I know what it is, of course. But pretty much it baffles me. So, I stick to what I know. If it doesn't carry a gun, I'm not sure what to do with it."

Maria giggled again. Dresden lost himself watching a light band of freckles that dappled the bridge of her nose.

"Why not? It's so important. It has such an impact on everything else, including physical security. Especially when you have little or no idea where a threat may come from. Being aware of every possible avenue of attack simultaneously ..."

They talked, sometimes excitedly, for the next hour, weighing and discussing and arguing the merits and pitfalls of security systems and their implementation and operation. Maria seemed to know his thoughts, read his mind, and often finished his sentences. They would have carried on had it not been for Valerio interrupting.

"We were just discussing grandfather's security issues," Maria said, standing and straightening her dress, her cheeks rose-colored.

Dresden was sure his cheeks looked the same. He looked at Valerio, who winked at him.

"Marcus, my uncle has to leave. But before he leaves, he would like to know if you are interested in helping him." Valerio looked from Dresden to Maria, a smile on his face.

"Definitely. I can do it."

"Great! I will let him know." He turned to leave but stopped. "Oh, and how long do you think it will take?"

Dresden looked over at Maria. She had half turned away from him, looking out over the stone wall to the sea. The evening sun highlighted her black, wavy hair. "Oh, I don't know Valerio. It could take … a while. A week, maybe?"

He caught Maria flush again and smile.

"Yeah, tell your great uncle a week should do it … at the most ten days."

Valerio snickered at Dresden, then walked away shaking his head.

Nine

San Francisco, California

The fragrant sauces and spices wrapped around Dresden like a warm blanket as he walked into Freddie's, a favorite of the lunchtime convention crowd. Waiters slung plates of food around like acrobats. Large pitchers of beer spilled as they were delivered to a table of men and women Dresden knew from First Watch. He recognized a few of them, but no one he wanted to sit with, so he found a table for two out of the way of the maddening crowd.

His waiter swung by his table like Tarzan. Dresden's pained, ragged expression prompted the man to say, "Do you need something for the pain, young man? A beer? A glass of wine? Something stronger?" Dresden winced and ordered only food. The waiter hung out, hand on hip for a moment, then shrugged and walked off. Jet lag, Dresden figured. His head was pounding. He waved the waiter back over and ordered two cups of coffee.

Dresden's phone rang; it was Robbie Coltrane. He covered his ear.

"Hey there, Robbie."

"Got your message. Italy, huh? Robbie said.

"Yeah, but I'm really feeling it for some reason."

"Eat a bad meatball?"

"No. Don't think so. Hey man, you about here? I ordered already."

"Sorry guy, can't make it. Sick kid," Robbie said, "and I'm on the late shift as well. Gonna be a rough one,"

A raspy cough sounded in the background.

"What? Can't a babysitter handle that?"

"Are you kidding? This is my kid. Hey, we'll catch up soon. I gotta go. Oh, oh hey Marcus, I may have some work for you if you're interested. We'll catch up," Robbie said, and hung up.

Dresden pocketed his phone and downed his first cup of coffee. The room swirled and an immediate need to splash cold water on his face overcame him. He jerked himself from his seat and made his way to a tiny bathroom outfitted for three that barely fit two. The cold water shocked him, but the dizziness remained. His tired eyes peered back at him from the mirror. As he reached for a towel the door swung open, slamming into his elbow. A shot of pain coursed through his body. The door retracted then opened again, hitting his back this time. Dresden swiveled to see who was banging him around. The door opened again and a man, roughly Dresden's build, with a shock of white hair, pushed past him. He stank of cigarettes and body odor. The man slammed the toilet seat up against the bowl with his foot and started to urinate, groaning as he did. He looked back over his shoulder to see Dresden staring at him.

"What? You a fuckin' faggot?" the man said.

Bold statement in this town, bud. What an asshole. He rubbed his elbow as he tried to flush out the guy's accent – thick and eastern European. Dresden was in no condition to tussle, so he left. His head swirled again, and he leaned on the nearest wall for a moment. As his head cleared, he overheard someone mention First Watch. Inching forward, Dresden looked in on several men huddled around a table in a private alcove.

"First Watch is in over their head. No, wait, maybe that's not it," the man said.

Dresden cocked his head to the side enough to get a look at the speaker. He looked familiar, but Dresden couldn't quite place him. A slight man with thin blond hair—a suit and tie, headquarters guy for sure. The man went on about First Watch and how they needed to move away from DOD and invest more in the private sector. The man's audience consisted of four men in well-tailored suits, slicked-back hair and plastic smiles. They all chewed on unlit cigars. Dresden slid a few inches forward, and saw two young girls, twelve or thirteen, maybe. One of the girls looked at Dresden, deadpan. The other looked frightened or bored to tears; it was hard to tell. Dresden felt for them. He'd been there. Lunch with daddy meant sit down and shut up and listen to the adults talk about nothing of interest to a twelve-year-old kid. Dresden leaned another inch forward and saw the old shithead from the restroom sitting next to deadpan girl. He pinched the bridge of his nose.

Limping back to his table, he drank his second cup of coffee. His head started to clear about the time the noise in the room began to die down. The restaurant was emptying out; lunch break was over. Dresden fell into step as the crowd moved back to the convention center like a pack of zombies.

The gathering of security professionals was co-sponsored by First Watch and DOD. Started seven years earlier, the convention had become a must-attend event. A veritable who's who in security operations, tactics, and technology. The year before, Dresden's second year with the company, he'd reluctantly attended the convention as a First Watch representative, gladhanding sweaty, overly excitable people he'd just as soon have throat punched.

This year Dresden, the varnish washed off, saw First Watch as a glossy mockup of what Roker had first intended. He didn't even really know why he was there. Habit, he guessed. Maybe even boredom after his week in Italy getting to know Maria. Dresden wandered the presentation halls until he came to a poster advertising a keynote speaker.

Sean Branch, Senior Operations VP for First Watch. Mr. Branch will be speaking to First Watch's long and valued relationship with the Department of Defense. A look back, a look to the present, and a look at what is still to come. 13:30 to 14:30.

He studied the photo of Branch on the poster. It was the man from the alcove at lunch, espousing how First Watch should cut and run from DOD. *Oh, this ought to be fun.*

The room was dark and almost filled to capacity. Dresden squeezed himself between two overweight guys breathing like they were on ventilators. Branch walked on stage, standing in the center for a moment and looking at the floor. He was more diminutive now, framed as he was by the big, empty stage. Branch held the silence to the point of discomfort. The people around Dresden began to shift nervously. Finally, Branch looked up and said:

"Dramatic? Intense? There is no better way to describe the last ten-plus years than dramatic." The crowd murmured. "First Watch has walked hand-in-hand with the Department of Defense the entire way. There to provide. There to assist. There to ..."

"Make a billion dollars," the guy in front of Dresden whispered.

"… there to train. And more. When First Watch started, it offered simple solutions to simple problems. DOD says they don't have enough men or women to cover a particular post? First Watch was there to provide the highly skilled personnel. As time went on …"

Branch moved around the stage, looking out at the audience. His image projected onto two large screens behind him. Occasionally, scenes of soldiers and First Watch contractors working together flashed in his place. He smiled when he caught an eye in the crowd. He looked serious as he mentioned DOD's issues; elated when talking about First Watch's achievements.

"The adversary has adapted almost as rapidly as we can provide solutions. In some cases, faster."

Dresden found the man charismatic and captivating, traits Roker did not possess. Roker was a nuts-and-bolts guy. This guy, Dresden thought, was a salesman, peppered with a smoldering intensity that held a hint of danger. Dresden could see why Roker was worried. He should be. Dresden had heard enough, though. His headache was coming back.

Outside in the hallway, he bought another coffee at a cart, then watched the people move down the halls to workshops, presentations, and the vendor hall. Except for the First Watch monolith of a booth at the center of the hall, the vendors were worth checking out. He especially liked the castaways at the perimeters and the back.

Dresden's phone buzzed. It was Lance. He'd gone back to Oman despite his better judgment. He'd told Dresden how he sat in the terminal at the gate until the very last moment, arguing with himself, but eventually got on the flight. Lance had texted him several times a day since. The drama at his site was reaching Mexican tele-novella proportions. First Watch had sent him a couple additional men, including a guy named Tippins who was a real ass-kisser and riding Lance hard about getting imbedded with Almasi. Things were particularly bad at the moment, as he'd been sequestered in his dorm room for the past day and a half.

Lance said Almasi was holding a secret meeting of a splinter group of the Middle Eastern and North African Financial Action Task Force, nine men of power and influence in the region. Lance's men were not allowed to be anywhere they could hear or see the members attending. They were to ensure the lane of ingress and egress was secure, and that was it.

Lance wrote that his room was his ad hoc TOC and gym. He'd done two hundred burpees in the last two hours trying to keep himself from putting a bullet through the wall. The good thing, he joked, was that Almasi didn't allow weapons in the *helps* dorms. Otherwise, who knows what would have happened.

Several people passed Dresden in the hall, talking loudly. His phone dinged—another text from Lance. *"Louisiana" by Percy Mayfield. I needed some sweetness right now and Mayfield was just that, pure sweetness.*

He could almost feel the utter desperations in his friend. The texting had been more frequent, elucidating his song choices, mostly about going home. Dresden, not one to wax poetic, struggled to provide what he thought his friend needed. *Stay strong brother* was his common comeback. This time he added, *Just a couple more weeks man, you can do it, hang in there.* Pathetic. He added, *Love the song, concur*, then paused before sending it. Dresden hit send and turned around, feeling a warm breeze on the back of his neck.

"Ciao, Marcus!"

Ten

San Francisco, California

"Maria?" Dresden said.

The woman beamed and gave him a hug. "Yes, it's me," she said, her voice muffled in his chest.

Dresden hugged her back, feeling awkward. His legs wobbled but his headache ran out of his head like a whippet after a rabbit. Dresden pushed Maria back and held her at arm's length.

"What the hell are you doing here?"

Maria giggled, flipped up her convention credentials, and said, "I *do* work in security. Or did you already forget me?"

A booming laugh startled the people nearby.

"No Maria, I haven't forgotten you. How could I? I just saw you yesterday!" Dresden pushed her out of the crowd. "Sooo, you just decided to jump on a plane and come to California?"

They found a bench among the throng of people, and Maria explained that she'd been coming to the Frist Watch convention for three years. She'd had plans to attend long before they met. Dresden, confused, confessed he didn't understand. Why hadn't she told him? They could have flown together. Maria said that was exactly why she didn't say anything. Her family situation was complicated. If they knew about Dresden, it would get even more complicated. Valerio was sworn to secrecy, and since he thought of Dresden as a brother, he was complicit. Everyone else would have ratted her out to her father—or worse, her mother.

Dresden admitted it sounded overly complicated. The headache, sneaking its way back into his head, crept around his temples like a goblin. He looked around the hall. He instantly hated the place and wanted to leave. "So you've been to San Francisco for three, now four years, and you've never seen the city?" Dresden asked.

Maria looked at him sheepishly. "No."

"Well we're just going to have to fix that, now won't we?" Dresden grabbed her by the hand and led her out of the building.

The theater let out onto a damp sidewalk in Lower Haight. No rain, just a thick, wet fog that enveloped the city while Dresden and Maria were watching the movie. People shuffled by under umbrellas and wrapped in parkas. Occasionally, someone scuttled by without either. They tucked themselves under the awning of the movie house. Maria jammed her hands into her jean pockets to keep them warm, and Dresden draped his zip-up hoody over her back and head.

"Better?"

"Yes, thank you."

"Let me check my phone before we head out, okay?"

Maria stared at a glass-covered movie poster, lit up like a shrine. An exceedingly handsome black man was running, briefcase in hand, down a busy street. Helicopters and police cars appeared to be chasing him.

One text. Lance asked if Dresden would be heading to Tennessee, and in response, Dresden reminded him he didn't work for First Watch anymore. Lance persisted. He hadn't heard from his lady friend in a couple days and was worried about her. It was just a feeling, though. They'd gone a few days without talking before, Lance admitted. Dresden knew the closer Lance got to coming home, the more neurotic he was likely to get. He texted that he would have someone look in on her if he couldn't, and Lance sent back the contact information.

Without reading the last text Dresden stuffed his phone in his pocket and stepped out to the edge of the sidewalk. He looked left then right, then back at Maria.

"We can catch a cable car to Chinatown in the next block. You good to walk that far?"

Maria smirked, straightened her back, and flung the sweater at Dresden as she passed by. They walked to the cable car stop. The trolley took them up and over a hill to Chinatown. From there, it was another short walk up a steep street to what Dresden considered the best Chinese food joint in town. At the front of the restaurant, a gaunt Chinese woman ushered them up a narrow set of stairs to the third-floor, cupping Maria's elbow the whole way. At the top, she handed them off like a football to another host. They were seated at what must have been the smallest two-top table in the country. Maria craned her neck out the open window, peering down to the bustling, neon-streaked street. A droplet of water splashed onto the back of her neck. She squeaked and sat back down.

"I hate that I have to go," Maria said, wiping the back of her neck.

Dresden was quiet. He folded and unfolded his napkin several times.

"Why this place for our last night on the town?" Maria said.

"Look around," Dresden said. He leaned back in his chair and grinned at her.

Maria looked. The paint was peeling. The tables wobbled. The walls were cracked. The stairs they'd come up were only fit for one person at a time. Every chair was mismatched. The place was so crowded there was no room to pass without bumping into those seated. The hosts and waiters seemed put out, or aloof at best. It was a disaster. She looked at Dresden, he beamed, and so she looked around again.

The smells were exquisite. The patrons, smiling and laughing and drunk or getting there. They gestured wildly as they savored their food. They talked loudly in direct competition with the rest of the room. On their tables were plates of noodles and fish, rice and vegetables, pork and beef. Steaming. Fresh. Sizzling. A pallet of color even Picasso would have been proud of. All served from a rickety-looking dumbwaiter in the center of the long, claustrophobia-inducing room.

"Thank you, Marcus," Maria said. She leaned back in her chair and knocked heads with the woman behind her. They both laughed, then apologized and laughed some more.

Escondite, California

Dresden's phone rattled on the nightstand. Sleepy, he grabbed for it and shut it off. AP groaned at his bedside. Dresden had gotten back to Escondite a little before two in the morning, snuck AP out of

Mary's backyard, and fallen straight into bed. Maria had called him on his drive down from San Francisco. It felt like they were in high school. As Maria spoke in hushed tones, he imagined her hiding under the stairwell, hand cupped over her mouth, whispering conspiratorially. He knew she was sitting on the bed in her hotel room, but it was all so juvenile and exciting. He dreamed of steep streets and fog and Chinese food. Of Maria's olive skin shining in the neon.

A shard of light bathed Dresden's face as he woke to the sound of seagulls squabbling somewhere outside. He was disoriented for a few minutes. A soft, dry breeze blew the smell of the sea into his room, and he remembered—it was the smell of his childhood. He was ten again for a second. Dresden rolled onto his back as his phone sounded. It was too early for Maria to be calling. Her flight was at noon, and she was going to call from the gate. The clock read 7:30 a.m. Dresden needed to go to the beach.

He sat on the steps off Delta street. The sun was up but not over the hills yet. The bay was calm, glassy. Small, waist-high swells lazily rolled in. Three surfers sat on their boards on the south side of the pier.

Dresden set his phone down on the wall beside him. It shuffled and bucked on the concrete. *Another call? Damn.* The phone sounded sick, coughing like an old man with tuberculosis. He picked it up and looked at the screen, then let out a long breath and answered it.

"Hello!"

"Marcus, we've been trying to get in touch with you man!"

"Who is this? I don't work for First Watch anymore. You can stop calling me." Dresden said. He went to hang up.

"Marcus! It's Fence, man!"

"Fence? What's up dude? Why didn't you—"

"Marcus!" Fence cut in. "Listen, I have to tell you, it's Lance. He ... he died last night in an attack at the compound he's—he was at."

Dresden heard nothing else. Smoke started to rise from the sand at his feet. A burgeoning flame flickered at the base of the fire. The smell of burning wood and flesh gripped his senses. Dresden froze, a faint pain in his hand pulsing with a subtle but increasing intensity. The crack of his phone brought him around. He pulled the phone away from his head. Small bits of glass fell to the steps.

"Fence! Fence! You there?" Dresden howled into the phone.

"Yeah man, I'm here," Fence said.

"Tell Roker that I'm going to Oman to do the after-action—"

"Marcus, I don't think that's—" Fence said, but Dresden had already hung up.

The crack ran diagonally across his screen. Dresden lay his phone in his lap and stared out at the ocean. Smoke churned like a tornado in front of him. The houses perched precariously on stilts over the water snapped like toothpicks, tossing their charges into the dark waters. They doused the flames but not his memory, not the visions. Dresden pressed his head with both hands to make them stop.

The shrill, sick sound of the phone shook him once more.

"What!" Dresden boomed into the receiver.

"Marcus! Are you okay?" Maria said.

"No! I'm far from okay."

"What is going on?"

There was a long silence, as Maria waited.

"There was an attack in Oman," Dresden said.

Another silence.

"Your friend Lance was in Oman, right?"

"Yes."

"Is … Is he okay?"

"No. He's—he's dead."

"Oh! Oh, Marcus, I'm so sorry. I—"

"He died while *we* were having fun! While we watched a movie and—and laughed. While we walked around the city and ate Chinese food. He died, and I was having fun. Laughing it up with you."

Maria's voice stiffened. "Marcus, it sounds like you are blaming me. Blaming our time together as the reason your friend died."

Dresden said nothing, just breathed into the receiver, fast and shallow.

"I understand your friend died. I can't imagine how that must feel for you.

Maybe this *was* bad timing. But you need friends right now, Marcus. I can ..."

She stopped, and still he didn't speak.

"I think it's—you know what ... I'll see you around, Marcus."

The line went dead.

Eleven

The Ozarks, Arkansas

The sky bristled with activity. High-altitude winds whipped thick gray clouds along overhead. The contrast was stark, the sky vibrant and torn asunder. The earth calm and whispering. Slow, shifting shadows danced between the tall white oaks. The Osage orange trees were still, except for a nearly imperceptible shimmer. Sean Branch stared out at nothing. Not the sky, not the trees, none of it. He waited in the tree stand, slumped with his rifle across his thighs. To his right, attentive in a tree stand five yards away, another man sat erect. The fellow hunter scanned the area with binoculars. Branch swiveled his head left. A third hunter, ten yards away, glassed the area through his Leupold scope mounted atop a Remington 700. Static crackled in Branch's ear.

"Boss, not much longer."

"I'm getting bored. Find me something to kill, Richardson."

"Yes sir. We're working on it. The guide says we should be coming up on a—"

"Just do it."

Branch hung his rifle on a metal step screwed into the tree trunk, missing it the first time and nearly dropping the weapon. He pulled off a glove, drew out his phone, and scrolled through his emails. Stopping at a flagged message, he entered a passcode to access it. Then he looked out at the trees, waiting for the encryption to work itself out.

Mr. Branch, we have isolated the incident in Oman. Damage has been insulated. The guard rail has been maintained.

Branch looked out at the gray bark of the trees around him for a moment, then wrote, *Good. Make sure it stays that way.*

Sean Branch had been the Operations Officer of First Watch for almost two years. Before he'd joined the company, he'd done his homework. Roker was the money guy but didn't have the business savvy of his father. He was a man who loved his country, his guns, and his men. He deplored having to sit in an office and feed the machine while everyone else was out getting the job done. Branch rubbed a narrow, aggravated wrist and remembered a year earlier when he'd approached Roker with a plan to revamp the company and give the boss more freedom. Roker had turned him down flat. He'd cut Branch off halfway through his presentation, thanked him for his time, and ushered him out of his office. He may have left Roker's office that day with his tail between his legs, but he'd sworn he would put his plan into action. He would be running the company within a year, before Roker buried it under the failing contracts with the DOD, some congressional action, or the big private clients going somewhere else. Branch thought First Watch was prime for ruin or revival. He was banking on the latter.

Branch's radio crackled again. "Sir, they're comin' your way." He put his phone in his pocket, retrieved his rifle, and found his reticle. Shots went off on either side of him as Branch struggled to acquire a target. A herd of well-fed White Tail bounded along a narrow corridor below him, broadside. The man to his right took out the lead doe; the man to his left a young buck. Both reloaded and shot again, and again both shots hit their mark. Branch tried to pull his trigger. Nothing. He'd forgotten to chamber a round. He released the bolt and a round slid into the chamber from the magazine of his Browning X-Bolt. Branch slammed the bolt forward and reacquired his sight. The last of the herd were about through the kill zone. More shots from his left and right. A man on a horse came crashing out of the brush and into Branch's scope. Branch took a half breath and pulled firmly on his trigger. The weapon kicked. When Branch looked over his rifle, the man and horse lay on the ground, both writhing.

Whinnies and screams comingled. The earth was no longer silent.

Branch slung his rifle over his shoulder as he walked to the horse and rider. The beast lay calm now. Breathing choppy and erratic. Neighing from time to time. The man, on the other hand, bucked with each breath of the horse. His shrill screams cut the air like a knife. He said he couldn't feel his leg. His left arm was twisted behind him at a grotesque angle.

Richardson trampled out of some bushes on his horse and deftly dismounted on the run. "What the holy hell!" He pointed a wagging finger at the two men from the tree stands.

"Which one of you dumb asses did this?"

"Wasn't me! I had each of mine dead to rights," said one of them.

"Give you shitheads bolt actions, so you won't spray up the world with an AR. And what do you do …" Richardson said, looking to the other man.

"Hell, I didn't do it. Give me the AR—I'll still kill the same deer." The man's eyes shifted toward Branch.

Richardson straightened.

Branch stared at the horse, peering deep into its lone bulging eyeball. He could see his reflection in the glassy orb. Panic befell the creature. It was dying. A bullet hole in its chest seeped a yellowish fluid.

The animal's lungs were filling with blood, making it increasingly harder for it to breathe. The horse bucked. The rider screamed in agony again.

"Sir?" Richardson said.

"Shoot the horse. Field dress the deer," Branch said.

"What about him?" one of the men said, like he was choosing between salad dressings.

"Shoot him too! Otherwise he'll talk when he gets to the hospital."

"We could leave him here. Like, maybe a stray bullet hit his horse and the beast fell on him. He died waiting to be rescued."

The rider panted. "No. No. Please! I—I—"

"No!" Branch said. He moved closer to the man and cocked his head, so they were looking at each other straight on. "He won't talk. Right?" The man shook his head vigorously, then bit his lip to stifle a yell. "Besides, what he does is illegal. If he talks, he goes to jail. Right?"

The man shook his head more slowly this time. Tears rushed down his face. Branch stared at the man. The guide shifted his eyes away from Branch's simmering stare. Branch slid his rifle off his shoulder and moved it to his waist, pointing at the mam's stomach.

The rider looked back and started to shake his head, whispering another "No."

"Sir?" Richardson said. He walked over to Branch. "Sir." Richardson leaned in to whisper in Branch's ear.

"Your weapon is off safe, sir."

Branch stalled for a moment, still eyeing the guide, then turned to look at Richardson. The man stepped back. Branch rounded on Richardson with a thin, tight smile, clicked his weapon onto safe, and shouldered it again.

"Thank you, *Richards*. Now shoot the horse and dress the deer. Let's go before I get bored again."

Twelve

Alexandria, Virginia

Senator Robert "Bobby" Markum traced the lines of red, white, and blue on the sign that seamlessly covered the windows of his campaign office. *Markum for President*. Rory Koepanger, his press secretary, had insisted they install the window dressing even though the start of the campaign was still six months off. "President," Koepanger kept saying in conjunction with other words, none of which Markum heard. Only *president*. President of the United States. The sylphlike man was still chirping away, so Markum forced himself to focus on Koepanger.

"Bobby, I think you need to go off script. You know, give your image a real boost. Let the people know you can roll up your sleeves and get to work. You need something polarizing, energizing, and less dreary than the other candidates. God knows they're putting the voters to sleep already and we haven't even started yet," Koepanger said. Markum watched him. The man irritated the hell out of him. An imp. Squeaky and nasal. If he wasn't so damn good at spinning and doctoring, Markum would have fired him years ago.

"Like that," Koepanger jolted up, pointing at the TVs on the wall. A scene of looters and rioters flashed across the screen. "Like that! Now that's energizing. But..."

"But what is it about that that would get voters behind me?" Markum said, more to himself. He sat up in his chair and watched a police car burn on a city street. His nerves tingle and snapped as the scene shifted to riot cops marching down a street. He'd been nine when the men came into his house, claiming to be police. They'd taken his father away. They hadn't taken him anywhere beyond the front yard, as Markum would later find out, but the damage was done. Police were not to be trusted.

Yet this could be something, he thought. He didn't want to admit it, but Koepanger may be right. *Why are we here right now?* Rioting and looting had become such a common occurrence. They seemed to spring up every several months. "So why are they rioting?" Markum finally said. "Besides the obvious, of course." The current round had sparked after another questionable detainment turned deadly. A black man arrested by a white officer dying in custody.

"Negligence. Corruption," Koepanger whispered.

"Yes, but not the police—the police are doing their job … right?" Markum said, still thinking out loud.

"Not very well if they keep killing people."

"True, but they are scared. Scared of what? But more importantly, we don't want to go after the police, right? They're not the bad guys. Maybe they're …"

"Ill-equipped?" Koepanger said.

"No. They are equipped—for Christ's sake, look at them, Rory. Helmets. Shields. Tear gas. Ten different kinds of weapons. They *are* equipped. They're … *too* equipped,"

"I was really referring to their mental state, or maybe their training," Koepanger bleated.

Markum wasn't listening. He stared out the window again. The Virginia sky was darkening, clouding over, afternoon thunderstorms rolling in. If that wasn't a metaphor for the current state of affairs in the United States, he didn't know what was. The idea of a rolling storm of unrest was intriguing to him. Not simply to find fault, but to be the one to begin to repair the damage. A quest for a leader of the future. Markum picked up a paperweight, a small statue of the Jefferson memorial. His father's favorite monument.

Twelve years in the Senate. An independent with an independent mind, which allowed Markum to think around the box, not just outside of it. Anyone could come up with some cockamamie idea.

The true genius was to see the box and improve it. *We are all in a box in one way or another.* Admittedly, this thinking had never gotten Markum very far. He had written and written but seldom gotten a law passed, and even fewer proposals signed. Nothing of consequence. In twelve years of laboring for the good of the people, nothing. His career was almost completely unremarkable. Markum worried over an idea festering at the back of his mind—maybe he was going about this all wrong. He was trying to be a workhorse; maybe it was time to embrace a wild horse mentality instead. That would be sure to shake it up, like Koepanger suggested.

This could be something. Something remarkable. But what was *it*? Maybe the question wasn't what, but where. Or, better yet, who? Markum watched the footage for another moment.

"Corruption is always a good angle," Koepanger repeated as he opened his laptop.

"It's too generic. Even if we spin it like a madman," Markum said.

"Okay, I see where you're going." Koepanger looked up at him.

"Do you? Cause I don't think you do."

Koepanger shrugged his shoulders, the injury washing over his face.

Markum wasn't looking for another campaign slogan. He was looking for something to stand behind, or better—stand in *front* of. Something that would make him appear to be leadership material. Presidential material. Markum looked back at the screen. All those police officers trained to handle riots and looters and mayhem, he pondered. Trained and equipped.

"We need a target. Something to point to. Someone to point to. Someone who benefits from this sort of thing. Who do you think benefits from this sort of thing?" Markum said.

"Well, I guess the FBI, maybe? I mean their budget goes through the—"

No, Markum mused. *This just makes the FBI's hands even more full. Someone who really benefits from this type of disorder.* A profiteer. Someone we … *I* can take down. Make culpable for the riots and the state of things. Markum let his mind meander some more as he studied the TVs. The news channels were starting to repeat the clips and images.

Where are we headed with all this? Mass riots in every city in the country? Governments shutting down? Maybe we're heading toward a national police state.

A police state. That sounds good.

Koepanger plucked away at his laptop. Markum picked up the remotes. He changed channels between Fox News, CNN, MSNBC, and a half-dozen other channels for the next ten minutes. Who? He watched what looked like a tank to Markum roll down a city street in the Midwest. A banner ran across the bottom of one of the TVs: *Indianapolis Requests Assistance from Private Security Company.* Markum changed the channel. A tall man in jeans, a hoodie, and a mask threw a trash can through a display window of a department store. Who?

"How about this?" Koepanger chortled as he sat back and turned his laptop for Markum to see. A band of men dressed in high-tech riot gear looked as if they were going to storm off the computer screen and into his office. The byline read: *First Watch, your total security solution for these trying and volatile times.*

Markum looked at Koepanger, who shrunk from his crazed look. Koepanger's eagerness made him want to strangle the man. Or maybe it was that the smug little guy had beaten him to it,

"This is fucking perfect," Markum said.

The door to the office opened and Maurice Stearns, Markum's campaign manager, stumbled in. He stood in the door with his back to Markum, shaking off his umbrella to no avail. The rain poured in the door and onto the carpet. Stearns turned to find the two men staring at him. "What is it?" he asked, an air of nervousness surrounding the question.

"Sit down, Maurice," Markum said. Stearns dutifully did so, still dripping onto the carpet.

The senator paced the room as he told Stearns and Koepanger his plan. Maurice, on no less than three occasions, attempted to interrupt. Markum held up a finger to quiet him. He explained that First Watch's boss would be their fall guy. He would propose a bill in congress to investigate him and his bulldog of a company. Dig into not only how they stole millions of taxpayers' dollars during the wars in Iraq, Afghanistan, and Syria, but how they were profiting from the misfortunes of the disenfranchised. Markum kept forgetting the man's name.

"Thomas Roker," Koepanger reminded him.

"Roker, right? Okay," Markum said. "So Maurice, what do you think?"

"Well, I—" Stearns paused. He was an accomplished worrier. Rubbing his palms together as if they were cold, he started, "Sounds kind of—"

"Sounds completely idiotic!"

Everyone's heads swiveled toward the door. A tall, sturdy man with shining silver hair snarled back at them.

"Jack!" Markum said.

Jack Lawson stood like a statue. His black trench coat was dry, with only a hint of moisture on his shoulders. He set down his black leather briefcase with its gleaming gold buckles on a nearby table, never taking his eyes off Markum. Lawson had slipped into the room like a ghost, a trait he'd picked from nearly thirty years as a spy, and one that completely aggravated Markum. Now, Lawson was Markum's hired hand, a fixer. Lawson knew everything that happened before it happened in the D.C. metropolitan area. He knew everyone that mattered in and out of the Beltway.

"Don't you think idiotic is a little strong, Jack?" Markum said as he sunk into a chair.

Lawson removed his overcoat like a magician removing his cloak. He placed it neatly on a hanger, then turned to the trio.

"No, idiotic is precisely what it is."

"Well now ..." Koepanger started, then shrunk behind his laptop at Lawson's leer.

"Robert, you are a hapless senator from a know-nothing state that has aspirations to be president. You have now decided, on a whim and no doubt some childish advice"—Lawson eyed Koepanger again—"to take on a crusade to save this country from what you believe is its inevitable descent into a police state. That, you say, has been orchestrated by none other than Thomas Roker." Lawson paused to let his words work their way around Markum's brain. "Is that what I'm to understand?"

The words stung, hard. Markum knew he had been grasping at straws. Searching for meaning. And knew Lawson was most likely right. He'd never been in the military, and knew little or nothing about private security contracting, other than the bills he saw for the wars Congress was financing. He didn't know the first thing about police work, other than what he saw on TV.

Markum *did* know one thing, though. The idea sounded good. It sounded great.

He stood, tucked in his three-day-old shirt, buttoned his wrinkled suit jacket, and flattened his tie. He ran his thick fingers through brown, lackluster hair and straightened his back.

"Yes, Jack, that's exactly what I'm saying," Markum responded.

Lawson looked around the room. Stearns shrugged his soaked shoulders and then hung his head. Koepanger flashed his most brilliant clown smile at Lawson.

"I still think it's idiotic, but if we are going to do this, everything has to go through me. And I mean *everything*. Robert, we will have to massage this Senate investigation well in advance of you moving anything on the floor, and—"

"Sure thing, Jack. You got it," Markum cut in. He knew Lawson would try taking charge. *Not this time, Jack. If I'm going to be President, and I will, I need to be in charge.*

Markum looked at the three men and landed on Stearns. "Now, Maurice, I think we should start by spitballing a plan to wrap the investigation into the campaign message. Something like … Markum for President. *The man to bring freedom back to the land of the free!"*

That was good. That was very, very good.

Thirteen

Muscat, Oman

A steaming droplet landed on Dresden's hand. Mist threaded out of the vent overhead. The airplane's cooling system struggled to treat the hellish air from outside. Welcome to Oman.

He reached up and closed the vent as a flight attendant, her makeup glistening like cake icing, handed him a cool, damp towel. Dresden attempted a smile but was not quite sure he succeeded.

The plane rocked forward and everyone cheered. It was short-lived as the plane stopped again with a jerk. They'd been sitting on the tarmac for over an hour, waiting on a gate assignment. Thankfully, the woman next to Dresden had finally passed out. She was a loud, non-stop talker on business travel with some insurance company. He'd bought her several drinks in the hope she'd shut up. He had to actively work himself off the ledge in deciding to not knock her out cold. Peace and quiet was what he needed and was in no mood for her antics. The thought of Lance dying played like a never-ending newsreel in his mind. The woman had stolen the space he needed to think about what he was going to do.

The plane surged forward again. A small group of college-age kids cheered, more as a joke than an expression of hope or relief. Dresden looked at his phone—he'd felt a ghost rattle and was sure Lance was calling. There was nothing. He put his head back on the rest. A modicum of sweat moved through the creases on the back of his neck. He felt the buzz again, but still nothing. This time, he thought of Jennifer.

In his rush to get to Oman, Dresden had forgotten to call Lance's girlfriend. On a layover in Tokyo, he'd found the woman's number and dialed, but it went straight to voicemail. Then the phone slid out of Dresden's hand as Jennifer's voice sounded on the greeting, beckoning those who called to leave their contact info and have a great day. Lance and Jennifer? Shit! The image of the two of them, happy together, slammed him in the gut. The second sucker punch from hell in twenty-four hours. Dresden tried several more times to reach her before he boarded his connecting flight. But still nothing.

The plane finally bounced into the gate, and Dresden texted Jennifer while he walked down the jetway. She was just going to have to wait. He needed to pick up his rental car and to get over to Almasi's compound, not wanting to stay in Oman any longer than he had to.

Al Azaiba, Muscat

Almasi's street was crowded with expensive cars popped up on the curb. Small palaces lined one side of the immaculate street. A long white wall stretched the length of the block on the opposite side. Almasi's compound. Dresden found a space a short walk from the gate. A thick glass portal separated pedestrians from the gate guard. The man looked at Dresden blankly as he slapped his passport on the window. The skinny man in his shiny, pressed shirt picked up a phone, listened for a moment, then told Dresden to return to his car.

"Someone will be with you soon," the guard said, not looking at him.

Dresden squinted up at the sun and leaned against the wall. His phone claimed it was 121 degrees. After five minutes, he glanced back at the guard, who'd picked up a mobile phone and was ignoring him. He went back to his car and waited. Two squad cars from the ROP pulled up beside him a few minutes later. An officer tapped on his window and asked Dresden to step out of his car. The gate guard gawked as the officers questioned him, then asked him to come with them to the regional police headquarters. Dresden looked at the gate booth as he got in the back of the squad car. A second man was standing behind the guard, watching the squad car roll away.

Dresden sat in the empty waiting room for an hour. A light overhead flickered, emitting a buzz like a bug lamp. A man in a black pinstriped jogging suit came out of an odd-shaped door and offered Dresden tea or coffee. He turned down both. The man said someone would see him soon, but another hour passed before he was led down a dark hallway to a single open door. The faded tag on the door read Crime Control.

Inside, a fat man with a severely receding hair line sat behind a government-issue desk. Piles of paper lined the perimeter. The room smelled of cigarettes and stewed lamb. When Dresden entered, the man hastened to get up. He knocked his knees on the desk, causing a stack of papers to shift and fall to the floor. Dresden bent to pick them up in unison with the fat man.

"Mr. Dresden, is it?" the man said as he stacked the papers back on his desk, fussing over them. "I'm Detective Arman."

"Nice to meet you, Detective."

"Would you please state your business in Oman?" Arman said. He struggled to fit himself into his chair.

"Business."

"With whom?"

"Mr. Badar Almasi."

"Yes, of course. Yet there may be a problem with that. You see—"

"Problem? There's no problem. I work for the company that provides security for Mr. Almasi. I'm here to do an assessment of the attack on behalf of the company." Dresden didn't bother hiding his irritation.

"That is not entirely true now is it, Mr. Dresden?"

"What?"

"It is my understanding that you were fired from First Watch several weeks ago. Let go due to an argument with the owner of the company. Is that not right?"

"No, it's not."

"So then, you are here in an official capacity. Fully sanctioned by First Watch to conduct an investigation of the alleged attack at Mr. Almasi's home?"

Dresden remained silent. He crossed his legs and laid his hands on his thighs and started tapping slowly.

The fat man picked at his teeth with a plastic toothpick.

Dresden finally spoke up. "Sir, I don't really know what is going on here. I'm guessing your job is to stall or divert me for some reason. To stonewall me so I can't conduct my assessment of the incident or reassure Mr. Almasi of First Watch's utmost concern for his safety." Dresden paused to rub his forehead. "Are you telling me that you and your Keystone cop outfit here and Mr. Almasi's knuckle-dragging cronies are going to impede me in conducting my assessment?"

The man coughed and spit, dropping his toothpick. "Mr. Dresden, there is no need to—"

Cops were all the same. Time for a change of plans. "Yes, there is. One of my closest friends died in that attack. I want to know what happened. I want to—Tell me one thing, Arman. Where is my friend's body?"

"Downstairs, in the morgue, being prepped for transport."

"I want to see him."

"I—that—"

"I want to see him!"

The detective looked away.

"You will need a positive ID, right?"

Arman stared at him through a haze of smoke.

The morgue was dark except for the examination table. Two dome lights cast bright rays that reflected off the stainless-steel table like the sun off the sea.

Dresden waited outside the room in the hallway, looking in through a window generally reserved for family. A kindly barrier to the smell of the deceased. Detective Arman stood an arm's length away as they waited for the body to be brought out. He puffed at his second cigarette since they'd left his office, blowing smoke away from Dresden.

"I will be going in when the body arrives."

Arman said nothing. He and Dresden had come to an agreement. The detective would let him see Lance's body, then Dresden would find a hotel for the night and book himself on the next flight back to the US. Dresden had no intention of upholding his end of the agreement, but he'd agreed, nonetheless.

Two attendants wheeled a gurney to the examination table. As they hoisted the black body bag up, Dresden opened the door and entered. One of the attendants protested, but the detective waved him off. Dresden had them open the bag, which they did, down to Lance's neck. He then demanded they open it completely, head to toe.

The body appeared to be untouched. Lance seemed to be wearing the clothes from the night of the attack. They were in tatters. Through them, one arm and leg were sorely disfigured. Dried blood still matted Lance's hair and caked his face and neck. Dresden had too many snapshots like this in his mind. He knew a dead man when he saw one.

Arman was talking, insisting the Embassy had given them instruction on how to prepare the body for transport, to ensure as little evidence was disturbed. *Probably too late.*

Dresden stood, hands by his side, staring. He knew it was Lance. But it wasn't. *What happened, brother? Give me a sign.* Dresden pulled gently at Lance's clenched fist. It didn't budge. His nails were caked with dried blood—and something else. Dresden looked closer.

Dried flesh. He'd been fighting. Fighting with someone. But with who, and why? Dresden leaned across the body to get a look at Lance's other hand. Nothing. The detective cleared his throat and wagged his finger at Dresden, then nodded at the attendants, who zipped up the bag. They lifted Lance back onto the gurney and wheeled him into the darkness.

Arman and Dresden stood in the hallway again. The detective explained that three mortars had been launched into Almasi's compound. One of them had hit the dorm where Lance was sleeping. The detective waited for Dresden to say something, then continued. "Okay, now you go to a hotel, find a flight home, and get a good night's sleep. Please don't leave your hotel until just before your flight, okay?"

Dresden savagely tossed Detective Arman against the wall. A blue-gray cloud of smoke streamed out of the man's nose and his cigarette flipped up and landed on his cheek. He started to squeal in pain, but Dresden covered his mouth and slammed him into the wall a second time, his forearm in the man's chest.

"Listen! You don't deserve to stand on the same planet as him. You will not tell me what I can or can't do." Dresden's brain rushed like a hot lava flow. Undaunted. A voice inside was screaming at him to stop, but another was egging him on. "You'd better tell your men, or whoever they are over at Almasi's compound, to let me in. If I have one issue, one eyeball in the wrong direction, I will come back and put you in one of those damn black bags. You hear me?"

Dresden thrust his forearm into the man's chest again, demanding an answer. Arman's eyes shifted to the hand over his mouth. Dresden withdrew it, then slowly released his hold. The man straightened his suit and patted his burned cheek. He moved like a sloth patting the ash out of his jacket sleeves, then bent to pick up his cigarette.

"Mr. Dresden, I think you have been misinformed. I would strongly advise you to go home. However, if you persist, I do not believe you will not find answers here within the ROP or with Mr. Almasi or his staff. The answers you are looking for are—are not *here,* with us." The man waved his hand down the hall. "Now please, a car is waiting for you outside.

"What are you talking about?"

"I will say nothing further. Please," Detective Arman said again.

They were silent as they walked to the car. The detective waved at Dresden as the car pulled away. He believed Arman but didn't know why. A small amount of bile made its way into his mouth as Dresden allowed his mind to see Lance lying there on the gurney again.

Dresden sat in his rental car, head on the steering wheel. No answers *here*—what the hell did he mean? The ROP squad car had stationed itself behind him. Lifting his head, he watched the booth at the gate of Almasi's compound. The security guard looked at him for a long time. Dresden started his car and was about to pull away when another man showed up in the booth. Idling, Dresden watched as the man came out of the booth and walked toward him. He was wearing dark gray tactical pants and a khaki polo, the contractor's uniform, but he didn't look like a Frist Watch regular. The man started waving at him to go. Dresden didn't respond. He moved like a man born to extreme heat. Only a slight sheet of sweat dotted his forehead. The man tapped on Dresden's window and told him once more to go. Dresden studied his face, but the man just waved again. The ROP car turned on its lights. Dresden cracked his window.

"Do you work for First Watch?"

"Go!"

"Where were you when the attack happened?"

"Go!"

"Who is the site manager now?"

Visibly irritated, the man leaned in, close to Dresden's window, a cloud of cheap cigarette smoke slipping through the crack. In a choppy voice, the man said, "O'Rourke was a thief. Now go away, or—"

Blood sprayed across the window as Dresden thrust the door open, too fast for the man to react. He fell to the ground and clutched his nose, yelling. The ROP car sounded its siren, and the officer got out but seemed hesitant to approach. The man rolled around on the ground, blood coloring the asphalt and his clothes. Dresden closed his door, rolled up his window, and drove away.

The call went directly to voicemail again. *Jennifer, where are you?* Dresden sat in the air terminal, ticket in hand. He'd played his cards all wrong and had nothing to show for his trouble. Detective

Arman had called him the night before to give him fair warning. Assault in Oman held serious consequences, even more so for foreigners. The detective sounded concerned, sincerely. It was weird. Dresden couldn't put a finger on it, but he thought Arman liked him. Like the man was trying to help him.

A glint off the polished planes blinded Dresden for a moment. His eyes watered. He was going to text Jennifer again, but instead brought up Lance's number. He wrote, *Hey brother. I've failed you so far. But it's not over. So, check this out. "In Hell I'll be in Good Company" by The Dead South.* He paused for a moment, then pushed send and waited for a reply.

Fourteen

Casper, Wyoming

People shuffled into the small church in twos and threes. A pair of oversized men in tight suits stood at the door, offering everyone a pamphlet. Dresden sat in his car. The weight of the scene kept him squashed to his seat, unable to move. He lapsed into a daze, not sure if he would be able to get out and go in. His phone vibrated in his suit coat pocket. It was Casper calling.

"Hey buddy, great to hear from you!" Dresden chimed, the relief of the distraction obvious. His son didn't say anything. Dresden heard him breathing. "Hey Casper? What's up buddy? You okay?"

"Yeah, I guess. Mom called and told me about Lance. I'm real sorry, Dad. I ... When mom called, she said she had some bad news." Casper was quiet again. "I thought it was *you,* Dad!"

Dresden's throat tightened. What should he say? What do you say? He was so bad at this. They never really talked about anything too serious. They'd developed a banter that never went anywhere. It was light and mostly meaningless, highlighted by awkward silences, too many to count. Casper worked out his words by humming. Sometimes it worked, most times it didn't. Dresden spent his time rummaging around an empty emotional vault, searching for what to say. Sometimes he wondered if Casper didn't like talking to him, if his son could do without their calls. Kind of like Dresden and his own father.

When Casper was younger, they'd had so much in common, so much to share. Even when they'd discovered Casper was basically a genius, certainly much smarter than his dad, none of that mattered. Dresden saw a little boy he loved, Casper saw a dad he loved, and that was all they needed. But after—Dresden stopped and shook his head.

"Casper, I'm okay buddy." Dresden listen to him hum. "So how's that old crotchety guy you call a mentor? Osuna? Huh? You guys still catching bugs out in the wilds of Ohio or wherever you are?"

At this, Casper laughed. "No Dad, we don't work in Ohio—Pennsylvania. And yeah, Doctor Osuna is doing great. We have made two new discoveries, and we are going to co-host a seminar in DC on the over-the-counter application of the medicinal aspects of three kinds of rare plant species. We think it may actually lead to the USDA and FDA to recognize … Dad, I'm sorry, I get really—"

"It's okay. I have one question. How are you going to fit all of that on a flyer or a poster? That's a real mouthful."

Casper laughed again. "Dad?"

"Yeah?"

"It's great to hear from you."

Dresden worked the tightness out of his throat before he said, "Hey listen, how about I come out and visit you. I have a few things to get done then, but would that—"

"Yes! Yes, that would be great."

Mickey Turrel tapped on Dresden's window as he hung up. Mickey was Lance's hometown buddy and best friend growing up. Lance had joined the Teams and Mickey had followed a year later, but for most of their careers they were on opposite coasts. Mickey tapped again.

"Come on, Master Chief. You can't hide in there forever!"

Dresden got out of the car and Mickey gave him a bear hug. The two men walked to the front door of the church. Dresden stutter-stepped, then stopped. Mickey made it up two steps before he realized he'd lost him. The men at the top laughed and helped Mickey get Dresden into the church.

Lance's family were lined up in front of the altar. The mourners shuffled past, whispering condolences and shaking hands. Some cried outright. Some were blank, emotionless. Lance would have hated this, Dresden joked to himself. He would have wanted to walk out into the woods and sit down by a tree with an aged whiskey. Or maybe have someone tie him to a surfboard and tow him into his last *big* wave. That was how Lance would have wanted to go out.

It must've shown on his face, because Mickey reminded Dresden that the wake and funeral weren't about Lance per se, but his family.

Behind the family, a group of Teams guys mingled like some kind of berserker horde. Their suits were stressed at the seams and chest. Unable to fold their arms across their chests, they shifted from leg to leg, hands in pockets. Slivers of tattoos poked out from the ends of their sleeves and the tops of their dress shirts like mice peeking out of a hole in the wall.

Dresden walked up and shook hands with most of them. A few pulled him in for a hug and slap on the back. He got a nod from the rest. Mickey stood by, looking over at Dresden several times.

"You got something to say?" Dresden asked.

Mickey turned to face him, his features tight. His eyes narrowed before he said, "So, Roker really fired you?

"Yeah, and goddamn, everybody knows about that? And no … I mean, I quit."

"Okay, you say so. Anyway, we need to talk." Mickey turned forward again. "Not here."

"Uh. Okay. Where then?"

"Later. Maybe the bar."

The back room of the tavern was packed. A private party. The majority were Lance's teammates, as well as some contractors he'd worked with, younger family members, a few strap hangers. All of them drinking to *remember*. That was what Mickey said they were doing, and everyone cheered. Dresden sat alone in a booth, twirling a glass of beer between his palms. He hadn't taken a drink and wasn't going to. The smell was enough.

"You're gonna warm that beer, my friend. You keep doin' that, it'll be no good," Mickey said. He crashed into the booth, knocking the table into Dresden.

"They serve it warm."

"Hah. Okay. I never liked that black tar shit anyway."

"So?"

"Yeah." Mickey looked out at the crowd. "So …"

"Just say it, man."

"Yeah, okay. Did Lance tell you what he'd been doin' out in Oman?"

"Same old shit. Site manager stuff."

"Nah, I mean the other junk. What headquarters was askin' him to do?"

Dresden sat silent and shook his head.

"I started gettin' emails a few months back from the ops guys," Mickey continued. They was askin' for weird shit about our clients. My guy out in Malaysia was cool about it; he seemed to get what they were tryin' to do, even if I didn't. Something about 'better integration.' Anyway, Lance said *his* guy was puttin' up some major resistance. Actually, it wasn't the client, it was his people. You get me?"

"No … not really." Small, fractured flashes of his conversation with Lance popped into his head but they were hard to put his finger on.

Mickey looked out at the crowd and took a drink of this beer. Two fingers wrapped around the neck to tip it back. "You made the right choice, brother—staying on the outside. Probably a blessing in disguise, you getting fired and all." Mickey rolled his bottle in his palms.

"Uh, Mickey?"

"Well, it's just I was down at headquarters, you know, and I heard some stuff. The kind of stuff that makes me kind of uneasy. You know, changes that are comin'. There was whispering about the Board taking over from Roker. About some congressional investigation that may be happening—you know, to take a look at what Roker's been doing. And then it got me thinking about those emails. I mean …" Mickey tapered off. He slid down in the booth, his head slumped, staring at his beer bottle.

"Uh huh. Mickey?" Dresden said.

"What?"

"That's it. That's all you had to say?"

"Yeah man. That's it." His mouth quivered, and Dresden saw the first salty droplet land on the table. He sat back and looked at his lap. *Shit.*

Team guys took up the pew behind Lance's family. The smell of mouthwash was pungent and hung in the air. The guy three down from Dresden had to be woken up several times. The tiny church was near capacity, yet people were still filing in. Mickey leaned down to put his water bottle on the floor, then looked over at the section of pews across the aisle to the left. He elbowed Dresden, nodding at a group of men. Most of the guys could have passed for Team guys, and maybe they were. One of them stood out though—Sean Branch. Dresden was becoming all too familiar with the man's thin, vulpine face and wispy blonde hair. He looked to be several inches shorter than the men who flanked him. Roker's stand-in, Dresden thought.

"That's the ops boss. There's somethin' about that dude. I don't know those turds he hangs with either. Richardson is the guy next to Branch, I think. The other three, no idea. They go with him everywhere though. Like a little Jay-Z entourage or somethin'. You know him? The ops boss?"

"No. Just heard his name a lot lately."

"I don't know about him," Mickey said again. "That douchebag will most likely take over for Roker if the Board has their way or if something else happens. I think that'll be my time to punch out."

Dresden looked at Mickey. A grin stretched like duct tape across the man's face as he nudged Dresden. The doors of the church closed. The late morning sun shone bright through the stained glass overhead. Oblong shapes of varying color marbled the church.

Mickey had asked Dresden to speak, but he'd declined. A priest presided. Several people spoke of Lance's life. His mom sat stoic through the entire proceeding. Toward the end, all the Team guys stood and filed past the coffin. Each man pounded a gold *Trident* into the hard casket lid with their fist. The jagged metal insignia cut into the men's hands, leaving drops of blood dotting the shiny veneer.

Dresden scanned the audience from behind the casket until he came across Branch. The man cast a lascivious eye toward him. No deflection, like a laser beam. Dresden locked eyes. Did he know about Oman?

There was another prayer, then everyone began to file out. Dresden made his way through the crowd, but Branch and his men moved out to the parking lot before he could catch them.

Weaving through the maze of parked cars, he barked Branch's name. One of the other men glanced back. *Those fuckers hear me*. Dresden stopped, not sure why. He watched Branch and his crew load up into their vehicle. The driver, Richardson, his eyes hiding behind dark wraparound glasses, stared at him through the rearview mirror. Dresden could have made it to the vehicle before they left. But why? What would Branch know that he didn't? Roker couldn't have possibly told the man what he wasn't willing to tell Dresden. Plus, as Roker put it Branch was gunning for him anyway. What a fucking mess. Dresden walked to his car and checked for a text from Lance.

Fifteen

San Francisco, California

A burst of laughter shot out from a second-story window across the street. Drizzle from an afternoon rain covered the streets and awnings of Chinatown, small droplets falling onto Dresden's face as he watched the window. He blinked the rain away as another burst of laughter rang out, followed by a clank of dishes and a mash of loud talking. Dresden looked at the door to the restaurant, where the same rail-thin woman stood guard. He thought of her ushering Maria up the narrow stairs. He smiled at her, but she didn't smile back. A couple came stumbling out arm in arm, laughing. Dresden looked up at the window again, then walked down the street.

Robbie was early. He was always early. Sitting in the back of the empty restaurant, the last booth on the right. A plate of pot-stickers simmered at the center of the table as Robbie wrote in a small notebook. A police band radio and two cell phones stood guard like a miniature set of sentinels. He looked up as Dresden approached the table.

"Hey guy!" Robbie said. He got up and offered his hand, taking Dresden's in a firm grip. Squinting, examining him, he said, "You look like hell. How are you?"

"Thanks, I needed that," Dresden replied drily.

"Not sleeping again?"

"No."

"Potsticker?"

"No."

Dresden put his elbows on the table, rubbing his temples with his fists. Robbie was right—he wasn't sleeping. He'd been home for four days since Lance's funeral. He couldn't run. Couldn't work out. There was no surf to be had. He just paced around his house, constantly.

Robbie had called, said he had a guy that needed some security work done. An assessment of a Knob Hill mansion that was being taken over by a non-profit historical foundation. Not much money in it, Robbie admitted. Dresden didn't care. He'd practically worn a hole in his floor at home. It was time to get out, get away.

So here he was sitting in a dark room with no idea how to get the visions out of his head. He looked up at Robbie. He knew Robbie had an idea, but he couldn't drag him into this. Dresden didn't even know what *this* was. Was everything that happened completely normal and it was Dresden who couldn't see it? Or were there giant signs pointing to danger that he was missing?

"It's probably nothing," Dresden said.

"Sure. You know I don't believe you, right? I know your instincts. I know you wouldn't be troubled if you could get around it. Those same instincts of yours saved my rear end a time or two." Robbie tossed a potsticker in his mouth. "Can I make a suggestion?"

"Sure. You're going to anyway," Dresden said, rubbing his temples.

"For as long as I've known you, you've dealt with the *external* like a true and valiant warrior. Undeterred, undaunted. But guy, I worry for you, because it's the internal you're ignoring." Robbie laid his wide hand over his own chest.

"So, what's your suggestion?"

"You're retired now. And you really don't *have to* work. Give some time and energy to what's going on inside. Look at your life more objectively, you know? Maybe get to know your kids better. It will help you sleep," Robbie said.

"Thanks doc," Dresden said as the waitress showed up. They prepared their teas in silence. Dresden watched his friend for a moment. His dark skin wrinkled at the corner of his eyes as he concentrated on adding honey to his tea. Robbie looked up and gave Dresden a crooked smile, his gray eyes full of wonder. The man's radio crackled and a female came on.

"Detective Coltrane? You have a 187 at 1010 Bush. Officers are on the scene." Robbie picked up the radio and responded.

He stood, dropping a cell phone into each of his suit jacket pockets and his notebook in his back pocket, and palmed the radio like a sword. Robbie put his hand on Dresden's shoulder. Dresden opened his eyes and looked up.

"I need your help. Professionally. I think I may have a missing person," Dresden said.

"Give me their info and I'll look into it. That it?" Robbie asked.

"Yeah," Dresden said, mashing his palms into his eye sockets.

"I doubt that. Call before you go off and do anything stupid," Robbie said. Then he walked out of the restaurant.

The bus left the curb, leaving the man exposed. He'd been tailing Dresden for over two hours. The man leaned on the back of the bench, arms outstretched like the barren legs of a stork. His long face looked drawn and exhausted. Normally, Dresden would have paid little attention to the man, except it was the fourth time he'd seen him. The guy, his coat heavy with rain, bent to tie a shoe that was already tied. Dresden wanted to laugh, but after nearly six hours of cataloging security issues in a dusty old building, he was too drained for mirth. Little slivers of Lance and Oman, and Jennifer, even Maria, popped randomly into his mind throughout the day. Scattered and fleeting, brief. But now, the flood gates had opened. This fellow and his apparent interest in Dresden had brought back every painful memory.

The streets were littered with people—walking, sitting, standing, moving about. The guy was not blending in well. Thirty minutes earlier, Dresden had decided to get off the street, just moments before it started to rain. His tail, with nowhere to go, attempted to wait it out.

Dresden decided to stop with the games. Break protocol. He left the narrow bookstore-café off Union Street in Cow Hollow that he'd ducked into and moved to cross the street. The man went erect like prey. Alert. He moved quickly down the sidewalk away from Dresden, against the flood of pedestrians. To avoid the flow, Dresden jumped into the street and ran along the gutter until a car nearly clipped him. The blasting horn made the man turn and look. Dresden locked eyes with him for a beat. Fear cascaded down the man's face. Then he was gone. Dresden stopped. Where did he go? A thin alleyway. Dresden moved to follow, then stopped. It was a blind alley. No good.

He had confirmation someone was following him. That was all he needed for now. Dresden sauntered back to the bookstore, looking back every dozen steps, then called Robbie.

You have reached the voicemail box of Detective Robert Coltrane, San Francisco Police Department. Please leave a message after the tone.

Dresden spoke hurriedly as he walked. Fractured bits of information flowed from him. Height. Weight. Complexion. What the man was wearing. The various locations he'd spotted him. Everything he could remember.

He didn't speak for a moment, then said, "Robbie, I need your help. I'm going home. Call me," and hung up.

Escondite, California

The bar stool swiveled with a series of creaks and cracks. Dresden turned left and right, trying to keep time with the music coming through the speakers overhead. The man behind the bar twitched but said nothing. Dresden, his elbows perched up on the bar, scrolled through his phone until he found the text thread with Lance. He watched his phone as if it were about to speak to him. Sometimes songs crashed into his brain like an epiphany. Sometimes he couldn't believe he'd never suggested one before. A song so obvious the reason for his neglect baffled him. "Passenger" by Iggy Pop was one of those. Now Lance was … *dead.* The word—so raw and disturbing. A metallic taste slid into Dresden's throat. He quickly typed, *top that brother!* and sent the message.

George Long, the bartender, topped off his water. It was George's place—a bar named after his dad, Hop-A-Long. The old man was a UDT guy, a Frogman who lost part of one leg on the beaches of France. It was a quiet place where Dresden could hide most of the year, though not when the tourists were thick at the height of the summer rush.

Dresden picked up his book, Cormac McCarthy's *Suttree,* and started reading again. George walked by and dropped a paper umbrella in his water, then walked off laughing. The bar filled as the afternoon wore on. Sundried beach-goers, road warriors, and sight-seers all stopped in for a drink or a bite or both. Dresden's phone buzzed. It was Roker. He slid off his stool and found an empty back room, away from the noise of the crowd. He opened a Zoom meeting window and watched Roker adjust his camera, then sit down at a conference table. Roker spoke, but nothing came out. They exchanged hand signals, then Dresden held up a remote. Roker looked at it, then back at him.

"How's that?"

"Better."

"I don't have long."

"Okay. Thanks for meeting with me, Tom."

"Uh huh."

"I don't think what happened to Lance was an accident." Dresden cut right to the point.

"Well of course it wasn't. Some assholes tried to kill Almasi," Roker said. "I'm getting some real heat for that. Some guys breathing down my neck. Now this stuff coming out of Congress. It's gonna make things a lot worse." He shook a piece of paper at the camera.

"Huh? What are you talking about?"

"Marcus, uh ... there's economics involved here. Big power struggles, and my sanity, at stake. I don't have time to go into it. You know all I ever wanted was to provide top-shelf training and support to this great country. That's all. Now ... now we're neck deep—I just don't know. First Watch can do so much more. We have the—ugh, I just don't know, Marcus." Roker looked off camera, then said, "Wait. Marcus, why did you call? You're reconsidering, right? I could really use your help and your skills."

What game was Roker playing? It was as if he didn't even know what's going on. This wasn't the man Dresden knew, who used to look out for all of his men like they were his brothers—his kids.

"Reconsider? No, I'm not reconsidering. I called because I couldn't get into Almasi's—"

"That's the prick down the hall. And anyway, Marcus, you don't work here anymore! What the hell were you thinking going to Oman? The man's—hey, you seen Jennifer? I need her back here. Tell her to contact the Board."

"What guy down the hall? What are you saying? Tom, really, I need you to focus."

"How about Jennifer. Have you seen her? Where is she? *We* need to talk to her," Roker fired off.

He picked up a cell phone on the conference table and started texting. Dresden waited, but the man kept looking at his phone. Where was his mind this time?

"Tom!"

"Yeah."

"I'm worried there is more to what happened to Lance."

"Marcus, really! Really, you have to drop this. You see this?" Roker held up a piece of paper to the camera again. "This is a letter, from Senator Taylor, stating that some shmuck senator is socializing the idea that Congress back an investigation into First Watch, into me. Before—" A phone on Roker's table buzzed. He picked it up.

"He's just talking about it. So what?" Dresden said, trying to get Roker's attention again.

"Dammit Marcus, in that town, *talking* is the kiss of death. He's doing that so it will have some legs when he goes to the floor," Roker said as he picked up the remote.

"Call me when you're ready to get to work. There're some situations you would be perfect for. Oh, and tell Jen I need her back here, *now*. I have to go."

The screen went blank.

"What the hell! Crazy bastard. What the hell?" Dresden shook his head and closed out of the app.

Sixteen

Santa Cruz, California

A mess of seagulls squabbled over the decaying carcass of a baby seal. Two men stood at the water's edge ten yards away from the ruckus, outfitted in full-length wet suits. They studied the waves moving toward them—six, maybe eight feet in height, and pitching fast. The sky above them was gray despite the encroaching midday hour. The rumble of thunder stopped their conversation. Small flashes of strobe punctuated the horizon. Then a crack like a horsewhip sounded overhead.

Six more surfers joined the first two. They pointed out to sea, at the waves, the clouds, and the lightning. Dresden looked back to see twenty more surfers moving down the cliffs. A man hunched over with age walked beside a teenage boy. The boy carried the man's surfboard along with his own. Stone Cold was what they called him. A legend of sorts. Surfed these same Santa Cruz peaks since he was five. He knew the guy that named this collection of breaks. Now Steamer Lane, but back when Stone Cold started, his crew called them the breaks on the west side. No name. Just a location, East Cliff drive—so the story goes.

More non-surfers lined the cliffs. Stone Cold made his way to Dresden, pulling the wetsuit hood off his head.

"I'm going to miss him."

"Me too, Stone."

"He brought us groceries every day that last month Helen was alive. If he couldn't make it, he had someone there to do it. Bingo here was one of those messengers. Weren't you, Bingo?" Stone put his hand on the boy's shoulder.

"Sure was."

"He was a wild man. But he had a heart too big for any one human. I thought I heard he had a girl. A steady one, that is." Stone laughed. A throaty, infectious sound. Dresden did too. But it didn't feel right, not yet. Lance would have been kicking him. Telling him to lighten the fuck up.

"He did. I called her. She never answered. I left messages, told her about today. I don't know," Dresden said, kicking at the rocky beach.

"Eh … love does weird things, young man."

"So are we going to do this or what?" someone yelled.

"Hell yeah, we're going to do this! What? Did you think there was ever a choice? This is Santa Cruz, man; we don't back down to a little storm action. And anyway, what would Lance have done?" JoJo said.

"Charge it, bro!" came from the crowd again. Everyone laughed and cheered.

"Alright then, it's decided. Listen up everybody ... find a swim buddy. SEAL Team style. Lance would have made us do it, right?" Everyone agreed. "Find a swim buddy and stick together; let's meet outside middle peak," JoJo said.

The group started to move toward the water. "Hold up, hold up." He bowed his head. JoJo gave thanks to Mother Earth, to friends, family, the ocean provider, and the god of our choosing. He asked the same gods look over the party of those left behind as they make their way out through the surf. He said amen, then boomed, "Alright, see you out there!"

Dresden asked to stick with Stone and Bingo as his swim buddies. They chose the channel to the left of middle peak. It turned out to be a good choice. Halfway out, they rode a rip that pushed them almost past the shoulder of the break.

Everyone made it outside and formed a circle. A large wreath of tropical flowers was placed in the center. Flower leis were tossed into the circle as each surfer said their piece. Some said it out loud. Some kept it to themselves. Dresden had planned to speak, but couldn't. He hung his head and thought of a time Lance, a few other Team guys, and Dresden did their first Hash Run in Dubai. At the end of the run, they sat in tubs of ice, their heads adorned in heavy, horned Viking helmets, singing songs and drinking from steins. They received their hash names with gratitude. Lance would forever have to answer to FCC, Fucking-Cray-Cray. And Dresden to Bad-Master-Baiter. He laughed out loud, then opened his eyes and tossed the lei in. His eyes were damp. He licked his upper lip. The salt of tears mixed with the sea salt.

The group broke up. Most of them lined up on middle peak and surfed. Dresden sat off to the side. Alone. A surfer he didn't recognize paddled over to him.

"Am I disturbing you, Master Chief?" he said as he labored to sit up on his board.

Dresden looked over at him. Few people called him Master Chief anymore. "I know you?"

"No, I'm at Team One. I'm from Casper. Senior Chief O'Rourke was kind of like my inspiration to join the Teams."

"Oh ... Okay."

They were silent for a while. A surfer caught a wave and sank deep inside the barrel. He hollered aloud as he reemerged, "That's for you, Lance!"

"Did you know him when he was in Casper?"

"Nah. My dad went to school with him."

"Oh. Were they friends?"

The young man laughed aloud, which surprised Dresden. "Nah, my dad hated him. Lance stole his girl and took her to the prom." He laughed some more, hard enough to knock himself off his board. Dresden laughed too. When the man got back on his board, he stuck out his hand.

"My name's Nick. Nick Reece. Petty Officer Third Class. It's an honor to meet you,

Master Chief."

"Call me Marcus. No one calls me that anymore. Especially my friends. How about we catch a wave or two?"

"Uh ... don't know how."

"What? What do you mean you don't know how?"

"I don't know how. Never been surfing before."

Dresden looked at Nick. The man was freaking serious.

"One of the guys let me borrow this board," he said somewhat sheepishly, as if he'd just realized how ridiculous it all was, "but I couldn't make it to the funeral and it didn't seem right to stand up on that cliff like a nub—no offense, of course."

"Well then we need to get you a wave!"

"Okay!" Nick said. He flashed a smile as big as Wyoming.

Nick never really caught a wave, let alone rode one. His best ride was on his belly—the only wave he didn't go over the falls on. Nick came gushing to the surface every time, laughing. And every time he clambered back onto his board, legs splayed out to the side for balance, and paddled back out to the lineup. JoJo nudged Dresden.

"The boy's either gonna kill himself or fall in love with surfing."

"Oh, he's in love. I'm sure of it. If he dies today, he will die a happy man."

"Spooky, huh brah? Reminds me of Lance, that guy does."

Dresden caught a wave in and waited for Nick. The kid caught a whitewash wave and darted toward Dresden, waving at him. They navigated the rocky beach and made their way to the top of the cliffs. A half-dozen or more cars and trucks were tailgating. Dresden stowed his board in his truck and changed, then met Nick at JoJo's truck.

He turned down a beer. Nick didn't. JoJo's wife had the grill going—teriyaki chicken and hot dogs. JoJo started a fire in a cut-down fifty-five-gallon drum. Dresden sat, shoulders slumped, staring into the fire. The mess he was in had slipped his mind for a while, and it felt good. He watched Nick talk up a couple Santa Cruz locals. Guys who would otherwise have called the boy a kook and pulled the spark plugs on his car. Nick wowed them with bull-riding stories and how surfing didn't seem much different. *Kid's good.* Dresden chuckled.

He took a walk to visit the other tailgates, ran into Stone Cold holding court and a van full of hard-core woman surfers that scared the piss out of him. They wanted to go back out after dark and charge middle peak again. They wanted him to come with them. The swell had picked up another foot or two since the tailgate started. He wished them well and moved on.

The man was standing near the road access to the parking area when Dresden noticed him. He was leaning up against a white Nissan Sentra. Rental Plates. Combat parked. No surfboard. No wetsuit hanging off a mirror, but he was intent on Dresden.

Nick asked him something when he got back to JoJo's tailgate, but Dresden didn't hear him. Instead he set his chair to get an angle on the stranger, who had gotten into his car. There was a familiarity about the man Dresden couldn't put his finger on. He *watched,* like the guy in Frisco. But it wasn't the same man, he was sure of that. Nick asked his question again, tapping Dresden on the arm.

"Uh … darn Nick, I'm sorry, what was that?"

"What is the biggest wave you've ever ridden?"

"A little over forty feet."

"Dang! That's what I'm gonna do," Nick said, then downed his beer.

Dresden looked over at JoJo and smiled. The man burst out in horse-bitten laughter, beer shooting from his nose. Slowly, Dresden turned back to get another look at the man in the Nissan. He was gone. A plume of dust was settling on the access road. Dresden dialed Robbie. It went to voicemail again.

Escondite, California

The first horn blast stirred Dresden out of his meditative state. He worked to separate the sensations that bombarded him. A bird squawked. A dog barked and a second horn blasted. *It's Robbie! For crying out loud, Robbie, why can't you use the doorbell like everyone else? Damn city boy.* Dresden leaned over his balcony. Robbie, head poking out of his car window gave an enthusiastic wave. He returned the gesture, if a little less cheerfully.

He went down to open the door, then walked into the kitchen. Robbie followed, stumbling over AP, who stuck his nose to Robbie's leg like a magnet.

"Something to drink? AP! Leave him alone—go!" The dog sauntered off.

"When was the last time you looked at your phone?" Robbie said.

Dresden stared at a point on the wall over his shoulder.

Robbie turned to follow his gaze. "What are you doing?"

"I'm trying to remember where I left my phone."

"Seriously? I'll take some iced tea. So, you didn't see what happened in Arizona?"

Dresden conceded he hadn't. He'd been doing his best to disconnect from it all. Nick had hung out at his house for a couple days on his way back down to the San Diego, and JoJo had tagged along as well. They slept, surfed and ate—that was it. JoJo had been the one to suggest the disconnect. He was worried about Dresden. Lance was dead, but he couldn't seem to get the circumstances of his death off his mind. The texts and emails of well-wishing had just made things worse for all of them.

"Okay, so you're done with your hippie-dippy trip-athlon and ready to greet the world again, right?"

"Sure," Dresden said, not so sure.

"Okay, well, first I think your friend Jennifer is actually missing. More on that in a moment. Second, there was another attack that stinks of some kind of weirdness. Well, it didn't right away, but now it does."

Robbie proceeded to tell Dresden about a cop buddy of his in Arizona. How they got to talking the other night. He was a gang guy with the Phoenix PD, Robbie explained. His buddy got called in to investigate a possible gang hit, maybe MS-13. The guy went to the scene and checked the place out, filed his report, done deal, didn't really think much of it. Except when the guy gets called to the carpet. The lieutenant says he's full of crap, because in his report the guy says that it was *not* gang related.

"Okay ... so what does this have to do with Lance?" Dresden said, settling onto a sofa chair in his living room. He felt more like taking a nap than listening to his friend.

"Apparently, my buddy knew it wasn't a gang hit. It was too clean. Sure, the hitmen were Hispanic. But that didn't mean it had to be a gang deal, or even cartel. But what bothered the guy was the fact that all but one of the guards had been drugged. The site manager had ended up with three bullets in him—one in the head and two in the chest," Robbie said.

Arizona, California, and Texas were all dealing with the direct fallout of mass migration from the south. Plenty of heavy-hitting gang and cartel members slipped across, hiding amongst those looking for a better life. Dresden knew not to assume that these guys couldn't shoot. Couldn't pull off a pro hit. More importantly was the sophistication of the hit.

A diversion team of delivery men took out the main body of guards. Two girls kidnapped, ages twelve and fourteen. Kidnapping was definitely MS-13's MO. But why kill the site manager and no one else? By all accounts, he wasn't even on the scene. The shooter drew him out and shot him. Lance hadn't been on the scene. Theoretically, he was a casualty of bad math. Except! Except for the flesh under his nails. What was that about? Dresden still hadn't teased that tidbit out.

"Whose house was it anyway?" he asked.

"The house belongs to none other than Tyler Baskin, the federal judged who's had more than his share of cartel and gang folks deported."

"And the girls?"

"His daughters."

"Hmm … I don't remember a Baskin being one of Frist Watch's clients."

"He's not. It's …" Robbie opened a notebook and flipped through the pages, "Uh … United Security Consultants, USC."

Dresden pulled himself to his feet. He filled a glass with water and wandered the kitchen and living room aimlessly. Oman. Arizona. Mortars and knock-out darts. Two site managers dead.

"I think you should seriously consider going back to Oman," Robbie said.

"No need—there's no answers there." Dresden sat back down.

"What do you mean?"

Dresden told Robbie what the detective had said. *Not here.* It was Robbie's turn to walk around.

"I'm going to go out on a limb here, but that was code. Not *here.* Not with the police. Not with Almasi and his *personal* staff. That leaves one possibility. And anyway, we aren't looking for answers, we're looking for clues that will lead us to answers."

AP came and lay down next to Dresden, who tugged on the dog's soft ear. *We?* Shit. I got Robbie hooked like a bloodhound. He's not going to let this go. I know it. Dammit! Maybe I can keep him at arm's length. I can't afford for him to get involved. Not if people are dying.

Dresden put his head back and closed his eyes. Two attacks in a matter of weeks. Two site managers killed. Two different companies. But both hits were similar in some way, Dresden pondered. He needed to get face to face with Roker. Maybe Robbie was right. Maybe he could get Roker to authorize him to get into Almasi's compound and check things out.

"So, you had something on Jennifer?" Dresden asked, his head still back.

"Yeah—well, not much. I ran a missing person's check. The basic. Got nothing. I called her number. The one you gave me. Got her voicemail like you did," Robbie said. "You told me her boss was looking for her, hadn't seen her, so no need to call her work."

He'd found a number for her parents. Gave them a call, acting like a bill collector. The husband, the dad, answered. He said they never heard from her but once a month. Robbie said he could hear a woman yelling in the background, who he assumed was the mom. The husband made excuses for his wife, said she and her daughter didn't get along. Then Robbie had tried credit cards, and came up with nothing.

"So, like you said, nothing really. Can you keep looking? I think she may be in trouble. Don't ask me why. But I owe it to Lance if nothing else."

"Definitely. What are you going to do?"

"I'm going to see Roker, in person."

Seventeen

Arline, Tennessee

The veil of sleep eluded Dresden, despite his trying. He normally slept well in hotel rooms. He read and drank some tea, but still, closing his eyes only brought the visions roaring back. The fiery scenes, the smells. All of it. He got up and called Casper, like Robbie had suggested. Ask about *him*—deep down, not shallow or cursory, but real, get authentic Robbie had said. Casper answered and Dresden flailed, clumsily dancing around the niceties trying to find a way to *talk* to his son.

"Hey Casper, do you … do you feel like you could come through in a pinch? You know, when things get bad?" Dresden asked. The words felt like chunks of glass in his mouth.

The boy said nothing. The silence kicked Dresden in the gut like a mule. He was positive Casper would hang up or ask him why he'd brought it up at all. Did he think Casper couldn't take care of himself? He was twenty-two and on his own; of course he could. This was a terrible idea. Terrible.

Casper didn't hum, but instead there was just silence, for a long time. Dresden waited, hoping, and finally Casper spoke.

"For years, I tried to live up to an image of myself as close to you as I could manage. You're my dad, so of course that's what I'm supposed to do, right? Then one day, something changed—I saw value in myself. I didn't really know it at the time, but Osuna helped me see that."

Dresden's was silent. *I never asked him to be like me, not once. Osuna. Damn!* Casper had a surrogate father because he was missing in action. Shit.

"Dad?"

"Yeah."

They tripped around the subject for another half hour, neither of them really able to commit to talking. They fell back into their old ways. Dresden's eyes drooped—he didn't want Casper to stop, but he couldn't stay awake. He woke a half-hour later, the phone pressed against his face, hot and buzzing. Casper had sent a text—*love you dad.*

All Dresden could think was, why?

The woman kept writing, so Dresden leaned in over the counter. Her round cheeks wobbled as she tossed her head sideways and looked out of the corner of her eye at him. "Good morning, may I help you?" Her voice cracked and pitched as she spoke. She didn't have the Tennessee twang. Foreign, Dresden thought. He didn't answer. The woman removed her hands from her keyboard, straightened her back, looked up at Dresden, and breathed out as she repeated, "Sir? May I help you?"

Dresden backed away. The First Watch lobby was empty. It usually was. Most people went in through the schoolhouse or tech buildings in the back. "Yes, I need to see Tom."

"Tom who, sir?"

"Huh? Tom Roker."

"Okay. Do you have an appointment?"

"No," he said." Never needed one before. Tell him it's Marcus."

"Marcus …?"

"Dresden."

"Please have a seat, sir."

Dresden sat. He sifted through magazines, expertly placed in descending order like timecards in a factory. He moved them around, looking for something to stove his angst. Nothing. Wait! One magazine featured Roker on the front cover. The man stood proud, in double-breasted suit, arms crossed at his chest, hair recently trimmed. It was an up-angle shot, a superman pose. There was a glint in the man's eye.

"Mr. Dresden?" the woman said, searching the waiting area for him. He was the only one in the room.

Sharp as a bowling ball. "Yes, I'm here."

"Oh, there you are. Well, it appears as though Mr. Roker is engaged at the moment."

"Okay, I'll wait until he's not engaged."

"Uh ... well sir, he will be engaged for the whole day."

"I doubt that. I'll wait. I can wait in his office."

The woman choked on some saliva. "I—don't ... let me call someone."

"Yeah, call Jennifer," Dresden said. He wanted to see how bad it had gotten.

"Jennifer?"

"Christ! Jennifer Nolan." This *was* bad.

"Hmm. Okay, let me see."

Twenty minutes passed before a pear-shaped man in a fawn-colored suit came out to meet him. "Mr. Dresden?"

"Yes."

"Can I help you?"

"Probably not. I need to see Tom or Jennifer. You know what? To hell with all this. I'll just call them. You can go now."

The man stared down at his blue shoes. "But Mr. Dresden—"

"No. Really, you can go."

The pear man left. Dresden made his calls; both went directly to voicemail. The doors down the leadership hall were badge-activated. Although it had been a very long time since he'd been to the lobby, he was sure the badge device was new. Dresden still had his First Watch identification card, dangling from a homemade lanyard of green parachute cord. He took it off and walked up to the keypad, placing it on the pad like the pear man had. As soon as he did, the device alarmed, a loud, shrill buzz that lasted five seconds. Dresden tried again with the same result.

The woman at the front desk jumped up in surprise, then horror after Dresden's second attempt. She was mortified, and seemed as if she couldn't manage to move, but finally bleated out, "Mr. Dresden, please!"

Doors beside him opened and two men came out—Sean Branch, followed by one of the men from the funeral. Richardson, if he remembered correctly. Branch wore a grin like the Joker. The shit-eatin' version. His demeanor was tight and agitated; clearly, he wasn't happy to be there or to see Dresden.

"Mr. Dresden, please follow me," Branch said. He led Dresden to a small, glass-walled conference room off the lobby. Richardson followed. Branch offered Dresden a seat at the side of the table, then slid like molasses into his chair. Richardson manned the door, giving him a hard stare.

"Where's Roker?"

"He's engaged."

"So, I've been told."

"My name is Branch."

"Uh huh. Okay."

Branch shifted in his seat, clearly not accustomed to being so blatantly blown off. He sat at a sideways angle to Dresden. When he spoke, he placed his chin on his shoulder, with his eyes half closed. Dresden tried to place his accent—Cockney maybe.

"Mr. Roker is very busy. Can I help you with whatever it is you're looking for?"

"No."

"Maybe there is a message I could pass on to Mr. Roker?"

"No."

"Well then, Mr. Dresden, it seems our business here is done. From here on out, please stay in your wheelhouse." Branch stood and motioned to the door. Richardson opened it.

Wheelhouse? What the hell's that supposed to mean? Dresden didn't get up. "How long have you been here, Branch?"

Branch didn't answer. He stood just as he was.

"Not much of a talker, are you Sean?"

Richardson moved toward Dresden. Branch raised his hand, and the man stood down.

Dresden leaned back in his chair, admiring his fingernails. So, he wasn't going to get to see Roker. Not here at least. But he needed to start playing this a little more tactically. *Can't keep going into the fray and coming out with nothing. What do you know, Branch? Let's find out, shall we?*

"Are you the reason I couldn't conduct my assessment in Oman?"

Branch rolled his head but said nothing.

"I'll take that as a yes."

He followed up with more questions, about the Oman police, the man with the broken nose, but Branch didn't answer anything. A small facial muscle near his temple jumped around the whole time.

"Quite the nervous twitch you have there," Dresden said, tapping his temple. "You have something bothering you?"

Branch motioned for Richardson. The man moved to Dresden's side.

"Well just so you know," Dresden added, "Roker and I go way back. I don't think he'll find this at all amusing. When he finds out, of course."

"For the record, Mr. Dresden, my sole objective is to preserve what Mr. Roker has built. My grandest hope is to play a part, however small, in making First Watch thrive." Branch ignored Dresden's comment.

Dresden stifled a laugh as he got up and walked to the exit, the other two men in tow. He stopped short and turned. "You're the ops guy, right?" He looked directly at Branch as he spoke.

Branch stood side-long to Dresden again and nodded with his eyes closed.

What a fucking weirdo. "That's good. Because, if you were training or the personnel guy, you'd be toast by now. Your balls would be hanging from that flagpole out front. The guys around here would've eaten you alive. Have a nice day," Dresden said, and punched the doors before stopping again. "One more thing—you wouldn't have any idea were Jennifer Nolan is, would you?"

Branch stiffened and shook his head.

A real, freakin' weirdo.

Dresden meandered to his car where he sat, stupefied by what had just happened. Shut down again, for the second time. No one would answer his questions. But it wasn't answers he wanted, right? It was clues.

Looking up, he saw Richardson watching him from the front door. Black wraparound shades hiding his tired eyes.

Big fat fucking clues. Dresden knew what he needed to do. He started his car as Richardson moved toward him.

Choto Bend, Tennessee

Dresden slammed his fist against the door. *Open the damn door. I know you're in there.* He kicked it for good measure. His fist, red, swelled and throbbed. Finally, the locks were thrown, and the door cracked ever so slightly. Dresden peered into one bloodshot eyeball surrounded by darkness. The door opened enough to allow Dresden to see Tom Roker in a pair of faded, navy-blue sweats and house slippers.

"What the hell are you doing here!" Roker said.

"I could ask you the same fucking question, Tom."

Dresden had left First Watch headquarters assuming that if he couldn't get to Roker at work, he'd try his house. He knew Roker's car, a gunmetal gray Hummer 2. He set up shop at a café off Choto Road, near a marina, and waited. It was the only road to the man's house, the only way for Roker to get home from work.

Two hours of waiting left Dresden wired on caffeine with his eyes feeling like sandpaper. A thought went off like a flash crash—what if Roker had never been in his office, never been at work? What if Branch, in his own weird way, was covering for him?

And here he was, hiding out. The weirdness seemed to never end.

Roker poked his head out and looked around like a bouncer at a speakeasy. "Get inside." He waved his hand at Dresden.

The house was dank. Dark sheets hung from the drapery bars. Tiny slivers of evening sunlight sliced away at the edges. Roker moved to the kitchen. An island the size of a ping pong table commanded center stage. A single dim light from the hood cast an eerie glow on the dark marble countertop.

"What the hell is all this, Tom?"

Roker took a glass jar of milk from the fridge, screwed off the lid, and tossed it in the sink. He drank straight from the container, a small trickle of milk escaping consumption. Dresden watched as it weaved its way through the stubble on Roker's chin. He wiped his mouth with the back of his sleeve.

Staring at Dresden, he said, "You wanna know something? It doesn't matter what you fucking do. Someone's going to want … you … ah, shit. What the hell are you doing here, Marcus?"

Here we go again—unfocused, incomplete, and meandering. "Listen, Tom, you gotta cut the crap."

"What are you talking about?"

"Oman. Lance. Stop dancing around this. You didn't even go to his funeral. You sent that freak man-boy Branch—"

"Hah. That's a good one. Man-boy. Hah!"

"Dammit!"

"Forget Oman, Marcus. There's a big 'ol grizzly bear of a problem out there. That shithead is gunnin' for my job. They are courting with unnatural bedfellows, I'm telling you. You think Oman was a problem? You wait! You wait. You'll see, Marcus. You will *all* see. You need to forget Oman. I don't like saying that any more than anyone, really I don't. But it's the price of doing business, and it's going to get worse before it gets better. I—I can tell you that, without a doubt."

"Forget Oman? Go to hell, Tom."

Roker looked hurt. "I need your help. I got a couple guys on board. They've been workin' it best they can. *We* can make this happen ... really. But this is going to take some grit. I need folks that can put aside their emotions and get the job done."

"Are you on that shit again? Whatever the hell that is that you can't tell me unless I come on board? Yeah, I got it, blah blah fucking blah. Tom—"

Without a word, Roker turned and walked out of the kitchen.

Jesus! Dresden felt a sudden thirst and searched the fridge for something to drink. Something hard. Nothing. He looked for a cooler or mini-fridge. Nothing. *Definitely for the best.* Dresden took thirty deep inhalations, exhaled fully, and held his breath.

Three minutes later, he slowly inhaled. Roker had disappeared. Dresden moved through the house like an apparition, sticking his head in room after room. They were empty. The kids' rooms empty. His wife's closet wide open and hurriedly cleared out. Bits of clothing were left behind, a layer of dust covering everything.

He found Roker splayed out on the floor, on his back, apparently of his own accord. Dresden watched him for a moment. Fast, shallow breaths caused Roker's stomach to rise and fall rapidly. He groaned with every third or fourth inhale, his eyes fixed on the skylight above.

"Tom? You okay?"

"Yeah. No. Not really sure. This is too much."

"What's too much?"

"All of it."

"Tom, I'm going to have to do something. I'm not sure what. I would appreciate your blessing. Your help. Figured you'd want answers as much as me. But I'm going to do it either way. Lance was our brother. He deserves to be—" Dresden stopped, not sure if there was a point anymore. He eyed Roker and tumbled into a thought that churned his stomach. What if Roker was part of the problem? Maybe he was going to the very people who were responsible for Lance's death. Robbie was right—he needed to get back to Oman. If he could see for himself what went down there, he might be able to figure out who was lying through their teeth, "Tom, you know what? I'm going to leave now. I would advise you, whatever you got going on, don't get in my way."

"But I thought—"

"Tom, I am sorry. Really, I am. I can't really relate to what you're going through. You know me and business don't mix well. But in some ways, I get the feeling you may have been your own worst enemy," Dresden said. He watched Roker's face, half-shrouded in shadow. The man's twisted expression dropped as if he'd just lost his last friend. Dresden nearly caved. Instead, he walked to the front door and left.

The girl at the café smiled broadly and handed Dresden his coffee before he ordered it. At a small, wobbly table, he sat for close to an hour. The image of Roker closed off in that big house made no sense. The man had never capitulated to anyone or anything. Why now? What had he done that was so bad he might lose his grip? Dresden knew his next step—Oman. But how to get there? He pulled out his phone and scrolled through his contacts, then stopped, scrolled back up, and hovered over the name for a moment before he pressed call.

"Fence? This is Marcus."

"Marcus! What's up, buddy? Man, it's good hear from you. How you hangin' in there?

"Thanks brother. Yeah, I'm doing good. Hey, I got a favor to ask."

"Shoot."

"Can you make sure I can gain access to Mr. Almasi's place in Oman."

"Dare I ask?"

"Well, Fence, I feel really bad about this—I know I don't work for First Watch anymore but … I need to get the post-incident assessment in Oman done. I tried, but—"

"What! I thought that was done weeks ago. Son-of-a-bitch! What the hell is Roker thinking? No, don't answer that. Hmmm …"

"Look, if it's too much—"

"No, no. That's not it. The one guy who could make sure that happens has been on my ass, and the rest of the Board of Directors' rear ends, about some whack-a-mole agenda he's cooked up. That's my two cents, of course. Anyway, maybe a little I scratch his back and he'll scratch mine. I'll call you back. But hey, if we do this, send the report and your travel expenses directly to me, okay?"

"You got it, Fence. And thanks."

Eighteen

Muscat, Oman

The jetliner pulled into the gate without delay this time. Dresden went first class, and although he didn't sleep, the visions hid out in the corners of his mind, leaving him alone for a little while. Long enough to rest and think.

When the seatbelt alarm sounded, Dresden stayed put. He'd been staring at an empty text message to Lance for the last fifteen minutes. Was he going crazy, writing a dead man? No, he was obsessing. There was a difference, he was sure of it. He needed to know what had really happened. He typed, *"Metal Health" by Quiet Riot* into the empty box and stared at the blinking cursor, then wrote, *don't worry man, I got your back on this,* and hit send.

The jet bridge was nearly empty by the time Dresden walked down it. Arman was standing at the gate, puffing away on a cigarette, holding a small sign that read *Drezdin*. Dresden laughed to himself as he walked up to the man. "Anybody ever tell you those things will kill you, Detective?"

"No. No one has ever told me that. You are the first, Mr. Dresden," Arman said. His narrow lips parted for a yellow-toothed smile.

"Marcus," Dresden said.

"What?"

"Marcus. My friends call me Marcus."

Arman huffed through a billow of smoke, then dropped this cigarette butt to the ground. He rubbed an off-colored mark on his cheek and shot Dresden a look. Pulling a pack of cigarettes from his suit pocket, he offered one to Dresden. Dresden shook his head and Arman stuck a cigarette in his mouth, then patted at his pockets for a lighter.

"Okay, it's Marcus then." The cigarette flicked around like a mosquito as he spoke.

Dresden and the detective rode in the back of the ROP squad car, Arman sitting quietly and smoking. Dresden didn't know the man, yet he had a sense Arman wanted to talk, but couldn't. The driver glanced into the rearview mirror every so often. Arman slid an envelope to Dresden, keeping it below the roving eyes of the driver.

We were not able to finish our investigation. Please share what you find out. If you can.

Dresden looked out the window as the city blurred. The colors blended like some psychedelic dream as they whooshed by. He looked back at the note, then retrieved a pen from his jacket and wrote: *OK.*

The ROP car pulled up in front of the Almasi compound, the whitewash wall blinding in the burning sun. The compound took up two, maybe three city blocks. A pair of security guards walked up to the squad car and opened Dresden's door. He raised an eyebrow at Arman, but the man's expression didn't change.

Arman got out of the car and put his elbows on the roof. "Mr. Dresden, I will take your bag to the hotel. A car will be here when you need it. Just call."

Dresden gave the detective a salute before he stepped into the guard shack.

Inside, Dresden was met by two men in suits. A thick coat of sweat masked their foreheads, their dress shirt buttons pulled tight. *Body armor under suits.* One of the men had faint bruising under his eyes and across the bridge of his nose. Dresden smiled broadly at him. The man did not reciprocate. The other guard patted Dresden down, then searched his backpack. As the man returned everything to Dresden's pack, a third man joined them.

"We cannot be too sure. You understand, right, Mr. Dresden?"

"Absolutely," Dresden said. He caught something off in the man's speech. Vaguely foreign, like the guy whose nose he'd broken.

The man jutted his hand out, its back to the sky. "Mark Tippins."

"Good to meet you, and thank you for orchestrating this goat rope. It's just a matter of paperwork. Gotta dot those i's and cross those t's, or the boys back in Knoxville, the ones paying our rent and groceries, get a little fussy, you know?"

"Yeah, well either way, let's get this over with as quickly as possible."

"Sure thing, you're the boss."

With three guards and Tippins in tow, Dresden surveyed the entire compound. He spent thirty minutes or more at each mortar point of impact. The guest house—where Lance had died. The building where Mr. Almasi had held his secret meeting. He walked the perimeter of the wall for another hour. Along the way, he asked Tippins to tell him what he knew of the incident. Tippins drew an impassionate look—conscious relaxation of his face. Dresden assumed the man would lie. Maybe he'd been coached. *Let's see.* Tippins described in some detail the events.

It turned out he lied *and* had been coached. Dresden knew that at the time of the attack, Tippins was seven blocks away from the compound with no possible vantage of Almasi's place.

He remembered Lance mentioning Tippins. Had he taken over because Lance died? Or was that the plan all along? *He's been bought. Or maybe something else altogether.* The other men slinked away as they walked to the gate, leaving only Tippins. The man hung his head and studied his once-polished boots, now scuffed and dusty.

"Can I ask you something?" Tippins said, not looking up.

"Sure."

"Did you know O'Rourke well?"

"Mmm ... I knew him."

"Well, I know this won't go in the report but—but he was a thief. And was totally fuckin' over the rest of us in the process, although we didn't know it at the time."

"And you're sure of it now?" Dresden said.

"Well, I shouldn't really say..."

Code word for 'I'm about to feed you a line of bull crap.' "But you're going to, right?"

Tippins looked up, his eyes glowing. "Knoxville has emails ... that's all I'm gonna say." He shut the door to the booth and walked into the compound. The gate guard returned to his post, boring holes into Dresden as he picked up his phone. Within five minutes, an ROP car was out front to escort him to his hotel.

The hotel room was plush, compliments of the ROP. Crisp sheets, pillows to bury your head into, and a glass step-in bath-shower big enough for four.

All that plus two hundred channels on an eighty-inch wall-mounted widescreen, and top-shelf room service, with juicy steaks to order and braised veggies. The concierge alluded to treats off the menu as well, but Dresden declined.

Casper answered the call on the second ring. Dresden, encouraged by their last conversation and egged on by Robbie, decided to try again. Robbie had cautioned him not to make every conversation an answer quest. This was virgin territory for Dresden, and it admittedly scared the crap out of him. But he'd worked over a batch of ideas, then landed on one: a confession. A shortcoming of his own. He told Casper that he knew that he'd hurt him. Left wounds to fester. Not physically, of course. But mentally.

Casper had been diagnosed with Fabry's when he was nine. Emily hadn't taken it well; it'd come from her side of the family. The boy, unaware of what it meant, took it in stride until he realized he would have to get an infusion every two weeks for the rest of his life. Dresden remembered those times. His hands ached now as he told Casper, how for about a year he'd attempted to put on a face and be okay with it, when in fact he was really angry. And that he knew now he hadn't been there for Casper in the way a good father would have.

His son was silent, humming again this time, his breathing choppy. Dresden cursed himself, sure

Casper would hang up at any moment. He changed the subject to how work had gotten more complicated and how he may have to put off his visit. Casper grunted and said he needed to go, but neither of them hung up. Dresden felt a noose tightening around his neck. He wriggled his toes to keep the toppling stool standing.

"Dad, I really don't want to go down this self-improvement road with you … not like this," Casper said.

"Is that what we're doing here?" Dresden said, genuinely surprised.

"Yeah. I gotta go."

Dresden heard a muffled, "I love you dad" right as the line went dead.

Despite the accommodations, he paced, restless as a penned stallion. He entertained himself for a short time looking for the listening devices. He found three. Bored, and wired, his brain on overdrive, he grabbed his watch, wallet, and shirt, slipped on his shoes, and went downstairs. Two in the morning, and the bar was overflowing. Slick men in business attire. Well-done women in next to nothing. A seedy element mingling between the cracks, pickpockets and working girls. Dresden headed into the street.

A taxi honked at him. "Where you need to go?"

"I'm going there," Dresden barked, and kept walking. The taxi drove off.

He walked through the city until morning began to dawn, then stepped into a café as the purveyor unlocked the door. After ordering a Turkish coffee and two pastries, Dresden sat at the bar in the window. The city was beginning to come alive. The ghost workers—the maids, janitors, cooks, and street sweepers—filled the sidewalks. He scanned his phone.

Finishing his third cup of coffee, he noticed the demographic of the streets had changed to Filipino shop clerks, Malaysian bus drivers, and Korean waiters—Asia in the Middle East. The unique crowd helped Dresden pick out the tall, lean man in the doorway, reading the paper. Dresden had seen him walk by at least once before. *That's it! If I can't snipe the fucker, I'm going to have to catch him.* For the next thirty minutes, Dresden did a rapid-fire map study of the city. Every street, every alley, every store and restaurant within a twenty-block radius. He found floor plans as best he could. He drew his route on a napkin, then stuffed the napkin in his pocket and walked out. He stopped and stretched outside until he was sure he'd been noticed.

On a bus, the lean man hid behind a large woman reading a book. At each stop, he peeked out from behind her to spy on Dresden. Dresden went through a park and a square, doubling back naturally a half-dozen times. The lean man kept his distance but was always there. Dresden used mirrors and large plate glass windows to keep an eye on his position. He wanted to maintain a persona of ignorance.

At stops along his route, Dresden took notes, writing down everything he could remember about Almasi's compound. He wrote it into his memory. After nearly five hours of touring the city, he ended up right where he'd planned to set his trap. As Dresden entered the Oman Avenues Mall, he spotted the second man. *Perfect!* In the mall, he found a bench by a fountain and called the number Arman had given him.

Arman answered with a yawn, and Dresden asked if he had someone following him. The detective said no. Dresden gave him a location to pick up his pursuers, but not before he busted them wide open. Arman laughed. *That's a first.* Dresden tore the pages out of the notebook and folded them, then stuffed them into an envelope.

He walked through the mall for about an hour and bought something for Casper, and something for Kelli and Robbie as well. He almost bought something for Maria. With three shopping bags weighing him down, Dresden stopped at a trash can near another fountain. He removed all the packaging of the items he could. All the stuffing. He ended up with one bag of trash, then felt around in his pockets and dumped the unneeded contents as well. That should pique their interest.

Dropping his tail took less than two minutes. He found a concealed positioned within eyeshot of the fountain and trash bin. For a while, he thought the game was up. Nothing happened. Around fifteen minutes later, though, the first man approached the trash can and sat down beside it. He pretended to read the paper, but his eyes didn't move at all. A few minutes later, a second man came into view, looking over his phone, eyes darting from side to side. The seated man gave him a head nod. The man pocketed his phone and lifted the trash can lid. With some skill, he removed the shopping bag and replaced the lid, quickly and quietly. He rifled through the bag and came up with a handful of pocket litter but nothing else. The seated man stood and rifled through the bag as well. Then the two men jerked up and dropped the bag.

Twelve ROP officers moved in, a couple with their weapons drawn. Dresden watched as the lean man and his accomplice lay face down on the ground. Arman came into view. *There's my boy.* He removed the contents of the shopping bag to find the envelope wrapped in the trash in the bag. He opened the pouch and pulled out the notebook pages halfway, then stuffed them back in. Arman put the envelope under his arm and walked away from the other officers. The phone buzzed in Dresden's hand. He opened the text message: *Thank you. Safe Travels. Arman.*

Nineteen

Escondite, California

The only real vice Dresden had, not counting coffee, was a breakfast burrito from The Terrible Taco, a little shack off the boardwalk. The burritos were served three ways, but Dresden always went for the grilled fish, ceviche, potatoes, eggs, cheese, and Pico de gallo. The one-foot square window served as both order and pickup point. Cooks yelled out names when the food was ready. Dresden grabbed his brown paper bag and found a bench on the boardwalk that really wasn't a boardwalk at all but rather a four-hundred-yard-long concrete walkway.

The tourists had started to thin out as summer was coming to a close. The locals now finding their way back to the beach enjoyed the cool afternoon temperatures. Dresden chatted with a few of the old-time surfers for several minutes. But mostly, he ate his food and watched the small waves ripple onto the beach. The biggest surf was yet to come, which made him think of Lance. This would be the first season they'd missed surfing together.

He picked up his phone and opened a text to his friend. In Oman, Dresden had settled on the idea that he would keep the playlist going for as long as he had the steam for it. A tribute of his own kind. He typed, *"The Magnificent Seven," by The Clash.* Joe Strummer claimed the song lyrics had been invented on the spot. Dresden felt like he was following suit. Making things up as he went along. His bumbling probably wouldn't end up with a classic hit, though. Dresden wrote a note to Lance, hit send, and opened another text to Robbie.

Nothing about the past ten days had set well with Dresden—Branch at Frist Watch, Roker at home, and most of all Almasi's place and Tippins. He knew Almasi's place had been scrubbed clean. The mortar impact points had been cleaned up but had yet to be repaired, and the staff briefed on what to say. Almasi had plenty to hide, Dresden assumed. A guy like that always had plenty to hide. Lance's death could easily reflect badly on him.

Dresden's phone buzzed. Robbie wrote: *I'll be in Escondite in the morning.* Dresden's phone vibrated again. It was Mickey. *Shit, I never hear from that guy,* he thought, then opened the text.

The message was three simple words: *check your email.* Later. He'd check it when he got home; for now, he'd enjoy his breakfast.

The next morning, when Dresden returned from his run, Robbie was sitting on the stoop, overnight bag and grocery bags flanking him. He looked up at Dresden and smiled. The two men went into the house, and Robbie headed straight for the dining room. Without asking, he cleared the hulking mahogany dining table. Then he turned on all the lights and opened all the windows of the bungalow, before heading back out to his car.

"Come with me. Grab the whiteboard and bring it in," he said over his shoulder.

Dresden obeyed. He watched Robbie unpack a backpack. Pads of paper and pencils, markers, pens, maps. A laptop. A file folder with papers in it. Robbie told Dresden to set up the whiteboard, and Dresden smirked and did as he was told.

"Sit down."

Dresden obeyed, again.

"Look, before we get going on ... I need to update you on your friend, Jennifer. I came up completely dry. So, I passed her info on to an FBI agent in the San Francisco office that handles kidnapping cases. He said he'd do what he could, so we'll see, guy." Robbie stuck his hands in his pockets.

"What?" Dresden asked.

"It's … It's just that there's not a very good chance—"

"She's alive. I know it. So, let's get moving on the other stuff and let your FBI man work his magic. Either way we'll know soon enough, right?"

"Yeah I guess," Robbie said. "Okay, well, there was another attack, and this time First Watch was in charge. It went down in Sri Lanka. You know the manager there?"

Dresden thought for a moment. "Overby. Rick."

"Yup. He's dead. Plus a whole bunch of other folks. Civilians and contractors. It's a real mess."

"Shit."

"Poop is right," Robbie said. "Oh hey, one more thing. I have a couple more bags of grocery in the car, back seat. Could you grab them?"

"Sure."

Dresden put away the groceries and made them some guacamole as Robbie gave him the details on the Sri Lanka attack. A restaurant along Colombo-Galle road in Colombo; a rich guy and his security detail. A front loader and two vans rammed the security detail's vehicles where they sat waiting on their principal. There's a shootout on a busy street at mid-day. Attackers, security, and civilians all shot. Inside, another man, or men, take out the principal and a woman he was meeting with. The site manager, Overby, was shot execution-style. Like in Phoenix.

Dresden started to feel a familiar tightness in his chest. Overby was a good man. Smart and outgoing, like Lance. Dresden shook off the weight of the information to stay focused.

"So, that's Sri Lanka."

Dresden moved to the whiteboard and wrote *Oman, Phoenix, Sri Lanka* at the top and separated them into columns. *Each attack, the site manager is killed,* he added below the locations.

"Can I ask you a question?" Robbie said.

"Sure," Dresden said, half listening.

"Why are you doing this?" Robbie leaned back in his chair.

The whiteboard became a blur—slowly putting the cap on the pen, Dresden realized he hadn't stopped to consider why. It was Lance, that was why. He looked over at Robbie and knew that wouldn't be enough, and it was a fair question. But it was one he didn't have a ready answer for. Robbie's expression told him he wasn't going to get off that easy. So why?

"Lance was my friend and a beast. A fighter. A man of real substance. I know something is wrong here. I know Lance went down fighting to his last breath. I intend to do the same to find out what happened." Dresden surprised even himself by the level of conviction he'd mustered.

Robbie pursed his lips and nodded. "Works for me, guy." Then he pointed back at the whiteboard and said, "The last attack. The site manager wasn't the only one killed."

"Well, the manager *was* killed, but there were other casualties, you're right. Let's put it that way, okay? Oh … hey, in Sri Lanka, are they pinning the attack on the Tigers?

"Maybe—JVP's another option."

Dresden read over the columns again. He wrote *Tigers/JVP* under Sri Lanka, and *MS-13* under Phoenix. "Did anyone get fingered or take credit for Oman?"

"Nope. Well, ISIL kind of did in Oman. So much for oasis of peace, right? And MS-13 is not confirmed."

"Okay, but it looked like them or some group of their ilk, right?

"Yeah, but there's been no request for ransom. You know, the girls are just gone."

"Shit, that sucks. You think trafficking?"

"Yeah. A target of opportunity, I'm guessing."

"Damn. That really sucks. Okay."

Dresden wrote *ISIL* under Oman. Three attacks. Three major criminal or terror groups. Three dead site managers. Two sites First Watch, one site not. What made that one different?

He moved to the dining room table and dipped a chip in some guacamole. All the attacks used different equipment. Weapons, vehicles, explosives.

Explosives! Wait a minute. Shit. Dresden ate another chip. He lost the thought for a moment. What was it? What was it? Dammit! He scanned his list again, then ran from the room and headed upstairs, Robbie yelling after him.

Dresden walked back down the stairs grunting as he flipped through photos on his camera. He handed the camera to Robbie, who flipped through the photos. Dresden had taken nearly two hundred pictures of the Almasi compound. Robbie glanced up and smiled. There were at least fifty of each mortar impact site. Except they weren't impact sites.

"These are explosions," Robbie said, looking up at Dresden.

"Ranger up, brother! You still got a little Army in you after all."

He hadn't put it together while in Oman. But the mortars were faked. Something had been buried at the sites. Explosions meant diversion. That meant all three attacks had been faked. Was the fake mortar attack meant to throw off anyone snooping around? Diversion, Dresden thought, was not unique to any particular group. Everyone was capable of employing the tactic. Two things troubled him, though. First, tacticians who employed diversions tended to have a signature, and second, why a diversion in the first place, unless to cover something up? These were sophisticated, well-orchestrated attacks. They were conducted for a reason, but not the most overt reason. Dresden had a suspicion he was trying to avoid. All three attacks were *connected*. But why? He wrote *diversion* down on the board under each column.

"I was thinking the threat was from a player outside First Watch. Maybe someone who had it out for contractors—or contractor leadership. But this is too much for a grudge deal, simple vengeance. The Phoenix attack is what makes no sense if we think it's coming from First Watch."

"Okay," said Robbie, "think about this. What if these aren't the first attacks, just the ones we know of? Have there been more attacks on First Watch contractors? If so, were they planned and executed? Were they part of a larger scheme? And lastly, is Phoenix a large diversion of its own?"

"Hell, I don't know! Jesus, you took that one way down conspiracy road—quick, fast, and in a hurry. Let's think smaller and stick with the three, for now," Dresden said, rubbing his forehead.

"Okay, fair enough," Robbie said.

"What else?"

"Hmm, how about, well … witnesses?"

Dresden hummed and nodded his head. "Good one."

Witnesses. People who saw the site managers die or get killed. Oman—no witness. Phoenix—no witness. Sri Lanka—two, but they ended up dead as well. Dresden wrote down *no witnesses* under each column, as he finished the last one his phone rattled across the dining room table. He ignored it. It buzzed to the edge of the table before Robbie grabbed it and shoved it into Dresden's hand. Dresden looked at him as if he'd just handed him an eel.

He swiped at his screen. "Crap!" Dresden tossed his phone onto the table and ran back upstairs again.

"You getting in your workout or something?" Robbie yelled.

Dresden returned with his laptop and began to sift through his emails. "Ah, okay, here it is."

"Here's what?"

Dresden had completely forgotten about Mickey's text and email from the day before. The email needed a passcode, but Mickey hadn't sent one. He texted him, then told Robbie what had happened. Robbie yawned and suggested they take a break. He'd pulled a nightshift then got in his car and drove the three hours down to Escondite. Dresden started to protest but decided against it as he watched his friend yawn again. They moved to the second-floor balcony.

Not able to keep his mind off topic for too long, Dresden tried different passwords for Mickey's email. Name, initials, birthday, all the usual stuff. Nothing worked. He checked for a text from the man. Nothing. He tried again with the passwords. Wife's name.

Kids. Hometown. Why was this even important? Probably just some lude picture Mickey wanted to hide from his wife and kids or something. No, anything out of the ordinary had to have something to do with ... Lance.

Lance and Mickey. Dresden punched in a six-digit combo. Lance and Mickey's two BUD/S class numbers.

"Got it!" Dresden barked.

"Jesus, guy, you scared me half to death," Robbie said, opening his eyes with a jolt.

"Sorry man." Dresden clicked on the first of nearly thirty attached documents. "What the hell?" He opened a few more of the documents handing his computer over to Robbie.

Robbie read what Dresden had pulled up and continued clicking through. Dresden found his phone and texted Mickey again. He let him know he got in, but that he didn't understand what he was looking at. Robbie grunted and said they looked like correspondence between people at First Watch. Lists of questions. Something about procurement of large sums of something, that didn't make any sense. There were spreadsheets full of numbers. Agendas and pick-up and drop-off schedules, but of what?

Dresden agreed. He knew exactly what a batch of them were. The client surveys both Mickey and Lance seemed to be so upset about. What bothered

Dresden most was Mickey's subject line: *here they are, I'm done, do what you do, peace out.* Mickey wasn't a quitter. So what was that about? He'd sent them to Dresden as if he knew something was wrong. Something big. Something weird. As if he knew Dresden would go after whoever killed Lance. *Mickey knows someone planned it.*

Dresden texted him again, but still no response.

"We need someone who can decipher these," Robbie said, bringing Dresden out of his haze, "you think someone at First Watch could ..."

"No, no one at First Watch. We have to assume everything from them is tainted."

"Okay, I can have some of the cyber-crime guys—"

"Whoa, isn't that like breaking every jurisdiction rule in the book?"

"Wow, look at the big brain on Marcus!"

The two men sat in silence. Dresden propped his feet up on the railing. Robbie lay back down on the chaise lounge. The sun bounced its rays off the green Pacific Ocean making the entire coast shimmer. They needed someone they could trust and who was as disconnected from First Watch as much as possible. Someone competent and trustworthy. Someone far away, not connected.

Dresden dropped his feet with a loud slap. Robbie once again jumped up out of a half-sleep.

"Dammit!" Dresden said.

"Darn it, what?" Robbie said, looking over him while wiping his eyes.

"I know someone, but—"

"Who?

"Maria!" Dresden waffled his way out of the depression in the lounge chair to sit up.

"Who?"

"Maria … uh, never mind. She's a cyber guru … person."

"Why her?

"Well, I know her. She does that cyber thing. But the biggest thing is she has no connection with First Wa—" Dresden stopped.

"What's the problem? Let's give her a call."

"She hates me. I was really rude to her."

"I hate to break it to you, but you've been rude to a lot of women, my friend. They still crawl all over you. Remember that young lass down in Darwin, she—"

"Maria's different."

"Oh, ho. *Different*. I see. So, basically, you're sweet on her. How charming. But back to business. Let's call her up."

Dresden lay back down, dropping his black sunglasses over his eyes. "It's not that simple. I said some really mean things to her. I doubt she'll even pick up the phone."

"Maybe. Maybe not. But if she does answer, you own it."

"Own it?"

"You know something, you are one hell of a warrior, but you're a terrible husband—boyfriend, guy-friend, whatever. Get the women's number, and let's call her."

Dresden found it, then sat for a minute with his thumb over the call button.

Robbie reached across and pushed Dresden's thumb down. "There, now it's all my fault."

The phone rang, and Dresden put it on speaker. He pictured Maria staring at the number, deciding whether to answer or not. *Hell, she probably deleted my number.*

A sleepy voice came over the speaker. "Marcus?"

Dresden didn't respond right away. Robbie slapped him on the knee. "Yes … yes, it's me, Marcus."

Maria said nothing.

"Uh, um. Maria, I want to apologize for saying the mean things I said to you when we last spoke. I was out of my head, but that doesn't make what I did, what I said, right. I'm sorry for being such a jerk. I know you weren't the reason Lance died."

Maria breathed into the phone and the time drew out. As Dresden took a breath to speak, she said, "Marcus, is that why you called?"

"Yes. I mean, yes … and no."

"You called to apologize?"

"Yes."

"Thank you."

Dresden's shoulders relaxed, and he found he could breathe again. "You're welcome. How—how have you been?"

"Good. Thinking about you, wondering how you were doing."

Dresden leaped from the lounge chair and slammed his fist on the railing without touching it, then sat back down. "Same here."

"So, what is it you wanted to ask me?"

"Who said I had anything to ask you?"

"You did. I can hear it in your voice,"

Wow! She is good, Robbie mouthed.

"Okay. So we have some emails. Nothing that makes any sense, though. Is there some special thing you can do to figure out something like that?" Dresden said, scratching his head, not understanding a word he'd just said.

"Does this have to do with Lance?"

"Yes."

"Why?" Maria yawned. "Why are you trying to find a reason for Lance's death other than that he died?"

Dresden was silent for a long time, while Robbie sat back and closed his eyes. He listened to static on the line and Maria breathing.

"Because Lance was an action guy. All action. I'm positive he went down fighting like a son-of-a-bitch—sorry for the bad words. But I intend to do the same. I want to find out what happened. I owe him that much."

The line was silent for a long time again.

"Maria?"

"Okay. I will send you a secure email address. Send what you have to it, and I will take a look. I won't know anything until I see it."

"Great! Thank you so much."

"Marcus, I'm going to go back to sleep now. Oh, and next time we talk, can it be just you and me?"

Robbie burst out in a silent laugh, and Dresden punched at him like they were in grade school.

"Sure thing, Maria. Sweet dreams."

"Thank you. Talk to you soon."

Dresden held his phone, staring at it. He listened to his heart slow. A wild euphoria spiraled through his mind into his throat.

The murmur of Robbie's voice in a distant room was the only thing Dresden could hear. The man barked happily into his phone, playing with his kids. Dresden thought of Maria, and his temples started to pound with each heartbeat. He reached for his phone and flicked through songs on Spotify till one caught his eye.

She's back man, he wrote in a text, *and I feel like I have a "Fever". Heh… you know, by Peggy Lee.* Dresden chuckled at his own stupidity. It was a welcomed diversion, though, and he even thought of going back to Italy. Finding a quiet pension where the two of them could … he stopped, sent the text to Lance, and set his phone down on the bedside table. He rolled over and closed his eyes and thought of Italy. His phone buzzed a few minutes later. Rolling back over, he looked at the screen.

Lance!

Hello Marcus, the message read.

Dresden didn't move. The phone slid to the floor. He shook off the shock, grabbed his phone, and backed out of the message. It was the right contact. The correct thread. Crap!

Who the hell is this? Dresden wrote.

He waited, glancing at his watch every few seconds. The time passed agonizingly slowly. Two minutes. Three minutes. Four minutes.

At almost five minutes, the response finally came.

You know.

Twenty

Escondite, California

The cool morning breeze off the ocean chilled Robbie and Dresden as they ran. The tune of uneven measures of rubber soles hitting the asphalt supplied the soundtrack. Robbie struggled, but he tried to hide it. Dresden slowed his pace.

Robbie laughed, then coughed a wet hack. "I really need to run more." He slowed down. "I gotta tell you something. I woke up last night thinking about our list." Robbie stopped, bent, and put his hands on his knees.

They'd reached the north end of Escondite. A dead end into a private residence. The land beyond the house wrapped around the bay like a blanket. At the point, small waves peeled off the rocks, crystal-perfect barrels a foot high. The horizon and sky meshed in a still blueness. The two men stretched. They said nothing for a while as Robbie caught his breath.

"Last night, I started thinking about who we could talk to. You know, in police work we try to find witnesses. I know, I know, we went over this already, but hear me out. We don't always look for someone who witnessed it firsthand. Sometimes, clues come from something someone heard, you know?" Robbie took a deep breath.

Dresden remained silent, but nodded. He wasn't quite sure where Robbie was going.

The man broke it down for him. In all three attack scenarios there were no witnesses to the killing of the site manager. But what about guys on the periphery? Well in Oman, Almasi or someone made sure all of Lance's men were well out of range. So, no chance there. Phoenix—all of the possible witnesses were drugged or out of range, like the gate guards. They were a mile from the house. No good either. So, Sri Lanka, technically no witnesses, but maybe the dead could tell a story. There were guys in the vicinity, right?

Robbie had gotten the names of all the men on the detail and ran them. Four of them were former Army, SF. It took him a little while, but he found a major who all four men had served under at First Group, up in Washington state. Then he found their NCO. Small world, of course—Robbie kind of knew the guy. Same Ranger Battalion, different Rifle Company, that sort of thing. So, he called him. The NCO said one of the men from Sri Lanka, Gallagher, was unaccounted for.

Dresden scrunched his face at Robbie and looked at his watch.

"What?"

"You did all this before nine o'clock in the morning? Wow, you really were in the Army." Robbie scowled at Dresden and rubbed his calf for a moment.

"So, you think he's out there. And if he's out there, and the media doesn't know, and no one else is mentioning it ..."

"Then whoever is behind the attack is covering it so *they* can get to him," Robbie said.

"And we need to get to him first."

"That's my thought."

"Does your buddy have any idea where he might be?" asked Dresden.

"Outside Reno."

"Oh. Uh, I wasn't expecting that."

Dresden found a map of the area on his phone. The NCO from First Group had a cabin in the mountains near Reno. Sun Valley. The NCO said the guy knew about it. Secluded, and outfitted pretty well. The NCO and his family used it to disconnect and do a little hunting, and Gallagher had tagged along on a couple occasions. It was mostly BLM land, Dresden noticed on the map. Desolate. He might not be there, but it was worth a look.

Robbie's brother had a friend who was a warden in the area, and he'd asked if the man could check the place out, see if the cabin was inhabited. The warden said there were fresh tracks leading up to the place. And he was sure, when he passed by the second time, that he saw a light through the scrub up where the house would have been.

"That's enough for me. Let's go check it out."

"Marcus, listen … I got to go home for a while. You know, read bedtime stories to the kids, get cozy with the wife, stuff like that."

"I got yah. No worries."

"If this pans out and you get somewhere with it, I have a bunch of use-or-lose leave …"

"If I find something out, you will be the first to know."

The two men started back toward Dresden's house.

"Oh, hey. Weren't you going to tell me something?"

"Yeah. Not now, still need to work it out a little more."

"Alright." Robbie jogged out in front of him. "Race you home, sailor boy!"

Twenty-One

North of Sun Valley, Nevada

Just a sliver of the cabin was visible from the road. Dresden parked the Nissan Rogue at the gate. He mashed the passenger side in against a tall manzanita to get the car as far off the narrow dirt track as possible. The gate was secured with a new heavy-duty chain and a commercial-grade lock. The cabin disappeared as he walked up the drive, hopping from side to side over rain ruts. The warden had been right. Fresh tracks, off-road tires. Dresden stood for a long time behind a chaparral bush at the mouth of the driveway. He wasn't trying to hide, really, so much as assess the situation a little before whoever was inside shot at him. Sneaking up was sure to get him laid out. Cooking grease was in the air, bacon maybe. The wind shivered and the leaves on the dry oak trees fluttered, but it didn't hide the branch broken by a boot to Dresden's rear.

"I'm here to help, not hurt Gallagher," Dresden said, and put his hands up in the air. There was no response. "One of your buddies from First Group let me know you might be here. He's worried about you."

"Don't you fuckin' move a muscle," came a hoarse, shaky voice. "Which buddy from Group?"

"Don't know. Never met the man. I'm here through Robbie Coltrane. He's pals with your former NCO." Dresden fingered a cold coin about the size of a silver dollar." I'm going to toss this toward you, okay?"

The man grunted. Dresden tossed it. He heard the man grunt again as he bent to pick it up.

"Start walking toward the cabin."

It wasn't much of a cabin, more of a plywood shack with a couple outbuildings made from old shipping containers. The shack, Dresden noticed, listed to the left a little. It reminded him of the houses in a German impressionist film, haunting and creepy.

"Sure thing," Dresden said. He walked forward.

"Turn around and sit down on the porch."

Dresden did as he was told, turning to face a tall, burly man with a thick black beard speckled with small bits of egg.

"What's your name?"

"Marcus Dresden."

"How do you know Robbie?"

"We worked out of JUSMAG in Manila together a long time ago."

"It would have to be," the man said. "You go down south with him?"

"Yeah. Mindanao. Zambo. Sulu. All the garden spots."

"You're not SF."

"No. SEAL.

Gallagher broke into an unexpected laugh. "They sent a SEAL to do a man's job. Damn Eddie's gone loco."

"I was expendable."

Gallagher laughed again. "So, you're *not* here to kill me?"

"No. But I do need to ask you some questions about what happened down in Colombo."

Gallagher switch his shotgun from his right hand to his left, then offered the right to Dresden.

For the next hour, Gallagher told Dresden everything he knew. Everything that had happened that day in Colombo. How there had been several attempts at Baldwin, but somehow Overby knew they were coming and either talked Baldwin down and stayed safe, or they were ready when the attacks came. If they came.

All the attempts had been poorly planned and executed. Some druggy paid a dollar to stick Baldwin with a homemade knife in a crowd, or something like that. But that day on Galle road—that had been different. There was nothing half-assed about it. When Gallagher came to the end, when he had to move Baldwin and the Sri Lankan woman out the back gate and into the stash car, that was when the shit got weird.

"Overby always wanted stash cars—you know, in case we had to bail from the SUVs," Gallagher said.

"Sounds like a solid plan."

"Yeah I thought so. We would get them there in advance. As far out as we could. You know, so as not to blow the site."

"Yeah, I got it."

Gallagher went on. Baldwin had had a favorite place to meet lady friends. Gallagher emphasized that the guy was married, with three girls. The restaurant had a small employee parking lot out back. Overby was supposed to cover while he got Baldwin to the vehicle out back. Except he got shot before Gallagher got the car door opened. He didn't know it right away, but he heard the shots near the gate. Gallagher assumed it was Overby. He shoved Baldwin and the lady in the backseat, then went around to get in and the glass in the back window shattered—two shots. Gallagher took cover at the front of the car. He looked in through the cracked windshield and saw Baldwin and the woman, their bodies slumped together, brain matter splattered all over. Gallagher hunkered down, drew his weapon, then took another peek.

"That's when I saw the guy. Tall, powerful-looking. Spiky hair and a square head. It's the details I'm missing. He was backlit by the sun, kind of ghostly. It was hard to make out his features. He floated toward me. I shot at him twice, and he didn't flinch. I'm a good shot. Especially at fifteen yards. Shit, it blew my mind. I looked down at my Glock. Did a press check. I had rounds. But that was all it took. I looked up again and he was gone. Disappeared. Fucking vaporized."

The two men sat quiet for a time, and Dresden mulled over everything the big man had said. It was true—the terror attack had been a front, a diversion. But for what? Two more questions popped into his mind: who was the hitman, and why did he kill more than just the manager this time? Most of all, why'd the guy let Gallagher live? None of it made any sense.

"What did you do after the mystery man disappeared?"

"I moved back to the gate. Found Overby, dead. Then left."

"Left?"

"Yeah. This was bad, man. For all I knew, the whole team was dead. There was no radio traffic, not a peep. Plus, a week or so before the attack, Overby had been getting really irritated with First Watch HQ. They were asking him to do shit. I don't know what, he wouldn't say. Sometimes he'd be all pissed or agitated and bark about HQ. It made no sense to us. So, there I was looking down at Overby … dead. I was confused. But I quickly realized one thing. I was a dead man too if I didn't move. It didn't matter if it was a Baldwin hater or—or someone at First Watch. I was a dead man if I didn't move, and move fast. Get out of the country. That was where my mind was at the time."

Again with the damn emails. What the hell was Roker up to? For a brief moment, Dresden thought he should join Roker and break this craziness up from the inside. Then he thought of Maria and hoped she could come up with something soon. He was suddenly exhausted, and looked over at Gallagher.

"So, what are you going to do now? You can't stay here forever."

"No. But I think I have to wait this out. I hope it was all about Baldwin, and when they see I don't or won't talk, I can just move on."

Dresden knew in his gut that that was the farthest thing from the truth. He knew Gallagher didn't believe it either. The man went to a plywood cabinet and pulled out a bottle of whiskey. Dresden hadn't drunk liquor in nearly ten years. But if there was a drink and a reason for which he might break his hiatus, it would be for Basil Hayden's bourbon whiskey and to toast a dead man before he died.

Dresden woke in the shack, disoriented. Gallagher lit the double-burner camp stove and put on a pot to boil water. As Dresden stepped outside to relieve himself, the chill smacked him like a fly swatter. He moved to a bush on the edge of the dirty sandlot, watching as the sun rose over the soup bowl of a valley. The scrub brush and scant oak trees reminded him of every old Western movie he and his dad had watched. Cold. Rocky. Desolate. *Why would anyone choose to live here?*

The smell of bacon grease careened up his nose as he came in the door. Dresden sat down on a plastic chair next to a folding card table. The big man handed him a cup of instant coffee. Dresden moved aside an issue of *The Economist* to expose the book beneath—a tattered and dog-eared copy of David Kilcullen's *Out of the Mountains.*

"Yours?" Dresden said. He held up the book.

"Yeah."

"Good stuff." *The man's a thinker*. Dresden took a sip of the grainy instant coffee, then laughed. "Man, for being a fugitive, you're eating pretty well."

"Well, you're my guest … it'll run out soon. The fresh stuff. There's a locker out back with all the doomsday provisions." Gallagher flashed a broad smile through his thick beard, this time peppered with bacon bits.

"You retire?" Dresden asked, sipping his coffee.

"Nah, got out. Loved being in the sandbox, but the bullshit just got to be too much," Gallagher said. "You look like the cake eater type."

"Nope. Enlisted."

"No shit. What'd you retire as?"

"Master Chief … E-9."

"No shit. That's cool. How about your family? Military?"

"Nope. Well, not my dad. My grandfather was. My dad was one of those, 'I didn't bust my ass to make a life for my kids so they'd go die in some foreign country' kind of guys. So, I joined at seventeen. Forged my old man's signature."

"Damn, they must have gone ballistic. How are they now? Twenty-something years later and you with all your fingers and toes?" Gallagher asked.

"No idea—haven't talked to them in years," Dresden said.

Gallagher picked up around the shack. Dresden checked his phone; nothing. No bars, no service. Gallagher punched play on a dusty old CD player.

"Texas Serenade" by the Gun Club came clawing out of the speakers.

"Damn … this your CD?"

"Yeah man, these are my boys. Well, a little before my time but I love them. Anyway, my older brother turned me on to them."

"Good shit man. You got taste. Unlike the rest of your greenie beanie brethren."

"Hah!"

Dresden wanted to start heading back to the coast, but he was worried about Gallagher. It was hard to leave despite all he'd learned and knowing how much there was to do. The seclusion was welcome. His phone not going off every ten minutes was a reprieve. The thought of his last text with Lance and the mystery man on the other end … With no way to do anything about it, he could put it aside, if only for a few hours. The dense fog that whitewashed his mind had started to lift.

"You going to be alright up here?" Dresden finally said.

Gallagher played hurt. "Yeah man, I can take care of myself. I just need to let this shit blow over. I may not be a big bad SEAL, but I can handle things. I just need to wait a little while before I get back into circulation, you know. Then I can find a nice comfortable place to hide out and try to make it to old age. Maybe up in the Northwest or something."

"You really think this is that serious, huh?" Dresden asked.

"Yeah. I do. If you had seen that dude, well, you'd know," Gallagher said.

"Thanks for the cot and grub."

"You betcha, brother. Anytime!"

"Alright, tell you what—I'll send you a care package in the next week or so. How's that sound?"

"That would be cool bro, I appreciate it."

"I'd better head out."

"Alright, stay safe and thanks for comin' and checkin' on me. I hope I helped.

"You did. Thanks. Keep your head down, man." Dresden offered his hand.

"Will do." Gallagher shook it, then turned and went back into the cabin.

Twenty-Two

Sun Valley, Nevada

Dresden inched down the driveway, making sure not to high center the Rogue. He parked out on the road near the gate, then grabbed a branch and swept the driveway clean of tracks. *That should keep a few folks from stumbling on him.* Dresden sat in his car for a moment, looking back up the drive. The afternoon shadows were long and awkward. As he pulled away, hundreds of random thoughts flooded his cranium. The fog was moving back into his head. He drove a mile or so without any recognition of doing so. A plume of dust ahead jarred him back to the moment.

A Ford F-350, an obnoxious jacked-up rig with an after-market pumper that belonged on a tank, belched black smoke as it barreled toward him in a tornado of dust. The truck made no attempt to move over as it got closer. Dresden shifted to the right as the blur of black metal passed. He watched his driver-side mirror take flight.

Motherfucker! Dresden checked his rearview mirror. A solitary arm clad in black stretched from the driver's window of the truck—a fist with a single digit pointed skyward. *Fuckin' desert rats!* He got out and picked up his severed mirror, then threw it in the passenger seat. As he sat back down in his car, he slammed his fist on the steering wheel.

The dust tried to settle, but the windless morning kept it suspended longer than usual. He put the broken mirror down after he hung up the phone with the rental car company and studied his rearview. Dresden wondered if the F-350 would come back his way. *Probably not.* The road went on for several miles. There were options too, other roads. He was wasting time. And for what, to kick the shit out of some teenage punk? Dresden needed to get to better cell coverage. He glanced at the broken mirror one more time. It sat there like a scared hermit crab tucked in its shell.

The windows fogged as he stared out at the stark landscape. Should he stop somewhere for the day and get a fresh start in the morning? Reno maybe. He was tired, but the idea was short-lived; he wouldn't actually sleep. He drove to a truck stop outside the city, gassed up, and grabbed some food and coffee. Then he bought a phone holder he could attach to the dash. He needed to talk with Roker, give it one more shot. But first, Maria.

Dresden opened a text and drove for a half hour as he worked out what to say. There was so much he wanted to tell her. He wanted to say everything and he knew he could. It was too much, though, so he kept it simple. Just the highlights. She responded right away.

I hadn't heard from you, so I thought the worst, she wrote. Dresden's heart pounded for a second or two off beat, a lump landing in his throat. He told her he was driving but that he would call her the following day and tell her everything. She agreed and said she had a lot to tell him.

Vivid images of Maria at the Chinese restaurant paraded through his mind. He snapped back to the moment, said goodbye, and texted Roker. The decision had been simple, really. He needed to talk with the man. It was something Gallagher said, but Dresden hadn't put it together until now—*someone* at First Watch. Someone? Dresden kicked himself for not catching it sooner. A VTC would be a good idea—he needed to *see* Roker.

Roker responded. *I will call in as soon as I can.*

Dresden turned on the car's Bluetooth and tapped saved favorites on Spotify. Ben Harper and his Innocent Criminals banged out "I'm In, I'm Out and I'm Gone." Turning up the volume, he worked on what he would say—or not say—to Roker. Talking to Gallagher reminded Dresden of something else. All three attacks were inconsistent with the tactics employed by the groups that were being blamed or taking responsibility. It was the signature that was all off. ISIL, MS-13, and the Tigers or JVP were unlikely to all use a diversion given the type of attack. The mission objectives were different too. Disrupt a meeting and kill conspirators—Oman. Kidnap and ransom—Phoenix. Kidnap, blackmail, and extortion—Sri Lanka. Oman was an oddball in another way, Dresden thought. There were *no* boots on the ground. And something else was pecking around his brain like a chicken in a yard. The Sri Lankan attack seemed familiar.

The music cut off. Dresden checked his phone. Casper. Dresden hit the button to take the call.

"Hey buddy, I can't really talk right now ..."

"Oh, well. Uh—okay."

Dresden stopped the cyclone in his brain long enough to see the flare go up.

"You know what? I'm glad you called," he said.

"Really?" his son replied, voice laced with surprise.

Casper launched into telling Dresden how he hadn't really wanted to hang up on him, but he hadn't known what else to do. He was really uncomfortable and kind of embarrassed. It was awkward, like one of those coming-of-age movies. It didn't feel right.

Dresden admitted he'd been in the same boat, especially about being uncomfortable. He said it was all Uncle Robbie's fault, and both men laughed. Dresden told him he thought they should try to get through the uncomfortable parts and talk. Casper agreed, and then was silent for a while.

"Dad, I want to see my grandparents—you know, your mom and dad."

The steering wheel seemed to swerve all on its own. Dresden jerked the car back into the lane. "Well. You know. I don't. Casper, what's this about, son?"

Casper drew a deep breath and fired his words through the phone like a belt-fed weapon, fast and deadly accurate. It was all about identity. Dresden knew his dad and even his grandfather. Good or bad didn't matter; he had *spent time* with them. Casper claimed he barely knew Dresden in any real sense, and to start, he needed to know his family. Where he came from.

The words hit hard, like a sledgehammer to the chest. It took Dresden a moment to pick himself up before promising to tell Casper what he wanted to know. But that wasn't enough. Casper wanted to *experience* it—good, bad, and indifferent.

Dresden was quiet again, scooping up his guts off the floor. He looked out into the darkness of the freeway. A Skype call sounded—Roker. Not now, dammit!

"Casper. I will think about it ..."

"Really?"

"Yes, but I have to go now,"

"Okay, okay. Great. Love you, Dad." His son hung up.

Dresden answered Roker and adjusted his screen so the man could see him. But Roker was nowhere to be seen. "Tom? You ... Jesus!"

Roker came into view. His stubble was now weeks old, but it didn't hide the gaunt cheeks, sunken eyes, and pallid skin. "You look like shit," Dresden said without thinking. Unfiltered. The darting back and forth in Rokers eyes was more pronounced, more erratic. *Definitely something with his CNS! Drugs? Can't be. What in the hell is going on?*

"Marcus, you have to find Jennifer. I need her. She's gone. She won't answer any of my calls or emails or anything. Branch, that snake, maneuvered his way into the Board's favor. They are actually considering his plan. He wants to move this company in an entirely different direction. The wrong direction. He wants to take me—he wants to ..." Roker coughed a marathon of phlegm and mucous. He was off the screen again. "To think I hired that asshole. And this is how he—" More coughing.

"Tom. Tom! Listen. I get all that, but you really need to shoot me straight Did you have anything to do with the attacks in Oman and Sri Lanka?"

"What? What are you talking about? Attacks? Why would I have anything to do with those attacks? I run a company built to"—he coughed even louder— "built to *protect.*"

Dresden could hear Roker throw up off-screen. When he came back on, he continued, "And what the fuck are you asking me that for? You've become an asshole, too. I have to take *care* of all of you. I have to watch my back all the time! Can't trust any of you. I'm going to do what I have to do to protect this company and my future."

"Tom? What do you mean by that?"

"By what?"

"By—you know, never mind," Dresden said. He looked off-screen for a while. The man was certifiable. The Board wanted him out, out of the business he'd built. It was cliché at best, but it made sense in some twisted sort of way. At the same time, it made no sense at all. It was too damn easy—get rid of Roker, and things would get better.

"Tom, have you seen a doctor for that?"

"Yeah. They have no fucking clue what's going on." Roker coughed. "Pneumonia or bronchitis or something."

"Answer me one question. What's with all the emails and data collection the site managers have to do?

Roker looked straight into the screen. His square face drooped. "You told Jennifer to quit, didn't you? Didn't you!" Roker squinted his eyes.

"No. Now answer my—"

"You have left the meeting now," a woman's voice interrupted.

Not again. Distracted, Dresden punched at his screen, trying to rejoin the meeting. A light like the sun instantly filled the cab of his car, followed a half-second later by the teeth-shattering sound of metal impacting metal. Dresden's head jerked to the left, bouncing off the glass. He looked back over his shoulder. His eyes were seared instantly with the Ford motor company emblem ablaze between two massive orbs of light; his small car slammed into the guard rail, wedged between the rail and what he could only surmise was a behemoth of a truck. Sparks flew, and the screech and grind of metal claimed the hearing of his right ear. The airbags hadn't deployed—the truck had hit the Rogue at just the right angle and speed. A second, maybe two, had passed, yet Dresden knew the wreck was deliberate, planned. The truck was pushing him down the guardrail. To what end, though?

He attempted to regain control of his car. He saw the end of the railing coming, and realized the truck was trying to run him past it. Dresden slammed on the brakes. Nothing. Emergency brake. Nothing of consequence. The giant truck belched diesel exhaust as the engine revved to the resistance. But nothing changed.

The guard rail was there for a reason. The drop from the freeway's right lane, past the shoulder, was at least a hundred feet down, possibly two hundred, at an angle only an extreme skier would appreciate. Dresden gripped the steering wheel and made sure his seatbelt was set. There was *one* chance. Past the end of the rail, the ground rose. A cut-through—a section where the highwaymen had blasted a path through the hill. His attacker was looking to push him through the small gap and over the ledge. If Dresden could clear the gap and run up the mound, he might be able to keep from tumbling down the mountain. Dresden gunned his vehicle—nothing happened. His bare rims threw sparks as the left wheels ground down on the asphalt. A second later, the car took flight.

Dresden breathed out slowly, letting his body go limp. The trunk of his vehicle whipped around as his car left the rail. For a very long second, the car seemed to hang, suspended in midair before gravity brought it crashing down. Dresden was whipped toward the passenger side, his seatbelt cutting into his shoulder and wrenching down on his waist.

A second later, the car hit the hillside and rolled several times before it came to a stop, upside down.

The car steamed and gushed. Metal creaked. Fluids dripped. Dresden was semi-conscious, but alert enough to know he'd been attacked, deliberately driven off the road. He was alive, and they wanted him dead. He couldn't hang around there waiting to be gutted or shot. His brain kicked in, but his body lagged. Adrenaline started to pump full speed ahead. He harvested what he could and reached for his seatbelt. Unlike in the movies, it snapped open easily, but was accompanied by an instant rush of pain in his left leg. *Damn!* For a moment, he'd thought he'd be able to walk away from the crash unhurt.

Dresden slid himself out of the window after clearing the passenger-side airbag. He wanted to be on the downhill side, in case his attackers were coming to check the wreckage. Even in the turbid light he could make out a figure moving down the hillside, halfway between the railing and the car.

The faint sounds of sirens wailed in the background. *Not possible.* Dresden tried to stand, but his left leg wouldn't hold him. A stabbing pain ran through his quad. He crawled farther away from the Rogue, into a bush. It would slow his attackers down, give him some time to think.

The man was closer. The siren wailed, louder now. A searchlight scanned the hillside. Dresden stared at where the man should have been, and the light illuminated him for a second. He was tall, well-built, powerful looking. A full head of light-colored hair, with a square jaw and a pronounced brow. The man clenched a side-arm in his hand. The light moved on, but the man's image was imprinted on Dresden's brain. It took several seconds, but then he could see the man's outline again. He stood his ground for a long time, then turned and climbed back up the hill. Dresden heard voices from down below as the man disappeared over the ridge. With a quick flash of lights, he was gone.

Dresden collapsed into the cold grass and composted underbrush, watching the reddish-pink clouds sail past in the early morning sky. *Casper … Kelli, how are you? I loved it when we lay in the backyard and you guys told me what you saw in the sky. A piggy, Daddy. Look, a piggy. Oh, oh look there, Daddy, that's a dragon. Doesn't it look like a dragon, Daddy? Sure does, sweetheart. What the hell am I doing wrong? You need to listen, Daddy. Just listen. And you will see.*

Dresden saw two men standing over him. Dark faces looming like death. But why two? *Listen, Daddy. Just listen.*

Too late, my sweethearts, they've come to get me. No time to listen anymore. I have to go now. See you on the other side.

Twenty-Three

Great Falls, Virginia

The wind blew down the Potomac River from West Virginia, cold with a reminder that winter was coming to Washington, D.C. Markum buttoned his long overcoat and instructed his security detail to remain with the car. The men looked at each other but got back in the car without argument. Now that he was making a stand against First Watch, private security, and Thomas Roker, Koepanger and Stearns agreed it would be best if he limited his own security detail. Perception management, they claimed. He'd fired half his staff. Lawson was furious and threatened to quit if he pulled another stunt like that.

The dirt trail wound along the cliffs of the National Park overlooking the rushing waters of the Potomac. Kayakers weaved through dozens of rock outcroppings and dropped down steep chutes into pools of foam. They were getting in their last thrills before the water became frigid. Markum found a large, flat rock ten yards off the trail. He used his binoculars to watch the watermen work their way downriver.

The trees rustled behind him. A man dressed in outfitter gear complete with wide-brimmed hat and water bladder backpack walked out onto the wide tabletop. He stopped an arm's length from Markum, who removed his binos and glanced at him. The man was taller than Markum, slender, and seemed unaware he was there.

"Great morning for catching sight of an Osprey," Markum said, going back to his binoculars.

"It is, except I'm looking for sharp-shinned Coopers," the man said.

"Riley, right?" Markum asked. He lowered his binos but continued to look forward.

"Yes, Senator."

"Bob. Call me Bob."

A friend had suggested Riley. He was a fixer, like Lawson, but with a different set of skills. Roker and First Watch had not rolled over as easily as Markum had anticipated. He wanted, he needed, an insurance policy. His friend had assured him Riley was his man.

Markum had tested him out over the last several weeks. Some odd jobs that needed an astute practitioner to handle. Riley had done well.

The two men kept their eyes forward as they talked. Markum watched the far side of the river canyon. People slid along the trails there. Markum made sure no one was watching them or taking pictures, but everyone seemed oblivious of the two men. The park was a favorite of his. Thirty minutes from the capitol building and his office. It was quiet and pocked with seclude alcoves such as this, where he could think or meet someone without drawing the attention of others.

When Markum mentioned what he wanted Riley to do, the man give him a quick glance with an eye of surprise. Maybe this wasn't his guy, Markum thought. Too late. He assured Riley that the plan did not include hurting anyone. Markum wasn't completely convinced of this point, of course. He explained that the plan would be instituted only if Roker didn't play along, and assured Riley that they were the only two that knew about the plan.

Riley would need a week to flesh out all the details. He suggested they meet again after that, and he could share what he had in store. Markum had learned enough from Lawson to know that was a bad idea. He didn't want to have any further contact with the man. Instead, Markum gave him the details of how he would signal him to execute the plan. An otherwise-innocuous mark on a window in a brownstone east of Lincoln Park, behind the Capitol. He also gave the fixer a bank account that had the funds and his payment already deposited.

Markum reminded him that Jack Lawson was on his payroll should Riley get the idea of taking the money and running.

"Does Lawson know about this plan?" the man asked.

"Like I said, it's you and me. That's it," Markum said.

Riley stiffened, but made no mention of backing out. He would have a plan worthy of executing in a week, and would start looking for the signal then. Markum should start watching the news channels within two days of leaving the signal.

The senator sensed an odd kind of irony in the venture. Hiring a private contractor to take down a private profiteer. Markum agreed to Riley's terms, though. Riley excused himself and left him to his own thoughts.

Markum's staffers had crafted a beautiful justification for conducting the Roker investigation. Sitting in his office, he'd found himself laughing after reading the document. He rarely used any of his staffer's words, preferring to do his own writing. This made him realize he should have read more of their work. Lawson had orchestrated a socialization plan that was moving along flawlessly. The Senate was within a few days of voting on the proposal, and already it had wide bi-partisan support. Both sides needed to hang someone for the state of the nation and bolster their party's candidate as the run for president warmed up.

Now, with the debacle in Sri Lanka fresh on everyone's minds, it was a shoo-in. Five US citizens dead including a prominent US businessman and billionaire—Miles Baldwin. A half-dozen locals killed or injured, gunned down by First Watch contractors. All in all, a complete shit storm. If the proposal made it onto the floor within the week, Markum thought, he would be on his way to shutting down Roker. With Riley's help, he was sure of it. But, more importantly, this would draw him clearly into the public spotlight. He considered his plan some more as he focused again on the river. A large bird of some type with a massive wingspan and a long narrow beak swooped low along the still waters below the falls. He thought he might take up bird watching. Seemed like the voters might like that. Markum's phone buzzed loudly in his chest pocket, startling him out of his daze.

"Hello Jack."

"Bobby, I think we may have a problem."

Markum started making his way back to his car. "What kind of problem?"

"It appears as though the First Watch Board may be replacing Roker," Lawson said.

"I fail to see why that's a problem," Markum said, jumping down off a rock ledge and back onto the dirt trail.

Lawson huffed into the phone but said nothing.

"Jack why are they thinking about removing him?"

"Incompetence, inaction, and I guess the Board is just generally worried he's lost grip with reality and is potentially dangerous."

"Jack, I'm going to ask you to repeat that one more time, at some point, but before you do, did you get this sumptuous morsel from a credible source, a very credible source?" Markum said as he waved to his security men getting out of the car.

"Yes, Bobby, otherwise I wouldn't be calling," Lawson said incredulously.

"Great Jack, this is just great! Meet me back at my office in an hour," Markum said, and hung up. He skipped three times before he noticed the looks from his security men.

"What? Can't a guy be happy in this town?" he said as he landed in the back seat of his car.

Twenty-Four

Karns, Tennessee

The windows were milky from both age and frost. Small, clear ovals punctuated the center of each pane of glass. Sean Branch used one of the clean spots like a looking glass, peering out into the yard of the old house. He held a rag across his nose and mouth, shielding himself from the unpleasant smells. The stink of years of wet, soggy dog and oddly odiferous woods burnt in the fireplace accosted his senses. They seemed to have saturated the peeling paper walls and dull wood floors. Branch tightened his coat around his narrow waist and turned to face the three men sitting on a sofa in the otherwise empty living room. He did not meet their eyes, instead looking at a stain on the wall above them, then started pacing.

The three men followed Branch as if they were watching a tennis match, their backs straight and hands flat on their knees. Branch could feel them, their eyes boring into him, waiting for him to speak. He avoided their gaze—he couldn't think under their eager stares. It was so damn cold in the house, he struggled to put two thoughts together. Branch stared for a moment at the sofa the men were sitting on. It had been yellow once, now a rough beige hue with dark stains where someone had laid their soiled arm or neck. Branch's stomach churned. The three men, apparently oblivious to the condition of the sofa, had sat down on it when Branch told them to, without a thought.

Branch had instructed the men to find a house they could occupy, a place where they could work. He needed an office away from First Watch headquarters, a place where they would not be interrupted. This was the best they could come up with. He'd become accustomed to Richardson, who always went first class. But then, those men were too close to the source, Roker. He needed men he could trust, outside First Watch, with an unbiased eye on the plan.

"We will make a fire, okay?" a fourth man said, bringing Branch back to the moment. He leaned on the door jamb that led to the kitchen. His long, thick legs crossed at the ankles, his wide, square shoulders filling up the doorway. The man wore black jeans and a long-sleeve black shirt, like the other three. He worked a toothpick in his mouth while he absently massaged the left side of his face. Three long streaks ran from his ear to his mouth. A light purple on his pale skin, they were yet to be scars.

"That's alright, Fedor. I don't intend to stay long. I will be back in a couple days and we can get started.

"Is there something we can do to help?" Fedor asked.

"I'm not sure. You have done well to this point. Maybe you need some time off? Some rest after your long flight?" Branch said.

"No sir. I'm ready for our next task."

Branch paced some more, primarily to stay warm but to think as well. It was getting harder. The three men had been working out of a rural motel for the last several weeks. Fedor had arrived the night before. This house would be much better, Branch mused. But he was not ready to move forward. A week ago, he was sure the First Watch Board of Directors was about to hand the reigns over to him. But they were waffling now. The events in Oman and then Sri Lanka had made them uneasy. His path was clear, and he reassured them that the incidents were the risks of doing business. He could handle it. Neither Almasi nor Baldwin had fired the security firm over the events. Well, Baldwin's wife almost had, but she had been persuaded to allow them to continue. Branch looked at Fedor.

A sound like children squealing while at play drew Branch back to the window again. There wasn't another house for a mile or more in any direction. Branch checked the front yard anyway. Nothing.

He heard whimpers but did not look outside again, and moved back to the center of the room as a gust of cold wind blew in from around the windowsill.

Roker was just about out of the picture. Branch was confident the Board viewed him as a major liability. He'd gone off the reservation, and there was no telling what he'd do. The man had made of a fool of Branch, and he couldn't let that stand. But he had to be patient and strategic in his view and approach. Also, he needed to have some assurance against any unforeseen elements popping up. That was where Fedor and company came in. But what to do with them in the meantime? Men like this, Branch calculated, could not be given too much free time. They themselves might become a liability he could not afford.

"Fedor, I'm going to assume since you choose the accommodations," Branch said, blowing through his hands and looking around the room, "you are okay with this place."

"Yes, sir. We are," Fedor said. He pushed off the door jamb and walked closer to the other men.

"How about our guests? Are they happy with the lodgings as well?" Branch asked, smiling warmly.

Without returning the smile, Fedor said, "Yes. Yes, they are settling in just fine, sir."

"Good, good. I appreciate you taking such good care of them."

"My pleasure, sir." At this, Fedor smiled.

Another gust of wind blew outside and made the doors in the house shudder and creak. Branch wanted to leave but felt he owed it to Fedor and his compatriots to show a certain amount of solidarity. Some intestinal fortitude. The cold didn't seem to bother the men. They showed no signs of discomfort. Branch would have to find a room to work and make sure it was heated, otherwise he wouldn't last very long. He would lose the respect of these men, and he would consequently lose control of them.

"How about TV and internet?"

Fedor had drawn a cigarette from a case in his back pocket. With it clasped between two fingers, he pointed at a large cardboard box near the front door. "Everything we need is in there. We will set it up tonight. It will be ready when you come back."

"Okay. Good," Branch said. He looked over at the box and the two wide-screen TVs leaning up against it. He had a flash of the Senate floor. In his office at First Watch, before he'd made his way to the old house, Branch had watched CSPAN, the senate vote on Senator Markum's proposal to investigate Roker and the company. He hadn't planned on an interloper like Markum. Branch had delayed his departure, as the vote was a close call. Thirty minutes past the time he'd planned to leave, the vote to set up a sub-committee to conduct an initial inquiry was as good as done. It would make his work more difficult, but not impossible.

With hands cupped around his eyes, Branch peered out at his car, which was parked on the dirt driveway. He pushed a button on a remote, and the yellow parking lights flashed on the Mercedes S560 as the engine came to life. A small wisp of cotton-colored exhaust covered the ground. Branch moved his hands down in front of his mouth and blew on them. It would take ten minutes for the car to warm up; it would be good to get warm.

"Sir," Fedor said. Branch turned around to look at him. "May I suggest that you use a different car to come here? This car will stand out, maybe."

A pain in his temple flared. Branch rubbed the side of his head. He held no real power over these men other than his position. He knew that. The balance of power could tip in either direction quickly. Fedor alone could kill him in seconds and he'd never be found. Manipulation was his greatest tool. That, and a heavy hand. But this was not the time for a punishment for speaking out of turn.

"Thank you Fedor. I will consider it," Branch said. He walked to the front door. The doorknob was cold through his glove. A small, faint cry of a child came again. Branch turned and looked down a dark stairwell that led to the basement. It didn't come again. He looked over at Fedor and the other three. "I will let you know if there is anything you can do. Otherwise, be here, ready to go in two days."

He opened the door and left.

Twenty-Five

Truckee, California

The recognition was swift. He was in a hospital. But why, and where? Dresden attempted to move his head. A thick slush ran from ear to ear, making him salivate. The taste of heavy metal was ripe and thick in his mouth. He opened one eye. A cup with a straw and a label, *Tahoe Forest Hospital.* Okay. Dresden moved his body a few inches. That covered where. Now why? He closed his eye and tried to move again.

Stop, Daddy. Your car tumbled down a hill. You could be really hurt.

Sleep came again. He was lost in a great void, falling. Startled, Dresden opened an eye again. Then both. The clock said 5:30—morning or evening? Evening. Okay. The shadows were long and the reddish yellow of a sunset. He closed his eyes again. For just a moment, he said to himself.

Awake again, he turned to look at the louvered windows. A bright reflection met him as he swung his head around. The white light tossed a scene of headlamps and screeching metal ambling across his view. He wrestled to get up, but couldn't. Dresden looked down at his arms and legs. They were bound to the bed. Dreaming. Nightmare. Shit!

Wake up, Daddy! They're coming. Stop, you're okay. But wake up and listen.

"I'm telling you, he's lucky. Real lucky,"

Dresden watched through half-opened eyes as two men in white coats came into his room. They looked like the reverse of Laurel and Hardy. One fat and short, the other tall and thin. They turned on a lightboard mounted to the wall and stuck an x-ray image up on it. With their backs to Dresden, they talked, their voices muffled at times and other times clear. They were talking about him.

Listen Daddy.

"A six-inch hunk of metal in his quad, that's it. Okay, so he's got a few bruises and a couple lacerations. But I mean, come on. Lucky as hell, I tell yah," the fat one said.

"I think he's lucky that highway patrol officer was so close and just happened to see him fly off the road," the tall one said.

"Yeah,"

"How'd the patrolman get down to him so fast? It's hard to get off 80 and onto the roads off Billy Mack."

"He was already there. Some folks reported a vehicle hanging out in and around the area.

The patrolman was there checking it out and bam—here comes this guy flying off the freeway!"

"Wow! See? Lucky. Oh hey, what about toxicology?"

"Residual. A small consumption over twenty-four hours old."

"Huh."

"Alright, well he's stable and I think he shouldn't cause you any trouble. I asked the nurses to check on him every ninety minutes until morning. Time for me to get out of here. I'm headed home to grab the kids and get some night skiing in," the fat one said.

"Sounds fun."

Both men left the room.

The nurse shut the door quietly. Dresden waited five minutes and for the clock to strike 8 p.m. before moving. He pulled the oxygen clamp off his nose and the drip from his arm, then found what was left of his clothes in the closet. His wallet, cash and credit cards, driver's license. No phone, though. What had happened to his phone? He crept down the hall to another room. It was empty. He used the phone book and a landline. He *was* lucky—there was a rental car company just three miles from the hospital. The place closed within the hour. Even with his bum leg, Dresden determined he could clear the distance. He reserved a car, then slipped out of the hospital.

Escondite

A beat-down plumber's work truck, backed up on a cell tower service road, faced Dresden as he exited the highway. If it had been lunchtime, Dresden might have let it slide. But it was almost seven in the morning. One of the men in the truck was sloppy. The man's binocular lens winked at Dresden as he dropped down the exit ramp. *They're here*, he said to himself.

He assumed they wouldn't take him in broad daylight. Well, not out in public anyway. They would be waiting *in* his house. Everything had to look inevitable. A late-night, highspeed car crash was logical. So this time, maybe a home robbery gone bad. They might be sloppy at surveillance, but the attempt to run him off the road, had it worked, would have left little doubt as to the cause.

He wanted to drive straight into his garage, but without his phone or garage door opener he was out of luck. He could use the push-button pad—the exposure would be for a minute, maybe two. It was his only option. Dresden assumed they would have searched his house. Bugged it. Staged men inside to attack him possibly. He had a weapon cached in a place the surveillance crew was unlikely to look, and he needed to get to it first.

Two blocks from his house, he spotted another surveillance guy. Escondite had a rhythm of its own. The guy stood out, badly. The car wreck hadn't worked, and it seemed they hadn't planned beyond that point. The surveillance package must have been hastily assembled, and it was showing.

The thing that ate at Dresden was why they hadn't tried to get him at the hospital. It took his beleaguered brain a while to remember his license. The license he was carrying was in a different name. Fully traceable, just the wrong information. It had bought him some time as they searched for him and couldn't find his name. He figured they didn't have the balls to go walking door to door in the hospital. Wimps. His house was all they knew, so here they were.

Dresden pulled into his driveway, punched the code into the pad beside the garage door, and stood to the side as it opened. He retrieved a Remington 870, 12-gauge shotgun with a 00 load from a hollowed-out surfboard. The weapon was loaded and had a shell in the chamber. At the door to his house, he punched in another code.

He moved through his house swiftly, one-man room entries on every room. Nothing. *Could they have missed me altogether? No, no way. The car's in the driveway; they know I'm here. They knew I was coming. Then why no welcoming party? They are on their way.*

He went to his bedroom, moved his bed aside, flipped up a carpet and opened a door to expose a computer bank and two CCTVs. He powered up the computer and entered a triple-verification password, and the computer screen came to life. At the next prompt, Dresden entered an additional set of coded passwords. The house was now on autopilot. Lights. Sprinklers. Music. TV. Sound effects. Running water. The works. Dresden retrieved a set of keys and a palm-sized notebook, then replaced the carpet and his bed. He moved downstairs and watched a couple CCTVs tucked into a closet in his office. Nothing, except he found a bug under the desk. He left it in place and moved on.

In the garage, Dresden bent to reach underneath the surfboard rack. He unlocked a master lock, then undid the hasp. At the center of the rack, Dresden pulled the rack open like a set of doors. Inside was a small steel door set into the wall, just big enough for a six-foot man bent over to walk through. Dresden opened the door and flipped on a light switch. The unused bulbs flickered gently as they warmed up. A concrete shaft the same size as the door lay in front of him. Dresden bent down and moved into the tunnel, pulled the rack shut, locked it, and waddled down the passage.

At the other end, Dresden fussed with another locking system, then stepped out into a small, dusty shed. He pulled at oil clothes to expose a vehicle. A non-descript, early model Toyota Tundra. Four-wheel drive, paint faded, crew cab with a cap on the back. Common enough. Dresden reached in his pocket for the keys, started the truck, and let it idle quietly. In a locked tool cabinet. Dresden checked a couple CCTVs with a series of camera shots from different angles around his neighborhood. An alleyway two blocks from his house. The front of his house. A few angles down different streets. He watched a man making a delivery walk up to the front of his house. The house took over and the man left.

Dresden grabbed a small bag on the passenger seat, containing a black wig, gold-rimmed sunglasses, and some makeup. Ten minutes later, he had turned himself into a fiftyish-looking woman, at least from the neck up. He hopped behind the wheel of the truck, pushed the garage door opener, and inched his way forward. Clear. He moved to the highway and headed south.

It was 650 miles before Dresden stopped. The truck was outfitted with an extra-large gas tank plus two additional tanks—approximately ten hours before he needed to stop to refill on diesel. Two bags in the back seat were full of what he needed for the road. Food. Water. Money. P-Bottles and a med bag. Enough of everything to get down the road a distance, to bug out of a bad situation. Like the shit storm he'd got himself into. Six hundred and fifty miles should have put some real distance between him and the whack jobs that were after him.

Jim Morrison croaked out "Roadhouse Blues" as Dresden pumped diesel into his truck. The wind whipped through an empty lot across the street. Trash bumped and swirled against a chain-link fence like a goose trying to find its way out of its pen. Ely, Nevada. A one-street town off the interstate, way off. Dresden knew exactly where he was going but wasn't in a hurry to get there. Back roads only. Dozens of zig zags. No hotels. No credit cards. Cash only. Bills collected over several years from different sources. The cash amounted to a little over fifty thousand dollars stashed in various compartments in the truck. Enough to keep him going for several months. In every cash compartment was a handgun, just in case someone decided to get stupid and pushed him to reveal his stash. No phone plans. Dresden pulled a gallon-sized zip-lock bag from a concealed compartment. Burner phones—throwaways. Dresden took one out, along with a prepaid card. He stuck the phone in his jacket pocket. During the night, he had stopped to change his plates to Utah, registered in his dog's name, AP Ruffin of Bent Ridge. Orville's handiwork.

"You a vet?" the gas man asked as Dresden went to retrieve his change.

"Huh?

"Vet. You a vet?" the man said, pointing at Dresden's leg.

"Oh, that. No. Tractor accident."

"Yeah? What done it?"

"Thresher accident back when I was a kid in Missouri. Nearly took my leg off."

"Uh huh." The man eyed Dresden and pushed the back of his chair against the wall.

Near Delta, Utah, he would cut south on Highway 257 to Milford. As he drove, he sent a text to Emily. A simple code. She knew the deal. She would let the kids know Dad was out of pocket for a while and to be careful. At Beaver, he weaved down Highway 153 through Fishlake National Forest, then through Angie. He was worried about Robbie. If someone had gotten ahold of his phone and Robbie called, that would be just plain bad. He made his way to Torrey, then Caineville and Green River. His phone was in the rental car somewhere. It didn't matter; Red would have patched Dresden's number to a secure line. They would be monitoring it. No need to worry about Robbie or Maria calling. He crept through

Spanish Valley in the middle of the night. He was out of Utah.

Stiff Little Fingers punched through "Safe as Houses" on the truck's CD player. Dresden moved his head to the grinding beat and worked to stay focused on his driving and nothing else. It was impossible. Oman and Lance. Sri Lanka and Gallagher. Jennifer and Maria. The men following him! And now he had been run off the road. And fucking Roker. What was that bastard up to?

No. No, this was not Roker. Were they even linked? What did he have to do with the site managers other than trying to figure out how Lance really died? Dresden slammed his steering well and focused back on the music. He would be in Maryland in a few days. No rush. Orville and Red would be there. He could work it all out then. *Let these shitheads search for me. Let them grovel and stress.* If they really wanted him dead, they should have done right the first time, cause there wasn't going to be a second.

Twenty-Six

Cumberland County, Maryland

The sun rose from behind the mountains with a reddish-green glow blazing through the leaves of the shifting perennials. Blinding rays of sun shot out like lightning or hid behind the crimson leaves, looking like the searing eyes of a demon. Dresden tossed his sleeping bag into the back-bench seat of his truck. The rumpus sound of migrating birds greeting the morning was akin to a construction site. Dresden sat up straight. Sweating. He'd slept, finally, but it had ended with a cascade of images. Some from his past, some from his present, all mixed in a surreal cocktail of terror for the future.

The crisp air dried his sweat as he walked shirtless down the trail and found a tree. He dumped his pee-bottles, then jogged barefoot back to his truck. He'd parked in a lot off a hunting trail—pulled in at five in the morning, around the time most hunters would arrive to set up before dawn. Four hours of sleep and he could leave without any questions. Dresden was an hour, if that, from his destination. But he needed the morning to sort out somethings before he arrived.

A chilly bottle of water over his head shook off the last of the sleep. He washed his face, brushed his teeth and hair, and then dressed. A long-sleeve, pale green, plaid collared shirt. Jeans. Leather slip-on work boots and a heavy canvas sandstone jacket, worn but not dirty. He threw a ball cap on the dash. No more board shorts and t-shirts. He'd changed his plates again in West Virginia, to Maryland Farm plates.

The heater blasted, warming up the cab and knocking the frost from the windshield. He sat and waited. He was in Appalachia. A local radio station played bluegrass and country. Old, *real* country. Through the static he could hear "Bright Morning Stars" performed by Gillian Welch. Two ovals spread upward from the dashboard like tiny ice breakers in the arctic. Maryland—he wondered for a time whether he should lay low. Orville was supposed to let him know if the heat was on, but he'd heard nothing in nearly two weeks. The urge to stay out of sight and just let it go had grown with every mile he drove.

Cumberland, Maryland

The Bark-less café off Baltimore drive was full, bustling and busy. Dresden took a stool at the counter, close to the door. A beefy guy who smelled of axle grease blocked his clear view of the bank across the street. The guy gave him a sneer when Dresden craned around him to look outside. The waitress slid over a plate of eggs, grits with a mound of butter, bacon, two fresh-baked biscuits, and coffee along with an eager smile. *When in Rome.* He thanked her, then sipped his coffee and glanced at the bank again. Thirty minutes until opening.

In the bathroom, Dresden checked his face and teeth. He'd been on the road for twelve days. Thick, reddish whiskers covered his face. He'd taken a shower at a truck stop two days prior. He was presentable and looked the part. Dresden fitted his ball cap over his now dark brown hair, dyed at the truck stop. He pulled the brim down low and washed his hands, cleaning the grit from his fingernails. *Okay, here we go.*

The bank had been open ten minutes by the time Dresden made his way through the front door. It was an old building, mid-nineteenth-century with thick concrete pillars covered in slate. Bared teller stands stood below narrow windows, cutting sunbeams into rectangles while lazy fans spun high above.

The receptionist flashed a smile as he approached the desk. He handed her a business card without a word. The woman glanced at the card then stiffened as he asked to view his safe deposit box. She looked up at Dresden. The corner of her eyebrow twitched. She asked him to take a seat, then walked over to a man stuffed into his blue suit like a sausage. The man nearly jumped after reading the card. He wrestled with his composure as he walked toward Dresden. Leaning forward like he might topple over, he stretched his puffy hand out. Dresden took it.

The man ushered him into a small viewing room. A younger man was grunting under the safe deposit box's weight, and he slammed it down on the table. The manager man shot him a look. Dresden was sure he heard him growl at the young man. Sausage turned to Dresden and asked if he needed any other assistance. Dresden shook his head and signed the log, *Conor Doyle.* A man forty years dead. Sausage bowed his head and closed the door behind him.

Dresden took several minutes to check the room over. No cameras. He removed a small device from his pocket and pushed a red button. A tiny light on the device glowed green. No listening devices—all clear. He pulled a small key from around his neck and opened the box. The lid popped up, revealing envelopes and papers clipped together, two Taurus G3's with extra magazines full of 9 mm rounds, and ziplock bags of cash, mostly twenties. Dresden found what he was looking for: a small metal box with a five-number wheel combo on it. Everything else in the box was a prop. But this, this micro-safe, was what he needed.

He opened the container half the size of a cigar box and removed a set of keys and another small notebook, putting the keys in his jeans pocket and the notebook in the inside jacket pocket with the one from Escondite. He stuffed everything back into the safe deposit box, then pushed the button on the wall and waited.

Mount Cinder, Maryland

The low branches scraped down the side of Dresden's truck like fingers on a chalkboard. He lost sight of the main road ten yards down the pitted gravel path. The truck pitched from side to side. A half-mile down the road, he came to a tall, wrought-iron gate built to withstand a beating. Dresden stopped, got out, and walked up to the gate. Hands wrapped around the stout uprights, he pressed his forehead onto the cold iron. Beyond the gate, a pristine blacktop wound its way into the dark woods like a rat snake. He shook the gate, and it didn't budge. After a moment, he pulled the notebooks from his jacket pocket.

The keypad required eleven pairs of numbers. Every page of his notebooks, from top to bottom, was covered in numbers. Thirteen columns, thirty-seven lines each. He turned to page five, line twelve, then counted back fifteen numbers to find the first digit to punch into the keypad. The keypad, until a few moments before, had been buried under ten inches of earth and grass. He continued this routine until all the pairs were entered. Dresden inserted a key from the safe deposit box and turned it to the left, then right, and pressed a green button.

Immediately, a motor began to hum. He'd initiated an elaborate system akin to a missile silo arming sequence, a complex set of signals ending in his safe passage and entry to the house at the end of the blacktop road. Like something out of a Stephen King novel—house eats unsuspecting passersby, Dresden joked to himself. The house in Escondite was a hideout. This house, the Doyle Lodge, was a fortress.

Dresden watched the gates close before he drove up the drive. A mile beyond the gate, the house came into view, a Yukon-style lodge with a towering A-frame made of heavy, rough-cut timber jutting up at its center. A sweeping porch wrapped around the front and down two sides. Enormous windows overlooked a twenty-acre front yard and a four-acre pond, with thick woods and mountain peaks in the distance. Visions of childhood romps in the pond and summers lost to the woods danced around Dresden's thoughts as he approached the house.

The beauty of the place concealed a more lethal side. AMI motion and noise sensors surrounded the house, ground sensors and a software system that could tell the difference between a squirrel, a deer, and a curious ten-year-old boy. That wasn't to mention the heavy-duty, concealed anti-vehicle barriers, bulletproof exterior lighting systems, and six parapets on the top floor providing 360-degree coverage. Every window in the house was double-pane bulletproof glass. Every wall was reinforced with steel plates and rebar. A fortress. Why? Because his father had lived a life completely consumed by fear.

Dresden walked in and dropped his bags in the foyer. It smelled just as it had the last time he'd been there. He peered up at the vaulted ceiling thirty feet above, made of polished timber segmented with planks of oak. An elk antler chandelier loomed overhead. The walls were covered with close-to-life-size paintings of men on horses wrangling cattle, vistas of rivers running through deep lush valleys. And pack mules laden with equipment led by pioneers skirting narrow paths in steep mountains. *The West in the East.*

In the kitchen, Dresden found an envelope propped up on the countertop, adorned with the letter M. He pulled the card from the envelope. A simple note in exceedingly neat handwriting stated: *Rail Spike. 8 am*. He looked at his watch—it was 1:32 in the afternoon. Good.

After a long shower, Dresden built a fire in one of the sitting rooms. With a grilled cheese sandwich in one hand, a glass of warm cider in the other, he sat next to the fire. The thought of lying low still wobbled like a pigeon around in his mind. Emily and the kids were safe. Robbie and Maria were safe. Jennifer—well, the FBI were on the lookout for her. What could he do?

Lance was dead. It came out so fast he couldn't stop it. Acid coated his throat, and the cider washed it down. He said it aloud: "Lance is dead." What good would come of sticking his nose where it didn't belong?

Dresden pulled a blanket up to his waist. The ornate swiss clock on the mantel read 4:06 p.m. The fire burned down to embers, leaving the room warm and smelling of pine and leather. It didn't help his dreams. The stilt houses on the water began to blaze as soon as he fell asleep and raged until 10:07 p.m., when his car hitting the side of the hill shook him violently out of his slumber. Not fully awake, he saw flashes of a man's face, in a truck near Sun Valley. Then again, in a small, poorly lit room somewhere. *But where?* Then once more—the man walking down a hill, his face glowing in the dark. He saw all of them superimposed on each other, different but somehow *exactly* the same.

Dresden was a broken man, falling to pieces.

A damp fog clung to the trees bordering the road. Fingers of mist slithered out from the trunks and crossed the blacktop at uneven intervals. Ten Mile Road dropped into the back of Mount Cinder, a tiny village built up around Maryland Route 36. Ten minutes from the Lodge, the mountain enclave had one market, one barber who off-and-on doubled as the town's mayor, and one place to eat: the Rail Spike. From the intersection of Ten Mile and Route 36, Dresden headed north a half-mile to the diner. The parking lot was packed with full-sized trucks, old American sedans, and a smattering of foreign compact cars. Every vehicle was well worn. Dresden had parked his cross-country truck in the garage at the house and drove another, slightly newer truck. This one was not as well outfitted; a handgun in the glove box was the only "amenity."

The diner was split down the middle by nine square tables, with a long counter on the left and seven booths on the right. The space was near capacity. Dresden spotted Orville and Red and ambled toward them, every eye in the place taking him in. Patsy Cline's silky voice quietly serenaded the patrons with "Just a Closer Walk with Thee." With his gaze unshifting, he made his way to the back table, sat down, and nodded to the two men. Orville and Red nodded back. The diner resumed its normal banter. A couple old-timers at the counter continued to stare. Red lifted his chin at them. The men turned around, but continued to spy on them through the mirror behind the counter.

Dresden ordered coffee and the standard breakfast. The two old men sipped their coffee and waited, their grizzled hands wrapped around thick coffee mugs. Orville on the left looked over his cup at Dresden. His silver hair was cropped close to his head, flat on top. The man's straight back was reminiscent of a Marine Corps drill sergeant. With a thick, stubby finger, he tapped on the cup. His ring finger and half his little finger were missing. Orville's deep-set blue eyes studied Dresden as he turned to Red.

The other man's long fingers gripped a coffee cup, he hadn't looked up from it since Dresden sat down. Red's shaved head was spotted with time in the sun, his jaw square and built to take a baseball bat. There wasn't a man, young or old, in Cumberland County who'd challenge the men to a fight, regardless of their advanced age.

"You make the drive alright?" Red asked. Still not looking at him

Dresden nodded his head. "Yes sir."

"You get in the house okay?" Orville asked, peering over his cup at Dresden.

"Yes sir."

"You get some sleep?"

"Yes."

"Good. You're going to need it. We're heading out in the morning," Orville said.

"Heading out? Listen gentlemen, I was thinking … thinking of lying low. Letting this blow—"

"No time," Orville interrupted. "We have a package to pick up."

"Yeah, you're gonna wanna pick up this package too," Red said, winking at Dresden.

The three men drank their coffee. Dresden eyed Orville. What was he up to?

Red coughed low and said, "You hear anything from your *friends*?"

"No," Dresden said, still staring at Orville. "Orville, I've been down this road and I don't—"

"Then this time, don't go it alone," the man said in a terse tone, ending the conversation. He leaned back in his chair and scowled at his coffee.

"Orville. Marcus. We don't need to work this out right now, right here," Red said. Orville leaned back like a bulldog loosening his chain. The other man continued, "The thing is, you made it here. The point of this meeting was to let the locals know you were in town. A *Doyle* was in town. Keep the questions and hearsay to a minimum—you know the deal. We did it. Now let's enjoy our meal."

The waitress dropped large plates of food down as Red finished speaking. There was nothing else to say, and Orville didn't look at Dresden again.

Twenty-Seven

Roanoke, Virginia

The four-seat Cessna 172S Skyhawk bobbled as Red maneuvered it in for a landing. He craned back and gave Dresden a smile. Dresden pointed at the runway. Red mocked him, the skin between his eyes knitting together.

The day before Dresden had arrived at the Lodge, as Red had explained on the way to the plane, Red had taken a call on Dresden's old phone line. It was Jennifer Nolan. She was on the run, though from what, Red wasn't sure. She claimed she'd been kidnapped and had escaped, and Dresden was the only person she could trust. Red told him that she'd sounded bad; coughing fits had broken up their conversation several times. Dresden thought of Roker.

The plan was simple. Red told Jennifer what to do. She had some money, but no cell phone. So she got one, unlocked with a prepaid card. She would have to ride a series of buses and trains and head for Ashville, North Carolina.

"Why there?" Dresden had asked.

It was Orville's idea. He'd conducted surveillance training in the town. The city was small enough to spot anyone odd, yet metropolitan enough for the three of them to blend in.

When they landed, Red would head out in a rental car, something flashy. He would run several preplanned routes, stopping at spots around the city. A decent counter-surveillance crew should spot him within a day or two. Dresden and Orville would hang in Roanoke for a couple days, then arrive in Ashville on the day of the pickup. They would make one run. If they didn't link up with Jennifer, they would have to start over. All Dresden had to do was sit tight and do what Orville instructed. That would be the hardest part of the whole operation, he knew it.

The wheels skidded along the runway and Red taxied the plane to a private hangar. Dresden struggled to get out of the back seat. His injuries were nagging at best and excruciatingly painful at worst. He was somewhere in the middle and couldn't move his right hip. Red eased him out of the back seat with the manners of a trained medical professional. Orville looked on with an air of disgust.

"You move like I feel," Red said.

"You look like I feel," Dresden said, wincing and croaking out a short chuckle.

"Ladies, do you mind? Red, I need to you to get on the road," Orville said.

"She's not going anywhere. You need to take care of Marcus here. Use the pool at the hotel, okay?" Red said as he looked at Dresden.

Dresden nodded.

"I've never lost a pickup, and I'm not going to start now," Orville said.

"Seems like he's only gotten crotchetier with age," Dresden commented.

"Yup."

"Get going, Red," Orville snapped.

Jennifer was alive. Kidnapped. Escaped. Sick and on the run. Running from what? Dresden pictured her locked up in some room. Of course she would escape—never one to lie down and take it. He imagined her pacing her enclosure like a jailed varmint, constantly looking for a way out, scratching and clawing. A more gruesome image scrapped its way into his mind. Jennifer's captures beating her or … or worse. As the vision inched its way into the light, Dresden stamped it away.

She could give them so many answers. Or maybe not, Dresden puzzled out. What if her kidnapping had nothing to do with Roker, Lance, Oman—all of it. Then what? But why call Dresden? That was the question, right? He would have an answer soon. All he had to do was endure Orville's long bouts of silence teeming with judgment and indignation.

Ashville, North Carolina

The sun dropped down onto College Street. In ten minutes, it would blind motorists heading west down the wide three-lane road. They would lose the advantage in less than four minutes, when the sun dipped behind the buildings. Orville and Dresden sat in a diner off South Spruce Street, sipping sweet tea. Orville looked at his watch, then nodded at Dresden. The two men rose, Orville paid the bill, and Dresden checked his simple disguise in the bathroom mirror.

Red was out on the road, running his route and hopefully dragging any surveillance behind him. His shiny red Toyota Camry was two blocks away as Dresden and Orville started their magnetic gray Ford Taurus. Red rolled past in the left lane. Orville pulled out and followed two cars behind. At College, Red turned left into the left lane. The afternoon traffic helped shield the well-choreographed movements of the pickup team. Orville turned left at College as well, then slithered his way into the right lane within the same block. The sun was beaming. *Perfect.* Dresden pulled the sun visor down and watched as a man walking into the sun held up a folded newspaper to shield his eyes.

The red Camry pulled over to the left curb. The back door opened and remained that way. A moment later, Orville pulled over to the right two blocks up. The back door opened.

"Nice car you have. Mercedes?"

Orville kept his eyes forward. "No, it's Japanese-made."

The car sank slightly, and the back door closed. Orville drove down the street as Dresden handed Jennifer a bottle of water without looking back. He could hear Jennifer drinking. Dresden suggested she lie down and cover herself. The water was laced with a mild sedative that would take effect in less than ten minutes.

Jennifer did as she was told.

"It will take us about thirty minutes to get out of town proper," Dresden said.

A soft whimper came from the back seat. Dresden looked at Orville. A minute passed with nothing, then it all came out. Orville turned up the radio.

Mount Cinder, Maryland

Dresden watched Red pull the blankets up to Jennifer's shoulders. Soft, low-watt bulbs illuminated the bedroom in a yellowish glow. Red claimed it would help her recovery. She would undoubtedly wake from terror fits over the coming days, maybe weeks. If the room was too dark or too light, it could be disorienting. It could cause Jennifer to regress, even have a seizure or worse.

Red got her to shower. Jennifer cried for long periods of time, then yelled as loud as she could, slamming her fists against the walls. In the end, she whimpered and huffed, slumped against the shower stall. She crawled into bed still wet.

There, Red gave her an antibiotic cocktail that included a stronger sedative. As the resident medic, he had to examine her wounds and determine what she needed in the way of further medical care. He assumed Jennifer would not volunteer for the examination.

After Red left the room, Dresden sat next to Jennifer. She tried on a smile that came out crooked and pained. In a low, hoarse voice, she said, "Thank you," though her eyes remained closed.

He could see her struggling against the sedative.

"I—I need to ..." Jennifer's eyes opened wide. Her body stiffened, and her eyes welled up.

"Jennifer, you rest. We can talk soon. Just rest. You're alright now."

"I need to tell you ..." Jennifer's eyes closed, and her body went limp.

Twenty-Eight

Mount Cinder, Maryland

Moonlight beamed through the window, waking Dresden. He rubbed his neck as he straightened his body. Jennifer moved fitfully under the covers and startled him. He stood too quickly, and a sharp pain shot upward from his quad, reminding him of everything. Dresden stared at her bruised and battered face. Her eyes opened.

"Marcus? That you?"

"Yes,"

"I—Have I told you anything about what happened?" she said.

"No."

She said nothing for a few moments as she looked out the window. "Oh," she said eventually, and looked up at him. "I can't make it out, Marcus. I'm sorry. I was in a room at first, I think. A room, and I was tied and bound and there was a bag over my—"

Her eyes filled with tears and her lip quivered like an earthworm on hot pavement. She closed her eyes and didn't open them again for a long time.

Dresden didn't realize she'd fallen asleep until he looked at the drip attached to her arm. It was connected to a monitor that gave her a dose if her heart-rate rose above a certain level. Dresden moved to the door, then stopped and looked back. He needed to find Orville and Red.

Music threaded its way up from the basement. Dresden followed it through the darkness of the house, finding a narrow hatch leading to a stairwell to the basement. Dipping his shoulders, he made his way down to the tight hallway below. Light seeped from behind a half-drawn door. Dresden pushed the door open and squinted in the bright light.

His eyes adjusted and he took in the room. A conference table commanded center stage, with room enough for ten people. Four whiteboards took up one wall, computers and associated equipment the opposite. Two wide-screen TVs mounted to the wall stared down the length of the table at Dresden. A command center. Go figure.

Orville saw him first but kept writing on one of the whiteboards. He coughed, but it sounded as if he didn't really need to. Red turned from the TV he was watching and waved Dresden over.

Red pointed at the screen. A scene filmed by a shaking hand on a mobile phone showed several people dressed in black approaching a car parked in a lot near a nature area or wooded park. Two men exited the vehicle and asked the camera person and his cohorts to move on. The scene cut to a silver-haired man apparently out for a run being escorted back to his vehicle. Two more men pushed him into the backseat of the car. The scene changed again; now the people in black were lying in front of and behind the vehicle. Balloons, flying from somewhere behind the camera, pelted the car, exploding in a vibrant shade of red. The camera zoomed in on the dripping paint, then went black. Red turned to Dresden.

"You know any of those guys? I mean the security guys," Red asked.

"One of them looked familiar," Dresden said.

"They all work for your former employer," Orville added, still writing.

Dresden looked around the room again and chuckled to himself. It was Orville who'd encouraged Dresden to join the military, to join the SEAL Teams. Dresden's father had never forgiven the man, but in a funny twist of irony he'd still made Orville and Red the lifelong caretakers of the fifty-five-hundred-acre Doyle Lodge. He'd even built each of them a small house at the far north end of the property, near the Pennsylvania border.

"The others, the ones dressed in black, they have taken it upon themselves to harass First Watch security elements. This is the second video like it in the last week," Red said.

"What's it all about?" Dresden asked.

"Markum ... Senator," Red said.

Dresden cocked his head to the side, an eyebrow raised.

"It's good publicity, I'm sure. It'll help the man get some votes come November. But it could just as easily get out of hand," Orville said as he sat down at the conference table.

"You should call it in, Orville—ask Jack what's going on," Red said.

"No need. I know Lawson. I'm sure of it. He'll defuse this if it needs to be," Orville said.

The men and women in black, enraged and engendered by Senator Markum's now-very-public push to conduct an inquiry into the operations of First Watch, claimed they were going to conduct "disruption operations" against the "soldiers of misfortune." Red claimed the congressional proceedings had taken a turn toward the constitutionality of what First Watch was engaged in around the country—and around the world. Sri Lanka brought that home. Red thought it was a complete smear campaign. Orville felt Markum had set a wildfire in motion that might ravage more than its intended target. Dresden, on the other hand, flashed to the last time he'd seen Roker. Gaunt. Sallow. Death-like. What kind of effect was this going to have on him? Branch was intent on taking over. Was he going to jump into this inferno with two feet? Damn, what a mess!

"Marcus, here's your phones," Red said, snapping him back to the moment.

"Huh?"

"Your phones. This one is your old phone—completely rigged. Don't use it unless it's directly related to what we are dealing with here, like talking to Roker for example. Everything on this phone will be recorded and traceable. This other phone is for general conversation. You need to call Emily, I suppose. It's encrypted and shifts keys every half-millisecond. This is your throwaway—you can do all the basic stuff on it. Social media, music and search engines, you know that kind of stuff, okay? If you have to give a number out to anyone other than us or the family, give them the throwaway Got it?"

"Okay."

"So, what now?" Orville asked.

Their faces shined like children at the zoo. Even Orville couldn't hide it. His expression was hard as granite, but his eyes glistened with delight. This was what they lived for. All they needed was a four-second call from Dresden, saying there was trouble and he needed help, and within a matter of hours they had the machine up and running again. In fact, Dresden wondered if they ever really shut the engine down.

He was going to walk away, let Lance rest in peace, but here he was. Dresden pulled a chair out, and after a long pause sat down. Twenty-four hours earlier, he'd been resolute—now, not so much. Orville and Red. Lance and Jennifer. He'd seen what these men could do, what they *would* do. He imagined Lance on his last day. What he must have gone through, the fight he must have put up.

"I have an idea," Dresden said.

"Let's hear it," Red replied, his voice eager. He turned in his chair and took out a notebook and pen.

On the drive up from North Carolina, the two men spoke only a handful of words. Orville drove straight through, so Dresden ruminated on the events. Why and how were the obvious questions. Why were site managers being knocked off? How had he made it onto their list? Whoever they were. Oman, maybe? He thought of the men following him in San Francisco and Santa Cruz and again in Oman. Someone must have been onto him when he went to First Watch. Did they want him dead for the same reason they killed the site managers? Maybe they thought he knew something. It made no sense. What about Roker? It all came back to Roker. But Dresden couldn't bring himself to believe the man would sign off on killing Lance; he just couldn't see it, despite how all the pieces fit so well with Roker as the puppet master.

So, if Roker seemed to be at the middle of all this, wittingly or unwittingly, it would stand to reason that Frist Watch was at the middle too. That the killer or killers were tracking their prey out of First Watch. What he needed to do was give them his scent and draw them out. The site managers had not had this foresight. Surprise was on the side of the killers, and so they went down easy. *Not me.*

Darwin—he would go to Darwin, Australia. Dresden needed a way to perk the killers' interest. If someone requested his services through First Watch, the killer was bound to find out. But he needed someone and someplace that was pretty much off the First Watch radar. He had just the guy in mind, and that guy was in Darwin—First Watch had nothing going on there. It was perfect.

He hadn't told the two men any of this, until now.

Orville was the voice of dissension. He didn't like Dresden being bait, or the three days with a super-tight schedule, planned down the letter. Dresden's friend was completely unaffiliated with First Watch or any American firm—he ran his own security company. They specialized in providing support to the UN. He'd been in East Timor for over a decade. They conducted straightforward counter-surveillance. They'd ID and photograph the guy, with no contact or connection to Dresden. It was perfect and better yet Darwin was a First Watch free market, so there was little or no chance Dresden would run into anyone he knows.

"Why go all the way to Darwin?" Red asked, tearing himself away from the TV.

"Because they'll likely have to bring someone in."

"What if they hire local guys?" Orville asked. Dresden had thought of that. It did pose a problem, until he remembered the three attacks. In Arizona and Sri Lanka, the site manager was killed in the same fashion. Plus, all three hits were planned by the same person. That was the connection Dresden hadn't made until recently. The diversion was the key. None of the attacks had needed a diversion. In fact, it wasn't a diversion at all. It was a cover-up—something for the authorities to focus on.

The men sat silent for a time. Stan Getz jammed away in the background. Red was the jazz man, fashioned after his idol, Cint Eastwood. Red still denied the fact, although Dresden could remember a time when Red had tried learning to play the sax. No one could stand the racket he made, so he quit and just listened.

The gate alarm broke Dresden's reminiscing—a loud banging sound, as if someone was slamming trash can lids together.

Red jumped out of his chair and moved to the bank of TV cameras. He smashed his finger onto a large button that silenced the alarm. A shot of the driveway was on the screen. Then the gate. He shifted the view to one of the wide-screen TVs, then jostled the joystick to drive the PTZ camera in. A compact car drove slowly toward the gate, then parked. The driver got out, and Red zoomed in and took a screen-shot of plate. The car's info came up on the second TV screen. A rental car. The driver moved to the call box.

"Hello?" a woman's voice came over the speaker.

Red moved the camera in for a close-up of the woman standing at the gate. The heavy rain distorted her face slightly. Dresden got up from his chair and moved to look more closely at the screen.

"Hello? Is Marcus there?" the woman said again.

Red shifted to the camera on the call box.

"Hah!" Dresden laughed, rising up and down on his toes.

"What? Red said, his jaw tight.

"It's Maria!"

Twenty-Nine

Mount Cinder, Maryland

Maria looked over her shoulder and winked at Dresden. He smiled, watching her walk down the hall, following Red. Sparks of excitement crashed with unease, all between flights of lightheadedness. Maria. Shit! He fell into a chair at the dining room table. His vision cleared and he noticed Orville sitting next to him. The man glared at him. He sure knew how to spoil a good thing.

"Would you please tell me what *she* is doing here?" Orville said. The words slipped out between his teeth like a viper's tongue.

"Well ..." Dresden started, then stopped. He was impressed, really. Maria had remembered his son's name, where he worked, and what he looked like. Enough to track him down and use all her womanly charm to convince Casper to help her find Dresden. Which wasn't too hard, he imagined. Casper was undoubtedly worried, and Maria could be very convincing.

"Before I got run off the road, one of the guys from First Watch sent me some emails. I forwarded them to Maria to take a look at them. She says whatever is going on, it's bad. When I didn't answer my phone, she decided to come looking for me."

Orville's eyelids lowered like a drawbridge, until they were almost closed. Red sparks flickered under his lashes. Dresden had faced down men intent on killing him and never flinched, not once. This old fart squinted, and it made him want to run from the room.

"She's pretty and smart and clearly industrious. What does she see in you?" Orville finally said. An unfamiliar smile stretched across his face for a brief second.

"I don't know."

"You know what this means, right? We have to bring in your friend Coltrane."

"Uh, why?"

"They are the only two who know anything about this. Maria is here. So, we can take care of her now. But Mr. Coltrane, I'd hate—"

"Don't say it. Just do it."

"Okay, I'll have Red make it happen. I will get a team on his family."

"Good." Dresden said.

He groaned as he rose, his injuries swelling and muscles tightening up like a knot on a wet rope. "I need to get a workout in or I'm going to be useless."

"Okay, I'll find you in a little while. I have something to show you," Orville said as he got up and left the room.

The pool water was cool and perfect for laps. Dresden did sets of short sprints—freestyle, breaststroke, and backstroke. An echo rang through the basement room as tiny waves buckled against the pool walls. His quad throbbed as he swiveled his legs up and down through the water. The wound had healed and scabbed over, yet the muscle underneath remained stiff and sore. The long drive hadn't helped the recovery process. He switched to breath holds. When he came up at the far end, he found Orville staring at him down the lane. Dresden swam the length and looked up at the old man.

"It's time I showed you around," Orville said, and walked out of the pool area.

"Okay, give me twenty minutes," Dresden said as the door to the pool area closed.

Orville was sitting on a long leather couch, watching Dresden enter the room. On the coffee table in the center of the room, Dresden noticed a large piece of paper—a bird's-eye view of the farm. Orville showed him the new additions to the property. The old barn that used to house horses was now a tactical gun range and kill house. A one-mile and three-mile obstacle course weaved through two separate parts of the woods. A close-in range for small arms and a thousand-meter range were spaced out at hundred-meter intervals. Orville explained that everything was designed to be concealed from the air.

It was impressive. Orville and Red had built everything themselves. The question that hopped around in Dresden's mind was: Why? The Lodge was private—an island, a big island among ever-shrinking parcels of land as the concentric rings of suburbia stretched farther and farther from Washington, D.C. What was once a secluded getaway for his dad would likely become just another tract of land with several hundred houses on it, or at least that was how Dresden saw it. So, what was this all about?

The answer was simple, really. His dad didn't want the property anymore, and Orville had designs to turn Dresden into his protégé. If he could coax him away from California, Orville could pass on his knowledge and tradecraft and make the Lodge his own private training grounds. Of course, Dresden wanted nothing to do with it anymore. When this was done, it was back to Escondite.

"When was the last time you were behind a long gun?" Orville asked.

"The last time? Well, it's ... it's been a while." Dresden struggled to stifle the thought of the last time he'd fired a sniper weapon.

"That's what I suspected. You're gonna have to put that behind you now, son. This won't be like the last time. I won't let that happen." Orville locked eyes with Dresden, who had to work to stay engage. The other man blinked. "Your training starts this afternoon. When are you heading to Australia?

"Day after tomorrow. Real early."

"Okay, good. Not much time, but first, we can get you back up to speed and lethal. Then, you do what you do best—shoot, move, and communicate. Got it?"

"Roger!" Dresden said.

A ball of dust followed Dresden into the house and settled as he filled a glass of water in the kitchen. Red took a bite of an overstuffed sandwich, lettuce and mustard hanging from his mouth. He pointed to a small stack of papers.

"You know what this sounds like to me?"

Orville grunted as he up-ended a glass of water.

"Sounds like the bait and switch the Afghans started using to get their kill count up. You know?

Attack and pin down the recon element, then lie in wait for the QRF to arrive and take them out too."

Orville had asked, more demanded, that Dresden do an after-action report on all the events related to First Watch and Lance's death. Red was the first to read it.

Contemplating the tiles on the floor and nodding slowly, Orville said, "Yes, each of the attacks was initiated with a diversion. I was thinking that they were similar to the Russian SOF method—using two unrelated elements to meet the objective."

"Failure of one does not constitute total failure," Red said through another mouthful.

"It does sound similar, but I get the feeling the tiger's still in his cave. That the real attack or campaign hasn't started yet, hasn't been launched," Dresden mused.

The refrigerator whirred for a few seconds, then shut off with a clunk.

"The game has only started," Maria said.

The men looked up in surprise.

"Maria," Dresden said, moving toward her. She kissed him on both cheeks.

"Did you get some rest?" Red asked.

"Yes. Thank you." She sat down at the table. "The attacks themselves are a cover for something. The files and documents you sent me, Marcus, are enough to give anyone the idea that there is a much bigger plan in place. The questions lead us to identity theft. The financials lead us to embezzlement or outright theft, and the attacks, well, they're meant to cover it all up.

The emails Maria had reviewed were not complete—mid-stream threads from accounts that led her nowhere. There were spreadsheets with figures and account information that meant nothing without the appropriate context. The clues were there in what wasn't there, Maria said. First Watch would undoubtedly have IT protections in place. Great protection. The kind of protection that could make following a series of emails difficult. Most of them had been encrypted at some level. Some more than others. The financials had significant protection. That made sense; the questionnaires were encrypted too, but with something different, something she hadn't seen before. So, she spent some time with the questionnaire and got the sense something was inherently wrong with them. The cryptic emails provoked a type of answer that any good hacker could use to infiltrate a system or steal an identity. Packet sniffing, Maria called it.

"Like phishing, but a little different," Red clarified for Orville and Dresden.

The room was quiet again after the explanations. Red handed Maria a cup of tea.

Orville filled his glass again. "Roker—what do you think of him, Marcus?"

"I think he's a good man. Well, he was … I mean, I'm sure he is, he's just in trouble and having to work it out in his own strange way."

"Would you say he is capable of orchestrating these attacks?"

"The thought has certainly crossed my mind."

"Then what stopped you from going all the way? Loyalty?"

"Uh … yeah."

The thinning trees outside waved like metronomes, leaves flickering on their branches. A squirrel ran up a trunk, delivering his stores to his winter cache. Dresden pictured Roker lying on the floor in his sad, empty home, a frenetic, confused aura surrounding him. The trees leaned in toward the windows, and the branches reached out and startled Dresden.

"We are talking about a man who runs a multi-billion-dollar company," Orville said, "an international company with ties to some of the wealthiest, most powerful men and women in the world. I know you, Marcus. I know you can walk away from wealth to some degree." Orville paused, his arms out, palms up as he looked around the room. "But most men cannot. We have to think outside the bounds of simpleton constructs such as loyalty or even our memory of someone. Roker was a good SEAL. He started First Watch for all the right reasons. But that time and that man *may* be long gone."

Dresden pushed his untouched food aside, sat back in his chair, and eyed Orville. The man had a point, but it was one Dresden was not prepared to accept.

The room was warm and smelled of jasmine incense. Jennifer was asleep. She'd woken up once for an hour. Disoriented, she'd spent most of the time trying to remember who she was and how she'd gotten there, clearly petrified.

Red tended to her with the help of Maria. Her voice seemed to soothe Jennifer, calming the woman. Jennifer had suffered severe trauma. They should expect very little from her, despite the urgency of the matter, Red advised. There was no telling how long it would take. Jennifer, for all intents and purposes, was not there. She seemed to trust Maria, but Red admitted he may be grasping at straws. They'd been able to talk for a few minutes of lucidity.

Maria told Dresden what she knew, what Jennifer had told her. About the room she was kept in. Her cell. How it was cold, with a dirt floor and a folding cot. How she woke, clad in nothing but a thigh-length t-shirt, otherwise naked. Dry heaves had racked her body as she took in her circumstances. Over several days, bits of clothing showed up.

Pants. Socks. A sweater. All piecemeal and random. The food was awful and unvarying. *Grechka.* Her captor would bark the word at her as he tossed the bowl on to the floor. Cold, hard, and tasteless.

Dresden wrestled with the memory of talking with Jennifer at the pool. Her worrying over Roker. Now, he stood next to her bed with Maria, who leaned against him and wove her fingers between his, gripping hard. He looked over at her and smiled, still unsure if he could trust himself. Dresden was relieved she'd taken to Red. Their mutual interest drew them together fast. But he could not afford to expose her to this. He shuddered to imagine what she would think if she saw who he might have to become. He had to protect her; Red was his best bet.

"She is lucky to have a friend like you," Maria said, looking back to Jennifer.

Lucky? There was nothing lucky about any of this. It was likely his fault she was in this predicament. He pulled Maria out of the room.

Thirty

Mount Cinder, Maryland

Robbie wobbled in, a heavy-looking overnight bag in his hand. Red followed close behind. Dresden and Orville were sitting in the dimly lit family room off the dining room.

The new arrival dropped his bag near the dining table and descended the steps, looking like a saddle-sore cowboy, and flopped down in an overstuffed chair across from Dresden. Red straddle an armrest across from Orville.

"So … this is some fine howdy doody you got me into, Marcus," Robbie said. He beamed through tired eyes and brilliant teeth. Robbie was clearly complaining as a mask to hide his childlike joy at the adventure of all of it.

"How was your flight?" Dresden asked. He leaned forward to get a better look at the man.

"Flight? Flight? Let me tell you, guy, it was madness. I drive my car to a parking garage near my office. I get in an SUV with someone who knows my name. I'm still not sure why I did that. Anyway, I'm driven to a farm northeast of Frisco. Get on a puddle jumper. Fly to Nevada … or Arizona … I'm not really sure. I don't know. Anyway, that guy lands on a dirt strip next to another plane. This one, the new one, is a jet—like those executive planes. Just me in this twelve-seater luxury jet. It lands in the dark somewhere. But I don't get off. We take off again, go to another strip somewhere. All I know is there was grass under my feet. Then I get in another small plane with this guy"—Robbie threw a thumb toward a grinning Red—"and then I land here after nearly nose-diving out of the sky to an airstrip. And by the way, I use airstrip loosely in this case. Oh … oh yeah, and this guy's on NODs on the landing, cause there's no lights on the air strip! We hop in a truck, and here I am."

"Well, I'm glad to hear your flights went well. You never can be too careful," Dresden said. He got up and stretched his arms out as he limped toward Robbie.

The man glanced at Dresden's leg, got up, and gave him a hearty hug. "Good to see you, guy. And alive!"

"Same here."

Dresden introduced Red and Orville. Handshakes were exchanged around the room.

"You hungry?" Red asked.

"Starved. Didn't eat. Glad I didn't. I think I would have painted one of those planes if I had."

"Good. Set up at the dining table." Red said. He moved into the kitchen and took the lid off a cast-iron skillet. The room filled with the smell of bacon and sage.

Robbie looked over at Dresden and slid him an envelope. Then he wrinkled up his nose and his eyes drooped, as he looked down and troubled a spot on the floor with his foot.

Dresden took the envelope, pulling out a folded sheet of newsprint. The Reno Gazette-Journal, with a section highlighted in green. The heading – *Man Dies in Sun Valley Blaze.* The subtitle read, *One fatality and 300 acres of BLM land destroyed in fire caused by faulty camp stove.* Dresden folded the paper up, returned it to the envelope, and handed it back to Robbie.

Robbie put his hand up. "All yours—and for what it's worth, I'm sorry Marcus."

Dresden looked at Robbie but didn't say anything. His vision blurred; he needed some fresh air. He left the room without a word.

A light dusting of early-season snow lingered the next morning. The sky, now a perpetual gray, constantly threatened more snow. Dresden's breath puffed out in white plumes. He held his head up, eyes scanning. Orville was out there, in the woods.

It would be his only indication something was coming. When he caught a glimpse of what he thought was the old man, it was too late. Dresden went tumbling to the ground. He'd stepped on a pair of coffee can lids made into a pressure plate switch hidden under some leaf debris. The switch set off several obstacles. Padded beams of wood swung at him from behind trees. He may have fallen, but he recovered well, with a graceful roll back to his feet. He continued running.

Dresden jogged onto the range, rubbing his leg. He could run, but the scar ached and the muscle beneath burned. Ignoring the nagging pain, he lay down behind his Steyr SSG PIV. He had thirty seconds from arrival at the range to make the shot. He pulled the butt of the rifle into his shoulder, acquired the sight, and minimized the scope shadow. Breathe out. Breathe in. Halfway out, then hold it. Applying constant pressure to the trigger, he made sure to pull straight back. The weapon fired, the suppressor cutting the sound down to a spit. Dresden reacquired the target and waited five seconds, then opened the bolt, and retrieved the shell casing. He got up and ran off the range.

"Ten circuits. Ten rounds," Dresden said.

"That's it?" Robbie said, his dark brown cheeks pushing against his eyes.

"Orville said tomorrow you're joining us."

Robbie tried to read him. Nothing. The color ran from the man's ebony face. He searched around for Orville, then leaned in and said, "Really?"

"No … but it was fun watching you squirm for a minute."

"Hah, very funny." He took a bite of his sandwich. "This house is something else, Marcus. I've never seen anything like it before. Your family owns it? I mean it's cool, but kind of creepy."

"Yeah, tell me about it. There's a lot of ghosts here."

"What?"

Red stomped into the kitchen before Dresden could continue. "The rest of us are down in the conference room. Care to join us?"

They followed Red as he wound his way through the house to the den. Dresden almost ran into Robbie as he stopped before fitting himself through the small opening to the basement room. He gave Robbie a squeeze to reassure him. When they entered the conference room, Dresden noticed Maria sitting at a computer, her fingers dancing across the keys. The expression on her face was something he'd never seen before, like a mad doctor from some old horror movie—intense and maniacal.

Dresden stood behind her for a moment before saying, "Is that C-plus-plus or Java?"

Maria's fingers stopped. She turned with such deliberateness it provoked Dresden to take a step back. The mad look remained but was laced with a hint of hysteria.

"I thought you said you didn't know about—"

"Eh, I've been reading. So, what is it?"

"Python," Maria said, her edge melting away. She reached for Dresden's hand. "Listen, we need to talk about these files." She shifted one of her two screens to a document full of numbers. "My best guess, and Red's too, is these are financials. I think—we think so, at least. Red says he has a contact that can run this down but wanted me to talk with you first."

"I really don't want to drag—"

"I know, but this is important. This man, Derek, can help us. I think we should let him."

Dresden looked down at her. "Okay," he said, still not sure.

Orville finished writing a single word in the center of a whiteboard: *Strategy*. He nodded to Dresden, who was pouring himself a cup of coffee. Red whistled to get everyone's attention.

"Okay, so this may be a little awkward, at first." Dresden looked around the room and saw friends brought together under less-than-fortunate circumstances. They were going to have to work together despite how much he wanted to go it alone—they were going to have to be a *team,* and he was going to have to lead them. His stomach tightened. A knot formed just below his sternum. Dresden was stepping up to be responsible for the lives of others again. He imagined himself running for the door when he glanced over at Orville. The man studied him and clearly saw exactly what he was thinking. A single wink, and Dresden knew there was no way out.

"But I think we are all here for the right reason," he continued. "So, to be effective, we need a strategy." He tapped the whiteboard. "We need to have a plan of attack."

With Dresden clearly at the helm the group, the team discussed their strategy. Maria and Red were going to white hat First Watch to see what they could find. Robbie and Orville were going to run down any deaths related to First Watch contractors, focusing on the site managers. On occasion, Dresden found himself drifting away, floating above it all, watching as a sort of pride filled his chest grew—like years before with a new platoon of SEALs. They had a singular purpose bolstered by inherent resolve and the drive to do the right thing. Maybe they could pull this off. Maybe, just maybe, he could keep everyone safe and bring closure to Lance's death. But when Dresden mentioned Darwin, both Maria and Robbie argued against it and the doubt came plummeting back. It took a full hour to tease out the details and reassure them it might not be the only way, but it was the only way at the time.

Dresden kept saying they needed to act fast. It was likely they'd lost the advantage. Orville was less convinced and assumed they'd be still looking for Dresden. The fact they couldn't find him would have them worried, and if he rose from the ashes, they would jump at the chance to kill him. This comment started Maria and Robbie arguing all over again, and the debate ensued for another hour, before Dresden said the eleventh hour had passed. He needed to pack and get ready to leave.

A soft knock at the door made Dresden stop. It came again, and he opened it. Maria. She looked sleepy and worn, and he reached for her hand and led her in the room. Sitting on the edge of a chair, she sighed and looked out a window. Dresden sat on the edge of the bed across from her and waited.

Still not looking at him, Maria said, "I don't like it, Marcus."

"I know you don't. But it makes the most sense. If we play around at this, someone else will get hurt or die. We have to move fast. Keep them off-kilter.

If we can." Dresden was not succeeding in reassuring her; he could see that.

Maria was silent again for a moment then whispered, "Will you be able to call?"

"Yes. But I plan to keep it limited," Dresden said. He got up and moved to Maria, grabbing her hand and lifting her out of the chair. He wrapped her in his arms, and she sank into him. It felt good. Real good.

"Maria, I need you to do something for me. This is going to sound weird." Dresden stopped.

"What is it, Marcus?" Maria pushed off him so she could look him in the eyes.

"I … I've been texting Lance. After he died. Several times. It was a game we played, and …"

"What's weird about that?"

"I don't know. Something about texting a dead man seems like … well, anyway, the last time I texted, he wrote back."

Maria's freckles seemed to swirl like a constellation as she squinted, "Okay. That is kind of weird."

"Yeah, and a whole lotta creepy," Dresden said.

"So, what can I do?" Maria said.

"I was hoping you could carry on the conversation," Dresden said. He explained the rules of the music game.

Maria frowned, on the verge of laughing. "Uh … Okay."

"Red's got it set up."

"I see. I can do that. I *think*."

"Cool. Thanks. I'll get you some songs to text him.

"Okay. Don't worry I'll figure it out. But what's this about?" she asked.

"I'm not sure yet. But if I don't keep it up, I think it may go cold and I'll—we'll never know."

"Okay."

"Oh, and one more thing. I don't actually think it's Lance ..."

"I got it, Marcus." And this time, Maria laughed and buried herself into him again.

"Thanks. It means a lot.

"You're welcome. Marcus?"

He wanted to stay there with her. He wanted to wake up the next morning and head back to Escondite with her. But he knew he couldn't, so he grabbed her hand and led her downstairs to join the others.

Thirty-One

Darwin, Australia

The remoteness of the outback, of the Northern Territory, never changed. Farther north than both Sydney and Melbourne, it felt as if it were the opposite. As if Darwin was farther from, not closer to civilization. Dresden pressed his head to the cool plane window and watched the bush stretch on like a shag carpet to an ant, occasionally broken by flat expanses of sandy, arid space. Alien and unforgiving. It was this remoteness that made Darwin one of his favorite places.

As the passengers disembarked, Dresden kept his eye on two men. When he cleared customs, he lost sight of his would-be pursuers. It was unlikely anyone would have been on the plane anyway, Dresden pondered. All Orville had given First Watch was a timeframe and a destination. And the last they'd seen of Dresden was on the West Coast, not the East, and especially not Philadelphia where he flew out of.

At the baggage carousel, he spotted the first guy, an aboriginal. His skin, dark as coal, flashed in stark contrast to his pearl-white shirt. The guy threw a quick glance and a nod to the other side of the room. In the reflection of a window, Dresden spotted the second one, a tall, exceedingly thin man. His cream suit jacket was draped over shoulders like the folds of a rhino's skin. A heavy sheen of sweat covered the man's pale, hairless head.

The thin man nodded at the aboriginal. Dresden continued to watch the reflection. The man's shirt billowed as the guy headed for the exit. These two were the local hires Robbie had been worried about. They weren't here to kill him, though—too clumsy. They were the eyes and ears. His target was out there somewhere, waiting.

With one eye on the rearview mirror, he drove to his hotel, sticking to the speed limit so as not to lose his tail. No quick lane changes or dramatic turns. Steady as she goes. The trail kept its distance, always two or three cars back. Dresden couldn't confirm it was the men from the airport, but it didn't matter. One way or another, they were onto him.

He parked out front along Esplanade and watched a family set up a picnic in Bicentennial Park across the street. Dresden thought of Casper. He'd meant to call his son, but everything had happened so fast after the crash. There was no *right* time for it. Maria had assured him she'd left Casper in a good state of mind, enough that Dresden had a little time to spare. That window was closing though, and Casper would get worried again.

Dresden walked toward the hotel entrance, then noticed the bald man from the airport. He was heading toward a large memorial statue in the park. Dresden moved to get a better vantage. He lost sight of the man for a moment, the thick trees of the park covering his movement. When Dresden caught sight of him again, he was walking up to another man at the railing overlooking the bluffs. He was tall as well, maybe taller, stout and with close-cropped blond hair—white-blond. The hair on Dresden's arm stood up. It was him.

Dresden almost made a beeline for the two men, wanting to end it right then and there. But no, that wouldn't work. He watched them a little longer, then scanned the area for any other surveillants. Nothing. They were overly confident. Good.

The balcony overlooked the park and bluffs ten stories below. His chair teetered as he waited for Casper to pick up. No answer. The message was short—*I will be in Pennsylvania in a few days. Can only stay overnight. Sorry. I will plan a longer stay soon. Love you. Dad.* He tipped his chair back, pushing his feet on the rail. There really wasn't time for the diversion.

But Robbie had convinced him he needed to do it. Casper was worried. "A good father reassures his children," Robbie had said. And there was no argument once Orville jumped in as well. He would visit Casper, that was that.

Ted Mink was the associate manager of the Cullen Bay Mariana and yacht club. His combover had thinned to three strands of waxed hair slapped over his pink scalp, and his neck and chin were fused. When he laughed, which he did often, flaps of skin shook like tectonic plates.

"Hello, Mister Dresden, so good to meet you. Great of you to come out on such short notice." Ted offered him a chair at a table snuggled in between two potted palms and a large plate glass window overlooking the harbor. Sailboats and motor-cruisers bobbed gently in their slips.

"I have to admit, I was getting nervous. Thought you might not be able to make it, and we would have to suffer another break-in," Ted said.

"No problem, Mr. Mink. I'm happy to help."

The break-ins were a spin, part of their overall plan. Ted was a close friend of Dresden's man in Darwin. The two men had a leisurely lunch. They talked of nothing—the weather, the harbor, good places to eat and drink. Ted was playing along perfectly, allowing Dresden to find his surveillance pals. He spotted them near the end of the meal.

Dresden spent three to four hours each day surveying the yacht club. The irony was he found a few security issues, real ones that he reported to Ted. After taking nearly an hour to consider what Dresden had provided him, the man laughed loud, his neck shaking like chunks of a glacier falling into the Arctic Sea. He clasped Dresden's hand with both of his and shook it vigorously, to the point Dresden's shoulder began to hurt.

Each day, Dresden walked and drove his planned routes, often catching either the thin man or the indigenous fellow. They were at best semi-concealed, always in a car, always backed in where no one else was. Worse, they drove the same car every day. Both men used binoculars to watch him, often flashing him with their lenses. They ducked into corners or strange shadows when they thought they might have been seen. He never saw the blond, not while he worked the harbor.

The man finally showed up in the afternoon when Dresden toured the town and the outback. Dresden walked along Mitchel Street, shopping. He drove to see the George Brown Botanical Garden and the Darwin Military Museum. Afterwards he'd find a small café and wallow away an hour or two reading, currently *The Moving Target* by Ross McDonald. He even went to Vestsy's Beach to the farmers market. The blond was much better—Dresden only caught the faintest glimpses of him.

Luckily, the counter-surveillance team caught much more. On the second day, they were able to get a series of clean photos of the man. Dresden wondered what the guy was waiting on. He'd given the blond several opportunities to move; he wouldn't have come all the way to Australia just to watch him. It didn't make any sense. But Dresden kept to his plan.

One evening, he walked from a café off Smith Street, through an open-air mall to the Deckchair movie theater. He used the mall to shorten up the walk. The blond followed. The counter-surveillance team was in an office on the fifth story of a building perfectly situated to take a hundred shots of the man as he sauntered down the narrow open-air mall.

The team sent the photos to the Lodge. Orville in turn sent a single cropped copy to Dresden's secure phone. No name. No stats. Nothing else. Orville added as short text, *Still looking for his file. The man's a ghost.* There was no doubt he was good. His only mistake was his car. Like the other two, he used the same rental every day.

Dresden had one last route to execute. If the man didn't take the bait there, he wasn't going to.

That night, Dresden tossed and turned, tortured by nightmares. Flashes of the blond man driving by in the black truck. Standing on the hillside clutching a pistol bathed in the sheriff's floodlight. Standing over Lance with bloody fists. Face to face in a small room. Sitting with a group of men around a table. Women too, young women, their faces like clay.

The images mashed and twisted. Dresden searched his memory. The small room and the other men, faceless and laughing. The women again, scared this time. He woke gasping for air. The images trundled away as he tried desperately to hang on to them, to make sense of them, but nothing stuck, and within seconds the dream slipped away.

Dirty sand blew across the two-lane blacktop. Dresden stared out the windshield at the desert south of Darwin. A lone gas station and café came into view like a mirage. The car directly behind him pulled off in a bowl of dust. The tires on the rented Toyota Land Cruiser buzzed beneath him. He slammed his brakes as a wallaby bound across the road. In his rearview mirror, the target car was a quarter-mile behind. The driver deftly placed himself in a position such that Dresden could neither make out the man's features or read the plate. If he slowed down, closed the gap, his cover would be blown. The same would be true if he sped up. It *was* the blond, he was sure of it. Dresden wondered if the guy had a clue. Chances were he knew the destination but not the route to get there.

National Highway 1 to Alice Springs was practically deserted. Just the two of them as far as the eye could see. The sun had set behind the horizon twenty minutes earlier, and now the stark blue sky was streaked with wispy pink and graphic shades of orange and red. A curtain of unfiltered darkness rose from the ground beside him. Two miles to his turn. Dresden flipped his lights on. As the darkness enveloped him, he turned on a band of LED floodlights mounted on the roof of his truck. He could regulate the intensity of the beam using a rio-stat on the dashboard. At full intensity, the beam would blind oncoming vehicles.

His turn was coming up soon. He looked back. A small sign marked it—*Mary River, next left, Kakadu National Park*. His truck bounced off the blacktop and onto a hardpacked dirt road. A plume of fine red dust exploded behind him. Dresden checked his side-view mirror. The chase car slowed and made the turn. The car hesitated, then took up the chase. *Good boy,* Dresden said to himself.

He absently fingered the small black box in the cupholder of the Land Cruiser's center console. Two buttons, one blue and one red. The clock on the dash read 8:43 p.m. He'd been on the dirt road for nearly thirty minutes. He could have stayed on the main road to make it to his destination; this added almost three-and-a-half hours. He'd scheduled a boar hunt for the following day, his last in Darwin. He decided to go the back way. Dresden was gambling the blond wanted somewhere remote to knock him off.

The trip odometer read forty-seven miles. Dresden picked up his speed incrementally, not wanting to lose his tail. He *did* need to get out ahead though. The Land Cruiser started to buck from side to side. As the road narrowed, the twists and turns came more regularly. The sides of the road curved up into a two-foot embankment, ragged and unmaintained. They were way out now. No houses, no people—alone in the vast wilderness of the outback. A road to nowhere.

Dresden lost sight of the headlights of the blond's vehicle. There were no turns or turn-offs for the next thirty-five miles. He picked up the speed again and kept his eyes on the road. Large potholes and washouts jostled his vehicle around. The jeep tilted sideways, threatening to tip. Dresden glanced quickly at his odometer—fifty-six miles. Two more to go. He glanced at the rearview. A glow in the distance. The blonde, nearly a mile away now. He needed a full mile between them, maybe a smidge more.

At 57.4 miles, Dresden punched it for another thirty seconds. Then he cut all his lights except for one tiny, wide-angle flood below his bumper. The light cast a dim, broad beam about ten feet in front of his grill. Dresden took a sharp left, then a hard right, coming around a full 180 degrees. He cut the last light. The grill of the truck was hidden behind a thick scrub bush. He got out and moved smartly—tossing a canvas over the windshield, he placed a big, high-intensity flashlight on the driver's seat and stepped ten feet to the side, his vehicle leaving the driver-side door open.

In one hand, Dresden held the little black box, the key fob with the two buttons. In the other was a pressure switch, tethered to the truck by a long electrical cord. Dresden looked back in the direction he'd come. Lights bounced along, flickering shadows dancing around in the sky, almost supernatural. The blond was less than five hundred yards away. He was moving fast, playing catch up. Three hundred. Now one hundred. His lights came into clear view. Fifty yards away. The blond didn't have the big set of LEDs. He was driving in a small cocoon of light. Twenty-five yards. Dresden stood in the path of the blond and depressed the button attached to his truck. Instantly, the LEDs mounted atop his truck shined at max intensity. He could see the man squint and raise an arm over his eyes. Dresden mashed the blue button on the black box. The lights on the blond's vehicle went out, and then Dresden pressed the red button. The accelerator pedal in the man's car went to the floor. He was blind, disoriented, and in a runaway car.

"Hold on or jump out—your choice buddy," Dresden whispered to himself.

The man's vehicle went screaming by Dresden, the left tire hitting a bolder and launching the car sideways into the river, hidden behind the blinding lights. Before Dresden could get his flashlight turned on, he heard the deep guttural grunts of prehistoric animals. Crocodiles! Dresden finally shined the light on the river, where dozens upon dozens of yellow-green, glowing orbs sparkled back at him. The effervescent bobbles descended on the blond's slowly sinking car. Dresden climbed onto the roof of his Land Cruiser and watched as the vehicle gasped for air through an open window. The big man scrambled out onto the side, his last vestige of safety slowly fading. He leaped from the vehicle, trying to clear the mass of crocodiles. As he plunged into the water, one of the beasts bit down on an exposed leg. A short-lived gurgle of agony shot from the water.

From the mayhem, a hand gripping a large knife rose out of the water. It stabbed the water several times before it went under for good. Dresden stared, waiting, a twisted perversion beginning to build in his gut. Vengeance and satisfaction. A mocking smile crept onto his face.

"I got him, Lance," Dresden whispered to himself.

But the moment of triumph was cut short. Several crocodiles were working their way toward Dresden, lumbering along, mouths agape, hissing. He shut off his light, swung himself into his truck, and pulled away as one of the massive crocs started to paw at the back of his truck. He shot sand at the creatures before his tires got traction. In his side-view mirror, the beast's eyes took on a satanic gleam, illuminated by the red and yellow lights of his truck. He waved at the animals and screamed out his window, cheering them on.

"Good work boys!"

Thirty-Two

Longwood Gardens, Pennsylvania

Outside the Conservatory, a chilly breeze whipped Dresden's jacket sideways. A large man trailing two teenage girls smiled broadly and held the heavy door for him. A coat of humidity enveloped him as he moved through the second set of doors. The ornate glass ceiling fifty feet above cast a misty light down on the large room. Dresden peeled his jacket off and slung it over his arm then stepped forward only to step back again as a gaggle of elementary school children bounced by holding hands. A woman followed close behind, explaining the different varieties of plants that surrounded them. She might as well have been talking to herself.

The building was a maze of walkways, stairs, alcoves, cubbies, and patios, all surrounded by lush plants from around the world. Rooms off the main hall displayed special exhibits: roses, orchids, desert plants. Dresden made his way to a green house near the rear of the building. The word *Bonsai was* stenciled on a small plaque near the door. He slipped inside as quietly as possible. A slight man in his late sixties stood at the back of the room, with a dozen or so college-aged men and women sitting in folding chairs before him. A young man, tall and lanky with a wave of black hair, sat on a stool beside the older man. Casper. The young man looked at his mentor, Dr. Takashi Osuna, with obvious reverence. Dresden recognized Osuna immediately.

Since the age of nine, Casper had followed the man's career like a rock band groupie. Dresden's ex-wife had finagled a meeting between the two when Casper was twelve. His career path was set from that moment on. When the young man looked in Dresden's direction, he squawked, covered his mouth, then looked back and forth between Osuna and the class, then pointed at Dresden. Osuna shooed Casper away and happily reprimanded the class for laughing at his assistant. Casper walked quickly toward Dresden. When he was clear of the students, he ran. Dresden braced himself. Unabashed, his son jumped on him and buried his face in Dresden's shoulder.

"Dad … you're alive!"

"Yes, buddy, I am. I'm fine. I heard you've been worried about me."

Casper lifted his face and surveyed Dresden's, his eyes damp. He wiped at them with the back of his hand. "Dad, I can't leave Dr. Osuna right now. Will you stay? We can go get some lunch together?"

"Yes, of course."

Dresden sat at the back of the class. Dr. Osuna was an engaging man. He wove story and Japanese folklore with fact and science. A PhD in biology by the age of sixteen, Osuna had left Japan to pursue his two other loves, botany and entomology. Casper had followed the same path. He'd missed beating his mentor, though. Casper hadn't completed his first PhD until eighteen.

Dr. Osuna spoke to the many uses of plants for health and wellness. When Dresden sat down, the good doctor was elaborating on the darker uses of roots and berries. The students were feverishly taking notes as Osuna discussed the effects on the human body and mind when one ingested *Atropa Belladonna*. Dresden found he loved the old man, maybe as much as Casper did.

Thirty minutes later, the three men were walking across a bridge that led from the Conservatory to the café. They found a table out of the way. The conversation flowed easily. Dresden sat quiet and let the two men talk. He was happy to have a break from the task at hand, and Casper looked happy too. Dresden had missed his son's infectious smile and corny jokes. Regrettably, Osuna turned his attention on him.

"How are you liking retirement, Marcus?"

"Fine."

"Why don't I see you more often—if, in fact, you are retired?" Osuna said, narrowing his eyes and allowing his mouth to curve in a mischievous smile.

Osuna, you old fox. Not this time. "Well, I never said I was retired from life. I still have to pay the bills, you know."

Osuna gave a look that said, *You're full of shit, Dresden.* "Ah, then what keeps you busy these days?"

"Dad! Uh ... didn't you want to get some rest? I can give you my keys. You can go to the house and I'll see you when I get home."

Osuna looked at Casper. The boy blushed and looked down at his food.

"Sounds like a great idea, buddy," Dresden said. He stood and looked at Osuna.

"I just flew in from out of country, and man my arms are really, really tired." Dresden flapped his arms like a chicken.

Osuna hesitated, then belched out a hearty laugh along with several slaps to his knee.

Interstate 70, Maryland

The brilliant green of summer was now muted and dull under the gray autumn sky. Dresden drove through the rolling hills pocked with barns and silos, lost in thought. He'd stayed one night with Casper, but promised to visit again soon. He hoped he could keep his promise. The exhilaration of Darwin had faded. He knew the men that were after him would likely find someone else to do the dirty work. This wasn't over. His phone rang and broke his rambling thoughts.

"How's Casper doing?" Robbie said.

"Good. Better now. You were right, it was the right thing to do. I think it was good for me too."

"Good to hear. You ready to get back in the fray?"

"Yeah."

"Great, cause when you get here, we have some work to do. We—*you* have a videoconference with Roker. Tomorrow morning. 5:30 a.m."

"What? How?"

"Red and Maria have been monitoring your old email. The guy has been trying to contact you for about the last four days. I mean manic, crazy stuff. Ten, fifteen times a day. So, start thinking up a plan. Orville's got some ideas, but I'm sure you know this guy best, So …"

Dresden stared out the window. Orville was right—he'd hung onto being loyal, blinding him. He would need to think more openly, just let Roker talk and listen, really listen. One more bruising, punishing bout with the man. *You better come clean, Tom.*

"Okay, thanks. I'll start stewing on it. Anything else?"

"Nope." Everyone's glad you made it out of Darwin.

"Great. See you soon." Dresden hung up.

A smattering of wet snowflakes fell on his window. The sky was smudged with light blotches of blue popping out from behind gray clouds. More damp snow fell, thicker, faster, and heavier. Slick patches dotted the freeway. An eighteen-wheeler swerved in front of him. He stepped on the gas and sped past the rig. He needed to get back to Mount Cinder. *Victories rarely have long legs,* Dresden thought.

Mount Cinder, Maryland

Dresden walked into the room in the basement and Orville turned down the volume on the TV. Dresden glanced up at the screen, a stream of edgy video clips playing on a loop on MSNBC. Several people dressed in black stood in front of an expensive SUV, a sparkling white Range Rover. They threw water balloons at the security men and the vehicle. The SUV dripped with red paint.

Still facing the screen, Orville said, "I predict two outcomes. Roker ups his game and we see more attacks of greater complexity, or he shuts down his efforts altogether."

"That's assuming, of course, that Roker is behind all this," Red said.

"Precisely, Doctor Watson!" Robbie said.

Red flicked the corner of a newspaper. "Listen to this." He looked up at Dresden. "*First Watch Is Not a Standing Army*, is the title of this article. Uh … Malcom Thurman wrote this. He writes, *It is ignorance that guides so many of our decisions today. Ignorance and overreaction. Let's take, for instance, the current debate surrounding Senator Markum's push toward deconstructing what he perceives to be a rampant rise in militarism in this country. Although there may be some truth to this claim, it is a weak and short-sighted view. The facts state otherwise. Criminals have become more sophisticated over the past two or three decades. The weaponry they possess and the tactics they employ are on par, in some cases, with well-organized militaries. This is not true of every criminal. However, police departments have had or have been forced to arm and train themselves equally as well. This rise in para-military police forces, that most in this county had only seen on TV until the last twenty years, is a direct result of the criminal element they must contend with to keep our citizenry safe.*

The insidious misinformation campaign Mr. Markum and his supporters have worked to spread has the general public believing two farcical fabrications. The first, that First Watch is directly responsible for the rise in our police departments arming themselves such as they have. The second and even more confounding straight-out lie is that First Watch is a standing private army held back by a thin leash tethered directly to Washington, D.C. Mr. Thurman goes on. But you get the point."

Orville looked at the ground and supported himself on the back of a chair. "It appears that we have a clear path ahead of us." He looked over at Dresden.

Robbie followed Orville's eyes, not realizing Dresden had come into the room. The same for Maria, who jumped out of her seat and moved to hug him.

"Marcus has identified the killer," Orville continued, "who we can safely assume got his direction from someone at First Watch. The prime candidate is Roker. With this kind of pressure"—Orville pointed at Red's newspaper—"a man might do something beyond his character. Well beyond."

"That, and factor in what Robbie found out about the events in the PI," Red said. He turned and looked at Robbie. "I think we're safe to assume Roker's wrapped up in this pretty deep."

Dresden looked at Robbie as he sat down. Maria slid into a chair next to him.

"I looked into the death of the Philippine site manager like you asked. The cause of death was a rare stomach virus including massive internal bleeding. The doctors who attempted to save him had never seen the virus before. CDC got involved. They'd never seen it before either. In fact, as I dug deeper, it wasn't a virus at all. But, here's the tough part. All three of the other attacks we are aware of, the intended target was the principal. Yes, I know what you are going to say ... what I'm referring to is the larger plan. In each case, no real effort was made to ensure the principal and those around him weren't hurt. The principal was in the vicinity of the attack. But in the case of the PI, there was no diversion, unless you call a killer that looks like a virus a diversion. So, the question is why? Because ... you're not going to like this, but let me finish—Roker and DeSoto are friends."

"There's another piece to this that makes for great television," Red said, and nodded to Maria.

Maria pushed her chair away from Dresden. She stretched and stalled, took a deep breath, then looked over at Red, who nodded.

"The emails. I was able to follow several of the threads, and they lead back to Roker. Like they originated with him."

"Okay," Dresden said as a spliff of uneasiness ping-ponged around his body, making him twitch. *Dammit, Roker!*

"And the financials—Red's contact, Derek and I have been working them over and we have found some unusual activity." Maria stopped. She looked at the clock on the wall, then back to Dresden. "We have a call with him in about an hour. Derek will be able to explain it better."

The news didn't hit as hard as he might have imagined. Roker was *dirty*. Okay, so Dresden would have to accept that. No. No! This wasn't just taking out the trash, kicking it to the curb. This was a friend, a teammate. But he *was* going to have to let it play out. No time for biases. There was a man behind the curtain, and until something better came along, it would have to be Roker. He would play along despite his doubts. It just didn't feel right.

"I'm going to check in on Jennifer," Dresden said without responding to Maria. He looked at her blankly then got up and left the room. The developments were too much. He needed to think.

Dresden knocked but heard nothing. The room was nearly pitch-black. He turned on a dim light and moved to Jennifer's bedside. The swelling in her face had gone down. The bruises had turned from black to a yellowish brown. Despite her coloring, she looked more herself.

On her bedside table, Dresden found a tablet of paper. A mangle of chicken scratch covered the first sheet and the two after that. He could make out clumps of words and sentences. *Darwin. Dresden going to Darwin. Found rod to use as lock pick. Floors creak. Can't get deadbolt to open. Cold. Markum making things more difficult. Wrapped in wool blank. The fuckers finally left me a sweater.* There was more, but he couldn't figure any of it out. He tore the sheets off the pad and watched Jennifer as she turned away from him.

The rain fell hard on the roof of the Lodge, overflowing the gutters and rutting out the front yard. Inside the house, the torrent sounded no worse than a summer drizzle. Dresden grabbed some juice from the fridge and made his way back down to the basement. The call with Derek had started. Robbie leaned back in his chair, his fingers clasped behind his head, eyes closed. Red hunched over the speakerphone at the center of the table and whistled low through his pursed lips. Like a guard, Orville watched from afar. Dresden took a seat at the table next to Maria.

"I did the forensics. I did it three times. That's what I came up with."

"You're sure?" Red said. He started another round of whistling.

"Positive. With what I have, it's pretty basic. I'd have to dig deeper, to you know, to get more. To tie it all together."

"So, you are sure the accounts are Russian," Red said, turning to look at Dresden. "You're sure there's a way to connect them to our POI … I'm not saying I want to. I just want to know if you *think* there's a connection." He leaned back and scratched his chin. His face pinched.

"Yes."

"And you're sure these are off-shore accounts, or…"

"Yes. Covered accounts."

"Dammit!"

"Want me to work through it?"

Everyone was quiet and looked from one to another.

Orville looked to Dresden. "Derek, hold on a second, okay?" He hit the mute button. "We know him, can vouch for him. He's good. No trace. It's your call though."

Dresden nodded.

"Derek, we appreciate your work to this point," Orville said. "It has given us something to think about. My ultimate concern now is exposure. This issue continues to evolve and has become quite complex. If you can give us a level of assurance that you will not expose yourself nor us, I would like you to go as far as possible."

"I can do that."

"Okay. Then please proceed."

Dresden spun a pen between his fingers. Site managers. Roker emails. Russian finances. Why would Roker kill site managers? What could they have possibly done? And the goddammed Russians. *Why are you mixed up with the Russians, Tom?*

The man who sat before Dresden was not the man he knew. Not even the man he'd known two months prior. He was gaunt, his cheeks hollowed, eyes empty vessels. He sat hunched as if willing the table to hold him upright. His voice hissed and cracked. A raspy cough indiscriminately injected itself as Roker spoke.

"Tom ... again, for the last time, I am not going to help you."

"Why not, Marcus?"

"Because you have committed murder. You've kidnapped Jennifer Nolan. And who knows what—"

Dresden and his team agreed the less Roker knew about what they knew, the better. Nothing about the white hat of First Watch or Russia or the PI.

"I have"—he coughed—"done no such thing. I—if you would just help me get this ..."

"Stop with that, Tom. That's a pipe dream."

"It's not. If ... I could just get some help to ... we—we could end this. We could end this witch hunt. I'm ... sure of it." His speech was punctuated by more and more coughs.

"Tom, you kidnapped Jennifer. You did—"

Roker raised a tissue to his nose as a trickle of blood ran from one nostril. Dresden's skin crawled. The plan was for him to play hardball with Roker. Total hardball, get him to crack. To spill. It was going against every instinct Dresden had about the man. He couldn't put together the sick, desperate figure on the screen in front of him and the idea that he was responsible for all that had happened. Lance. Jennifer. Gallagher. Everything.

"You killed her."

Roker sat back. He pushed the heels of his hands into his eyes. A loud groan crackled out of the speakers. When Roker squared off with the camera again, his eyes burned. He sat up straight and leaned into the camera as if trying to look into the room.

"Marcus ... and whoever else is listening," Roker boomed into the mic. "I didn't have anything to do with the fucking attacks overseas or here in ... in Arizona! You hear me? I didn't kidnap or kill my assistant Jennifer! Did you hear that?" Roker put his hands on the camera and leaned in closer. "I didn't do any of those things. You fucking got me? Marcus, you miserable son-of-a ..." The menacing façade broke ever so slightly. He diverted his eyes toward the floor. "Marcus ... they are coming. They are after me. You and the others were supposed to be the cavalry. But no more!" Roker looked up into the camera again and shouted, "I will defend the wall until someone worthy, someone who can—" The line went dead.

Dresden wiped his hands on the table. No one spoke. Robbie made to, but stopped. Maria moved to her computer and started working again. Dresden stood and walked around the room slowly. Roker was sick. Was that what stress could do to you? The man had lost thirty pounds, at least. Why would he do this? Kill his own men? Why?

Because he was sick. What if we got him some help? Dresden stopped pacing and looked from Orville to Red. They had the answers, but were waiting on him, waiting on Dresden to work it out on his own. Roker was sick. He'd kidnapped Jennifer to cover up whatever he was doing. Did she actually know anything? They had to get to Roker, get him some help.

Red's phone rang. Everyone jumped.

"Hi Fred," Red said as he walked out of the room.

"I think we need to get to Roker," Dresden said to Orville as he watched the other man leave.

"It seems like the obvious choice," Orville said.

"Especially considering his lieutenants," Robbie added.

The two men turned to look at Robbie, confused.

"I'm with you, Orville. I think Roker is behind this. Call it detective instinct, but I looked into First Watch's leadership, did some digging. I looked at the guys who would benefit the most from Roker being out of the picture. They all seem to pan out. You know, ex-military, cop, something like that. Like your buddy Branch," Robbie said, glancing at Dresden. "He seems pretty legit. British SBS, six years. Worked in security in Canada for a spell. Nuclear plants. Impressive resume. Went to Oxford, knows three languages, that kind of thing. They're all like that. So, although they may benefit from Roker losing his gourd and the Board pushing him out, they don't seem the type. We have to have better access to all of them to be sure. But that's some basic facts and my gut talking."

"Branch sounds like good leadership material," Orville said, nodding toward Dresden.

"I don't like the guy," Dresden blurted out. And he didn't like being on the outside of this. Everyone else had it in for Roker. Or was he just that blind?

"Well, just cause you don't like someone doesn't necessarily mean they're wrong for the job," Robbie said.

"I haven't met anyone yet who likes him," Dresden said.

"Marcus, what he's doing is consistent with what anyone would do if handed such a bag of alley cats. He's trying to shore things and get the company back on its feet, or keep it there. And he's got the Board of Directors' blessing," Orville said.

Ignoring both men, Dresden asked, "Where in Canada did you say he worked?"

"Uh ... a couple places short-term, but mostly Montreal."

"You said he was in nuclear security?"

"Yup, and intelligence for a short time."

Red wandered back in and gave Maria an odd look. "Dresden, you got an hour to kill?" he interrupted

"Hmmm ... Sure, I guess. Why?"

"Oh, I just need a little muscle, that's all," Red said.

Thirty-Three

Mount Cinder, Maryland

The night air was crisp and refreshing. An odd job with Red was just the distraction Dresden needed. The two old men were the unofficial fix-it men of the area. They had a gift for wrangling in derelicts without a fight, or much of one anyway. Red had a knack for dousing a simmering pot about to boil over. They were headed for the Cinder Motel a mile north of town on Route 36.

Red pointed his truck off the blacktop and into the dirt lot of the motel. Fred was out front, waving as they drove up. Red grabbed a stout stick from behind his seat, got out, and placed it on the hood. The manager shook Red's hand and gave Dresden a nervous glance.

"They're in 310. Four of 'um," Fred said.

"They hurt you?"

"Nope. Just got kinda wild when I tol'um there wasn't no hookers in Cinder."

"Why'd you do that?"

"Cause they said they was looking for a woman. They don't speak so good. Foreign, I think," Fred said, sticking a finger in his mouth to pick at his teeth.

"Armed?"

"Nah, don't look like it. Not the type."

Red looked at Dresden and nodded. They walked to 310. Both men stood off to the side of the door while Red knocked softly. A chatter burst from behind the door. Dresden recognized it as Italian. The door swung open as someone said, "Pronto?"

The man in the doorway was tall and lean, almost Dresden's height but more of a runner's build. Blond hair and light blue eyes. His complexion was fair and ruddy around his cheeks. He looked to Red first, then Dresden. As his eyes met Dresden's, he popped off a few excited words of Italian, and the rest of the men in the room rushed the door to see. A round of "Mamma Mia" flew out of their mouths as the men gawked at Dresden.

"Mr. Dresden, my name is Primo," the man said as he offered his hand.

Dresden and Maria sat next to each other on a small sofa. The steam from their ciders intermingled as they watched fat flakes of snow drift in and out of the rays of the floodlights outside. A blanket of white fleece covered the yard. Laughter drifted out of the kitchen. Maria smiled over her cup, warm as the ceramic in his hands.

Laughter boomed down the hallway toward them again. Despite Maria, Dresden's stomach roiled and tightened. Four more bodies to add to his list of liabilities. He had to get rid of them as soon as he could. Maria reached out and touched his arm. Caught up in his thoughts, he didn't look at her right away. He walked through scenarios of how to get rid of them. When he managed to see Maria and not impending doom, his stomach settled a little.

Stay on task. Montreal in the morning. Test the waters, see if these guys are really serious. Was Darwin a fluke? He needed to find out, close the loop on the idea. If they get on him in Canada, then he would know. He'd be sure. Branch seemed like a good enough reason to go. The man was next in line to take over First Watch, and a little background check couldn't hurt. Orville wasn't convinced the ploy would was worth it. After Darwin, the man was sure they'd be on him if he came up for air. They wouldn't let him slip by a second time, and that could spell real danger.

Red called for Dresden from the kitchen. He looked at Maria, the warm smile fading some. Maria tucked her feet up under her and moved closer to him.

"So? Who are they really?" Dresden nodded his head toward the kitchen. "Boyfriends?"

Maria turned to look at Dresden. "Jealous?"

"Not really. Maybe a little."

"Good. Let's keep it that way." Maria looked back out the window.

"Fine. But what's their story?"

"Incursori. Valerio picked them. My father sent them."

"Okay. But why?"

Maria slid back and looked at the ceiling. "My family is very tight. Very close. My father worries about me. He has someone watching me all the time. No, not watching me … but …"

"Watching *out* for you?"

"Yes."

"Why?"

Maria shrugged her shoulders. "Hmm … because I'm a Fiondella."

"And I'm supposed to know what that means?"

"No. Not yet. But you will. When the time is right."

Dresden paused, then said, "would it make you feel better if I had a swim buddy?"

Maria gave a conspiring grin. "Swim buddy?"

Dresden laughed and explained, pulling Maria off the sofa.

"Yes, a swim buddy would be great!" Maria said.

"Okay. What's this?" has asked as she handed him an envelope.

"Inside," Maria said, tapping the envelope with her finger, "is every text message I sent and received with your mystery man. I think you need to be very careful with this, Marcus. He is dangerous. I don't know how I know, but he is. Plus, if he's connected to all this, and I'm fairly certain he is, you should be very cautious."

He drew her into him and hugged her. "Okay. I will, and thank you."

They made their way into the kitchen, as Maria snagged Dresden's hand from the back. Dresden closed his fingers around hers. The four Italians, their backs to the pair as they came out of the darkness, turned in unison, their faces blank. The man in front, Primo, shifted his gaze from Dresden to Maria then back, then cracked a smile. Dresden studied the men. Two of them were squat, with deep olive skin and black tousled hair. The last was a couple inches shorter than Dresden, with dark eyes, a long nose, and slicked-back hair.

"So, I thought you couldn't speak English."

"I do and Segundo does. Trece and Quatro a little less. It is a cover for us. Play dumb. You know?"

Dresden looked around the room. Eight pairs of eyes looked back at him. A squad. He put his hand on Primo's shoulder and said, "How would you like to go to Montreal?"

Jennifer woke screaming and banging the walls at 3:30 in the morning. Red tried to calm her, but eventually asked Maria to help. Dresden looked on as she rubbed a salve on Jennifer's bruised palms, while the woman babbled incoherently about her escape. About using the makeshift lock pick and crawling up the stairs to the first floor of the old farmhouse.

She didn't know why her legs wouldn't work. In her memory, her legs were fine, and then they weren't. Her ribs hurt. Her face hurt. But why? She couldn't remember. She did remember finding a man's jacket with money in it. A shed with dead people stuffed in it. An old man and two girls. She remembered stumbling into the woods, running.

Jennifer tugged at her hair, clearly trying to remember more. A tear trickled down her face as she apologized to Maria over and over. She confessed she didn't want to remember. Just wanted to push it all from her mind, all of it. But she knew she needed to tell them. She knew it was important. Maria assured her it would come in time, and changed the subject to soothe her. Jennifer succumb to her exhaustion and fell asleep.

Dresden and Maria continued watching her from a sofa. Maria lay her head in his lap and fell asleep.

Then Dresden dozed with no visions, just darkness. Peaceful darkness.

Montreal, Canada

For most of the flight, Dresden caught Primo up on the story to date, from meeting Lance at the reunion to feeding the guy to the crocs in Darwin. Primo took it all in. The man's youthful, boyish face belied his intellect. He asked Dresden questions he couldn't readily answer, all relevant and necessary, yet still unanswerable.

"So, you don't think Roker had anything to do with it."

"No, I'm not convinced it's Roker. I'm not convinced he's at the head of this. It just makes no sense to me. I have a buddy up here. I'm pretty sure he knew him. Branch, I mean. If we can get some inside info on him and check him off our list, well then there's one less person to worry about. Plus, if he's not the schmuck I think he is, maybe we can go to him and he can help to straighten this out."

"Okay, but why don't you just help your friend, Roker?"

There it was, the billion-dollar question. Dresden had been dancing around it ever since he got himself run off the road. What if he'd just joined

Roker? Would things have gone so haywire? Could he have just walked away if things went bad, or could he have changed things from the inside? Maybe stopped all this madness? He looked at Primo and knew he owed the man an answer.

"You know what I think, Marcus?" the man continued before he could respond: I think you are a good friend. But you have your limits. We all do. In life as in war, we must use our head and our heart to make the right decision. Not one or the other, but both. Your friend Roker may have gotten himself into something bad. You tried to warn him in your own way, but he did not listen. That is what I think."

"Hmm."

"But now what? Are you going to help your friend? You think he is *not* involved, and if he is sick, then don't you think you should try to help him?

"That's the question, isn't it?"

The rooftop restaurant of the Hotel Halgen, with its unobstructed view of the Notre Dame Basilica, was closed. Too early for dinner, too late for lunch. The restaurant was empty. Jericho's cousin owned the high-end bistro and had set up the meeting. They sat at a small table near the window that basked in the gray light of the late fall day.

Dresden and Jericho hadn't seen each other in over ten years. They spent the first hour catching up over coffee. Primo sat quietly and listened. Jericho was thick around the neck, a man who looked like he'd be more comfortable in a cage match than running the city's police force. Jericho had risen through the ranks. Captain in the Canadian SOF, then superintendent of the RCMP. Then head of security for a couple nuclear plants, and finally he was nominated by the mayor to take over as chief of police. Jericho still held himself like the soldier Dresden had met in Haiti, after the fall of Aristide.

"So, I know you didn't come all this way just to shoot the shit with me, Marcus."

"No ... well yes, of course I did." Dresden smiled broadly at his friend. "But, no, I also wanted to ask you about a couple folks you might know."

"Okay."

Dresden had three names he thought Jericho might shed some light on. The first two were would-be lieutenants of whoever took over for Roker. Men who'd been to Haiti. One worked for the UN, the other for a Canadian security firm. Jericho said he had met the man who worked for the UN. A good man, easy to work with and very competent. He didn't know the other.

"And the third?" Jericho asked.

"Do you know a Branch, Sean Branch?"

Jericho's face twitched. He lowered his gaze to his coffee and spun his cup. Looking back at Dresden, the man sat up straight and said, "Yes." The word sliced the air like a shiv in a prison shower.

He walked through the little he knew of the man. Branch had worked beside him for the short time he was in nuclear security. Jericho had run into him again as a Mounty in an investigation into Russian involvement in stealing information related to nuclear materials information and Iran. Branch was an outlier in the transaction, cleared of any suspicion.

Jericho stalled and rolled his water glass on the table.

There was an unease in Jericho, as if the man was unnerved by the memory. He looked at Dresden, his lips moving, but nothing came out.

"I'm still unsure about the Russian deal. He came out clean. I mean squeaky clean. That's what bothered me. No one comes out of situations like that squeaky clean. Also, the guy's just creepy." Jericho stopped again and looked out the window. "I highly doubt he had anything to do with what you have described. I don't think he's that sophisticated. He's smart and a little conniving, but not a leader, not a planner. Not when I knew him anyway. I have little hope for First Watch if he is put in charge."

Dresden dropped the subject and listened to Jericho and Primo talk. Russia again. Another less-than-stellar report on Branch. Roker had hired him. Could Roker and ... Dresden stopped. Was he on the right track, or was he fixated on Branch because the man seemed like a weasel? Maybe Orville was right—maybe he was losing sight of the big picture.

Primo grabbed Dresden's arm as a horn sounded. A taxi flew past him, inches from his toes. Rue de Bleury was coming alive. He needed to get out of his head and pay attention. Another taxi made its way through the intersection, headed down Saint Jacques as Dresden jumped onto the curb. He unzipped his light running jacket and tied it around his waist before looking up the street.

The same taxi had pulled to the curb twenty yards away. Its fare jumped out. A tall blond man with broad shoulders and square jaw. Dresden's skin pricked, nerves fired, sprinting toward his heart. He grabbed Primo's arm. The blond turned and walked to the doors of The Collection Café. What the fuck? It wasn't possible.

Dresden collected himself, then moved to the glass doors of the café. He spotted the man climbing a wide set of stairs before disappearing at the top. Dresden looked at Primo then moved through the heavy doors himself. Sprinting up the stairs, he managed a glimpse of the blond as he walked into a glass-walled conference room. Dresden walked up to the coffee bar and asked the attendant if they had any meeting rooms to rent. They did. He said he'd forgotten the room number for his meeting with his friend. The attendant cocked his head—they had *one* room, and it was occupied. Dammit.

Primo nodded. Dresden pointed at his phone, then started to chat up the barista. Primo used the pillars, tables, and coffee bar to cover his movement. With his phone, he snapped as many pictures as possible. The barista craned his neck to get a look at Primo.

"He's Spanish. Loves architecture," Dresden said, smiling broadly and waving his hand around the room. "It's beautiful in here."

The barista wrinkled his face and walked off.

Outside on the curb, Dresden and Primo jumped into a cab. Jericho's phone rang in Dresden's ear. There was no answer. Primo worked to send the photos to Red. Dresden hung up after leaving a message, then looked over at the Italian.

"I think we are going to make a great team," Dresden said. His phone rang in his pocket. It was Red. "Perfect timing. You won't believe what just happened."

"What's that?"

"I saw a fucking ghost, but this time I got a picture."

"Uh, okay.

"The picture's headed your way now."

"Okay. Hey Marcus, we have another problem. Apparently, Roker now believes that Senator Markum is behind this whole thing."

"What?"

"Yeah, and it gets better. He's alleging that Markum is behind the group that is harassing his security details. Maybe behind all of it—killing the site managers, the whole thing. Supposedly he had enough proof that the FBI has opened an investigation into Markum."

"No shit, huh?"

"Yup."

Maybe Roker had something on the director of the FBI.

"Orville thinks you two should head to Tennessee, try to talk with Roker again," Red said.

"I think that's a great idea," Dresden said, and hung up.

Thirty-Four

Choto Bend, Tennessee

Dresden followed Primo through a patch of woods. The man raised a fist, and then they both took a knee and listened. The din of the furnace unit hummed. Nothing else. Primo glassed the perimeter of the yard while Dresden surveyed the interior—no lights on. It was after midnight. The yard was lit up like a prison, though. Dresden fingered a small key fob in his jacket pocket. Another one of Orville's toys.

They planned for Primo to cover Dresden as he got into the house. It wasn't the smartest plan. Roker would likely shoot Dresden as an intruder. On the other hand, Dresden was sure he wouldn't just let him in the front door. Not now, not this time. Dresden needed fifteen minutes with the man, that was all. He adjusted his earpiece and tested his radio. They hadn't spotted anyone, but he knew they weren't alone.

Dresden signaled to Primo. Before he moved, Dresden checked for the key fob in his pocket again. The fob had four buttons on it this time—red, blue, yellow, and green. Dresden started across the lawn. As he stepped into the light, he pushed the red button. All the lights went out. Sensors, alarms, everything. Dresden sprinted for the back door. Out of his other pocket, he drew a tool that looked like a mini-power drill. He jammed it into the keyhole and pressed the trigger. It opened. Then the deadbolt. Dresden entered the house in one swift movement, then pushed the green button. The lights came back on. *Six seconds.*

Shadows crisscrossed the walls in deep pockets of darkness. Dresden slid his back down the wall, allowing a few seconds for his vision to adjust. His earpiece crackled as Primo whispered that he had visual on one *tango*. Dresden pressed the radio's PTT button twice.

He removed the punch-dagger from its sheath, placed it between his middle finger and ring finger, and made a fist. The knives were Orville's idea. No firearms across state lines. Maybe they could pick one up if they needed to. Dresden moved from the basement to the first floor. He waited and listened. The house creaked, as the furnace kicked on for a few minutes. No lights. Primo came over the radio again. Dresden paused as the man said, "One tango down. He's a professional. Armed with a suppressed Keltec CMR-30." *Shit, these guys came prepared.*

Dresden had been to Roker's house three or four times. Not enough to remember where all the furniture was, but enough to remember the general layout. The boss's bedroom was on the second floor, at the end of a long hallway.

A minute passed before he found the stairwell. Dresden resisted the urge to sprint to the top and get it over with. Near the landing to the second floor, he leaned down and used the blade of his knife to look around the corner at floor level. Hard to tell. Nothing to the right. A dim light to the left. Roker's room. The earpiece crackled again, as Primo whispered the code for trouble. *Crap! So close, can't turn back.* He depressed the PTT button on the handset three times to acknowledge receipt of the message, but to inform Primo that he was going on.

Hope you can hold them off.

Primo came across again in a hushed tone. "Three tangos down. More on site. Location unknown."

Dresden laughed to himself. He depressed the PTT again, then stood and moved up the stairs. The dim light from the end of the hall lit the light-colored carpet. There were four rooms down the hallway. Not a time for formality. He would bypass them all and get to Roker's room.

Dresden moved the dagger at chest level, ready to jab. In Roker's room, he flowed down one wall to the corner and crouched. He let his eyes adjust to the space. Light shone from a bathroom, and there was a large sitting area with a set of French doors that led to the bedroom. He moved around the area, checking everything. At the closet, he stopped. The door was ajar. He crouched again, and moved to the hinge side of the door. With his back to the wall, he pushed hard on the panel. It swung open fast and bounced back a little. As he was about to stand when a long arm swept out from the dark closet. A knife meant for his head lodged itself into the wall above him.

The man stalled and tugged on the knife. Dresden, still in the crouch, rose and grabbed the man's wrist and arm, spinning him into an armbar. He struck the man in the armpit with a quick jab of his fist. His attacker, stunned and disoriented, was easy to manipulate. Dresden drove the man's face into the floor. Before the guy could rise, Dresden gave him several hard kicks to the ribs and a knee to the back of his neck. The man slumped to the floor. He was a big guy. The assassin tried to get up again but failed—tough, too.

Dresden swept through the bedroom. Roker was nowhere to be seen. He came back into the sitting room. Primo fired off in his ear. Multiple tangos approaching.

Dammit! Dresden looked to the closet. The man was getting to his feet. He gave him a kick to the face and moved swiftly to the hallway door, where he held up in the doorway for a moment. Window?

Or back through the house? *Whatever you do, get out of the fatal funnel now!*

Too late. A searing pain shot through Dresden's left side. He spun, reaching for the origin of the pain. A throwing knife protruded from his back. Dresden tried focusing on the man stumbling toward him, but froze. The light from the bathroom lit the man up. The jaw, the white-blond hair. The man fell to his knees. Visions flew like sparks in Dresden's brain. The driver of the truck. The man on the hill at the crash. Montreal! The bathroom. *The bathroom? What the hell? Snap out of it, man! Now!*

The blond raised his arms in a boxer stance. As he moved closer, Dresden saw the knives in each hand. He tightened his grip on the punch-dagger. *His ribs. Go for the ribs.* He lifted his knees as he walked. Hands up in surrender. "Muy Thai," the blond growled, blood spittle dripping out between sharp, crooked teeth. The big man lunged, but Dresden side-stepped him an inch and slapped down hard on the back of the guy's neck as he passed. The man fell onto Dresden's rising knee. A gust of wind and the distinctive crack of bone accompanied the move. Dresden jabbed the punch-dagger into the man's back several times. He fell in a heap on the floor.

No waiting. Go now!

He moved into the hallway as Primo fired another volley into his ear. Men were coming in the front of the house. Dresden turned and looked back at the blond. He was spitting out Russian, or something close to it. Dresden ran down the stairs and out of the house, then hit the red button on his key fob again.

Primo shinned a dim blue light from the wood line. Dresden stumbled into the trees and went to his knees, breathing heavily. The pain drifting up and down his side. He looked down at the man on the ground. Dresden's head swirled again, more violently now. He stared, his mouth agape, and rocked side to side. The man at his feet, the blond. Square jaw. Blue eyes. *I must be losing my fucking mind.*

Primo, now aware Dresden was in distress, lifted him and moved him through the forest. Dresden looked back at the dead man. Then the house. Then the blond there at his feet. It wasn't possible. The guy worked for Roker. *That means* ... Primo was talking, telling him to hurry and move. Right! Gotta move. Gotta get out of here. Dresden glanced back one last time at the house. A man, bent over, staggered out of the basement door, his white hair shining in the bright lights of the backyard.

Tennessee River, Tennessee

Primo aimed the small boat to the northern tip of Park Bend, away from Roker's house, tying off the handle to keep it on course. The small engine puttered. No one was following.

Dresden lay on his side, arched over one of boat benches and breathing quickly. Primo put the web of his hand around the knife handle and pressed hard against Dresden's back. He pulled the knife out and threw it overboard. Dresden stripped as quickly as he could. Primo prepped an ace bandage and gauze he retrieved from his cargo pocket. As soon as Dresden was down to nothing, Primo stuffed the gauze into the wound to stop the bleeding. He wrapped Dresden's torso with the elastic bandage. Dresden dressed again and lay down in the boat. The men didn't say a word. Primo glanced back several times as he guided the boat across the river, but still, no one followed.

They left the boat and trailer at the front gate of the rental facility. Primo had wiped it down and Dresden had taped a hundred-dollar bill to the outboard. When they were an hour south of Knoxville, they found a motel. Primo sanitized and stitched Dresden's wound. He was lucky—the knife had cut into the thick, meaty muscle that ran from his armpit to his waist. No real damage, just a lot of blood. His heavy canvas jacket had suffered the worst of it.

Dresden showered and dressed in fresh clothes. Sitting on the bed, he fingered the hole in his jacket before he put it on. His phone buzzed.

TR in hospital. Coma. Need to verify. O, was all the text said.

TR? Tom! "Crap. You got to be kidding me!" Dresden said aloud.

Knoxville, Tennessee

A cluster of news vans littered the parking lot of the UT Medical Center. Thomas Roker in a coma was bound to be news. Dresden and Primo sat in their car, looking for familiar faces wandering around the hospital. Orville wanted them to verify it was Roker, not another game piece. Dresden considered asking Primo to go in but decided against it.

Dresden had a hunch pecking away at him. It was something Casper had said about plant and insect venom, and how the PI site manager went down. The guy could have run across it on his own, but maybe it had been *given* to him. How about Roker? What if he'd been drugged? Dresden sent Casper a text and waited. His son replied ten minutes later.

After reading the text, Dresden said, "I'm going in—gotta get something for my son."

Primo scrunched his face. "Uh, okay. What can I do?"

"Keep the car warm and make sure we can leave," Dresden said as he got out. "And fast," he added, looking through the window.

Twenty minutes later, Dresden hurried out of the ER. Primo brought the car up and Dresden moved to the driver's side. He handed a small bundle of towels to Primo and told him to drive away, fast. Once the man was gone, he sent him a text—*Meet me in front of the greyhound bus station in two hours and get a new car. Oh, and make sure you shake that towel and don't stop.*

From the shadow of a tree, Dresden watched the sliding doors of the ER. Two men came scampering out—one holding his head, the other his stomach. He'd pushed both of the men down a stairwell, but apparently not hard enough to kill them. Before they could spot him, he moved out of view into the darkness of the parking lot.

The Chevy Impala rolled up to the bus station right on time. Dresden stepped out of the shadows, crossed the street, and got in. He grabbed the bundle of towels from Primo, who took quick stabbing glances at Dresden.

"You want to know. Don't you?"

"Yes. Of course."

"Roker's blood. A vial of it."

Primo's eyes grew wide with excitement. "So he *is* in a coma?"

"Most definitely. I'll explain it all later. Right now, we need to get the vial to this address." Dresden handed Primo a wrinkled piece of paper. Then he held up the bundle. "And we need to mail this to my son in Pennsylvania as soon as possible."

Thirty-Five

Mount Cinder, Maryland

The knock at the door was soft and tentative. Dresden said to come in, but nothing happened. He foisted a pair of pants on as he walked to the door. Maria looked up as he swung it open. Her face fell as she considered his naked torso. She made an attempt to touch one of his wounds, but pulled back as if she'd be shocked. He struggled to get his arms in his t-shirt, and Maria helped him. Facing her, he saw a new determination.

"You okay?" he asked.

"No. But that is not important now," she said, waving her hand as if shooing flies.

"Okay. Were you just checking on me, or did …"

"Jennifer is awake and asking for you. But Orville wants to meet in the conference room first. Somethings happened with your senator," Maria said, and moved to embrace Dresden. "We can check on Jennifer after." She pulled him into a firm hug. Then, as if suddenly aware of her boldness, she pushed him off her and walked to the hallway. Amid it all, he knew he was losing her. Their innocent banter was gone. They only related to each other through a series of disasters. She was hardened and not herself, he thought, and sighed.

"Maria. It's over, and I'm okay. I will heal, so … so don't worry. Okay?" Dresden smiled at her.

Maria looked at him, or maybe through him. "Let's go. You move like an old man."

The smell of coffee and printer cartridge ink and dry erase markers assaulted Dresden as he stepped into the room. It was warm and buzzing with activity. Orville noticed Dresden and Maria come in and waved them to sit at the conference table. The Italians were huddled off to one side, Primo's hands flying around as he spoke. Robbie and Red, deep in debate, didn't look up. Orville waved Primo and his men to sit as well. The urgency was palpable—any sense of relief Dresden had had now slipped away.

"I have it on good authority that Senator Markum will be brought in for questioning—"

"On what Roker came up with?" Dresden interrupted, anxious to get to the point.

"Yes, and what happened this afternoon," Orville said.

Dresden looked at him, confused.

Orville continued, "The Black Shirts, as they are called now, took their show into the daylight and into a public forum. To a rally for a potential presidential opponent to Markum. The Black Shirts shot water guns of red paint at the candidate's security detail. Someone in the crowd—well, several people—grabbed a few of the Black Shirts and beat them. Bad. Markum tweeted about it. Apparently unaware of the beating and brawl that ensued, he tweeted that he applauded the Black Shirts' efforts to expose First Watch."

Roker in a coma, cause unknown. Markum out of the picture for trying to influence an election. Branch destined to take over First Watch. Definitely not right as rain, but good enough.

Dresden said, "I don't see the problem?"

"The problem is, we have to assume there's still someone after *you*. What are *we* going to do about that?" Orville asked.

Orville was right. It wasn't over. Maybe if he laid low now, it would all pass. He looked around the room.

"Okay, I get that. But what if I simply walk away ..." Dresden trailed off—hearing himself, he knew that wasn't possible. For whatever reason, he was in this deep. They would hunt him down until they finished the job.

"Marcus, Roker was responsible for this. Markum sped up the timeline for sure. He hired someone to orchestrate these black shirts, which made Roker—"

"It *wasn't* Roker!" a hoarse voice blurted out. Jennifer, pale and listless, leaned on the door jam.

Maria jumped and ran to her. She guided Jennifer to a chair at the head of the table. Red filled a glass with water and put it in front of her, then sat next to her along with Maria. Jennifer looked over her glass at Dresden. Her eyes sparkled with tears. Dresden gave her a feeble smile. The woman sighed deeply, her breathing clipped and painful. She started to talk, then stopped. Maria put her hand on Jennifer's.

Jennifer took another deep breath. "Tom had nothing to do with it. Any of it! It ... it was..." her lips quivered, and her body shook.

"You don't have to—" Red started.

"Yes, I do!" Jennifer said, laboring to take a deep breath again. "Branch. It was Sean Branch!"

The room fell silent. A drip of water rang like a bell in the metal basin. Everyone sat frozen and perplexed. *Branch?* The truth Dresden already knew still hit him like a sucker punch. Roker was not the one, but Branch. The moment of levitation in the room ended with Robbie slamming his fist on the table and grunting, "yes!"

"Jennifer, my name is Orville," the old man said, leaning toward her.

"I remember you. You and Marcus picked me up in Ashville."

"Yes. Jennifer, I don't want to sound insensitive, but we are kind of under, well ... how do you—"

"Know? How do I know it was Branch? I understand. We need to catch that bastard and cut off his—" Jennifer blurted out, then blushed, looking around the room. She sat up straight as if empowered, but lost the momentum and hung her head. Her body jerked with a bout of raspy coughing.

A cloud of lead descended on the room. Heavy, oppressive, sodden with dubiety and exasperation. Red left and came back with some tea. Dresden stared at the whiteboard again. Orville wrote on a pad of paper as Maria talked softly with Jennifer.

"Would you be willing to tell us what happened? If this is too overwhelming ... too many people ... we can wait or make other accommodations," Red encouraged.

"No," Jennifer said flatly. The determination was back. "Are you going to hunt him down and ... if you, all of you, are going to get him, then I will tell it all. Everything."

Everyone nodded.

Dresden said, looking straight into Jennifer's eyes, "Yes."

Jennifer kept his gaze and began. Dresden moved uneasily in his chair as Jennifer relayed the last hours of her captivity. She'd heard one of the men say Branch's name and knew right away it was him. It was an accident, she thought. They'd been careful to use no names. They even called her only *the woman.* But it was him. Him all along, his voice—that slithering voice of his, she said. She had fallen and made a loud noise while trying to listen through the ceiling. All of Branch's men came in her room at the sound. Three of them, she thought, but wasn't sure. They took turns on her, punching and kicking her. They stripped her naked and took *turns.* She passed out, assuming she was dying. When she woke, she escaped her room, her cell, and found the old house empty. They'd left. Gone, moved out. She found a jacket with money. Some clothes. She also found the shed with the bodies. The old man, who she figured owned the house, and two girls—young girls. Jennifer slumped, and Maria supported her. She looked over at Red. He grabbed Jennifer under her arm, and with Maria's help lifted her out of the chair and walked her to the door.

"Jennifer, I have one more question. I'm sorry," Dresden said, "I know you need to rest … but can you describe the men, the men who—who attacked you?"

"Yes. I will never forget them … never. Tall. Thick. White-blond hair. Brutally square jaw. Frightening blue eyes. One had scratches down his face and another teeth like a shark. But they were all … all the same. They—they could have been one man."

"Okay. Sorry, one more question. How many of them were there?" He knew the answer, but wanted to be sure.

"There were three … maybe four. All the same—exactly the same," Jennifer said. Her eyes welled up and looked at Dresden, pleading to make the nightmare stop.

"Thank you, Jennifer. Thank you very much," Dresden said, and nodded at her.

Tears started to stream down her face. "No Marcus … all of you. I'm the one who is thankful."

Thirty-Six

Blairsville, Georgia

A tractor trailer rushed by, spraying dirty water into the motel parking lot. Branch rubbed his narrow chin as he watched the pool of muddy liquid swirl around. The lights of the motel sign came into a murky focus as the water settled. Oasis Motel. *Sure,* Branch thought, *sure.* He pulled his coat in tighter, wiped the rain off his shoulders, then knocked on the door behind him.

Fedor opened the door, a cloud of putrid-smelling air followed him. Cheap, stale cigarettes. Branch stifled a cough and strutted into the room. Andrusha sat on one bed, watching videos on a phone. He didn't look up from his device. Branch walked to a lopsided table and a single chair. The carpet squished under his feet.

The corner of the empty bed squeaked as Fedor sat down across from Branch.

"Where the hell is Mischa?" Branch said, waving his hand in the air.

"Mischa? No idea. He never returned from Australia," Fedor said. His voice was thick with anger.

"And Sasha?" Branch said, his face tightening.

Fedor mashed a cigarette out in the soggy carpet. "In the Tennessee River."

Branch straightened his back and pumped his fists. "Dresden," he said under his breath.

Fedor crossed his legs and leaned forward. He took a long drag of a new cigarette and blew a puff of smoke over Branch's head. "Yes. Dresden."

"It is not safe here anymore. We will need to leave. All of us," Branch said, waving the smoke away.

"But what about First Watch?" Fedor asked.

Branch had spent some time thinking about that. With Roker effectively out of the way, he was in charge. The Board had said as much. The Board also knew that the Senate wasn't easing up on First Watch. Markum was on the precipice of disaster. Some seemed to think he'd taken the whole thing too far, gotten caught up in his own net. Regrettably, the Senate as a whole was not backing off. They basked in the light of success as they continued to highlight the perceived illicit nature of First Watch's affairs around the world. They'd already crucified several of their own, men who were deep in Roker's pockets or vice versa.

Branch didn't need to be in the office to manage his "candidate" selection program. He could maintain his position of power within the company and keep his side work moving forward from abroad, for a while at least. Let the smaller fish fry. Let the lesser security companies answer their subpoenas. The Senate would tire of it all. The public would lose their taste for it. Some new social media event would go viral and enrapture the lemmings. Then Branch could come back. Plus, he had a bigger problem. Dresden.

The man wouldn't just let it go. But why Darwin? Montreal, Branch understood. Dresden was learning what he could about him. From what, some old police investigation? Good luck with that. But why go to Australia? No matter. Branch looked at Fedor. Whatever flippantness he'd had was gone. Whatever Dresden had done to Mishca and Sasha was perfect. Fedor and Andrusha would not let the men die in vain. Time to take Dresden out of the picture, for good.

"What about the house?" Branch asked.

"Wiped clean."

"And the guests?"

"Dead,"

"All of them?" Branch said with a tinge of surprise.

Fedor nodded and rubbed the scars on his face.

"Listen," Branch said as he rubbed his hands and looked at the water seeping out of the carpet, "Dresden doesn't know anything. And if he does, he knows very little. And that very little is probably confusing at best. He seems to have some idea that I may be of interest in all this—that, I think, is fair to say. So, we got him. We can lead him where we want him to go, and he will undoubtedly follow." Branch stopped and looked at Fedor, who was nodding his head. Branch continued, "He is one man. But apparently, I misjudged him. He *is* dangerous."

Fedor stood with a massive thrust of his arms and legs.

"But he is still *just* one man, my friend. He will tire and make mistakes. When he makes a mistake, we will be there to take advantage of it. But I don't want to do it here, in the US. I want him somewhere he will be at a disadvantage. Not somewhere too foreign, though," Branch said, standing and walking toward the door. He couldn't stay in the room any longer.

"Where then?" Fedor asked, leaning against the wall near the door.

"I always wanted to go to France," Branch said as he reached for the doorknob.

"France," Fedor said, followed by a grunt.

"But first I must find a suitable *candidate* … then we will leave. I will be in touch. Maybe two days. Be ready."

Branch slammed the door and walked to his car. A girl of about twelve looked up from her phone and smiled at him as he opened the door. He smiled back. His stare lingered on her. The girl's smiled faded and she moved into her hotel room.

Thirty-Seven

Alexandria, Virginia

Like the womb, the darkness gave Markum comfort. He could hide in the dark. Make plans there. The whir of his mind slowed in the void of light like a machine running out of gas. The heater turned on and pushed a stream of cool air across his face. He shuttered and watched the cars pass outside, flickers of headlights reflecting off the walls of his campaign office. The crunch of ice under the tires. He was alone, like always.

It's not over, Markum thought. He set down the steaming paper cup and wiped his palms on his pant legs, then got up. With a fingernail, he absently picked at the corner of the window dressing. Peeling already. Shoddy workmanship, like everything else in this town. *It's not over,* Markum professed to himself again. He pulled hard at the corner and ripped a three-foot section from the window. It hung like a dead man draped over the saddle of a horse.

A dead man. Not me.

Markum fell into a chair in the middle of the office. His feet patted the floor as he spun himself in a circle. With his back turned, the office door opened. He spun quickly to see who it was. In the dark, the figure looked like a lump of clay. The man removed his coat and dragged his shoes on the mat, not making a sound. When he raised his head, a car passed and lit him up in a ghoulish red glow. Lawson.

A desk lamp came on and Lawson's face, cast in shadows, looked down at Markum. The man stood erect and paced behind the desk. He glanced over at Markum from time to time. Words danced on Lawson's lips. Markum could see it. He could feel it. It was coming.

"They are coming for you. I hope at least you are aware of that," Lawson finally said. He took a seat behind the desk as he spoke.

Markum said nothing.

"They are coming for you, and I will be nowhere to be found when they do. You are on your own on this one, Bobby."

"I've always been alone, Jack. Always."

"No, you haven't, you dim wit. I've always had your back."

"Little good that did me, huh Jack?" Markum said, looking straight at Lawson.

The shadows twisted the man's face even more. "I should take you out back and shoot you like a rabid dog. You have dragged everyone through the mud. Me. Your campaign staff. Everyone that believed in you. Even those lunatics you hired, the Black Shirts, chasing First Watch around. You thought you'd get away with that? You're... you were running for president. And Roker? The one man besides myself that could have been an ally ... and you drove him into a coma."

Markum jumped out of his chair and made a moved toward the desk. "Is that what you think? I'm the reason Roker is in a coma?"

"Yes, you idiot. All of this is because of you. Who else would be stupid enough to do what you've done?"

"What is it you think I've done, Jack?"

"You cut up the vegetables and browned the meat and stuck them in the pressure cooker. Then, in all too common Bobby Markum style, you left it to tend to itself. Now. Now ..." Lawson said.

Markum walked to the front door and looked up the street. Then down. The icy rain had lifted. He watched a man exit a car, arms out to his side, then walk to the front door of the Italian restaurant across the street. Ice. Slippery like politics. Never know when you'll take a tumble. Not now. Not me.

"They are coming," Lawson said behind him.

"Who, Jack? Who's coming for me?"

Lawson sighed. His chair creaked. "The FBI, Bobby. They are coming to take you in. To question you about your involvement in all of this." His voice sounded distant. "you won't be able to wea sel your way..."

"So, is that what you"—Markum turned—"came to tell ... me?"

Lawson was gone.

Markum adjusted the chair in the middle of the room to face the front door. He looked down at himself, shoes scuffed and pants rumpled. He found his suit jacket and put it on before straightening his tie as he walked to the front door. The street was nearly empty. Dark and gleaming. Markum slowly scanned the street. There was no one on the sidewalk. *Lawson was full of shit—there's no one coming for me.* He pulled another strip of the window dressing off. It fell to the floor and curled like a man being kicked by a gang, fetal and afraid.

The blue and red lights flashed against the walls. Markum watched them grow, then moved to his chair, checked himself again and sat down. He folded his legs and pinched the crease of his pants. *It's not over. This is just a bump in the road. Just a bump.*

Thirty-Eight

Mount Cinder, Maryland

"Faster!"

Dresden released the magazine from the well of his Sig Sauer P226, slid another magazine in and chambered a round, then holstered his sidearm. On the sound of the timer, Dresden drew his weapon and fired three shots, each one knocking down a saucer-sized metal plate at twenty-five meters. He depressed the release button for the magazine. It slid out and fell to the ground. At the same time, Dresden removed another magazine from his belt, loaded and chambered a round, and fired three more bursts of 9-mm ammunition. All six plates down.

"Better," Orville said. "You look pretty good. But this is just the square range. After lunch, let's get you on something a little more dynamic." His voice trailed off.

"What's bothering you?" Orville said after a moment.

"I guess … I wanted it to be over."

"And now?"

"Now? It feels like we're starting from ground zero," Dresden said.

"I see," Orville said. He looked down the shooting range. "Well, maybe it will give us more time to get you back into shooting shape. Let's pack it up and head in."

The conference room felt stale and cold. Red was hunched over his keyboard, his expression drawn as he stared at the computer's blank screen. He looked up and wrinkled his face as Dresden and Orville walked in. Primo turned and dipped his chin.

"No update yet from Tennessee," Red said.

"Back to square one," Dresden replied as he slid slowly into a chair.

Red's expression wandered as if he were meandering through a fantastical museum, every new exhibit more fascinating than the last. Then his face lit up.

"Well, not exactly. We know a few things," Red said, sitting up straight.

"Such as?" Dresden said.

"For one, the doctors have no clue what caused Roker's coma."

"That's helpful?"

"Yes, it means that there may be more to this. Maybe, wait, maybe like the guy in the PI."

Dresden pulled at an earlobe. More? But what? Casper—did he get the vial?

"And the emails, they are definitely leading us down a rabbit hole. Which must mean something," Maria said as she came into the room.

"Okay," Dresden said, "but could we just be reaching?"

"Sure, but we won't know until we get into their system. *We* are sure there's more. It's a matter of finding it," Maria said, looking at Red, who nodded.

"So, what's that going to take?"

"Time. We are running a version of a PenTest," Maria said. She looked at Dresden, then elaborated. "Penetration Test—it's what we use to find vulnerabilities in systems."

He knew the emails were important. Maybe they would point a boney, accusing finger and give them direction. Point to Roker. Point to Branch. Roker and Branch? His stomach churned at the thought. Point to someone or something! Anything. The blond. The blonds! Branch's henchmen.

Robbie walked in, yawning, a steaming cup of coffee in his hand. "Boy, aren't you the somber bunch."

"Orville," Dresden said, ignoring Robbie. The old man looked up. "The blonds. We need to find out who they are. They weren't at Choto Bend to protect Roker. They were there to kill him!" Dresden stood up, an image in his mind of Roker in his house, alone, shot by his own gun. *Apparent* suicide. That was what they were there for. Only Roker beat them to it.

He needed to talk with Casper. Dresden looked at Robbie. "Help Orville find out who the blonds are. I'll be back in a little while." Then he addressed everyone: "We need to find Branch, find out as much as we can about all the emails, and find those men. Those are our most immediate tasks. Let's get to work."

Dresden stepped outside into the cold, old snow crunching under his boots. Everything of the last few months was flowing through his mind at once, not a babbling brook but a class-five rapids. He text Casper and stuck his phone in his pocket, then blew steam from his nose and watched it float away. So much had happened. Where to start? He thought of Roker trying to talk him into joining him. Branch, when he went to find Roker. He pictured the men around Branch. There was Richardson and those other guys at the church. Who else? Dresden checked his phone. No response from Casper. He called him and left a voicemail. A tree sloughed off a blanket of snow. Had he ever seen the blonds with Branch? Were they Branch's guys, or was Branch working for them? Damn! Dresden looked at his phone again. Casper. Dammit, come on! Why did he get him involved? His chest ached when he thought of something happening to his son. What if the men found the trial of the vial and traced? He'd wave off Casper, tell him to forget it, say it was a joke or something.

Two days went by in a blur as the Italians and Dresden spent the mornings working out and down on the range. In the afternoons they rolled on the Jiu Jitsu mats and did more shooting. Between sessions, Dresden checked in on the rest of the team.

The sound levels in the conference room rose and fell, waned and ebbed. Dresden sat and watched it all. He was not idle though. His mind raced. There'd been no contact from the guy with Lance's phone. Casper still hadn't written or called. Maria had broken through a wall and gotten into First Watch's exterior system. But she and Red were stumped. They hadn't slept in over twenty-four hours.

"Yes!" Maria shouted, throwing a stack of papers in her hand.

"What?" Red asked, rubbing his eyes and yawning.

"Jennifer sent an email from her office less than an hour ago."

"What the ..."

"She sent an email from her desktop in her office at First Watch."

"How's that possible? You sure it wasn't sent remotely?" Red said. The look he got from Maria was all he needed. "And she doesn't even have a device to send an email on. Hasn't wanted one."

"Give me a minute," Maria said.

The room was still, holding its breath. Dresden looked at his phone. Nothing. Robbie walked in and Orville motioned for him to be quiet. He nodded, sat down, and handed several sheets of paper to Dresden. Each sheet was topped with an official header for Interpol. Below the header was a color photograph. Eyes as menacing as Charlie Manson's stared back at him. The blonds, with their shocks of white hair.

Andrusha, Mischa, Sasha, and Fedor.

The photos must have been old. One of them was missing the three scars on his face. But Andrusha was easy to pick out with his shark-like teeth. He looked at Fedor. There was a subtle difference about him, a deeper intensity, maybe even something psychotic. Dresden read the write-up. Quadruplets. Identical. Russian. Spetsnaz. Combat vets. Specialized as drivers. Familiar with small arms and hand to hand, primarily judo. All four had been released from service under less-than-auspicious circumstances.

"Got it," Maria shouted again. "I knew it. I knew it!" She looked around the room. "Oh, sorry. When I saw Jennifer's email, it made me think about Roker's emails. So, I followed ..." She looked at Dresden and smiled. "Let's say I figured out that Roker's emails did not come from his office or his computers. They did originate, however, from the same place Jennifer's just did."

"What did Jennifer's email say?" Orville asked.

"Hmm, okay, here. She sent this to the Board of Directors—*I am overwhelmed and overcome by Roker's illness and I need to get away. I will be in Europe and will have my cell phone and laptop to handle any business.*

"Europe, huh?" Orville said.

Dresden knew the look. The old man was putting something together. Orville rubbed his thumbs on one another, then stopped. "Robbie, when you were looking for Jennifer—did you ever find anything about travel?"

Robbie shook his head. "In fact, if I remember correctly, her parents said she'd never been out of the country." He nodded his head, and then his face lit up as he swung his chair around to his computer. "Give me a second," he said, holding up a finger.

The brothers' eyes stared up at Dresden from the conference table. He shuffled the papers together and hand them to Orville, watching for the man's reaction. There was nothing as he scanned the sheets. Finally, he looked up at Dresden.

"It's a good thing there's only two left. Let's hope he was one of the first," Orville said, pointing at Fedor, "cause this one looks like the worst of them."

"Here it is," Robbie barked. He flashed a smile at Dresden and Orville, "Jennifer has never applied for a passport. She couldn't leave the country if she wanted to. Well, not to Europe anyway.

Orville's phone chirped. He flipped through emails for a moment, then handed it to Dresden. Dresden looked back at the man with his brow furrowed. Orville shoved the phone at him again. Reading, Dresden rolled his shoulders then stopped and looked up at the old man. His stone face unnerved Dresden.

"What is it, Marcus?" Robbie asked.

"It's too much is what it is," Dresden said, looking at the ground. "They found where Jennifer was held. An old man's house, a recluse of sorts. They found him dead in a shed along with two girls, like Jennifer said. The same two girls that were kidnapped during the Arizona attack. They're Tyler Baskin's kids."

"Shit," Robbie said, drawing out the word into a whistle.

Primo and his men came into the room.

"Is everything okay?" Primo asked.

"No. But we are going to do our best to make it that way," Dresden said, putting his hand on the man's shoulder.

"That we are," Orville said. "We are going to Europe."

"Europe?" Dresden said, his head swiveling toward Orville. "Why? And who's *we*?"

"That email from Jennifer was code. She doesn't speak or write like that. I know. And it doesn't matter anyway, it wasn't from her. We know that. That email does two things. Sends a coded message to someone in First Watch—maybe Branch's cronies—and it puts Jennifer right in the middle of any investigation into Roker's coma and death, if it goes that way," Orville said, staring at Dresden. "As for who? You, me, Maria, and Primo and his gang. Red needs to stay here and mind the shop and monitor Jennifer's recovery. Robbie is his backup, plus I think he should take a furlough and go home for a bit and be with his family."

Everyone nodded in agreement. Orville came back around to Dresden. *The old man never loses his touch,* Dresden thought. *So, Europe it is then.*

"Okay, Europe," Dresden said. "Where in Europe?"

"Italy of course," Red said beaming.

Orville walked into the dark sitting room and stood next to Dresden. The old man looked spry and unfazed. Dresden straightened and pulled his shoulders back trying to deny the weight that seemed to be dragging him to the bottom of a lake. Small dabs of snowflakes landed on the window.

"You know, this was the kind of thing your father was good at. Problem solving."

Dresden coughed. "Orville, you give me more credit than I deserve."

"No. I don't. You may wrestle with things inside that head of yours. But when you're done with your mental WWF, you are Johnny on the spot."

"Well it sure doesn't feel like it." Dresden rubbed his eyes. "I mean, what about Emily? What about the kids? I royally f'd that up. And Maria—I mean, we haven't even had a second date." Dresden forced a smile. "And now this. All of this. All the ups and down. We've gone backwards, not—"

"I'm not so sure about that. You're letting the big picture get in the way of the little things."

"Yeah?" Dresden shrugged. That was it, that was all he was going to get from the man?

"Yeah."

"Mister Marcus? Mister Orville? Are you here?" Quarto asked, shielding his eyes.

"Yes, Quarto, we're here."

"Oh good! Come please. Miss Maria, she found something."

The men followed a harried Quarto. Soft sobbing met his ears and Dresden pushed past Quarto jogging to the conference room. Maria jumped out of her seat and darted for him. She was stricken and shaken, and her heartbeat raced. Dresden had questions, but he kept quiet and held her.

"Uh ... Maria was—Maria, maybe you should leave," Red said. He ringed his hands together as he waited.

Quarto walked her out of the room.

Red mumbled something intelligible then said, "Maria was searching the system and came across some spaghetti code, a tangled mess of code. She found some hefty firewalls and heavily protected databases, not on the First Watch system but linked to it. She used a *hamster* to root it out." Red stopped and stepped aside. The exposed computer screen displayed a half-dozen headshots of girls. Young girls. Eleven to fourteen, Dresden guessed.

He looked at Red, his expression vacant. "I'm not sure what I'm ..."

Red's face was stern, but Dresden noticed his hand shaking as it moved the mouse. The man didn't look at the screen as he spoke. "What we saw cannot be undone. I hesitate to show you this, but I think you need to see. Maria found one of Branch's private databases."

What were at first innocent headshots became more and more graphic. More sinister. Dozens and dozens of shots of young girls in varying degrees of undress. Then completely nude and posed. Forced poses, evident by the terror in their eyes. The photos turned to sex—young bodies twisted and bound in grotesque ways. Then Branch, with them, naked and dominant. The sick bastard smiling. His hands all over them. Who would do this?

Dresden's hair stood up. His face started to burn, and a sudden urge to smash something overwhelmed him. Red put a hand on his shoulder. The photos were about to get worse, much worse, demonic even. Why would anyone keep files like this?

Young girls' lifeless bodies pierced his psyche. Photo after photo. Skin mottled, pale and blue. Dresden coughed loudly, turning away.

"There are over four thousand photos in all," Red said.

His ears started to ring. He could hear the screams and cries. Looking back, he grabbed the mouse from Red and flicked the ball. Photos spun like a slot machine, spinning and landing on sickening image after image. Again, he flicked the ball—girl after girl. His throat tightened as images of his own daughter flashed through his mind. Her smile. Her charm, so full of life. What if … Red started to speak, but Dresden held up his hand. He didn't notice Red usher everyone out of the room. He was alone with the demon himself.

Thirty-Nine

Over the Atlantic Ocean

The images flew by like apparitions; they crawled like ghouls from a dark ooze at the recesses of Dresden's mind. They battered his brain, unrelenting. Red was right—he would not be able to un-see what he'd seen. The hollow, vacuous eyes. The terror. Sheer terror. Blue, green, dark eyes that had once sparkled, dull now with fright. Skin sallow and gray. Pale and blue as the blood drained from them. Dresden wondered why Branch had killed them. A dark thought crossed his mind—*it was better than living.*

Branch was a weak man, but this, this perversion, this sickness must have made him feel strong and powerful. Dresden thought of Maria as the girl's faces continued to ravage his mind. He imagined the same images ripping at her sanity, tearing apart the goodness in her soul. He had done this to her, had allowed this evil into her life. It was his fault.

He pressed his face against the window and watched the clouds pass. Spots of blue popped through from time to time. The sky was dark up ahead, setting Dresden's mood. A can of beer fizzled on his folding table. Dresden brought it to his nose and breathed in, then asked a flight attendant to take it away. The obligatory first-class questioning began, and Dresden reassured her it was fine, he'd just changed his mind.

Desperate for a distraction, he fumbled for his throwaway phone. The screen lit up, and within a minute he found what he wanted. He reclined his seat, lay his head back, and closed his eyes as David Bowie's "Starman" squeezed its way between the blood-soaked visions. Bowie's deep melodic voice punched away at the haunting images. His highs shattered the pictures in Dresden's memory, past and present. Sleep came before Dresden knew it.

Milan, Italy

The landing gear squealed and woke Dresden. He'd slept for the remainder of the flight, the images of the girls fading with every mile. His focus had returned, narrow and on target. He was in Milan, on his own, for three days. Three days of preplanned surveillance routes with Primo and a cohort as his unseen overwatch. There would be no contact, complete radio silence. And of course, he was the bait again. The radio silence didn't include contacting

Casper, Dresden thought. He needed to talk with his son, make sure he was okay.

The hotel was a couple blocks from the storied Piazza Del Duomo. Dresden finished his sandwich as he watched the plaza below. Despite the late hour, people crowded the square in front of the massive, spired cathedral. They walked arm in arm or sat on steps and benches or in the cafés that lined the piazza. There was no point in trying to sleep. He grabbed his jacket and made for the plaza.

Dresden found a bench, sat down, and people-watched for thirty minutes. A favorite pastime. A chilly breeze blew past his neck, forcing him to pull his scarf up. Two men leaning against a motorcycle caught his eye. One of the men was staring him down. The man's face, partially concealed in shadow, gave him a menacing appeal. Ghost hunting, he was seeing things that weren't there. His secure phone buzzed with a text from Casper—*Can you talk?*

"You rang," Dresden said after Casper answered.

"Dad, where are you?" Casper asked.

"Uh, well I'm outside at the moment."

"I mean is it okay to talk?"

"Yes, if you're using the phone we sent you."

"Yeah. Okay, I am. Okay. Listen, Dad that *thing* you sent me was in pretty bad shape. We've been working on it for a few days. I think it's been a few days. Not sure, anyway. Doc O, he wants to take a closer look at it, says there's something wrong with it. Not sure what he means."

"Okay," Dresden said. That explained the not answering his phone.

"Yeah, I don't know. But Dad?"

"Yeah?"

"Thanks. This is cool, you know, helping you out. It's really cool."

Dresden stifled a laugh and smiled instead. "Okay. You're welcome. Although, I should really be the one thanking you for hanging in there with me."

There was a silence, then Casper said, "Dad? I gotta go."

"Casper—answer your phone next time, okay?"

"Okay, will do. Be safe, okay? And I love you. Gotta go. Bye." His son hung up.

Dresden looked at the ground, rocked his head back and forth, and tittered. His cheeks, tight, began to ache.

He resumed his people-watching. A flash or two went off in front of the basilica. Its dramatic spires stabbed skyward like the raised spears and swords of a hundred medieval soldiers. Eventually, he swung back around to the motorcycle men. There were three more now. All of them short, dark-skinned, dark hair, Hispanic looking. South American, maybe. Dresden's skin itched. Branch? Already?

Dresden pocketed his phone and wondered if Primo had a bead on him. He rose and stretched his arms, then sauntered down the center of the plaza straight toward the cathedral. More than halfway to the church, he veered off course, then stopped short. One of his pursuers overcommitted. The man stutter-stepped and changed direction. There was no need to hide, Dresden decided. They weren't going to shoot him down in the middle of the piazza. That wasn't Branch's style—he'd want plausible denial. Maybe a mugging? How about a dark street or alleyway?

Dresden turned off the piazza, skirting past cars parked up on the curb off Via San Raffaelle. The shiny cobblestones glowed in the streetlights. The clack of the men's hard leather soles echoed off the buildings and cobblestones of the narrow street. At nearly one in the morning, he took his posse down an alley off via Giorgio Pallavicino. A dead end, where Dresden spotted the diminutive Fiat 128 coupe parked deep enough into the alley that one of his pursuers would have to commit. Two of them did. Dresden leaned his back against the tiny car, pressing his hands into a pair of gloves as the two men struggled to hide. No shops. No off alleys. Nothing. They stepped like toddlers, unsure of themselves. Dresden got in the car, started the engine, pulled out, and sped back down the alley to the main street, waving as he passed the men.

A mobile surveillance team was on him within four blocks. These guys weren't kidding around. Dresden's adrenaline spiked as he buzzed through the narrow streets, the two Lancia Delta Integrals trailing close behind. He came to the Piazzale Giovanni de Agostini roundabout, off Via Stromboli, and wove into the inner circle. Completing half of the circuit, he took a hard turn out of the roundabout and screamed down Via Ulpiano, a narrow one-way street.

Dresden lost one of the cars with the maneuver, but the other came within inches of his bumper determined to follow him. The Fiat skidded over a set of train tracks, sparks flying out from under the car. His pursuer did the same. Small pats of wet snow hit the windshield. Bright lights blinded him as he flew through an intersection off Via Camilio Ugoni. A royal blue La Forza SUV skidded in behind the Lancia. Impressive driving. Time to stop polluting the air, Dresden chuckled to himself. He gripped the steering wheel harder as he turned onto Via Calabria, then took a quick turn down a private drive.

The gate to the abandoned train yard was overgrown with vines and bushes. Dust billowed behind him as he picked up speed, getting out in front of his pursuers. The car's tires squealed as he turned into an open bay door of a warehouse. He rolled out onto the ground and watched the car slam into a distant wall, stopping dead with a loud thud. Steam rose from the smashed grill. Dresden moved. Train cars and machinery sounded in the distance, shrouding the La Forza's approach. A light flashed. They were here. Men yelled over the noise.

The SUV crept forward, then stopped and backed up, the passenger pointing to the Fiat. Three men jumped out dressed in pressed slacks, shiny leather shoes, and shimmering black leather jackets. They looked like they were ready for the club, not a mugging. The men drew machetes from the rear of the SUV. One of the Lancia arrived and more men spilled out, machetes in hand. One of them, with large drooping shoulders, stayed with the SUV. Another staged himself at the warehouse door, and the rest walked cautiously toward the battered and hissing car.

Dresden came up behind the big man at the SUV and hacked at the man's wrist, loosening his grip on the blade. The man spun wildly as Dresden snatched up the blade and thrust the dull side into the man's throat while bringing his knee into the brute's groin. The big man and Dresden dropped behind the La Forza, out of sight. A loud groan left the man as Dresden put a heel to the back of his neck. A train car lumbered by fifty yards away as he slipped into the SUV.

The door sentry's lazy glance turned to panic as Dresden whipped the La Forza around and headed toward the gate. He glanced at the rearview mirror. Men piled into the Lancia. The car lurched forward and wobbled on flat tires, then stopped. One of the men got out, kicked a tire, and punched at his cell phone. "Whoa man," Dresden yelled out loud as he hit the main road and slowed down to the speed of the traffic. His temples pulsed. Sweat ran down his face, and he licked at his salty upper lip, noticing the music playing in the background. He turned up the volume and the cab filled with the chirpy beats of Cumbia.

He wasn't out of the woods, and he needed to keep his wits about him. The other Lancia was out there, somewhere. *Can't hang around here for three more days. Dammit! Now what? Breath and think.* His old phone rang—the number was unfamiliar, so he let it go to voicemail. A moment later, the same phone chimed. The La Forza had Bluetooth, and Branch's voice slithered out of the speakers.

"Hello? Marcus Dresden? This is Sean Branch, VP and Head of Operations at First Watch. I would like very much to speak with you." The voice on the phone was soft and melodic. "At your earliest convenience, of course. I believe it would be in our mutual best interest to clear the way for a more productive working relationship. I would like to propose that we meet and discuss how we can better facilitate and incorporate your particular skills as part of the larger effort to improve the scope and capability of First Watch. I know you were, and still are, a trusted agent of Thomas Roker. I have the utmost respect for the man and have been deeply disturbed by the direction his health has taken. He has struggled so valiantly to keep this company afloat. His deteriorating condition has left so many elements of the business needing urgent care. I believe that you may be able to help us rectify and repair the damage that was inadvertently done by Mr. Roker's failing faculties. So, I humbly ask you to return this call as soon as you can. I want to address this matter as soon as possible, before it balloons out of control. Thank you, Marcus, in advance for your assistance. Goodbye."

Shit! The man was a fucking genius. "If I wasn't onto you Branch, you bastard, I'd fold and believe your bullshit," Dresden said out loud. He drove, not sure where to go. His hotel was bound to be covered. He had what he needed on him. But where to? His secure phone rang.

"Hello."

"I need you to get to Lyon, France, right away," Orville said.

"Uh, well, I'm kind of busy at the moment."

"Drop the routine and move to Lyon."

"That's just it—I'm in the middle of fending off some rabid dogs."

"What? Really?"

"Yeah we just went at it for the last couple hours. I'm driving one of their cars right—"

"Hold on … let me call you back." Orville hung up.

"Uh … okay." Dresden said. Orville not knowing what was going on made him uneasy. His stomach rumbled loudly. Hunger. How could he be hungry right now? He spotted a Lancia, and his shoulders tightened. The car sped past him. Strands of blond hair flew from an open window. A convenience store sign flashed ahead, and Dresden pulled over and parked the SUV in the shadows. He sat and watched for several minutes before he went inside. As he came out, his phone sounded.

"Hello."

"Okay, dump the car. Get a train to Lyon," Orville said.

"And just leave these guys behind? What if they have info …"

"They have nothing to do with what we're doing. They are not connected to what we're—"

"Well, damn, who the hell are they?"

The line was quiet for a moment. "This is not really the time. There's a train leaving in thirty-five minutes I need you to—"

"I'm headed there as we speak. The least you could do is explain—"

"MS-13. They're MS-13. Quarto sent me the pics they got. Two of the guys popped on Interpol."

"MS-13? In Milan? Italy? I'm—"

"Yes. Let's talk about that later. I need you to focus on getting to your next location ASAP!"

"You're going to hate me," Dresden said, "but one more thing. Branch called."

"We know. That's why you're going to Lyon. Now go."

"Roger that."

Dresden hung up and continued to wipe down the La Forza. MS-13? Son-of-a-gun. Another song started to play on the car stereo. A song caught his attention and he punched eject. The silver CD slid out like a snake's tongue. Dresden pulled on the disk and held it up to the light. *Los Hermanos Flores*. Well at least these assholes had good taste in music.

Lyon, France

Get to the La Part-Dieu, near some hotel, Orville had said, then call.

An overnight train through the Alps and here he was, matching the name of the hotel with scribbled words on a crumpled piece of paper. He looked up at the broad, hunter-green awning with the words *HOTEL MARIANA* painted on it. Colorful flags flapped in the light breeze. The building was clean, with mirrored glass windows and square concrete bricks that checkered their way up to the roof above. Dresden pulled his phone out and dialed Orville, but there was no answer. He pocketed his phone and checked the street sign, Cours Émile Zola. This was the place. He dialed again, but still no answer.

Dresden walked into the lobby. It was sparse but tidy, like the outside. A middle-aged man with sandy blond hair and glasses hanging down on his nose sat behind the wood-paneled check-in counter. Dresden presented his passport. *John Dillon*. The man clunked away at his keyboard as Dresden looked around the small lobby. The host drew his attention to ask what size room he preferred. The elevator door opened. A man stepped out and a flash of blond hair in Dresden's periphery caused him to look.

It was Andrusha.

If the quadruplet registered Dresden, he didn't show it. But his eyes darted to the carport door. Dresden reached for his passport. The host held onto it, tight. Dresden looked at the man and yanked the passport away, but that was all the time the big blond needed. Dresden bolted through the door after Andrusha. He caught up to the big man and threw a hammer fist into his back, knocking Andrusha to the ground. But the man rolled forward and landed back on his feet. Glancing back at Dresden, he took off running.

What the hell? Why hadn't he stood and fought or drawn a gun or a knife, something? Dresden caught him again. This time, the big man was struggling to breathe. He turned and faced Dresden. *Okay. Here we go.* Dresden drew his belt through his pants loops. Andrusha sank into a defensive pose, smiling, his crooked grin showing as his eyes narrowed, and suddenly his breathing was under control.

Ah great!

Andrusha stomped toward Dresden, taking a couple steps forward then back as Dresden lashed out with his belt buckle. He was fast. Andrusha swept at Dresden's legs, followed by a couple quick jabs. On the third sweep, Dresden caught the man's leg in a loop of his belt and cinched down hard and fast. Hopping on one leg, Andrusha leaned forward, grabbing at him. Dresden yanked the man toward him, crashing into him with an elbow to the face. He walked forward, lifting Andrusha's leg as high as he could. The man stumbled and fell, rolling to his feet again.

Damn, this guy's good.

Crouched on all fours, Andrusha smiled through bloody teeth, then took off running up the garage ramps. Dresden lost sight of him, and two levels later he stopped and listened. Nothing. The blond was gone. Then the squeal of tires filled the parking garage. Andrusha had gotten behind him.

Dresden ran to where he could look out onto Cours Émile Zola. At street level, Dresden spotted a black BMW X5 tear out of the garage exit below. The BMW skidded into traffic, narrowly missing other cars, and was out of sight a moment later.

Forty

Lyon, France

A look of terror streaked across the desk clerk's face, his hands pawing at Dresden's fist wrapped around his throat. Toes dangled, the sound of shoes scuffing on tile following every flail of the man's legs. His eyes bulged and white, bubbling spittle coursed from his mouth. Dresden snapped out of his trance as spit landed on his cheek. Andrusha was gone, and this impish man was unwilling to give up his room number. Dresden, his filter non-existent, pounced on the clerk, slamming him against the wall.

Focus, dammit!

He looked at the host and released his grip, noticing a bluish tinge to the man's face. The clerk dropped to the floor and burbled out the room number between deep heaves for air.

In the room, Dresden tore off the sheets and flipped through the mattresses. He rummaged through Andrusha's luggage, the dresser, and the closet. Nothing. He dumped out the contents of the trash on the floor. The faint wail of sirens sounded in the distance. Sitting on the floor, he opened twisted pieces of paper. The pitch of the sirens became louder. He stopped and shoved the bits of paper in a pocket in his backpack. His phone rang, and he tapped his earbud without looking at the screen.

"Yeah!"

"What are you doing?" Orville said.

"I'm tearing through this asshole's room!"

"Whose room?"

"I don't have time for this. The guy we're looking for, one of his goons was here in the hotel you sent me to," Dresden said as he grabbed a towel from the bath and started to wipe the place down.

"Wait. What? You're *in* the hotel?"

"Yeah. The one you told me to go to."

"Did our POI see you?"

"I'd say so! We played tiddlywinks in the parking lot for a bit." Dresden stood at the door, taking one last look. Had he missed anything? No, the guy was a professional—he'd leave nothing behind.

"You were supposed to call me when you got in the *area* of the hotel."

"Well, goddammit! I called, but you didn't answer, what the hell did you expect me to do?"

The line was silent for a moment. "You're tired. You've been going non-stop for days. You're not listening to me. You're going to make mistakes. Stop. I need you to listen right now."

Dresden stood in the hall, the sirens getting louder. Three blocks away at most. His chest rose and fell like a racehorse hitting full stride. He worked to calm himself. No more mistakes. Orville was right, so he listened.

"Get out of there. Get far away from there. Go across the river. I'll get you set up someplace you can rest. Call me when you're clear of there, okay?"

"Okay."

Dresden found an exit at the back of the garage; the breakout bar didn't budge. Dresden kicked the bar—still nothing. The police were out front. The front desk clerk hadn't seen him leave. That meant he had a minute, maybe. Dresden body slammed the door three times and got it to open a few inches. Vines from the outside held the door in place. He pushed through the narrow opening, shoving the door back shut. He stepped into the alley as a police car whined to a stop on the main street, Rue Léon Chomel. He ducked back into the shadows. Get across the river. As the officers made their way to the front entrance to the hotel, he hurdled a fence and dropped down into the small lot of an office building. Get across the river.

The taxi ride was a blur. Andrusha running away, his shark teeth gnashing through a sardonic smile, played on an endless loop in Dresden's mind. Why hadn't the man fought? Tried to take Dresden out? Wasn't that what they wanted? It was noon when he found the hotel on the other side of the Rhone. A small non-descript place off a side street and another side street. Dresden showered and got in bed to rest, to slow his mind. Instead, he lay there, staring up at the water-stained ceiling for two hours.

He found a navy-blue jogging suit and a pair of soft deck shoes at a department store. *Make do,* Dresden thought. The sun was grabbing at the sky-line of the city, pulling itself down as Dresden set out running at a breakneck pace. He wanted to sweat, to hurt, to beat the maddening thoughts from his head. He was going to make a lot of mistakes if he couldn't focus.

The old phone vibrated in his pocket. He looked at the screen as he slowed. The pounding in his head faded as he slowed his pace. Knoxville area code. He dropped down on the walkway along the Quai du dr Gailleon as he answered.

"Hello?"

"Marcus! So good to hear your voice. Are you out of breath?"

"Yes … who is this?"

"Aww, I figured you'd know me as well as I know you. Sorry friend, this is Sean Branch."

"Branch." *You murderous bastard. Say it. Say it. No!* "Good evening, or afternoon Knoxville time or whatever it is."

"Yes. Knoxville time. Yes, and you are in California, I suppose."

"Branch? Why are you doing this? I just need to know—"

"Doing what? What are you talking about, Marcus? I called you to ask you for your help. Did you get my voicemail? I need you *here,* in Knoxville, to help me get this company turned around, and—"

"Cut the shit, Branch." *You slimy bastard. Come on, say it!* "I don't believe an ounce of your bullshit. You have your hand in all that has gone wrong with First Watch, you ..." *You kidnapped Jen. You killed those—* "You ..."

"Yes? I what, Marcus? How 'bout I say it for you? You're innocent of all that I'm accusing you of, Mister Branch. You *want* to say that you're the reason things have taken a turn for the worst. If you had come and helped Roker in the first place, helped put his plan into place, we wouldn't be here right now."

"Fuck you, Branch!"

"Well, Marcus, I'm going to take that as a no, for the second time. The second time you wouldn't help your *good* friend Roker, and now you won't help me. I for one am going to be sad to see you go."

"Branch, you like to play games, don't you? You know someone has to lose. I think it might be your turn," Dresden said, a drop of acid burning the back of his throat.

He was losing his cool. He'd lost his cool. He wanted to take the man somewhere dark and hateful, kicking and screaming, and make him pay. Not now. Not yet. Cool down.

"Marcus, I must say this has been a most enlightening conversation, but I have to go. You see, I have a company to save. I will expect your *resignation* soon. Maybe by close of business tomorrow … the next day at the latest." Branch hung up without waiting for an answer.

"I don't fucking work for you, asshole!" Dresden screamed. The few people within earshot glance his way, throwing furtive, irritated looks.

Dresden stopped along the river near the Pont de L'Université bridge, but barely noticed the fins of the nautical center towering over the building like the sails of a tall ship. He dialed Orville on his secure phone.

"Marcus."

"Yes. I just got off the phone with Branch."

"I know. Red is working on locating the call. Get ready to move—I'll call you back as soon as I know where."

Somewhere in France

It took an hour to reliably trace the call. This time it was Marseille. They were playing to Branch's tune. Orville wasn't coming out with it, Dresden thought. But they were searching and hunting for a break. Orville was likely seething at the idea of not being in control, not being out ahead of this by now. They'd guessed right—Branch was in Europe. Or was he? He could have sent the messages and gone the opposite way. Andrusha could have been decoy, a *diversion*. Did Branch know what Dresden knew? Did he know about Jennifer? He must have known something. Did he know about Roker? If he was on the run, why didn't he just run? Why give Dresden a road map?

The metal wheels of the night train to Marseille scraped on the tracks, providing a gritty industrial soundtrack as the locomotive sped through the dark countryside. The rhythm of the car swaying and gently pulling and pushing forced Dresden to nod off into a fitful sleep. The fire was back, the flames rising out of the water. A man, his face half-burned, yelling at him.

Dresden woke and punched the seat cushion next to him. Breathing heavily, he took out his old phone and found Lance's number and typed a text,

Where is your soul, my friend? Is it angry and unsatisfied, or is it in a place of peace and tranquility? I don't know. I'm hoping for the latter. Hope this helps bro – wherever you are, ask them to play the Black Crowes, "Soul Singing." He waited, thinking about the man who had Lance's phone. Fedor? He punched send. Dresden found the song on his throwaway and hit play before he closed his eyes and fell back asleep. The fire smoldered but didn't flame up again.

Marseille, France

Bleary-eyed and still tired, Dresden checked into a hotel with a view of Parc Borély in the Sainte-Anne district of the city, a stone's throw from the beaches of the French Riviera. The smell of the sea filled his lungs, and his mind drifted to memories of Escondite, of Casper visiting with him. The idea of them lazing on the beach and him teaching Casper to surf knocked around in his mind. The thought lingered, leaving him smiling. What if? Maybe it would be a good thing. The idea waltzed away after the elevator dinged loudly.

In his room, he lay down on the bed, sleep overtaking him almost instantly. He dreamed of nothing and woke a few hours later, his body racked with a sluggishness only a run could cure. The windows, left open, ushered in the early morning sea air, damp and fragrant. He breathed in deeply. A strange euphoria overcame him, replete with a small sense of something he thought might be hope. It faded, replaced by the sense of evil. They were here. They were out there. *One by one,* he thought. *Take them out one by one.* With his exercise suit and deck shoes on, he headed downstairs.

Avenue be Hamburg was empty and wet in the early-morning mist. He sped through the botanical garden and Parc Borély. KISS hammering out "War Machine" in his ears. He was being hunted. Depriving his senses wasn't smart. But at the moment, he was beyond caring. In a way, the music helped him focus. He kept his head on a swivel as he jogged by the stately Chateau Borély and over to Huveaune, to a flat expansive park along a white sandy beach. At the memorial des Rapatries D'Algerie, he started to climb the winding roads that led to the Basiliqque Notre-Dame de la Garde. At the top, with Motorhead's "The Game" still growling in his ear, he stopped to take in the city below, shrouded in mist with glimmers of the sun poking through. The route was nine miles round trip. Plenty of places to spot his would-be assailants. Plenty of places for them to set up. They were close-in guys. That was Branch's style. No snipers, he guessed.

From the Basilique, Dresden's route meandered down to the old port of Marseille. He jogged around the bucolic Palais du Pharo poised on a point at the mouth of the old harbor. Only small patches of mist remained as the deep blue-green Mediterranean glistened at the horizon. The air warmed and the streets came alive as he ran. Dresden stopped for a moment at the Statue de Missak Manouchain, then looped around the quai Marcel Pagnol, a bundle of floating buildings and moored boats. Halfway. Nothing. *They are out there.*

Back at his hotel, Dresden let Clutch's thumping "Binge and Purge" play out as he stretched near the entrance to his hotel. He thought of Primo. Had they seen him? Had they seen anyone else? Dresden's secure phone buzzed. A text from Orville read, *Go for a run same time tomorrow morning. Same route, Okay?* Well, I guess that answers that. He typed, *Okay,* and walked into the small café beneath the hotel. It was bustling with men and women heading to work or out for the day. Three women at a table next to Dresden squawked loudly. Happily. Dresden glance toward their table, and one of the women flashed a brilliant smile at him. She raised her eyebrows. Dresden smiled back and raised his cup to her, then returned to reading *100 Poems of Seamus Heaney*, a dogeared book he'd grabbed from the book share shelf.

Dresden's secure phone buzzed again, another Orville text: *Get plenty of rest today. Stay in as much as you can, off the streets. Okay?* Dresden looked at the woman at the table next to him. Her two friends turned to look at him. They beamed with conspiracy. Dresden nodded toward them, downed his coffee, and left. Outside he typed, *Okay.* Complete with a sad face.

The next morning, the lonely streets were covered in a fine damp haze, the morning sun not yet poking through as Dresden loped along, warming up. His earbuds were in, but no music was playing. He could *feel* them out there. The air was charged, or maybe that was just him. Either way, he'd centered himself and was back on point. Picking up the pace, he moved down Avenue Clut Brey but slowed again when he entered Jardin Botanique, the botanical garden of Parc Borély. He propped a leg up to stretch at the head of the parking lot. Two men, a hundred yards away, stretched as well. *Hello there, gents, glad you could join the party.* Another two minutes passed as he finished his scan of the area.

Running again, he listened for the men to fall in behind him. The distinctive patter of shoes landing on the path out of time with his own was the signal. The sound was faint; he put them at thirty yards. On a long curve, he spotted two more, maybe a hundred yards in front of him. The pair running at him barked loudly with laughter, gently pushing at each other. The men behind him maintained their distance.

Ahead, a wooded tunnel of vines divided Dresden and the men closing the distance in front of him. *That's the spot,* he thought. He would be boxed in, concealed from view. Perfect. Dresden picked up his pace. The men in front didn't notice, didn't change their pace. The men behind were in stasis, keeping their distance. In front, the two men picked up their playfulness; their pushing and shoving intensifying. Dresden could see how this tactic might work with some banker, an office manager, or a sloth-like aristocrat. Sorry to disappoint you, gents. As the men prepared for Dresden to pass, one of them shoved the other, forcing him to fall into Dresden. Except he stopped flat, and the man fell to the ground.

The man still standing stared at his comrade wriggling on the ground and didn't notice Dresden move in. He landed four savage blows to the man's solar plexus, the distinct sound of ribs popping followed each blow. Dresden followed this volley with a furious stomp to the other man's inner leg, a debilitating blow to the femoral nerve. The man, writhing more now, stifled a scream and reached for his leg.

Fast footsteps punctuated by the sound of grinding gravel caused Dresden to glance behind. Two seconds, maybe three until they were on him. He fell to a knee, patted the men down, and snatched a radio and an asp from one man. The radio was tethered to the man by a long cord and taped to his ear, slowed Dresden. He yanked hard as he sprinted away, leaving the man yelping.

Moving through the park gates and onto Avenue Paraque du Borély, Dresden serpentined through the low-flung trees of the grassy median. He'd opened some distance, but now the two men were closing on him again. He needed somewhere to hide, someplace to get behind them. Up ahead, the busy Avenue du Prado loomed. There.

Dresden assumed they were desperate, not going to make good decisions. But they would regroup fast. Call in reinforcements. Then he'd be screwed. He shoved the radio bud into his ear. A pantheon of French flew across the air waves; he couldn't understand a word. But he knew they were figuring it out. He sprinted toward the intersection, to the corner.

Turning onto Prado, he was immediately out of eyeshot. He ducked behind a large community trash bin. Rounding the corner three seconds later, the men sprinted past. Dresden jumped in behind them and moved up silently. Their bodies bobbled and heads spun as they searched for him through the pedestrians, parked cars, and traffic.

One of the men looked over his shoulder just as Dresden smashed down on the other man's Achilles. The man hit face first on the pavement with a loud, audible crack of his skull. The other man tangled up in his own feet stumbled to the ground. Dresden moved through the two men, landing a heel to the back of one of their necks, flattening the man to the ground. The other man, now regaining his composure, received a foot to the groin and a knee to the face. The man rolled onto his belly, holding both his nose and his crotch. Dresden landed a fist to the back of his neck to encourage him to stay down.

Sprinting from the scene, Dresden then slowed to a walk a block away and scanned furiously. Those were hired hands, local thugs, meant to tire him out. A diversion, again. Where was Andrusha? Which shadow would the man jump from? *Run the route. Run the route. Stay alert and run the route.*

Forty-One

Marseille, France

A horn blasted as Dresden dashed across the wide Prado and rounded the corner onto Promenade Georges Pompidou. The short, violent fights played around in his mind. He'd taken the men out of the battle, but not the war. His vision blurred and sharpened as adrenaline coursed through his veins like a bullet train. He slowed his pace and focused on short strides, on getting enough oxygen to keep his mind alert as he climbed up to the Notre-Dame de la Garde. He stopped in the parking lot and watched the winding roads and trails he'd just run. Nothing. Where were they? They would be on the other end down by the harbor—the next attack was out there, somewhere.

The soggy grounds of the palace were sad and uninviting this time. Manicured shrubs and trees drooped under the weight of the rain and fog, frowning as Dresden ran by. The dark Mediterranean Sea mirrored the turmoil surrounding him. Small, angry white caps crashed against the sea wall. He shook his arms and rolled his shoulders as he ran. *Where is it?* Dresden rounded the quay. Don't make me wait another day. Come on, Andrusha—come out and play, he said to himself. A black streak darted from the shadows of the floating docks. The sound of a man's footfalls pounding on the concrete. Unaccustomed to running. Dresden slowed and moved to the edge of the quay, as the man's shadow cast among the unsettled waters churned and bobbed like the deadly mouths of a hundred piranhas.

Dresden eyed the harbor master's office five yards ahead its floating barge bumping gently against the quay. Dresden stopped abruptly, forcing Andrusha to leap on him. His crooked teeth grinding in Dresden's ear, the big man growled as Dresden dove off the quay. Andrusha clapped down on his neck with one arm, the other around his chest. Dresden felt him heave as the cold, dark water enveloped them.

Kicking and swimming, Dresden made for the bottom, the big blond still strapped to his back. He punched at his side, not letting go of his neck. Dresden inadvertently kicked Andrusha in the groin, making him lose his grip on a knife he'd drawn. The pair swam into the shadows of the harbor master's barge above, the darkness closing in on them and Andrusha giving no indication of letting go.

Searching for something sturdy to grab onto, Dresden felt around in the dark. His hand hit something hard—a pylon. He grabbed ahold, barnacles slicing into his hands and arms, shredding his thin gym coat and t-shirt. He locked his arms down on the stanchion before Andrusha could pry him free. The big man shook and quaked. His grip loosened, then tightened for a second more before he let go and bolted for the surface. Dresden reached out and grabbed a pant leg, holding a thrashing Andrusha for a ten-count. When he let go, Dresden felt the whirl of water as the man flailed and kicked to the surface. Only he wouldn't find the surface directly above him.

Surfacing between two boats a moment later, Dresden watched the harbor master's barge. Nothing. He swam to the seawall at the far side of harbor, glancing back every three or four strokes. Still nothing. His clothes drained as he dragged himself from the water. A pond of red-brown water was pooling on the concrete, but Dresden didn't notice. He was intent on listening for sirens or a scream or a mad rush of people scrambling to gawk at a floating body. But nothing like that happened. *Number three down,* Dresden thought. *You're next, Branch. You're next. And Fedor, how about you? You killed Lance, didn't you? the scars gave you away.* He twisted his pack around and drew out his old phone. He removed it from an airtight case and sent a text.

Hey there, I'm just hanging out, relaxing after a swim and was thinking about you. So, what's your favorite long play song? I like "Green Grass and High Tides" by the Outlaws. Let me know.

La Spezia, Italy

Dresden heard Primo in the background. "I have an idea," the man said as he walked out of the room. He watched the man leave through a fog of sleep and exhaustion. A fire blazed in a stone fireplace, sotted black. The room was rustic, full of earthen scents and smells. It was warm and inviting and oddly familiar. Maria floated into this view, looking like a dream. She smiled and handed him a warm cup of tea. The aromatic steam rose from the brim, and his stomach rumbled with hunger. A warm hand touched his cheek. He looked up. Maria was still smiling. "Rest," Dresden thought she said, and then he fell asleep.

A heavy, billowy blanket stretched across him. The bedroom looked like the room he'd dreamed of. He sat up, head pounding. He'd slept. He'd dreamed, mostly bad. Branch. A group of men. The blonds. Young girls. The men laughing—lots of laughing at him. And some more men sitting around a table. Fragments at best.

A set of clothes were draped over a chair. After dressing, Dresden made his way toward the faint sound of talking and laughing, downstairs maybe.

A fuzz like cotton candy coated the edges of his vision. He stood in the doorway of a family-style kitchen-dining room a moment before anyone noticed, Orville with his back to him. Three of the Italians were there, and Primo was waving his hands, telling a story. Maria, her face radiant, grabbed his arm and guided him into the room.

"Where am I?" he asked Maria.

"You're in my grandfather's guest house in La Spezia," she said, a cloud of concern passing over her as she inspected his face.

"Oh. That's why it looks familiar," Dresden said. He pulled a chair out from the dining table and eased himself into it.

"Hungry?" Primo asked.

"Starved!"

"I hate to get right to it but ... well, Primo came up with an idea," Orville said, "a way we may be able to learn a little more about our friend Branch. I think it would be worth following up on. Maria and Red have made significant headway into their end of things. When you get back, we can discuss all that. Branch hasn't called back again. You, Primo, and Valerio leave in the morning to run this idea down."

"Okay. Uh ... what about Marseille?"

"It's covered. We can discuss it more tomorrow night when you get back. Why don't you eat and get some more rest? If anything comes up, I will let you know."

Valerio drove, while Dresden sat in the passenger seat with Primo in the rear of the BMW M8 Grand Coupe. Dresden wanted to ask where they were going several times, but stopped himself. Valerio took hairpin turns, drifting into the oncoming lane. Dresden kept his mouth shut and held on. For a while, he focused on getting comfortable. Every joint in his body ached with every turn. He focused on the scenery, the trees going by in a blur. Occasionally, the foliage parted. In the distance he spotted tiny villages, larger towns; red-tile roofs, and castles and cathedrals atop lonely peaks jutting out of lush, fertile valleys. The clouds parted and rays of sun doused the snow-covered Alps ahead, in the distance.

They stopped, once, at a roadside café. They each had a *thimble of death* and a breakfast bun and shared a pallet of dried, flavorful meat before they sped off again. The coffee worked to revive Dresden some. His phone buzzed. It was Fedor, or the person he assumed was Fedor at least.

Hello my friend. I'm glad you are back. Long play? Very American. If I have to, I like "So What" by Ministry. Live, 1989.

Dresden shook his head. Ministry, dammit. Forever tainted. He would never be able to play the band again. He should have never asked. He stuffed his phone in his pocket without responding. The man must not know about his brother yet.

Four hours of high-speed driving landed them at the foot of the Alps. Bormio, Dresden read as they passed into town. Valerio veered off the main road onto a narrow, winding lane with no markers. The car seemed to float out of the trees as they climbed into the mountains surrounding the village. A jarring turn onto an even narrower, rutted dirt road left Dresden rubbing his hip. A well-kept house popped out of the woods at the end of drive, a chalet-style building with a steep-pitched roof and decorative wood awnings. A gingerbread house.

The front door cracked, and a slight, elderly man stepped into the doorway. "Pronto?" he said with a proud bend to his back. He stared directly at Dresden, and the haunting gray eyes unnerved him. Valerio drew his attention and introduced everyone.

"I am Augustus—please, please come in." He led the group to a large table of thick timber, its surface polished by a hundred or more years of use. Dresden rubbed his hand across the table, amazed. Augustus set a plate of meat and cheese and pickled vegetables on the table, another plate of bread and butter and several bottles with no labels. Water. Wine. Grappa.

"Eat, please," he said, waving his hands at the food.

Valerio leaned toward Augustus and spoke to the man in hushed, conspiratorial whispers. Augustus took long glances at Dresden, then back at his food. He nodded as Valerio continued to speak, still studying Dresden from time to time. When Valerio was done, Augustus rose, bowed slightly, and moved to Dresden's side, his eyes steady and grave. Dresden felt the man's thin hand on his shoulder. Augustus grunted once, patted him on the shoulder, then left the room.

Primo rose from the table and looked down at Dresden with a raised eyebrow. Dresden turned to see a barrel-chested man filling the doorway. His chin hung on his chest as he moved forward, his eyes floating around the room. Valerio stood, and Dresden followed suit. Augustus pulled a chair out for the big man and helped him into it. He sat with a loud grunt and a short laugh. He flipped his hand, and Valerio and Dresden sat down. Primo remained standing.

The big man tried lifting his chin to look at Dresden. His pale blue eyes were as bright as a ten-year-old's, surrounded by aged leather. Dresden watched the corners of his mouth eke into a smile.

"You can call me Enzo."

"Yes sir. I am Marcus Dresden, sir. Very good to meet you, sir," Dresden said, a little too loud.

Enzo chuckled. "Likewise, son."

Augustus filled everyone's glass with Grappa. Enzo reached for his glass and raised it in the air. "Salute."

Primo downed his drink, then tapped the table twice with his glass before speaking to Enzo. His Italian flowed from him like a song. Dresden only caught every third or fourth word, but he was sure Primo was telling the old man about Branch and the Russians. About First Watch and the site managers. Enzo, his chin back on his chest, watched Primo with his intense eyes, nodding from time to time. Enzo thanked Primo when he was done and told him he should have stayed in the military, that he would have made a great officer. Primo blushed and sat down.

Two photos lay on the table in front of Enzo. He tapped them with a thick, wrinkled finger and glanced around the room. Dresden recognized the photos—Branch and Fedor. Enzo hummed, then turned his bulk in his chair to face Dresden.

"I was a junior officer after the war."

Dresden was sure he was referring to World War II, but he didn't ask.

"I'd only been in long enough to see the war end. Not to see any action. My war was the cold war and the rise of communism. Not much of a war at all, of course. But the kind of war that bred the wars we see today. Wars of invisible adversaries. They have a fancy word for them now." Enzo shook his wrist as if it would jog his memory. "Asymmetric wars. Yes. That's it. We all know why this happened. And of course, it is not new. The invisible enemy has been around for millennia. The forever war has been around for millennia. So, men have become very good at this asymmetric warfare. They have spent decades finding new and more perfect ways to wage war without actually fighting. Now cyber warfare. We have proxy soldiers that are truly invisible!" The old man cracked a smile, pleased with his own joke.

Dresden laughed too and felt the man's rough hand pat his. Wishing he understood where this was going, he struggled to focus, still exhausted. His patience had worn thin in the past months. He looked over at Valerio, who winked at him. *Stay focused. Listen.*

Enzo continued, "But you, my friend, are dealing with a very dangerous manifestation of this war." The man pushed the two photos in front of Dresden.

"This man? No." Enzo's finger hovered over Fedor's photo before moving to Branch. "This man? Yes." He kept his finger on the photo of Branch. "This man is what we call a *cameronite,* but much worse." Enzo took a long sip of his wine, then set it down, letting his fingers tiptoe along the bulk of his glass before starting again.

"Vladimir Putin is responsible for this man!"

Dresden pinched the bridge of his nose. Putin? Shit! The damn Russians again. He leaned back in his chair.

Enzo explained that Putin, in all his wisdom, saw fit to develop an even more robust asymmetric arsenal than before he first came to power. One of the programs was code-named *Vtoraya Kozha.* Putin knew his country was going bankrupt, even then, in the beginning. Enzo laughed and said that Putin was very greedy by nature. So, the man had invested a lot of time, energy, and talent into Russia becoming a cyber threat powerhouse. A great way to steal money. But most people were unaware of the less overt programs, like *Vtoraya Kozha.*

The world had enough capital to keep his country running, Putin figured, and definitely enough to make him a very wealthy man. All he needed to do was figure out how to take it. Of course, this couldn't be done outright. There had to be a strategic element to it, but with a tactical answer. Putin had shown through the years how ingenious and crafty he could be, so no surprise there.

Rubbing his finger along the rim of his glass, Enzo said, "One of the many possible answers was *Vtoraya Kozha.* This man is a *former* agent of the

Russian government," Enzo said before he licked his finger and looked at Dresden.

Russian agent. Son of a bitch. Dresden rubbed his temples. He was trying to keep pace with the old man, but was falling behind. Asymmetric warfare. Russian agents. It was too much.

"Sir, I ..."

"Enzo."

"Enzo, I don't—"

"Believe me?"

"That's not it exactly. I'm just trying—"

"You don't have to try. Just listen," Enzo said, patting Dresden's hand again. "This man, Branch, right?

Dresden nodded.

"He was one of twenty test subjects of project *Vtoraya Kozha.* He was recruited to undergo extensive psychological challenges to build him into a walking *uomo de argilla,* uh ..." Enzo looked around the room.

"Clay man," Valerio offered.

"Yes, clay man. He can mold himself to be whoever he wants to be. The intent was not to only change *skin* like the code name might imply, but to go much deeper. This is *dark psychology.* The people who participated in this program could, in theory, convince you that they were the person they were attempting to take over. The idea was that Putin could periodically put one of his agents in *place* as the head of a multi-billion-dollar company, or a billionaire himself to drain their accounts. Slowly, over three or four years. Nothing anyone would really take notice of." Enzo paused. He tapped the photo of Branch and pushed it in front of Dresden again.

Dresden picked up the photo. Branch stared back at him, his snake eyes narrow and deceitful. He knew something was off about the guy, but this was almost *too* unbelievable. At the same time, it explained so much. It was all meant to cover up his real intent—to steal millions of dollars from First Watch clients. He looked at Enzo, who smiled back at him.

"The program was shut down about ten years ago. Most of the candidates who underwent the training developed such deep psychological problems they had to be hospitalized. No one actually was ever employed. The program was deemed a failure. This man started the training when he was only twelve. He was in the program for about eight years before it shut down. He should have been committed with the rest. I heard stories about one individual from that program who escaped; all the other participants went insane. They're locked up in a hospital in Poland. But this one, Branch, he has been making his way through the world finding 'candidates' to take over. He has been on the 'program' as he understood it. Of course, he is clinically insane and consequently very dangerous. As I know you know."

The men were silent for a long time. Dresden watched Augustus clear the dishes away and busy himself in the kitchen. Enzo refilled his glass of wine and offered some to Dresden, who shuffled between the photos of Branch and Fedor. He thought of the text; Fedor's apparently innocent interest in music. It was all too surreal. He was shaken from his daze by Enzo patting his hand again. The old man offered him a flash drive. Enzo's now-tired eyes looked through Dresden for a long moment before he stood with the help of Augustus. Dresden stood as well and offered his hand to Enzo. The old man looked at his hand, then reached for his shoulders and hugged Dresden.

Patting him on the back, he whispered in his ear, "Mr. Dresden, please, for your safety, do not go back to Milan, okay?" He pushed off Dresden and looked up at him as a father would a son.

"Okay."

"Okay then. *Ciao,* my friend." He pointed at the flash drive and added, "I hope this helps."

He pushed off Dresden's shoulder, then nodded at Valerio and Primo and walked down the hall and out of sight.

Forty-Two

Bormio, Italy

A camera shifted its focus in and out, finally resting on a crisp picture of a man at a table. His body slumped and his head hung listless to one side, as if he were asleep. But his eyes belied his posture—they were wide, with an anxious glare. Dresden adjusted the computer screen to shade it from the sunlight coming through the Audio window. He turned up the volume so Valerio and Primo could hear from the front seat. A second man walked into the frame and sat across the small table from the first. He looked at the camera for a moment. It was Branch, but not exactly. The slumped man and Branch looked similar. The skin on Dresden's arm rippled with sensation. The second man, who Dresden was going to assume was the Branch he knew, started speaking low and slow. A bit of an Eastern European accent slipped in and out of his speech.

"What is your name?" Branch asked.

"Branch. Sean Branch," the other man said with a distinctive English accent.

"Sean Branch," Branch said, then asked again, "What is your name?"

"Sean Branch."

"Sean Branch. What is your wife's name?" Branch said.

Dresden's mouth dried out. He leaned in and watched Branch closely. Every time he repeated the other man's words, he moved his mouth and face more and more like the other man. The video went on for another four hours. Dresden sped through sections until he'd seen enough. His body shook and ached, and sleep poured over him like an afternoon thunderstorm. He drank some water to wake up long enough to ask Valerio a question.

"Why didn't Enzo use this to catch Branch?"

"He did, but he never thought to look outside Europe. We think Enzo is the reason the man chose Branch as his candidate. Enzo has made it his life's work to catch the man. Branch is so arrogant that he sent that video to Enzo just to toy with him. Enzo is not the man he once was, and he assumed the Russian had taken the form of Branch to hide in the UK. But he couldn't find him.

"So, he gave up," Dresden said.

"No. He became sick."

"Oh—then why not pass it on to someone else?"

"No one believed him. They thought the video was a hoax and the *program* an urban legend," Valerio said, raising his eyebrows in the rearview.

La Spezia, Italy

Twisting in her chair, Maria beamed with excitement. Orville started to speak, but Maria ran over him, going on about how she and Red had been able to make their way into several of Branch's accounts and databases. She faltered, her face clouding over, clearly remembering the girls and all the photos. She admitted she'd been scared at first to open any of the man's files. But Red had been there, on the phone, helping her along. She was quiet for a moment, staring down at her hands, but when she looked up, the excitement had returned.

Her speech was jumpy and clipped as she talked about how Branch had set up an entire proxy system to monitor First Watch's system. Branch had total control of the company's online presence and infrastructure. It was massive in scope. But what Maria was most excited about was a series of emails she'd found from Branch to the Russian FSB.

Branch had been communicating with the FSB for approximately two years, about the same amount of time he'd been at First Watch. He'd told them, in so many words, that he'd found a suitable candidate and a company worth "working on." Maria explained the emails were completely one-sided. There was no trace of a return email from anyone within the FSB. And now, in light of what Dresden had learned in Bormio, it was clear that Branch was on his own.

Orville waited patiently for Maria to finish. She looked at him sheepishly and mouthed sorry. He winked at her, then looked to Dresden. The contrast was drastic, Dresden decided, and figured Orville was about to drop a bomb. The old man had spent several days reviewing the emails Dresden had originally received, then asked Maria to find a complete set that had been sent to one of the site managers.

"The questions were not only an extra burden on the site managers." Orville rolled the balls of his feet on the floor. "The clients didn't like them much either. They were detailed. The craftsmanship of the questions was what caught my eye. It was like finding a puzzle within a puzzle."

Orville had laid the documents out side by side. In them, he'd found a series of questions. Questions that if taken individually were of no consequence, but collectively painted a very detailed picture of the person answering. More of a personal character profile than straight data collection. It was behavior the questions were after.

"Branch was searching for candidates. He was identifying men of wealth he could not only steal from, but possibly assume their identities." Orville stopped again. He stared at Dresden. "I found two men, both billionaires under contract with First Watch, who had completed Branch's survey. Both men are dead. Worse, they'd died after suffering long bouts of mental and physical duress. They were both removed from their posts as President or CEO of their respective companies by the Board of Directors. Their families left, afraid of the madness that had taken over both men. I'm fairly certain Branch must have *stepped in* for them during their illness. We discovered large assets from each man's company had been shifted into closed accounts. We aren't able to prove it yet but..."

Dresden immediately thought of Roker, which of course was why Orville was so hesitant and nervous. He'd been wrong about him, about Roker

"We are not going to let that happen to Tom!" Dresden said.

They needed to get Branch out in the open, on their radar instead of the other way around. But how? They had no way of contacting him. Red had redialed the old numbers. No good. As suspected, they'd been routed a dozen more times through various servers and proxy lines. So how? They were effectively at Branch's mercy, and it was driving Dresden mad.

Dresden went for his phone, hoping Casper had texted. Instead, Emily had called and left a frantic message that Casper hadn't checked in with her in several days. He stared at his phone, willing Casper to text. Nothing. He called Osuna, but still no luck. It was a *good* sign Osuna wasn't answering, but it was unlike Casper not to respond to his mom. He blindly swiped at his phone, spinning through his contacts. A second later, Lance's number stared back at him.

He tried calling, but got Lance's voicemail. He sat, hunched over, thumbs poised over the pad, but nothing happened. Was this Branch? Dresden wondered. No, it was Fedor. But he could get to Branch and that was all that mattered. Dresden started tapping at the glass keyboard.

You know, I haven't asked you your name. So, for now, I'm going to call you asshole, okay? So listen asshole, you tell that shit bag Branch that if he's any kind of man he'd fight his own fights. Stop sending chumps. Send in the A-Team next time. Oh, and I want my friends phone back. His name was Lance by the way and a real good dude and he's going to enjoy watching me kill you. You and Branch. One last thing, play "Bad Moon Rising" by Credence, cause that's what's comin' asshole!

That ought to get his attention, Dresden thought. He waited for a reply, but none came. *That's right fucker, run to daddy, you fucking tattle tale.* Dresden flipped back to Casper and sent another text. No reply. It was time to change tactics and find him.

A chainsaw buzzed in Dresden's dream. It hummed its way through to his deep sleep, the chains' teeth slicing apart the veil of slumber, letting in slivers of light. He tried to run from the noise, from the saw. He hid behind a tree or a log. But the machine kept coming, chewing up everything. In his dream, he covered his ears and screamed. Still the chainsaw buzzed. Dresden sat up straight as the grinding machine came down on his head. He gasped and wiped at his sweating face. At his bedside, his old phone rattled, bouncing along the surface of the nightstand. He grabbed it and growled into the receiver.

"Yeah!"

"Did I wake you, Marcus?

"Fuck you, Branch," Dresden said, jumping from his bed and running to find Orville.

"Marcus! You disappoint me," Branch said, his voice tight.

"I have a tendency to do that. Especially with people that are trying to kill me. You *are* trying to kill me, aren't you Branch?" Dresden burst into Orville's room and put the phone on speaker.

"Yes. You should have taken the hint when I had my man run you off the road. This is not a game you want to play, Marcus. The stakes are much higher than you can imagine. Your small, feeble brain cannot handle the extent of what is going on here ..."

"Now there you go, Branch, insulting me again. I see you got my text message."

"Message? I'm not sure I understand what you are talking about. Anyway, I called to give you—"

"Sure, sure, you're gonna play dumb. That's not like you."

"Stop talking. I don't know anything about any text messages!" Branch barked. The line went quiet. The man resumed his slow, forced speech. "You will listen, and that is all you will do, you—"

"Hey ... hey Branch, I hate to cut you off, but are you going to go on some crazy 'I'm a psychopath, you shouldn't mess with me' rant? Cause I'm not really interested. In fact, it's pretty cliché. If that's all you can come up with after going to that Russian finishing school for psychos, that's pretty pathetic. Let's just drop the act, okay? You want me dead. I want you rotting in prison. I definitely want your lap dog Fedor under six feet of manure. So, let's cut the shit. Tell me where you are, and we can do the dance. How's that sound?"

The line was silent for several seconds.

"Branch? You still there?"

"I know where you are. I will finish this."

"No, you don't know where I am, or you'd be here right now getting down to business."

Branch screamed into the phone, "I'm going to cut you into little pieces! And feed you to the—"

"To the fish? Yeah, yeah. Jesus, don't you sick-os ever get any new lines? Listen, I'll be seeing you around the schoolyard. You show me yours, I'll show you mine, and we'll see who comes out on top. Whatta ya say there, buddy?"

The line was silent again for several second; only the sound of heavy breathing crackled through the speaker. Dresden imagined Branch pressing the phone into his face, drool running from the corner of his mouth and his neck muscles bulging, about to snap. A soft click, and Branch was gone.

Forty-Three

Porto Venere, Italy

A fishing boat motored into the choppy, troubled sea. Dark clouds cast oblong shadows across the Chiesa di San Pietro, the workman's scaffolding giving the ancient building the feel of a proud old woman with a walker, limping along. Maria sat on a wall looking toward the sea as Dresden paced behind her.

"I don't know what to do," he said. "Why hasn't Red called back yet?

"Look at this scene, Marcus," Maria said. "Someone sat here a thousand years ago and pondered the ways of the world. Don't you think?"

Dresden stopped and looked over the wall.

"Yes, I would say so."

"And it will happen again many times in the next thousand years," Maria continued, not looking at him.

Dresden reached for her hand and held it. Her warmth and calm ran up his arm and through his body. What were they? He looked at her, so happy just to *be*. He stared at the ocean for a tick. But what were they? Two ships passing? Two cars crashing? His mind was scattered, still racing from the call with Branch. He was looking for a port to dock his thoughts. His pulse bounced erratically. He looked back to Maria and felt her hand again. It didn't matter what they were. His pulsed slowed.

This place, he thought. He would remember this place and Maria no matter what came of them. It was her home. A home away from home for him. A glimmer of Branch flashed through his mind, but his resolve was steady now. Branch had never had a home, Dresden pondered. Or maybe the program had been his home, and someone had ripped that away from him. So, he was looking for a home.

That was it!

"A home! That's what Branch is looking for. A candidate—a place to hide!" Dresden nearly yelled at Maria.

"Excuse me, sir!" a voice came from behind Dresden.

Dresden turned to find a finely dressed Carabinieri officer climbing the stairs toward them.

"Yes? Can I help you, officer?"

"Yes ... yes, she must get down from there. It is not permitted to sit on the wall. It is very old. The sign. The sign," the officer said. He waved to a sign in Italian. "It says you are *not* permitted ..."

Maria turned around to face the officer.

The young man's eyes jolted open. "Ms. Fiondella? Ms. Fiondella! Excuse me! Excuse me, I'm very sorry to have bothered you." The officer looked over at Dresden, "Sir, I am very sorry. Please forgive me." The officer tipped his hat to Maria and moved away quickly.

Dresden looked at her, waiting on an explanation, but he didn't get one.

"So? What was that all about?"

Maria shrugged and fashioned a childish grin. "I'm a Fiondella ... that's it."

La Spezia, Italy

The car ahead, a gun-metal gray Maseratti Quattroporte sedan, floated down Maria's grandfather's driveway like a cloud. Maria motioned for Dresden to pull in behind the big car. Dresden stopped as she grabbed his arm, whispering, "Wait." The car rose as the passenger removed himself from the back seat. An oak tree of a man emerged, straightened his suit jacket, and looked back at Dresden's car. The man's mouth curved into a comical smile. Dresden looked over at Maria, then back at the man. *Daddy*. Crap.

"Okay, now," Maria said. She tapped Dresden's arm. He watched her glide toward the big man. Daddy's little girl—his only girl. His palms became damp. Crap. Dresden approached Maria and her father, offering his hand. The big man smiled again, less fiendish this time. That was a start. Dresden shuddered.

"Mr. Fiondella, it's very good to meet you, I'm Marcus Dresden."

"It is good to meet you, Marcus. It's a good, strong name. Too bad your last name is not Aurelias." The big man smiled broadly, slapping Dresden on the shoulder and laughing. "You can call me Gaspare." He tightened his grip. "Unless of course you are interested in my daughter; then, you will call me sir and leave the country!" The big man laughed even harder and added a wink.

Maria elbowed her father, her soft features hardening.

"What? I like him." Gaspare threw out his arms and looked down at his daughter.

"How can you tell? You just met him."

"Oh, I can tell by the way you look at him," Gaspare said, reaching for his daughter and winking again at Dresden.

Maria wriggled free and stormed ahead, waiting at the front door.

As they walked into the house, Gaspare handed Dresden a thick envelope. "This is the information your Mr. Orville asked for."

"What? Already?" Dresden said.

On the way back from Porto Venere, Maria had asked her father to find any information he could on European billionaires, chiefly Spain, France, Italy, and Germany.

Gaspare looked to Maria. His eyes sagged. "He does not know?" he said as he climbed the stairs to the house.

Maria stood in the doorway, hands on her hips. "No, father. He will. Soon, but not now, okay?"

Maria's father shrugged his shoulders, slouching like a little boy who lost his toy. "Okay, your way."

Gaspare let his daughter walk on as he held Dresden's arm.

"I understand you had some trouble in Milan."

"Yes."

"Please don't go back there again, okay?"

"I … I don't understand. Someone else told me the same thing yesterday."

"Enzo. Yes, he is right. You don't know?"

"No."

Gaspare explained that there was a striking resemblance between Dresden and a man named Heir Abendroth of Germany. Heir Abendroth was an anti-gang specialist brought in by the city of Milan to combat their rising South American gang situation, predominantly MS-13. Milan had acquired the unfortunate title of Little El Salvador, as Gaspare admitted. MS-13 must have mistaken Dresden for Abendroth.

"Well that explains a lot!" Dresden said, nodding to Maria's father. "Thank you. I will do my best to stay out of Milan!"

Orville organized the dossiers, 257 in all. He sat back and looked at Dresden, beleaguered. Where to start? Everyone agreed it was unlikely Branch would hide in plain sight, living out of hotels and rental properties. He might be leaving First Watch behind altogether, but there was no telling for sure. They agreed Branch needed a way to hide, and what better way than to use his 'skills'? That was what he was trained to do. It seemed he would attempt to find a candidate within Europe's billionaire population.

"Let's start with physical likeness," Dresden said, a little too loud.

The room became a beehive of activity. Orville managed a whiteboard with possibilities. Piles were made of the unlikely, least likely, and so on. They focused primarily on those men located in France.

Dresden stepped out of the room to take a text from Emily—*still no word from Casper.* Dresden wrote back that he would call him again, and Osuna too, and if he didn't get anything soon, he would call in a favor and get someone out there to check on him. He stared at his phone as he walked back into the room.

"You okay Marcus?" Gaspare asked, coming to his side.

Dresden looked at the man's weathered and creased face shining back at him.

"Yes. No. I ..."

Maria stopped what she was doing and watched them. Dresden stood up straight and looked to Gaspare.

"My ex-wife. She's worried about one of my kids, my son." His vision glazed over and he looked past Gaspare. Then it clicked.

"Everyone, we need to look for any of the men on the list that have children. That have girls. A boy and a girl will do, but preferably just girls. Pre-teen and teenagers."

Dresden looked over at Maria, her face green.

"Okay, we're on it," Orville said.

"How many are we down to?"

"Twenty-three," Orville barked out.

"Only nine have children within the age range," Primo said excitedly.

"Okay, how many of them with boys? Or better yet, how many have only girls?"

"Three," said Orville.

"Alright, let me see them," Dresden said. He cleaned off a large space on the table and lay the three files side by side. The first one had two girls, ages seventeen and nineteen. The second had three girls ages six, seven, and nine.

"This is it," he said, looking at the third. "This is our guy! Francois Pelletier. This is definitely him—three girls, eleven, thirteen, and fourteen," Dresden said.

He pulled out the photo of Pelletier. It was all there. He had the same bone structure in his face. He was slight and short, even fair-haired. The three girls. Perfect. He knew Branch would think so too.

Primo and his men tested the surveillance equipment while Dresden worked with Orville and Gaspare to narrow down where Branch would be held up. Francoise Pelletier had three homes. One in Annecy, in the mountains in the northwest; one in Bordeaux near the coast; and a third in Paris. Orville and Gaspare felt strongly about Paris. Dresden had his doubts. He asked Maria to locate the Pelletiers. Red was tracing the latest call, but it was proving more difficult to pinpoint than the last two.

They were at a standstill. Stalled again. After rubbing his face and groaning, Dresden moved to where Primo was working on a laptop.

"Live video feed," Primo said. He handed Dresden a device that looked very much like a phone or a small, ruggedized tablet.

Maria interrupted; the Pelletier family was out of town, due back in Paris in a few days.

"That's great!" He thanked Maria and went back to Primo.

"This is perfect, Primo," Dresden said, a spark of energy reigniting in him. If they could find Branch and get eyes on him, the tables would turn, he was sure of it.

"You will be able to watch everything here," Primo said, pointing to the device. "When we get into position, I will set it up and you can monitor both video and comms. Plus, we will be recording it."

"Got it!" Maria howled as she jumped from her seat. "The call came from Annecy."

Dresden looked at Orville and Gaspare. Primo looked to Gaspare as well, who nodded vigorously to the young man. Then Primo and his team scooped gear and equipment into each arm and scrambled out of the room.

Forty-Four

La Spezia, Italy

The call came in at two in the morning, thankfully waking Dresden from a dream full of fire. Casper's chirpy voice shuffled the grogginess out of his head. Still, Dresden only caught fragments of his son's report. Something about a nasty venom, blood being bad. Dresden asked Casper to hang on as he splashed some cold water on his face and walked outside into the winter chill.

"Okay, can you start over?"

"Sure—the blood you sent me was in pretty bad shape. But Doctor O was able to find patches of it he thought would work. That took a while, though. Second, it took even longer to isolate the toxin in his blood, cause, well, it was pretty well hidden. That could have been because of the damage to the blood, but anyway. We found it! It comes from a rare insect found only in Afghanistan, and it made no sense in the beginning cause, like, the Daddy Long Legs spider—Pholcus Phalangioides, whose toxin is very dangerous to humans but will never harm us cause the spider can't bite through our skin—this bug is the same. So, someone had to have figured out how to *weaponize* it." Casper took a deep breath and added, "It's crazy, but true!"

Weaponize? Afghanistan? The Russians, again! They sure loved to poison people, Dresden mused.

"And then the last thing is, well Dad, this is the bad part—there's only a couple possible cures, very rare. And …" Casper stopped and cleared his throat.

"Go ahead, it's okay. You have done an amazing job, and this is all very helpful. Really."

"Okay, well, we found that the toxin has been in his system for a very long time. Probably administered through a lot of doses, if it had been weaponized like I said. Also, Doctor O says there was toxin that was only hours old in the blood you sent. So …"

Dresden drifted. He thought of the two men he threw down the stairs at Roker's hospital. Branch had been poisoning him like the other two billionaires Orville had found. Which meant …

"Dad, your friend is going to die if he doesn't get some help. He may already—"

"You rock! Thank you so much for all your help. I will get *Uncle O* to get him out of there. Thanks again, buddy, this is huge!" Dresden said, about to hang up.

"Dad?"

"Yeah,"

"Doctor O's worried about you. Worried you're mixed up in something bad," Casper said, his voice low.

Dresden stood where he was. Casper's cover was weak. Osuna wasn't worried—or maybe he was, but that wasn't what Casper was saying. "Buddy, I'm fine. I have a great team here, and we are going to catch this guy, and—and then I'm going to come see you and maybe you can come stay with me for a while in Escondite. Maybe go see your grandparents. How's that sound?

The line was silent for a long time. Then Casper said, "Perfect, Dad. That would be awesome. Love you."

"I love you too, buddy. Oh, and dammit! Almost forgot, call your mother, she's freaking out," Dresden said.

"Okay Dad," Casper said, laughing as he hung up.

Yellow grass filled the screen of the device Dresden held in his hand. A text box popped up reading, *Comms check*. Primo and his team were online and in position on a hill a few hundred yards from the Pelletier mountain house in Annecy. Dresden typed, *Video and text good*. The screen jiggled, then came to rest on a house beset by dim lights. The view was from the back of the house. Dresden's heart sank. The house looked deserted, boarded up for the season. The screen panned the length of the building and zoomed in on sections that were hard to see. It was a nice house. Big, with an expansive backyard. Orville and Gaspare watched over his shoulder. But his mind was already calculating options. Maybe he was wrong. Or maybe they were too late. Was it possible Branch had moved on? Shit. The screen went out of focus again for a few moments. A text popped up again: *Mounting camera on spotting scope.* Okay, so they had eyes on the mountain house. The house came into focus again. The sweep this time was smooth and the detail sharper. Dresden typed back, *Looks good. Will monitor. I have the notification set to alarm if you text.* He waited a moment. Primo responded with a thumbs up.

Dresden turned to Orville and Gaspare. "We need to check the other houses."

"Already did," Orville said, looking to the other man.

Gaspare smoothed out his pants with the palms of his hands. "They have not been to the Bordeaux house in three years."

"We have credit card charges about three days ago near the Annecy house," Maria said.

"So, they have to be there," Orville said.

"Then why doesn't it look like it?" Dresden said.

"Let's sit tight. Red is monitoring their email accounts and credit cards. If they are somewhere else, we will get a notice," Orville said.

Maria sat next to her father and moved close to him, watching Dresden as Gaspare put his arm around her. She shot him a crooked smile then stuck her tongue out and giggled. Gaspare looked down at her and frowned. She snuggled in even closer. Daddy's girl, definitely.

Orville coughed and drew Dresden away from the scene. The old man looked as spry as the day Dresden had dropped this mess in his lap. Yet now there was an air about him. Again, he seemed unsure of himself. He rolled his shoulders and started to speak, then stopped and sighed. He was troubled, and it was starting to show.

"There is something we need to consider, Marcus," Orville said, letting the words hang.

"Okay, what's that?"

"We have built a solid case against Branch. All the work that Red and Maria have done. Derek and the financials. You. Even Casper. I'm thinking we—" Orville stopped again. He slid forward on his chair and rubbed his dry hands together. "I think we should consider turning it all over. After we can get a fix on Branch, we should turn it over to the French police."

A flood of anger rushed through Dresden, then subsided. His head lifted off his shoulders and the room started to spin. What? Give up? Standing abruptly, he stuffed his hands in his pockets, paced, and shot looks at Orville. Quit—that was what they wanted to do.

Orville sat back and gave furtive looks at Gaspare. Dresden felt his anger pulse again. "It's a conspiracy, Lance," he mumbled to himself. "They're not going to let me finish this. No! That's stupid." Maria shook her head. Dresden stopped walking and stood over the three. He looked from one to the other, trying to read them. It was Orville and Gaspare. Maria was not in.

Dresden breathed and settled his nerves. In a flat tone, he said, "I hear you. But I'm not convinced the police will take on Branch like we have. How can we be sure? How—"

"I can take care of that," Gaspare interrupted.

Dresden cocked his head. "Sir, I'm confused."

Gaspare looked at his daughter and bellowed, "You still have not told the poor man? Why do you do this, Maria! I'm so sorry, Marcus."

Gaspare labored to push himself off the sofa. Dresden grabbed an arm and pulled.

"My daughter must be so embarrassed by her family that she would not tell you ..."

"Papa!"

"Hush!" Gaspare said, waving his hand in the air.

Maria slumped and crossed her arms over her chest. "Gentlemen." Gaspare stood to his full height and rolled his shoulders back. "I'm Gaspare Giovanni Fiondella, Comandante Generale of the Aarma dei Carabinieri ... retired, four months ago."

A laugh started deep in Dresden's gut, rumbling up through his body. It promised to be momentous but ended up as a disappointing croak. The room filled with spontaneous outbursts. Even Orville cracked a smile. Dresden wiped tears from his eyes as he worked to say something without laughing.

"Well hell, Gaspare!" Dresden finally said, still wiping his cheeks, "and here I was thinking you were the head of the mafioso! Dammit, man!"

At this, Gaspare spawned a fit of laughter. "Marcus, my dear friend, this is Italy! Mafioso, police, it is the same thing!" Gaspare roared and fell back onto the sofa, landing on Maria, who squealed and attempted to work her way out from under her father's bulk. When she did, she stood, looked at the three men with disgust, rolled her eyes at them, then marched out of the room. Dresden, still laughing, called after her. She turned back just before leaving the room and winked at Orville.

The laughter faded as an alarm sounded, growing with every passing second. Dresden reached for the surveillance device. Orville and Gaspare sat up and Maria poked her head back into the living room. Dresden swiped at the screen, then entered a passcode, and the dark screen shifted to a grainy green picture.

A text box popped up. *Watch the screen to the lower right.* Dresden responded to the text, then leaned the small tablet against the centerpiece of the coffee table. Maria leaned over Dresden and reached for his hand. The small group watched intently. Dresden blinked and Gaspare barked—there! He'd missed it.

The screen was focused on two windows. The stone walls of the house bordered the screen on three sides and the gutter of the roof on the fourth. Gaspare said he saw a sliver of light, a mere flash of bright green, light up the screen for a half-second. There it was again! The flash—they all saw it this time. Dresden grabbed the device and texted, *Got it. A flash of light. Correct?* A couple minutes passed, and one more spark of light filled up the lower right of the screen before Primo returned with a simple, *Yes.*

The image on the screen began to pan out. Soon the whole house was in view. There were no lights. Another text came through. *There is a quarter-moon, mostly hidden tonight.* Maria looked at Dresden and the bridge of her nose scrunched. He explained how night vision worked off low light. Had there been more illumination, a full moon for example, they may not have caught the light. Dresden returned a text. *Roger, great work, standing by*. He looked back to Maria, but her expression remained the same. Dresden grabbed both her hands in his, and she gave a nervous look toward her father and tried to pull them away. He didn't let her.

"Maria, the light means they are there. Someone is in the house. Someone who does not want us to think they are, is in the house. They must have covered the windows, but they missed a spot or something. We have them. Branch is there!"

Recognition streamed across Maria's face; her eyes lit up and her brilliant smile returned. She nodded, then leaned in, kissed him on his cheek, and looked at her father again and blushed.

Gaspare's baritone chuckle bounced around the room before he said, "We should go."

Forty-Five

Near the Italian border

The yellow beams of the Maserati's headlights shone out ahead, onto the dark highway. White strips zoomed at them, skirting by the car one by one. Dresden turned and met Maria's uneasy gaze; he smiled and looked to Orville. The man's head cocked off to one side, his hands twitching in his sleep. Dresden looked back to Maria, but she was now looking out the window into the scrum of darkness.

"A flicker of light—that's what we're going to get the entire French police up in arms about," Maria asked, still looking out the window.

"No, not just the light. The kids. The girls. They hadn't been outside once, all day. That isn't very French, don't you think?" Dresden said. "And of course Red's locator put Branch there at the time of the call—and the Pelletiers' credit cards."

"And, we are not going to get the *entire* French police involved, just a small part of it," Gaspare added.

Maria stirred. Dresden thought of their conversation back at the house. She didn't like the idea of handing everything over to the police. Dresden said he didn't either, but that he trusted her father. It ended there.

He turned and saw Gaspare's eyebrow raise and his shoulders shrug.

"We should be there by 8 a.m.," Gaspare said. "You should sleep. We have time and we can do nothing." Gaspare looked at Dresden again.

Dresden checked the surveillance device. A good signal, but nothing new. Rolling his jacket up, he wedged it between his head and the window. His eyes felt as if they were glued open. He pressed them shut, and his eyelids ground against his eyeballs like gravel. Squeezing them tighter, he concentrated on the hum of the car. Finally, his eyelids relented and stayed in place.

Satory, France

The vibration came before the chime of the alarm. The surveillance device slid on Dresden's leg as he reached to silence it. He wiped at his mouth and rubbed one sticky eye as the screen came to life. A text box flashed, *two men spotted outside, not able to ID*. Dresden whispered to Gaspare, who returned a thumbs up. Dresden started to tell Maria, but she was asleep. Same for Orville. Besides, two guys out front of the building was still no confirmation of Branch.

Dresden sat up and took a long draw on his water bottle. The cool liquid went a long way to waking him up. He leaned over the device and typed, *We are on the move. Will fill you in later. Stay safe*. The sky opened up as the sun peeked over the horizon behind them. The skyline of the city came into view. Were they doing the right thing? Primo and his men and Dresden could have taken out Branch by now. But at what cost?

The car bumped over a low-rolling speed hump and shook Dresden back to the present. Gaspare pulled up to a gate, showed his ID, and received a crisp salute from the guard. Dresden tried his best to make out the sign as they entered: *Groupe d'Intervention de la Gendarmerie Nationale*. Intervention?

"GIGN," Gaspare said out of the side of his mouth.

"Oh. Right. This is where your friend is?"

"Yes," Gaspare said as he pulled the Maserati into a parking slot.

Gaspare and Orville waited at the front of the car. Orville moved his hips around in a circle while Gaspare looked on, amused, ignoring the stares of the police officers as they walked by. Dresden opened the door for Maria, who stumbled lifting herself out of the car.

"I'm not awake. Need a coffee," she said, leaning against him.

"This is a police station—I'm sure they have some inside. Do me a favor and head in with Orville, okay? I need a moment with your dad," Dresden said to Maria.

Her head tilted and the corner of her brow lifted, but Dresden didn't say anything more. Maria shrugged her shoulders. "Okay. I need the coffee."

Dresden watched the two walk away, then turned to Gaspare. "Are you sure about this? If we get them involved, there's no turning back. Right now, we can go wrap that bastard up and have him—"

"Yes, I'm sure, Marcus. You hand him over after *we* take him down, we have to answer for all that. This way, they are involved from the start. They take credit for it, and extradition is no question. If he happens to die in the rescue, then the blood is on their hands ... not yours. Much easier to explain."

"Okay. I guess—"

"I know you want to take him down yourself. I want that for you, believe me. But you are letting your ego get in the way of the bigger picture. Plus, my friend, Phillippe, he will make sure you get your chance to, let's say, make an impression."

"Hmm ... are you sure he will do it?"

"I'm sure. Philippe is known for focusing on *what* needs to get done and less on *how* it gets done. He will follow the letter, the rules to get approval, but he will do the minimum. With as little interference as possible. If anyone knows how to make this work, it will be Phillippe," Gaspare said, and put his heavy hand on Dresden's shoulder.

Dresden shook his head and looked away. "Okay. We're all in or all out."

"All in!" Gaspare said.

The double doors to the front office opened. A man whisked by; his eyes fixed straight ahead. He glanced at the bench as if it were an afterthought. His embattled expression changed as he caught sight of Gaspare lounging there. The man looked to Dresden and Maria and Orville, then back to Gaspare. "Come," he said. This must be Phillippe.

His stride was long despite the length of his legs. His movements were crisp and full of efficiency, like those of a professional athlete. Phillippe held the door for everyone, then closed it behind himself. "Please sit," he said, motioning to the sofa and assorted chairs scattered around the office. Dresden sat on a small wooden stool parked next to an extensive library. Law. Military. Special Operations. Police.

Criminal Justice. History. Psychology. Dresden visually roamed the room until he came back to the man.

The man gave Gaspare a hard look.

"My brother!" he finally said, and grabbed Gaspare, pulling him in for a hug and kiss on each cheek. Both men beamed at each other. The man broke away from Gaspare and sized up Maria. "Mi amor! You are more beautiful than before. How is this possible?" Maria blushed and the man hugged and kissed her.

"Phillippe, I would like to introduce Marcus and Orville," Gaspare said. Phillippe moved to the two men and gripped their hands heartily.

"I'm very glad to meet you. You are friends of Gaspare, you are friends of mine."

"Thank you, sir," Dresden said, "we appreciate your help.

Phillippe shot a look at Gaspare that did not instill confidence in Dresden. Gaspare laugh and slapped his friend on the back.

"This is my good friend Major Phillippe Chesneau, head of the Groupe d'Intervention de la Gendarmerie Nationale. You probably know them as GIGN," Gaspare said, looking at Orville. Then he turned to Phillippe. "We need your help."

Phillippe looked around the room. The smile was gone, replaced with a stiff lip. "Yes, of course. What can I do?"

Dresden stood and handed a thick envelope to the major. The man took the file and laid it on his desk, removed his suit jacket, placed it on a hanger, then sat down. Dresden waited. Phillippe folded his hands over the envelope. "Before I open this, can you tell me what this is about?"

Dresden spent the next forty-five-minutes relaying the highlights of the previous weeks and months. Phillippe waited a moment, then blew through his closed lips and tapped on the file.

"You think he has taken a French citizen and his family hostage?"

"Yes."

"In Annecy?"

"Yes."

"How do you know he is at this location, Annecy, and not at one of the others, Paris or Bordeaux or somewhere else completely?"

"We have—" Dresden stopped. Phillippe raised an eyebrow as Dresden started to explain.

"I have my men on it. On location," Gaspare jumped in.

"Active members?"

"No."

"Good." Phillippe tapped the envelope, then got up. "You think he is going to ... *take over* Mr. Pelletier?"

"We learned about this from Enzo." Gaspare added.

"In Bormio?" Phillippe said, his face brightening.

"Yes."

"Okay."

"All of the email, financials, and other evidence is in this envelope. Everything, yes?"

Phillippe said, waving his hand over the envelope.

"Yes," Dresden confirmed. He stood and paced in his small corner of the office.

Phillippe leaned forward and lifted the receiver to his desk phone. He rattled off orders in French, then hung up and turned to Dresden. "Sir, you are a security contractor, correct?"

"Yes."

"Do you have your own company?"

"Yes," Dresden said.

The door to the major's office opened and a petite woman in her forties handed him a stapled stack of papers. Phillippe sat down and flipped through them, scribbling every so often. When he was done, he looked up at Dresden and held his gaze for a moment, then turned to Gaspare. A subtle dip of the Italian's head was all Phillippe needed. He slid the stack of papers toward Dresden.

The major shuffled back in his chair, looking at the ceiling. "Sir, I believe there is a threat to Francois Pelletier's wellbeing." Phillippe stopped, looked at the four of them, then looked at the ceiling again.

"I employed a private security company to conduct all the appropriate background research and surveillance necessary to develop this target package." He stopped and looked at Dresden, a fiendish grin painting his face.

Dresden's hand poised over the paper, pen in hand hung as if suspended by a string. Gaspare nodded. Orville nodded. Maria smiled. Dresden let his hand drop and signed the papers.

The small café filled as the afternoon rush shuffled through. Maria played on her phone and leaned against Dresden. She'd said nothing for over an hour. Dresden let it be and absently rubbed her arm. He sipped at his third cup of coffee. The sun was past the midway point in the sky and shone in the windows of the café. It seemed to jerk slowly toward the skyline. Seven hours had passed and no approval. Phillippe would task one of his branch units in Dijon or Orange. A three-hour drive from either location to Pelletier's house in Annecy. Phillippe could also engage a RAID unit in Lyon if need be; RAID was an hour-and-a-half away. But without approval, he could do nothing. Dresden ordered another triple-shot espresso.

He put his head back against the wall and allowed himself to think of something other than

Branch. He wondered about Roker, whether Red had been able to affect a recovery. Despite everything, Roker was a friend, and he couldn't afford to lose another one to Branch. It always came back to that monster. Damn.

The bell over the door rang, and Dresden opened his eyes. Orville walked to the counter, ordered something, then came to Dresden's table. The old man sipped his coffee and looked out at the street. Dresden wondered when the last time was that anyone had eaten a real meal. Orville looked down at the ground.

"The major got the approval. TOT is 0100," he said, raising his head slowly.

Before Dresden could answer, a pitch of the tablet's alarm sounded. Orville crowded into the booth. Three transit vans popped onto the screen. Maria put her phone down. Three vans; no plates to run. A driver and passenger lingered near each of them. Dresden texted, *How long?* Primo wrote back, *Twenty minutes.*

Dresden asked Primo to zoom in on one of the men. Their outfits were all the same—dark, single-color tactical fatigues. Close-cropped hair. AK style weapons slung over the shoulders, maybe AK-74s, a Spetsnaz favorite. Branch would be on the move soon. Dresden glanced at his watch—4:34 p.m. Too much time until 1:00 a.m. The snake could slither out of sight by then. They'd have to hope he stayed put.

Forty-Six

Satory, France

Phillippe slammed the phone down. "Dammit!" he growled, his head dropped below his shoulders like a gargoyle hunched over his desk. When he looked up, his cheeks were crimson and a small vein curled around his temple. "The team has been delayed. An accident due to the heavy rain. The entire freeway is blocked. There's a possible chemical spill as well." Phillippe stopped and sucked in a breath. "The team is looking for alternate routes but everything will add a least two hours."

"Primo still has eyes on," Orville said as he looked to Dresden.

"I'm sorry Marcus," Phillippe said, dragging a hand through his thick hair.

The two men locked eyes for several seconds before Dresden shook his head. He still said nothing. It wasn't Phillippe's fault. He knew that. It was that asshole Murphy again. There was still time, Dresden told himself, trying to be convincing.

"Okay. We have eyes on. Unfortunately, Primo and his team are a thirty-minute hike from their vehicle. We could split them up, send two to their vehicle. Or ... can we get any local units in the area to cover the entrance to the property and follow if need be?" Dresden said.

"I'll check into it," Phillippe said, picking up his phone.

Dresden retrieved the surveillance device and wrote a text to Primo: *Team's delayed. No idea of ETA. Will update ASAP.* Dresden flopped his head backward and stared at the ceiling. He noticed Maria, upside down, smiling at him. The tablet sounded. *Two men came out a few minutes ago. Fully kitted up. Still no sign of HVTs.* Dresden turned to Maria and read the message out loud. Gaspare and Orville exchanged looks.

Phillippe hung up the phone and said a local unit would take up station in less than ten minutes.

The device sounded again. The screen displayed three men in tactical gear, one of them sweeping his hand from left to right, eventually landing in the center, pointing directly at Primo's position. Phillippe interrupted, asking if the tablet had Bluetooth. A moment later, the scene showed up on the flat screen on the office wall. The camera shifted, following the three men as they marched single file directly toward Primo.

"The team hasn't moved. Still thirty minutes from the target," Phillippe said, consulting the map on his desk.

Dresden looked back at the screen. Small droplets of water landed on the camera lens. A cloth covered the view and wiped the dew away. Shit. A hand covered the lens for a moment. Primo texted, *Starting to drizzle here. Fitting hood on camera/scope. Fifteen minutes for tangos to clear the distance.*

"Tangos?" Maria asked.

"Bad guys," Orville whispered, leaning in.

Maria nodded.

Dresden's fingers hovered over the keypad as he watched the three men walk forward. They were less than halfway to Primo. One of the men broke off, walking perpendicular to the position. The camera lost sight of the other two men for a few seconds. Dresden tapped out a message. *Five minutes out. Break contact. Compromise eminent. Understand?* The text box popped up on the big screen. The two men were back in view as another man broke off in the opposite direction from the first.

The text box opened on the widescreen. *Roger.*

Leaning into Orville, Maria whispered, "I don't understand what's going on?"

"Marcus wants Primo to pull chocks when he thinks the bad guys are five minutes from his position."

"Oh. Okay."

The last man stopped and turned to face the house. The camera ratio widened. The entire house came into view. Dresden looked at Phillippe and tapped his wrist. Phillippe grabbed his cell phone and sent a text. A moment later, he shook his head at Dresden. *Dammit! I hope that local guy can keep up,* Dresden thought.

He looked down at his shoes, then followed a line in the linoleum. The crackle of gunfire filled the room. Dark figures flooded from the house, plumes of gunfire popping all around the transit vehicles. The camera panned down in front of Primo's position. The man was firing at the house.

What the hell!

The camera panned out again and caught the vans speeding around the house and out of view of the camera. The screen shifted once more, and the man down the hill from Primo was on the move, running toward them, and a second later the screen went blank.

Dresden huffed, his breath choppy and incomplete. He slammed through the double doors that led to the parking lot. Outside he bent over, hands on knees. The asphalt swirled like the cosmos. He heard Maria asking him something, but waved her off, told her to leave him alone. Standing, he started walking. He had no idea where, just away. *Shit, shit, shit!* He tripped, his foot falling in a pothole in the sidewalk, then looked around. Where was he? It didn't matter.

His brain pulsed. A fire fight? What the hell was that about? What the fuck was Branch up to? He leaned against a chain-link fence that bowed to his weight. His stomach tightened and made to heave, but nothing came. Phillippe said the locals had no contact with their guy. Was he dead? Branch was on the run. But a fire fight—why? The same men who were in the house had fired on their own men. *Dammit, Branch.*

Primo! Dresden pulled the surveillance device from his pocket and typed, *what's your status?* A car horn blared, and its bumper narrowly missed Dresden's hip. When he looked up, he was in the middle of an intersection. *Gotta find someplace to get my head straight.*

The boulangerie was empty, and Dresden found a seat at the back. *Branch, why would there be a fire fight at your hideout?* The cappuccino was milky and smooth. He sipped at it as he swiped through Primo's messages, making sure he hadn't missed anything. He sent another text. His secure phone buzzed. It was Orville. *Where are you?* the text read. Dresden stuffed the phone back in his pocket without answering.

His phone buzzed again—*Was the video feed recorded?* Great question. *Yes,* he texted back. Dresden found the link. He played the video back again and again. He plugged in his earbuds and turned up the volume. There was nothing but wind and leaves until the shots sounded. The shots—he listened again. It was fake-sounding. Just the speakers, he told himself. But no, that wasn't it. They were fake. They were blanks!

A staged fire fight—why? *Branch, you'd chosen a candidate—Pelletier, right? Were you becoming Pelletier? But why the drama? Because you are Pelletier! Right?* What was it Maria had said? The Pelletiers were scheduled to be back in Paris. When? *Dammit! You were on a timeline, weren't you Branch? Had to leave the cozy mountain retreat, and you were leaving as Francois! But what if you weren't?*

What if the transformation wasn't complete? Did that matter?

Dresden stared out the window. His phone buzzed again, Maria this time. He swatted at the keypad and sent her a short reply—*I'm ok. Be back soon.*

So, Branch had needed to move back to Paris, and now he was François Pelletier. *And you have an instant family. A wife. Three girls.* Visions of Branch's conquest database loomed in his mind. Dresden slapped his head to shake the images free. *You needed to endear yourself to your new family, didn't you Branch?*

Dresden played the video again. There he was, Branch, being ushered into the van. Dresden moved the time bar backward. His family comes out of the door in the middle of the fire fight. They stand there for a few seconds, huddled together. Then two men moved Branch out, but take a brief halt in the action. Branch, now Pelletier, looks over at his wife and three kids.

Deliberate, Dresden thought. He dialed Orville's phone.

"Marcus, where—"

"I'm on my way back. Let me talk to Phillippe."

There was a rustle as the phone was handed over.

"Hello?"

"Phillippe, can I ask you to do something please?"

"Yes, of course," Phillippe said.

"Get your men, your best fucking surveillance men, over to Pelletier's Paris house as fast as you can. And Phillippe, make sure there is no way they get spotted."

"Okay, but—"

"No time to explain. I will later." Dresden hung up and asked a waiter where he could find the Groupe d'Intervention de la Gendarmerie Nationale.

He walked for fifteen minutes before stopping. Nothing looked familiar. He was trusting chicken-scratch instructions on a paper napkin. His old phone buzzed in his jacket pocket and he fumbled for it, pressed it against his face, then started walking again.

"Marcus, did you see them?" a man said in a low voice tinged with a French accent.

"Who the hell is this?" Dresden said, knowing exactly who it was.

"Did you see them? I know you're smart. You found them, didn't you? Or maybe it was that girl of yours. She's the computer expert, right? Did you see them, Marcus? Their soft skin. Their eyes."

Dresden stopped walking. "You're a sick bastard,"

"Sick? No, I don't think so, my friend. They say that the love of a child is the purest. I can tell you ..."

A knot formed high in his throat. "You're finished, Branch," Dresden said, almost saying Pelletier.

"Branch, oh yes. Branch. I don't think you will find Branch anymore. He's moved on. Been retired." There was a pause, then, "I'm tired. I need to rest. As always, good talking to you."

Dresden put his mouth over the microphone and said, "You slimy, sick fiend I'm going to find you and break every bone in your body—"

"I doubt that, Marcus. Not now. I must go, my friend." Branch hung up.

Dresden started running toward the police station.

Phillippe rubbed his narrow chin as he stepped heel to toe in front of his desk. Orville, Gaspare, and Maria sat like school children on the sofa, hands on their knees. Dresden looked over at them. The weariness showed on all three. No real sleep. A couple dozen missed meals. The tether was wearing thin. Maria gave him a small, worried smile. Gaspare wrapped her in his arms, attempting to comfort her.

Phillippe grunted then said, "Okay." He eyed Dresden. "Okay, we will do it."

"Major, I have one other request," Dresden started, then looked back at his team. "I want all of us on the team in some capacity. They have worked too long to—"

"I understand. I will make accommodations for you. Anything else?" Phillippe gave Dresden a knowing look.

"Yes, may I suggest a blocking force and air assets? We cannot afford for him to slip away again. We just can't afford it." Dresden stood and bent over the map on Phillippe's desk. He stabbed his finger at major intersections in a semi-circle around Pelletier's house off the Seine.

Phillippe followed his finger, then leaned to the side. Looking to Gaspare, he said, "Why ... why, my friend, do the Americans always come in and think they can tell us what to do!"

Gaspare let out a bark. "Because sometimes they are right!" Then he put his arm around Orville and squeezed him. "But just sometimes."

Phillippe's surveillance team confirmed the arrival of Branch's transit vans in the sleepy Saint-Germain-des-Pres district of Paris early the next morning. His assault team was already on high alert and working the plan. They were assuming ten to fifteen security personnel, well-trained and armed to boot. They knew of five friendlies but were planning on an additional three to four to contend with. Dresden and his team were not allowed to sit in on the mission brief, but Phillippe ran through the details in his office. The man personally took charge of the mission, which didn't surprise Dresden. The major concluded his private brief, asked if there were any questions, then excused himself as he needed to brief his superiors.

"Any news from Primo?" Maria asked softly, putting her arms around Dresden's neck.

He laughed to himself, amused by Maria's forwardness in the presence of her father.

"Yes. They are all safe and headed back to La Spezia."

"Oh, good," she cooed, her warm breath in his ear. Suddenly she straightened and tapped Dresden on his shoulder. "What kind of security does Pelletier have at his Paris home? I mean does he have a managed online system?"

"Yes," Dresden said.

"May I have that?" Maria asked, reaching for the surveillance device.

"Uh, sure." He handed over the tablet.

Dresden watched Maria walk away. Another wave rolled past him as he turned to Gaspare and Orville.

"I know I shouldn't even ask this, but are you sure Branch is headed to Paris?" Gaspare said.

"I'm certain."

"How can you be so positive?" Orville asked.

"Gentlemen, if I told you, you would call the whole thing off. Please, just trust me."

They both shrugged and nodded, though their expressions remained vacant and doubtful.

"Okay," Orville said, "we are going to get a couple hotel rooms near here, get washed up and maybe some sleep. How about you?"

"I'm staying here. I don't want to miss a thing." Dresden pulled maps of Paris out of his pocket and beginning to review the streets around Pelletier's house. Gaspare shrugged, and Orville patted Dresden on the shoulder. Then they left the office.

The convoy rolled through the blocking force barricade a little after midnight. It was the beginning of winter in Paris—the tourist season over, a Sunday night, and the streets were next to empty in the city of light. Dresden was crammed into the back seat of an extended cab truck. The driver glanced at him from time to time but didn't say anything. Phillippe, in the passenger seat, called for the convoy to halt and for the on-scene commander to do one last vehicle check. Ten vehicles in all, over fifty men plus a twenty-man QRF standing by on helos with the blades turning.

Fifteen minutes later, Phillippe got the thumbs up from the assault team commander. Dresden pulled out the surveillance device and powered it up. A scratchy gray-and-white picture came on the screen. Maria had hacked into the Pelletier security system. The system came complete with camera shots from both inside and outside the house. She'd also hacked the city's transit system cameras, which she admonished Dresden to not show to Phillippe or her dad.

He watched the front of Pelletier's home, a four-story townhouse snug between two others of similar construction, its gray façade faded in the grainy picture. Dresden switched to the interior—nine thousand square feet of living space, including eight bedrooms and servants' quarters in the basement. A courtyard out back stretched to the street behind, Rue Guénégaud. It was a fashionable city estate that belied the fact Pelletier owned the whole block, including the semi-circle drive set back off Quai Conti, which was an anomaly in this part of town. A tinge of familiarity tickled the back of Dresden's consciousness. But why he didn't know, not yet.

A slew of chatter filled the cab as the convoy started moving. A stone pushed its way into Dresden's throat, followed by nausea. Phillippe looked back over his shoulder and gave him a thumbs up. The hairs on the back of his neck wavered. He looked at the tablet screen. The house was quiet. Lights out. He flipped through the other camera angles. No activity. He felt a pain in his stomach. Could he be wrong? No. The transit vans had shown up. Decoys? No, dammit, no second-guessing, Dresden scolded himself.

The driver pulled the command vehicle over and the remainder of the convoy sped by, disappearing in the blackness of the night. Dresden handed Phillippe his Paris map and pointed to the house. Phillippe gave a thumbs up and pointed to a spot on the map about two blocks away from the target. Dresden marked it with a sharpie.

Phillippe helped him out of the back seat, and the two men moved to the rear of the truck, to the command center. Monitors and radios came to life. This was it. This was as close as he was going to get to the action. His face slacked as he slumped onto a stool. A knock at the door and Gaspare climbed into the cramped space. He paused and put his hand on Dresden's shoulder, then moved to Phillippe.

Dresden watched as if detached and floating above. The three men huddled expectantly around a computer monitor. A shaky picture jumped around on the screen. A body camera. The camera squeezed in close to the man in front of him and everything went black. The assault team leader was in the train. The driver flipped through scenes on the TV. Dresden looked down at the device in his hands, where the picture was the same. He flushed with a renewed enthusiasm. This was going to work. He thought of Maria and tapped Gaspare on the arm and gave him a thumbs up. The big man gave him two thumbs back and mouthed, *Oh yeah.*

The monitor lit up again and Dresden looked down at his device. The assault team entered the front door with four men alternating directions. The driver flipped the TV screens to the rear door. The same, a four-man entry. Dresden looked again at his device as another quartet moved through the front door and up the stairs to the second floor. Dresden looked up.

The monitor displayed the team leader's camera. The area was dark. Dresden switched to the second-floor camera on his device.

Six men, two abreast, moved down the hallway, ducking into rooms in pairs. A door on the right opened and a half-dressed man stepped out, buttoning his pants. He turned and saw the squad. Dresden gripped the device. Before the man could level off his weapon, he was shot twice in the chest. Dresden held his breath. The shots had been suppressed, but would the dropping body roust anyone?

Dresden breathed as the team moved forward. From the rear, eight men moved up another set of stairs to the third floor, the bedroom floor. Branch would be asleep there. The driver switched screens again. Team members were leading three people out the front door. A man and two women. The staff, Dresden assumed.

The third floor was lit by small night lights at floor level. Two team members entered a room and came out with two of Pelletier's girls. They shuffled the girls down the hallway, making it to the stairs as bullets ripped down the narrow corridor. One of the team members slid to the ground, shooting before grabbing his leg. He was swiftly pulled to the back of the train. The team concealed themselves behind ballistic shields and moved forward. One of the tangos dropped, then the second followed close behind. The bullets stopped. Dresden watched as the third girl was pulled out of another room.

A man with bright white hair wrapped his AK around the corner where the hallway turned. "Fedor!" Dresden blurted out.

Fedor held the trigger down until his magazine was empty, then ran back to cover. The assault team moved up a few feet short of the corner. The team donned gas masks as two men readied canisters. A plume of smoke erupted in the hallway and spread along the floor like mist in a swamp. Fedor stepped out into the hallway, bare-faced, and let loose another volley of rounds. Wood and plaster flew from the corner of the hall, covering the assault team in dust and debris. Another team member fell to the floor, clutching his chest.

The assailant changed magazines in the open, the gas climbing up his legs like a vine. A smaller man covered in a blanket dashed out of a room and fell in behind Fedor. "Fucking Branch," Dresden muttered. The big man walked backward as he fired. He pushed the smaller figure into a dead end with only a closet left for safety. Branch opened the closet and stepped in. He beckoned Fedor to come, but the big man waved him off, marching forward. Two more canisters spit gas into the corridor. The assault team rounded the corner as Fedor changed another magazine. The team unloaded on him as white clouds of tear gas consumed him.

The closet, Dresden thought. The closet. He remembered now.

The creak of plastic snapped Dresden out of his rage. He loosened his grip on the device and eyed the crack running down the glass. His vision blurred as he looked around the small space, his face hot and hands aching. He reached back and fumbled for the door handle, looking to Gaspare, Phillippe, and the driver. The three men were in an even tighter huddle, Phillippe firing off orders. Dresden slipped out into the dark night.

Forty-Seven

Saint-Germain-des-Prés, Paris, France

Dresden moved a block away from the truck before dipping into the shadows of a doorway. The brisk walk chilled his face. Freezing in place, he stood staring blankly at the Seine, not really seeing it. A car buzzed by, its tires screeching on the damp asphalt. Dresden shook his head and looked down at the doorstep, then his hands. Jacket in one and tablet in the other. He needed to move. He put his jacket on and stowed his tablet, then patted his pockets, checking for his phones and silencing them all. Fitting a ball cap on his head, he tucked in his hair. Lastly, he patted the back pocket of his pants for his punch-dagger.

This wasn't over. Branch was going to get away.

With a finger, he followed the red line on the map. Gaspare and Phillippe chatted happily, because they thought it was finished. Phillippe called for a head count, officers, friendlies, and tangoes alike. Branch would be found in a closet, and Fedor, dead. That was the consensus.

But that isn't it, is it Branch? You're going to get away, aren't you? Dresden picked up his pace to a near run, then forced himself to slow. He didn't want undue attention. Not at this hour. Not with what was going on a few blocks away.

He turned on Rue Séguier and barely noticed the gates at Passage Dauphine as he ducked through the lucky short cut to Rue Mazarine. The narrow streets buttressed on either side by five- and six-story buildings made cardinal directions impossible. Streets shooting off at odd angles further complicated it. Dresden slowed at each intersection, double-checking his map. Walking down the wrong road could cost him valuable seconds, even minutes.

Rue Guénégaud. At the corner, a busy cocktail bar lit up the street. A group of four crashed through the doors, laughing and hugging. Their voices echoed down the street. Dresden watched the lounge patrons. They drank, talked, ate, completely unaware of the drama taking place up the road. He stuck to the right side of the street but counted addresses on the opposite side.

There they are, he thought, his nerves downshifting. Halfway up on the left, Dresden spotted a series of colored doors. Navy blue. Hunter green. Blood red. Big doors that opened onto the tiny sidewalk. Some opened to fashionable shops and small boutiques. The doors were covered in fresh paint and bright brass door handles. The other doors passed into small workshops and garages, all in a deep state of disrepair. Dresden stopped and counted. Number 16. Number 12. Number 10. Number 6. Number 6 Rue Guénégaud. This was it.

He moved into the darkness of Number 6, closed the door, and dropped the broken padlock on the floor. He crouched, his back against the door, and let his eyes adjust. Soon he could see the dusty car that filled most of the space. He blinked to see better in the yellow din. The walls were lined with shallow shelves and tools hanging from pegs. A small, rickety-looking closet took up the back wall. His vision improved and he shuffled to the back. Rummaging through a bent and dented trash can, Dresden found a thick metal pipe and sized it up.

A faint rattling sound came from the closet. A mouse, maybe, but it wasn't. Dresden tucked himself between the closet and the trash can. More rattling. The closet door popped open an inch. A stream of dusty yellowish light fell onto the floor. Then a foot tapped tentatively at the floor, and a body quickly followed. Dresden stepped forward from his hiding space, reared back with the pipe as best he could, and swung. The pipe landed against the figure's chest with a loud snap. Shapeless and contorted, the figure bounced off the car and dropped to the floor, writhing and sucking in air. The man opened his eyes and stared up at Dresden, holding his chest. Branch! Horror, shock, and disbelief shaded his face. He went lunatic and spat at Dresden, unable to form words. As Branch's face bulged and reddened, he squirmed, feet kicking, stirring up dust and making bits of trash take flight. Scrambling away from Dresden, he hissed and spat again.

"You! You. How? You! You couldn't just stop. Leave me alone …"

Dresden stomped on the man's calf with the heel of his boot.

"Yahahaha!" Branch screamed.

Then Dresden brought the pipe down on the man's knee, shattering it. Branch shot backward, his spine curved in a painful arch. He howled, rattling the small shed. Dresden kicked the man in the neck to quiet him, then knelt down and whispered in his ear.

"I want you to think of everyone you've killed. Every little girl who will never live a normal life because of you. I want you to think of them as I break every bone in your body. Every … single … bone." Dresden trailed off as he stood.

Branch curled into the fetal position, muttering loudly. His voice sounded refined and smooth, no longer like the Branch Dresden new.

"Spare me. I'm not who you think I am. I am … I am—"

"Yeah Pelletier, I know. Too bad you didn't start out that way, you shit-bag—I might have believed you," Dresden stepped down on one of Branch's hand to hold the man's arm in place. He raised the pipe above his head and swung.

A strobe light went off, and Dresden was blinded. He felt his body slam into the car before he could put it all together. He'd been punched in the face. Rolling on his back, he found Fedor standing over him, pipe in hand. Sweat poured from the man's ashen face as Dresden scrambled backward. He got to his feet.

The goon took a swing but missed. Dresden drove forward and landed several punches in the big man's stomach. Fedor brought the pipe down on Dresden's back, forcing him to the floor. He landed on Branch, who howled again. Fedor fell back into the closet.

The man wallowed, shifting from side to side like a cockroach stuck on his back. Dresden stood panting, watching Fedor beat against the sides of the cabinet trying to find purchase. Branch wriggled and squealed, dragging himself to the door. Dresden reached down for the man's belt and slammed him into the concrete several times, then stood blinking and heaving. A whoosh of cool air passed his face as Fedor's fist slid along his cheek. The big man stumbled forward, off balance. Dresden helped him down to the ground with a shove to his back.

Fedor rolled over onto his back, chomping for air. Glassy, bloodshot eyes pleaded with Dresden, crazed like a downed zebra waiting for the first lion to tear off a chunk of flesh. The man slid up on his elbows then fell back again. The shirt under his jacket was soaked dark with blood. The big man mumbled between choppy and erratic breaths. Dresden tore himself away from Fedor's gaze to find Branch patting at the door, flopping like a fish out of water.

A hand grabbed his ankle as Dresden moved to Branch. Fedor stared up at him again, his eyes now vacant and besieged. The man rolled his face to one side, exposing three long scars to the dim yellow light. A hot flash pulsed through Dresden as an image of Lance's clenched fist consumed him. Dresden looked up at Branch grappling with the doorknob, then back down at Fedor. Twisting his ankle, he pulled free of the murderer's feeble grasp.

Dresden stomped on each of Branch's thin shoulder joints. A loud, audible snap came with each. Branch arched his back again and opened his mouth to scream, but Dresden stuffed it with a rag and taped it secure.

Kneeling next to Fedor, he looked into the man's watery eyes. He wanted to watch this man die. Dresden looked down as Fedor wrapped his long fingers around his forearm, his grip flaccid and benign. With his other hand, the man rooted in his jacket pocket. Dresden stopped him. "Friend," Fedor mumbled, barely audible. Dresden pulled the man's hand from his pocket; Fedor coughed and spit more blood, then opened his fist for Dresden too see. A phone fell to the ground as the man's grip loosened for good.

The secure phone buzzed in his pocket. Then his old phone. Then his throwaway. *Goddamn Orville! Hold on, I'm coming,* Dresden said to himself as adjusted the bundle over his shoulder. The bundle squirmed, and Dresden gave it a punch. He tipped his hat to an elderly man and his dog. The dog sniffed madly and barked once before the man hushed him. Red and blue lights flickered down the street, dancing off the buildings as Dresden strutted toward the unseen source. His phone rang again as he neared the corner.

"Hello?"

"Marcus! Where the hell are you?" Orville yelled in his ear.

"Look behind you." Dresden hung up and rounded the corner.

Orville, with the phone still to his ear, turned, peering into the darkness past the squad cars. Gaspare, Phillippe, and Maria followed his gaze, and then Gaspare threw his hands toward the sky.

Maria closed the distance between them so fast she crashed into Dresden.

"We were so worried!" She pounded him on his chest. "What did you do? Where did you go? What—what is that on your shoulder?"

Dresden bent and whispered in Maria's ear, "I will tell you everything. But you'll have to wait a minute ... I have to apologize to someone first." Dresden walked up to Phillippe. "I tried to play the game the best I could. And you did the best you could. I know that, and I'm very grateful for your willingness to help us. So, I want to give you a small token of my appreciation," Dresden looked around at his team then heaved the bundle off his shoulder onto the hood of an assault team car.

Phillippe looked at his leader, and then both began to rip at the burlap-and-tape bundle. A gasping Branch flung his head from side to side, whining through the rag stuffed in his mouth.

Phillippe looked up at Dresden. "Apology accepted!" He barked and started laughing, a broad and boyish grin punctuating his face.

"Marcus, one question. How?" Phillippe said between laughs.

Dresden looked at the Pelletier house. "Well, let's just say it's a good thing Mr. Pelletier took my advice and put in that tunnel." Dresden looked at the ground and scuffed his shoe on the asphalt.

"Most of them rarely listen to me, let alone act on it."

Phillippe started laughing again and slapped his team leader on the back. Dresden shrugged and started to walk away, then said to Phillippe, "Oh and the other guy, the big blonde. His body is at Number Six." Dresden said pointing down Rue Guénégaud.

Turning made Dresden's head swim and spin, and he started to fall backward, but Gaspare caught him under his arm. Orville and Maria shapeshifted a dozen times, so Dresden focused out into the distance. The Seine sparkled under the streetlamps and King Henry the IV stood tall and proud astride his horse on the Pont Neuf. His stomach groaned and he thought it was the dead king grumbling. Mad. Crazy and disgruntled that he was dead and useless.

Dresden waggled his head and focused on Maria. Her eyes strained with worry as she fretted with her jacket zipper.

"You guys hungry? I'm really hungry. Is there any place good to eat in this town?" Gaspare chuckled and slapped Dresden on the back. "Food is good. A man must eat."

The Seine rushed by as Maria and Dresden walked along the Quai. The sun, peeking between the buildings, threw shades of pink and orange into the fair blue-black sky. An early morning mist hung on the edges of the river as the streets and sidewalks filled with humanity and life. Dresden flipped Lance's phone around in his pocket. Another phone buzzed—it was Robbie. *How'd it go? You get the bastard? Call when you get home*. Dresden chuckled and wrote back, *Got him! Now go play with kids*. He pocketed his phone, then looked over at Maria.

She moved closer to him and ran her arm through his. Now what? He looked down at her—Maria's face shone like a sun-kissed flower. *Now what?* he repeated to himself.

"Marcus, I'm going to go home with my father. I—" She stopped and pulled him to the railing. "I want very much to stay with, to have you. Oh, this is not right," she said, looking up at him.

This was hard. There was no way for this to work. Or was there? Not now. And yet Dresden wanted it more than anything. Almost anything.

"I have unfinished business," he finally said. "Some things I need to take care of. A promise I made. Maybe after that, we—"

"Yes! Yes, after that. It's important to keep your promises," Maria said, the strain on her face melting away. "Besides, you have never met my mama. She makes Papa look like a teddy bear." She giggled and pulled him in close.

This was the right thing, he convinced himself. He *would* have to talk with her. Learn *how* to talk with her. Be someone she could count on, be there for her. But that would take time.

His secure phone rang. He held it up for Maria to see.

Casper flashed a toothy grin into the camera. The lens shifted in and out of focus and bounced over to a man sitting up in a bed. The picture grew fuzzy, then cleared. Sun beamed in from an unseen window, and Roker waved at the camera.

"Hey, Marcus. It's been a while."

"Yes. Yes it has, my friend," Dresden said, his chest tightening. The man sitting before him was a shell of the man he knew. "How are you feeling, Tom?"

"Terrible but great, all at the same time."

"I bet. You doing okay?"

"Yeah, I … I can't remember much. Lots of memories lost, or fuzzy and fractured. But maybe that's a good thing."

"Yeah, I think it is. I'd have to apologize for a whole bunch of things I'd rather not remember."

Roker laughed, then coughed and grabbed at his chest. "You and me both, pal." He coughed again. "Thanks Marcus. I owe you and everyone."

"You got it brother. Keep doing the right thing."

Red leaned in. "Hey Marcus, the other guy look as bad as you?"

Dresden turned his bruised face to the camera. Red winced. Fedor's first punch had left him with a half-swollen eye and badly bruised cheek. "What do you mean?" Dresden said.

Casper turned the camera back on him. "Hey Dad, I look forward to seeing you in a few days. Don't forget where to pick me up, okay?"

The corners of Dresden's mouth were beginning to hurt. "Sure thing buddy. Love you!"

"Love you too, Dad." Casper waved then hung up.

Maria gripped him in a tight hug again. Dresden hugged her back and kissed her on the top of her head, then lay his cheek down in her soft hair. Perfect. Just perfect.

Forty-Eight

Longwood, Pennsylvania

Dresden looked up into his rearview mirror. Casper hugged Dr. Osuna for a long time. When they separated, he could see the old man wipe his eyes. Casper stepped back from the man and bent into a deep bow. The doctor returned the gesture.

Casper turned and walked away, glancing back as he made his way to Dresden's truck. Osuna shooed him every time he looked back.

Dresden re-read a text to Lance. *Hey brother this it. It makes no real sense anymore to text you since... well I have your phone. But I thought what the hell, one more time. I'll put it out there in the ether, maybe you'll pick up on it. But hey man I hope you don't mind... I have two this time. I know it breaks all the rules... the rules we never really enforced, anyway. I have two songs for you, bub. And to make matters worse they're from the same band. Ok, I won't keep you in suspense any longer. The first one's "Gang's all Here" by the Dropkick Murphys It's just to remind you that you will never be forgotten, you will always be in the lineup with the rest of us! And... the second one, is cause, well if we'd have grown old together, I'd of wanted to make sure we were "Going Out In Style"! Love you brother. Peace out!*

Dresden looked up again, then hit send as Casper climbed into the truck.

"You good?"

"Yeah. I ... I'm good." Casper looked into the side-view mirror. He waved back at Osuna. The old man waved back.

"Okay. Hey, check this out." Dresden pulled a photo from his pocket and handed it to his son.

"What's this?"

"It's your room in Escondite."

"What? When did you have a chance to ..."

"It's always been there. I just haven't had the guts to ask you to—you know, to come visit," Dresden said. He looked out the window.

"I'm not even going to ask why you drive around carrying a picture of a bedroom in your pocket."

"Well—" Dresden stopped, then smiled at Casper, and both men laughed.

He started the truck. Casper looked over at his father. "Dad, can I pick the road trip music? You know ..."

"What? Hell yeah, go for it. Let's see what you got!"

Casper pulled out a small disk case and opened it. He'd burned a bunch of CDs for the journey, realizing his dad's truck was old as hell. No Bluetooth. No Sirius XM. Nothing. Just a twenty-year-old CD player. Casper selected his first disc and slipped it in the player.

The scratching sound of *The Dammed* cranking out "I Think I'm Wonderful" came over the speakers.

"Oh yeah! *The Dammed*?" Dresden said. "Man, you're pulling out all the stops right from the get-go. Great pick, Casper. Where'd you learn about these guys?"

"I picked up a thing or two from you along the way, you know?" Casper said. He leaned over and turned up the volume, then scooched down and put his feet up on the dash.

Dresden's cheeks started to ache as he drove the truck out of the parking lot. He took one last glance at his side mirror. Osuna waved and gave a thumbs up, then turned. Dresden thought he saw the man's shoulders droop a little. He looked over at Casper, his head back and eyes shut, mouthing the words to the song. Sinking into his seat a little, Dresden guided the truck out onto the main road and found Pennsylvania state highway 1, heading west.

Did you enjoy this book?

PLEASE LEAVE A REVIEW

Reviews are the most powerful tool in my arsenal when it comes to getting attention for my books. Honest reviews from committed and loyal readers like you are gold. Your review will undoubtedly go a long way to helping others click that purchase button. And if you liked the book, I know you will want others to read it not to mention how grateful I will be for your kind words.

You can leave a review at my ***Amazon Book Page***. Please enter the following in your search bar and it should take you directly there:

amazon/waves-of-deception-marcus-dresden-1

Thank you very much!

ACKNOWLEDGMENTS

Thank you, Andrew Watts and Jason Kasper of Severn River Publishing, for saying no – then showing me the indie-publishing lighthouse. To Rick Campbell for taking the time to talk to me and introducing me to Andrew. To John and Lisa Campbell, John Fitzgibbons, my Dad and Aaron and Olivia Clevinger for reading my very first draft, your encouragement and advice helped me start on the second draft. To Stuart Bache for an awesome cover and Mark Dawson for teaching us all the indie-publishing ropes. To my wife Sofia for making sure I didn't take family time to pursue this project, because I would have. And lastly to Dylan Garity, my editor for bringing it all together, ready for the next one Dylan?

DISCLOSURE

This is a work of fiction and nothing more. That's it!

Okay, I know you need more so here we go, any comparisons or similarities to real and actual nouns (people, places and/or things) were not intended. However, elements of said nouns may have been used as a matter of inspiration. Any likeness to real or actual events is purely a matter of coincidence. The use of specific tactics, techniques and procedures were meant to enhance and lend validity the story and its characters – not to divulge national secrets. The author is amused that you've read this disclosure and hopes you loved the book and will give it a favorable review and pass it on. Thank you.

ABOUT THE AUTHOR

Brian Grogan served as US Navy SEAL for over two decades. He is a veteran of the Iraq war and Desert Storm. He spent his down time surfing, running ultramarathons and mountaineering. As of late he works as a security specialist and farm hand. He lives with his wife and two boys in western Maryland.

This is his first book – thank you for reading.

You can find out more about Brian at bgroganbooks.com or contact him at brian@bgroganbooks.com

Made in the USA
Las Vegas, NV
30 January 2021